The
BOUND

D1563156

Also by K.A. Linde

ASCENSION SERIES

The Affiliate
The Bound

Adult Romance Series

AVOIDING SERIES

Avoiding Commitment
Avoiding Responsibility
Avoiding Intimacy
Avoiding Decisions
Avoiding Temptation

RECORD SERIES

Off the Record
On the Record
For the Record
Struck from the Record

ALL THAT GLITTERS SERIES

Diamonds
Gold
Emeralds
Platinum
Silver

TAKE ME SERIES

Take Me for Granted
Take Me with You

STAND ALONE

Following Me

The BOUND

THE ASCENSION SERIES
book two

K.A. LINDE

Visit my website at www.kalinde.com
Cover Designer: Sarah Hansen, Okay Creations,
www.okaycreations.com
Photography: Lauren Perry, Perrywinkle Photography
www.perrywinklephotography.com
Editor and Interior Designer: Jovana Shirley, Unforeseen Editing,
www.unforeseenediting.com

ISBN-13: 9781682308769

To Meera and Kiran,
for allowing me to fictionalize you.

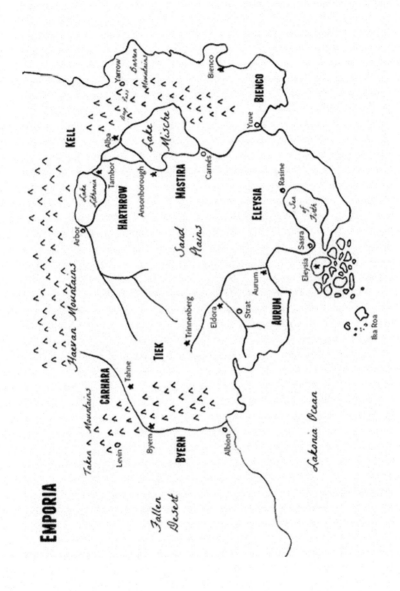

PRONUNCIATION GUIDE

AHLVIE GUNN: AL-VEE GUN

ARALYN STROHM: AIR-UH-LIN STRAHM

AONIA: A-OWN-YUH

AURUM: ARE-UM

AVOCA: AH-VOK-UH

BARKELEY IOLAIR: BARK-LEE I-O-LAR

BASILLE SELBY: BAH-SEAL SEL-BEE

BRAJ: BRAHJ

BYERN: BY-URN

CARO BARCA: CAR-O BARS-UH

CEIS'F: SEE-ES-EF

CREIGHTON IOLAIR: CRAY-TUN I-O-LAR

CYRENE STROHM: SAH-REEN STRAHM

DAUFINA BIRKET (CONSORT): DAW-FEEN-UH BUR-KET

EDRIC DREMYLON (KING): EDGE-RICK DREM-LIN

ELEA STROHM: EL-YA STRAHM

ELEYSIA: EL-A-SEE-UH

EMPORIA: EM-POR-EE-UH

EREN: AIR-EN

HAENAH DE'LORLAH: HAN-UH D-LOR-LUH

HAILLE MARDAS: HAYL MAR-DUS

HUYEK RIVER: HOO-YIK

INDRES: IN-DRESS

JARDANA: JAR-DON-UH

JESALYN DREMYLON IOLAIR: JESS-UH-LIN DREM-LIN I-O-LAR

JESTRE FARRANAY: JEST-RAY FAIR-UH-NAY

KAEL DREMYLON (PRINCE): KAYL DREM-LIN

KALIANA DREMYLON (QUEEN): KAL-EE-AH-NUH DREM-LIN

KEYLANI RIVER: KEY-LAHN-EE

KRISANA (ALBION CASTLE): KRIS-ON-UH

LEIF: LEEF

MAELIA DALLMER: MAY-LEE-UH DAL-MER

MATILDE: MUH-TILD

NIT DECUS (BYERN CASTLE): NIT DAKE-US

REEVE STROHM: REEV STRAHM

RHEA GRAMM: RAY GRAM

SERAFINA (DOMINA): SER-UH-FEEN-UH

SHIRA: SHEER-UH

VERA: VEER-UH

VIKTOR DREMYLON: VICK-TER DREM-LIN

PROLOGUE

JARDANA'S BODY HUMMED WITH VICTORY.

Ever since she had returned to her rooms to find a note addressed to her from Prince Kael in their secret code, she had known that tonight was the night. Everything would change between them. Their little dalliance behind the scenes had gone on long enough. It was time to make this official.

She was a Byern Affiliate, raised to be one of the most respected women in the entire country. And not just that, she was in a position to *rule*. Already, she was Assistant Director of Internal Affairs for Her Majesty, Queen Kaliana. Soon, she would rise from Assistant to the actual DIA for the Queen herself. The Queen's right-hand woman. Her most trusted Affiliate.

And, if things worked out as she suspected they would tonight, she would even surpass that and become a Duchess, ruling over all of Albion, her husband second in line for the throne. A woman could get used to that.

She tugged the black cloak low over her brow. The note had been clear that she was not to be seen when she left. Long ago, she had figured out more than one passage in and out of the castle grounds where no one would stop her from leaving, even in dire times, such as now with Affiliate and High Order murders and that annoying Cyrene's disappearance.

Truly, Jardana believed Cyrene was just trying to get more attention, as if the King's pretend interest wasn't enough. She turned her nose up at the thought. No, King Edric cared nothing for that girl. That was why Cyrene had vanished in the first place.

Jardana rolled her eyes. Cyrene made her blood boil. At least Jardana wouldn't have to deal with Cyrene again after tonight.

The trek to her rendezvous point wasn't that far, but she held to the shadows and avoided people. If Kael wanted a private proposal, then she would be happy to oblige him.

She passed a woman in a dirty frock, who jumped backward at the sight of Jardana.

"Get out of the way," Jardana snapped irritably.

The woman dropped into a hasty, clumsy curtsy. "My apologies, miss."

"Don't you know your betters? I'm an Affiliate, not some lowly commoner."

Her eyes rounded. "Forgive me. I meant no offense, Affiliate."

Jardana glared at the woman. "Her Majesty will be hearing about this."

And then she strode away, listening to the woman's pleas, with dark laughter buried within herself.

She reached the secluded building that Kael had mentioned in his letter. She had memorized it before leaving and promptly burned it in the fireplace. No one was to know what was happening.

Approaching the door, she tapped out the code—three taps, pause, one tap, pause, one tap, wait.

The door creaked open, and Jardana hurried into the house, locking the door behind her. She tipped back the hood on her cloak and surveyed the room. It was completely empty, not a single piece of artwork on the walls, not a single chair in the room, not even a scrap of rug to break up the stone floor. It was dismal.

Why would he propose here?

"Jardana, is that you?" Kael called.

She turned toward a narrow corridor and followed his voice. "Yes, it's me."

"Good. You came."

"Of course."

She walked down the corridor, into the open room, and stopped in her tracks. Candlelight flooded the bare room. A wooden table was in the center, and on top of it was a small book. When Kael turned to stare down at the pages, the air in the room seemed to shift with him. She had an eerie feeling that she couldn't exactly place.

"You wanted to see me?" she said, losing some of her bravado.

"Yes. Shut the door behind you."

Jardana swallowed but closed the door and strode to his side. "What are you reading?"

"A book my father left me."

"I didn't know King Maltrier had bequeathed you anything," Jardana said. "What does it contain?"

"A great deal of things that are very important to the country."

"Has King Edric seen it?"

It was the wrong thing to ask. Kael's head snapped up to meet her, and his eyes were storm clouds. His pupils dilated, and he looked furious. She should have known better. She knew how much Kael despised his brother. He was the chosen one, born for greatness, given everything on a silver platter while Kael had to wait in the background, was looked down upon by his peers, and struggled to attain such greatness as his brother had already achieved.

"Edric was not always the golden son," Kael growled. "Once, my father chose *me* above everyone...above Edric. He left me the most precious thing in his possession, and today, we will see his plans begin to come to fruition."

Jardana smiled cruelly. She loved when he spoke like this. "Yes," she told him, "together, we will take over the world."

"We most certainly will," he said with that charming smile she knew all too well.

He reached out and dragged her flush against him. "You trust me?"

"Implicitly," she told him.

They were going to rule the world together. She would be his queen, seated at his side, second only to the Queen. Her ambition had never been higher than at that moment. She could practically taste it. She would sit atop the golden throne, looking down upon all the worthless citizens. She would have full command of the Affiliates, and they would do her bidding and her bidding alone. It was what she had been born for. Her mother had always said that she would be supreme.

"Then, we must be made as one," he breathed against her neck.

She couldn't hold back the gasp. *Finally.* "Yes. Oh, Kael, yes."

The knife plunged into her back so fast that she never saw it coming. It struck her so precisely that she hadn't even had the chance to cry out, just as he had planned it. Blood poured from the wound, soaking Kael's hands and falling onto the stone floor.

"For you, Father," he said. Then, he chanted the words that his forefathers had chanted before him, which translated from the ancient tongue to, *"Life freely given. Power freely taken. Drawn from you. Give thus to me. Cast off the light and plunge into darkness. I surrender."*

As the life drained out of Jardana's once vibrant body, Kael claimed the life force for his own. There was no greater force on earth than the power he was claiming from flesh and blood. Their connection, so deeply entrenched over the years, only intensified the white-hot power now at his disposal.

It was in that moment, as the power flooded his body, that he finally understood why his father had murdered his mother.

1

The
WATCH

EVERY SINGLE PART OF CYRENE STROHM'S BODY ACHED.

She dismounted from her proud dapple, Ceffy, and dropped to her feet. Her knees nearly buckled underneath her, and she tried to shake off the stiff soreness that had come from riding day in and day out. Even her fingers were cramping from gripping the reins so tightly.

Pulling her bag off of Ceffy's saddle, she prepared her horse for another long day tomorrow. Her hand reached inside the bag before it fell to the ground at her feet. She removed the golden pin of Byern from the bag and affectionately ran her fingers over its climbing vines. It was the mark of an Affiliate, the highest position in the land, save royalty. It pained her not to wear the pin anymore, but she and her companions had all agreed that it was too recognizable. So, it lay, tucked away, in her belongings.

Cyrene stifled a yawn and covered her mouth to try to bite back the exhaustion. The last thing she wanted was for anyone to see her weariness. She had been the one to convince her friends—Maelia Dallmer, Ahlvie Gunn, and Orden Dain—to flee their home country of Byern. So, she was the one who had to remain strong throughout this journey, no matter what was thrown in her face.

From an early age, she had dreamed about finding adventure and traveling the world. She just hadn't expected adventure to be this tiresome.

Maelia hauled the packhorse through the open clearing and immediately began to set up camp. Orden scouted the hilly roads far ahead. Ahlvie had already tied up his horse, Belgar, and was collecting firewood. They had been on the run for a few weeks now and had settled into a routine.

"Cyrene," Maelia said, grabbing her attention, "Ahlvie should have been back already?"

"Already? He hasn't been gone that long," she said.

But then her eyes caught the location of the sun, and she frowned.

"I don't like for him to be too far out with Orden gone and guards on our tail."

"I'll find him. Don't worry."

"Take that with you." Maelia pointed at a heavy broadsword hanging from Ceffy's side.

Cyrene looked at the sword with disdain. "I'll only be a minute."

"I'd feel better if you had it with you," Maelia said.

The sword was an unfortunate necessity. The group had left Albion, the second largest city in their home country of Byern, with no trouble. By the time anyone had noticed that they had left, Cyrene had thought the coast was clear.

Oh, how wrong I was.

News had traveled quickly that King Edric Dremylon of Byern believed Cyrene had been kidnapped, and a hefty reward had been issued for her return. So, even if she could tell Edric that she had not been kidnapped but instead escaped to fulfill her mission to get to Eleysia and discover how to use her magical powers, no one would hear her story. Not to mention, everyone, including herself only a couple of months ago, believed magic was nothing more than a myth.

But magic was more than a myth. After a near-death experience where she had faced a deadly Braj, her powers had manifested, and even if she was in love with the King, getting out of Byern had been a necessity. Edric would never have let her go if he had known the truth...of any of it. So, it was partly her fault that he believed she had been kidnapped, and now, their departure from Byern had turned into a game of duck and cover with guardsmen in pursuit.

Cyrene must have made a face at Maelia's suggestion, and she fixed Cyrene with a stern look.

"The sun is setting, and the Hidden Forest is notoriously dangerous. You've heard the sounds at night. Strange inhuman howls and creepy slithering noises." Maelia shuddered at the thought. "Just take it."

Maelia had a way of ignoring Cyrene's protests. Even though the sword was clunky, Maelia was used to a world where a sword was the best defense. So, Cyrene untied the sword from Ceffy's side and laced it around her plain blue dress. It dragged down her waist, and she bent slightly to the right to try to adjust it.

"There."

"Thank you," Maelia said. "Be safe."

Cyrene ground her teeth and set out.

After the first week of trekking aimlessly through the woods, she had cursed her parents for not giving her a proper education on tracking, positioning, and other such important matters. She had thought that all she needed to know could be found in books. But the only book she had brought with her held text that only she could see and read. It was a riddle wrapped inside a mystery.

As she followed the most obvious pathway through the trees, her eyes scanned the ever-darkening sky. They needed to build a fire before they lost all light. Her stomach growled louder than those weird noises.

A rustle of voices sounded in the trees nearby, and Cyrene hastily hid behind a large bush. With a shuddering deep breath, she peered around the corner.

Six Byern guard were in full armor. Each had a headpiece tucked under his arm. The man currently speaking was sporting the royal colors of her homeland with a plume of green and gold feathers jutting from the top of his helmet, the telltale sign of a Captain of the Royal Guard.

"You're sure you saw someone coming this way?" the Captain asked.

"Certain, Captain," the guard answered at once.

"Then, where are they?"

"Sir, we've sent out Rorick and Naelan to sweep the perimeter of the area. They couldn't have gone far," another man said.

Not six guards.

Eight.

Eight against four with two of my friends missing, and I'm unable to properly use a weapon. Now would be a great time for me to be able to use my magic.

"I don't like these woods. If we don't hear back with a definite destination by nightfall, we'll make camp.," the Captain said. "There's a small creek not far from here on the other side of the embankment. Meet there. Now, move out."

Cyrene's heart hammered in her chest. Orden had said the guards who were trailing them were gaining ground, but she hadn't thought that he meant *this* much ground. She needed to get back and warn Maelia. She didn't know where Ahlvie and Orden were, but she had to do what she had to do.

When the Captain heeled his horse away from her, she breathed out heavily.

As soon as he was out of her line of sight, she bolted back to Maelia. Adrenaline pumped through her system, fueling her body, and lightening her steps.

She tiptoed around the next tree, careful not to barge into the clearing in the event that the guardsmen had already found Maelia. But Maelia was standing there with her sword in hand, easily swinging it back and forth while pacing the space.

Cyrene walked into their camp as Ahlvie burst into the clearing. He dropped what little firewood he'd still had in his arms.

"Guards," he choked out. "Everywhere."

"What?" Maelia squeaked, gripping her sword tighter.

"They're swarming the woods. I don't know how many there are, but I barely missed two of them."

"I saw them too," Cyrene said. "I saw six and they said the two you saw were out on patrols. So eight of them, and one is a Captain."

Maelia's face paled. "A Captain?"

"Creator!" Ahlvie said. He spat on the ground.

"Did you find Orden?" Cyrene asked Ahlvie.

"No. He was still scouting. I don't know how he missed the guards. They're right on top of us."

"We'll have to make do without him."

She didn't miss the glance between Ahlvie and Maelia. She knew as well as they did that Orden was the only reason none of them had been caught yet. He was an excellent tracker and seemed to know these woods like the back of his hand.

"With or without him, it's clear that we can't stay here," Ahlvie said.

"Agreed," Maelia said.

"I overheard them say that, if they didn't find anything by nightfall, they were going to make camp on the other side of the creek, due west of here."

They all looked at the sun hovering above the horizon. Nightfall would be here soon enough.

"Ahlvie, you know better than I do, how feasible it would be to get us away from here without drawing notice," Cyrene said.

He was more than adept at navigating the woods than either of them. His family was from a small Third Class village, Fen, leagues north of the country's northernmost city, Levin. The Taken Mountains trailed off into foothills, and a forest surrounded his village. He'd said it was nothing like the enormity of the Hidden Forest, but it was certainly different than Cyrene's First Class background with Affiliate and High Order parents or Maelia's life in Second Class with two Captains of the Guard as parents.

"We'd be sitting ducks," he told them. "We'd have more luck hiding and leaving before first light. That should give Orden sufficient time to return. I don't want to leave him behind."

"Then, we'll do that. Maelia, start packing in case we have to make a run for it. Ahlvie, find something to use as cover. I'd rather not move the horses. They'll draw too much attention. We'll set up a watch, and I'll take the first shift. You two are better with a sword, if it comes to a fight, so you should rest."

Without complaint, they immediately went into action.

Ahlvie returned with some foliage and branches for camouflage. The horses were obscured from sight by a large tree and shrubbery, and in such a short amount of time, there wasn't much more they could do. Ahlvie selected an area near the clearing to wait out in until sunset.

No one said a word. They huddled together and hoped for the best. It had been a long journey already, and they had too far to go to quit now.

A noise in the woods off to their right alerted them that someone was coming. They each took in a sharp breath. A small opening in the branches provided Cyrene with a peephole to view the heavy black boot stepping into the clearing. Her heart stopped as the Captain came into view. Maelia and Ahlvie tensed next to her.

He walked forward, his eyes searching the ground for prints to track. Ahlvie had covered their footprints as best as he could before throwing fresh leaves on the ground, but if the Captain overturned the wrong leaf...

She didn't want to think about it, and they all strained not to make a single sound. The Captain's head cocked to the side in the direction of the horses. She prayed to the Creator that they were as concealed as she thought they were. When she had made a pass by the horses, she couldn't see them. But one sound would give them all away.

The Captain took a step toward the horses and then tentatively took another, like he wasn't sure what he would find there. Cyrene was panicking, the closer he got. Ahlvie reached out and gripped her arm, as if he knew she was about to do something irrational.

When the Captain was practically on top of the horses, one of the other guardsmen barged into the clearing at a breakneck pace.

"Sir! Captain!" the woman cried. She stopped and saluted the Captain.

"What is it, Naelan?" he asked impatiently. "I'd be surprised if anything could hide from you with you trampling around the grounds like that."

"We found something up the western path. Jaela instructed me to inform you at once."

"Thank you, Naelan," he said dismissively.

"Sir," she said, saluting before retreating.

He followed Naelan out of the clearing, glancing back once before disappearing entirely. When he broke the tree line, Cyrene sighed in relief. She couldn't believe how close they had come to getting caught.

Unfortunately, their excitement was dampened by the news Naelan had delivered. They had found something along the western path. *Is Orden that something?* No one wanted to voice the concern.

They waited until dusk fell before removing their camouflage. Soon, night would follow, and Orden still hadn't returned.

"What do we do?" Maelia asked.

"We can't go after him." Cyrene hated the answer.

"We can't leave him either," Ahlvie said.

"No," she agreed, "we can't. If they apprehended him, we'll have to get him back. But it's too dark to go marching through the woods, looking for him, now. They'll need me before they can return anyway—Orden won't suffice—so that should buy us some time."

"Not the kind of time I prefer," Ahlvie grunted, scratching the back of his head.

"Me either," Maelia said.

"Either of you have a better solution?"

Maelia and Ahlvie slowly shook their heads.

Cyrene nodded. "All right then, let's bed down for the night. Don't unpack the horses. Let's just find somewhere hidden to rest for a few hours."

"Somewhere hidden in the Hidden Forest?" Ahlvie asked, cracking a half-smile.

"How can you even joke right now?" Maelia asked.

She glared at Ahlvie, and his smile vanished.

"I'm taking first watch," Cyrene interjected.

"Let me," Ahlvie insisted.

"You need rest. I couldn't go to sleep now if I tried," she insisted. "Now, go!"

Her friends set out their bedrolls, and Cyrene found a perfect location to stand guard. Her sword was hanging from her belt with her hand holding the oversize pommel as she stared forward into the darkness.

2

The
WOODS

CYRENE AWOKE WITH A START WITH HER BACK FIRMLY PRESSED against a tree, cursing herself for the fatigue. Her surroundings were pitch-black, and she knew she had been out too long already when she was supposed to be on watch.

Just as she turned to go wake Ahlvie to take over, a chill crept up her spine. She stilled, her eyes roaming the dark forest before her. She could feel someone was out there, but she found it hard to believe that the guards would venture back into the forest at night.

A low guttural growl told her that *something*, not someone, was stalking these woods.

Wolves?

She steeled herself against the rising panic. She could do nothing if she was immobilized by fear. She had to get to her friends and warn them of the danger.

Internalizing every ounce of preparation that Orden had tried to instill in her over the last couple of weeks, she crept like a wraith through the tree line and caught her first glimpse of the beast as she approached. With the forest obscuring the starlight, she could only attempt to ascertain the enormity of what lay before her. It stood taller than her, even while crouched on four legs.

Thankfully, it hadn't seen her, and she wanted to keep it that way. Even if this was the only creature of its kind in the woods, she didn't want to engage with it.

Breathlessly, she waited for the beast to pass out of her sight, and then she hurried to the edge of the clearing. When she saw what awaited her, her hand went reflexively to the sword at her side…not that it would do her much good.

Five more of the creatures filled the area. Their fur was as black as night while their eyes glowed yellow in the meager moon light. Their sharp claws curved out of their massive paws, and fangs the size of her forearm gleamed wickedly. They were not quite wolf or bear or leopard. Something more deadly, something…wrong.

Cyrene was thankful for the still night. No breeze to pick up her scent and send her to her death.

After an agonizingly slow minute, she reached her friends, still wrapped up in their blankets. Maelia slumbered lightly, her hand resting on her blade, poised for the ready. Ahlvie was covered from head to toe. Cyrene could only tell he was there because she had already known.

She bent down to wake them, but movement in the clearing held her still. The beasts were on the move. A low growl signified that one was dangerously close to her. She watched them fan out in a circle. Cyrene had never seen anything like it, and their behavior made her skin crawl.

When she turned back to check on Maelia and Ahlvie, a giant monster stood over them. Spit dripped from one vicious fang, as it was ready to devour its meal. It opened its powerful jaw, prepared to attack.

"Maelia!" Cyrene screamed in warning.

Her friend woke instantly, released her blade from its scabbard, and blocked the beast with such elegance that no one would have guessed she had just been asleep. Ahlvie scrambled out of his bedroll and reached for his weapon.

But the monster was already engaged with Maelia, and it growled its fury at being parted from its meal. Ahlvie tried to divert its attention, but the beast lunged for Maelia. She parried its blows, match for match. Her moves were graceful and precise but fiercely deadly. She ducked and rolled, lashing out at the tough fur, and she fended off the jaw that meant to crush her. She was panting from exhaustion when she finally landed an impressive killing strike. The monster fell to the ground in a pool of putrid black blood.

Ahlvie gagged at the sight of the dead animal. "What the hell was that?"

"I don't know," Maelia answered. "I've never seen anything like it."

"There are at least five others," Cyrene told them.

"Five?" Maelia gasped.

Ahlvie shook his head in disbelief and then assessed the body. His nose wrinkled as he poked the beast. "It almost looks like—"

"A wolf," Maelia finished.

Cyrene shook her head. "Worse. They feel wrong."

"Really wrong," Ahlvie agreed. "We need to get out of here."

"Now," Cyrene said.

Maelia assessed the situation and then nodded. "Let's get the horses and make a run for it. We can't kill five more without backup."

"The only backup in these woods are the blasted guards," Ahlvie spat.

Maelia sharply eyed him. She seemed to be in her element. "They might be our only choice."

Get caught by Byern guards, or get killed by monsters in the woods?

They didn't have to make that decision because, at that moment, another creature appeared. Making its way toward Cyrene, it pounced. She screamed in terror, and on instinct, she raised her sword to meet the creature. Miraculously, the blade bit into the beast's flesh. She gave it a thrust with all her might, and it drove through the creature, up to the hilt. Black blood gushed out of the dead animal. It smelled horrid as it covered her arms and coated her dress. The beast landed heavily, nearly on top of her, and Ahlvie shoved it aside to release her from its grip. She scrambled to her feet. Her hands were shaking as she tried to yank the blade out of the beast. When she had no luck, Ahlvie put his foot on the beast's side and wrenched the blade free, handing it back to Cyrene.

Two more beasts appeared. Maelia and Ahlvie were a murderous lot, fighting off the two that had come at them, but nothing they did seemed to dissuade the monsters. They couldn't keep this up, and the monsters knew it.

Cyrene rose to her feet and took a deep breath. *Okay, I can do this.* She could make her powers bend to her will. No matter how much time she spent reading the insufferable book or trying to make her powers emerge like they had when she killed the Braj, they had refused to budge. But this was life or death. They *had* to work this time.

Closing her eyes, she tried to remember what the book had said. She reached deep within herself, to the core of her magic. There, it supposedly lay dormant and untouched, ready to do her bidding. The faintest trickles, like the flutter of a butterfly's wings, brushed against her. She tried to hold on to it, to do anything to help her friends, but it was like grasping at thin air. She released her breath in a loud gasp.

She could have torn apart the enemy with her anger at her own ineptitude. Just as she went to reach within herself again, a fang bit into her arm.

She went down hard on her knees. Her sword clattered to the ground at her feet, and fire seared her flesh. She couldn't bite back her piercing shriek. Maelia broke from Ahlvie's side and sliced through the beast that had attacked Cyrene. The thing dropped with a shuddering cry next to Maelia.

Cyrene's arm was on fire. It felt like poison burning its way through her soft flesh, and she worried that the monster's teeth carried venom, like the tip of a Braj's blade. She shuddered at the thought, but she couldn't do anything at the moment. *Escape first, and assess my wounds later.*

Maelia and Ahlvie hauled her to her feet, Ahlvie scooped up her sword and replaced it in its scabbard, and the pair ushered her toward the horses. Cyrene found her stride and started forward at a brisk run, leaving the dead beast behind them. They almost made it to the horses when nearly a dozen creatures attacked.

By the Creator! What can we do against a dozen when we barely survived three?

"Get the horses," Ahlvie barked as he and Maelia engaged the first.

"I won't leave you!" Cyrene yelled.

"Go!" he screamed.

"Ahlvie!"

"Go!"

He shoved her in that direction, and she wouldn't gainsay his honor by denying him.

And so, she took off at a sprint. She had little hope that she could make it to Ceffy or that the horses would outpace these creatures. But she had to try.

Just as she was nearing their hidden location, she walked right into another pack of beasts and froze.

She was no warrior.

She didn't even have control of her magic.

She was just a girl.

But she would not go down without fighting these mongrels. Her hand was shaky as she removed her sword once more. Despite her muscles screaming in pain, the sword felt lighter and steadier than ever before. It had to be her adrenaline. She was sure. Her body hummed to the tune of the battle, and she took a steadying breath. Underneath the animal's yellow eyes, she saw a flicker of understanding about her movements.

She was ready.

"Come, beast," she snarled.

The first one lunged for her but was struck down at her feet with an arrow through its menacing yellow eye.

A battle cry erupted behind her, and a woman soared through the air. She landed lightly on her feet with an ice-white blade in her hand that appeared to be an extension of her body. She was tall with pale, almost white, blonde hair. She wore fierce camouflage britches and a shirt that hugged her form. Her blade whirred through the air, slicing and cutting.

Cyrene was dimly aware that others had joined the battle, but her eyes were locked on the incredible movements of this woman who was unlike any woman she had ever seen. She had ethereal beauty yet a ferocious ability.

After what could have been minutes or hours, a spatter of dead creatures lay at the woman's feet.

Cyrene whirled in place and found an even more gruesome display. More humans, unlike she had ever seen, fought the beasts. Their fighting style was delicate and precise. They looked like they were dancing rather than fighting, yet they were efficient in dispatching the creatures.

Cyrene couldn't spare their saviors too much thought though. She had to get to the horses and save her friends. She took one unsteady step toward the horses and then sprinted. To her shock, the horses remained, unharmed, though they were in a frenzy from the commotion. She went to Ceffy's side at once, but a scream stilled her steps.

With a resigned sigh, she untied the reins and hoisted her weary body onto Ceffy's back. She heeled the horse in the direction of the scream, her steel blade withdrawn before her.

Just as she entered the clearing, a beast sank its teeth into the beautiful stranger's side.

"No!" Cyrene screamed.

The beast jerked around, leaving the woman for death. It prowled toward Cyrene with ten more beasts on its heels. Ceffy reared up in horror at the unnatural creatures before them.

Cyrene held on for dear life. She was sure this was where it ended. They had come to kill, and they meant to see it to the end. She would need more than a blade to get out of this mess.

Cyrene steeled herself and then slid down Ceffy's side. Cyrene knew that she should have run as far and as fast as she could. But it would not have been fast enough. Her sword sank into the dirt, as if in defeat. When she released her weapon, she imagined she saw a smirk on the monster's face.

But it didn't know that, in that moment, the odds turned.

As Cyrene recalled all that she had learned from her magic book, gold letters danced across her vision. She would not yield.

The gateway to her power opened with barely any effort. A dull ache hit her core as the well of energy intensified within her body. The ache grew as more and more power flooded her system, and she coughed and clutched her chest as it filled her to the brim. She doubled over and dug her hands into the fresh dirt. There was too much. The pain was raw. She couldn't grasp control over it.

Creator!

It was as if she would suffocate from the intensity of it all. She couldn't survive this—not the creatures and not the magical torrent taking over her body. Her ears were ringing, and she ground her teeth against the inexorable pain lashing out at her bones, scraping and tearing her from the inside out.

"Don't," cried out the ethereal woman lying at Cyrene's feet.

Cyrene didn't know what the woman meant. All she was aware of was the pain and that she had failed.

Her head tilted to the sky, and with a breath, the dam broke. Her power lashed out of her in a deafening boom, rushing over the monsters like a tidal wave. She heard a crash and saw a beast had dropped to the ground. Another one dropped. And another. Then, they all dropped.

Cyrene clawed tooth and nail across the ground toward the girl. She had no energy left, and darkness beckoned her, but this couldn't all be for naught.

"Are you okay?" Cyrene croaked.

She reached out to touch the girl to try to offer some comfort.

"What *are* you?" the girl breathed.

Cyrene blacked out before she could answer.

3

The FEVER

CYRENE HAD THE DISTINCT IMPRESSION THAT SHE'D BEEN HERE before. But where here was, was not a where but a when.

The pain was gone, replaced by nothingness. She was present but distant.

What's going on? What happened in the woods? And why am I now here? Where am I exactly?

The last thing she remembered was magic burning her body from the inside out. *Is this death? Have I crossed some unnatural barrier?*

She began running through the dark. Her feet pounded on the dirt road. She was in sturdy boots that should be making far too much noise, but there was a tickle at the back of her mind that held the silence.

Before Cyrene could attempt to figure out what was happening, she abruptly stopped running. She pressed her back against a shadowed stone wall and tried to calm her breathing. Two men walked by, holding mugs of ale, and they were all but carrying a young woman between them as she regaled them with some lascivious tale.

Cyrene tried to move forward, but nothing happened. She couldn't even move an inch. She willed her pinkie to bend, and still, nothing happened.

Then, Cyrene realized why this all felt familiar. She'd had this feeling once before. Dread filled her from head to toe, but she wasn't sure if it was her own emotions...or the person she was trapped in.

Last time, it had been Serafina, the Domina whom Cyrene had heard about since she was a child.

Two thousand years ago, Serafina had been a tyrant, and Viktor Dremylon, the great ancestor of King Edric, had destroyed her tyrannical rule to raise a righteous society. Thus, the Class system had been created to differentiate the people into leadership, military, and mercantile workers.

But, when Cyrene had first encountered Serafina in a dream, Serafina had been only seventeen—like Cyrene herself—and she had been in love with Viktor. But she had discovered that she had magic and was to become a Doma.

For much of Cyrene's life, she had thought that Doma was just a name for the ancient High Court with the Domina as their queen. After going through the Doma Ascension ritual in Serafina's own dream, Cyrene now knew that Doma wielded magic. In fact, Cyrene herself was Doma.

But that did not explain why she was hiding in a shady alcove or what she was about to encounter.

The woman waited another minute before turning the corner and reaching a high hedge. Cyrene felt the prickle of the bush as she stuck her arm through it, pressed against a hard wall that opened at her touch, and then pushed her way through both. Cyrene found herself in a stuffy small pantry and wondered what she was doing here.

"Sera," a man said gruffly, grabbing her around the middle and crushing her against him.

Tears sprang to the woman's eyes. "I've missed you."

Cyrene felt as if she were intruding, but at least she now knew that she was in the same body. Serafina had allowed her access once more.

The man drew her face into his hands, and Cyrene recognized him as Viktor Dremylon. He had the same blue-gray eyes as the Dremylon royalty she knew at home—King Edric and Prince Kael.

"You came," Viktor whispered.

"I said I would." She sounded a bit defensive.

"Of course you did. I thought you had forgotten."

"I've never forgotten before."

Viktor brushed her hair back out of her face, and she closed her eyes at his gentle touch.

"Run away with me," he said.

She sighed, and Cyrene could feel Serafina's inner turmoil. She wanted it as much as she could feel the impossibility of it all.

"Just think," he continued, "we could have our own home tucked away in the south. I'd show you the ocean and the beautiful sandy beaches of Albion. We'd have children, the most beautiful children, Sera. As beautiful as their mother. Can you see it?"

"Yes." And she could. And it hurt worse than anything else in the imaginable world.

"Have that life with me."

Serafina turned her head and sighed again. "You know I cannot."

"You went to the Doma for control of your magic, and you have it. Come back to me, my love. Come back to me."

"I've always been here. I never left." Her hands were shaking. "Can't you see that I am no better than I was?"

He took her hands in his, and they stilled. "I can help. I ground you. It'll go away. You don't *need* it."

The thought of being without her powers made bile rise in her throat. Her magic was as ingrained in her as breathing. She couldn't go without it any more than she could go without air.

"You don't understand," she cried, wrenching her hands out of his grasp. "I *do* need it. I do, Viktor."

His eyes turned stony. "Why do you have to give in to this when you have everything you could ever want here? You would never want for anything with me!"

"I would want this," she said.

A shiver of magic surged up through her. Cyrene immediately recognized it, but it didn't rip through her. It felt more like a trickle of water rising up out of the river. More of a life force than an all-consuming inferno. It was bliss.

Nothing happened for a second.

Viktor gave her a disapproving look. Then, suddenly, they were both in the air, only a couple of inches but enough to startle Viktor and have him reach out for her. When he touched her, they unceremoniously dropped back onto the floor.

"Sera! You said you wouldn't!" he cried.

"You have to understand. There is no other way for you to know, Viktor. If only you could feel the energy that flows through me. It is life."

"It is poison," he spat.

Serafina took a halting step back. Cyrene felt the words, as if it were a punch in the gut.

"It has poisoned our relationship. I want my love back."

"I'm right here."

He shook his head. "The girl I knew would never have believed so much in this. Magic taints you, Sera. Please, think about our cottage on the beach." He took her wrist in his hand. "*That* is what your life is supposed to be."

"This is my life, Viktor." She tried to pull her hand back from his, but he wouldn't let her go.

"So then, we're done?"

"No!" she cried.

"Because they'll never let your kind marry such a lowly citizen. It doesn't matter that I come from an aristocratic family. I'll never compare to your magic. Is that it?"

"Viktor, no. Please! You're distorting it."

She yanked on her arm, and hysteria rose in her chest.

Cyrene wanted to knock him upside the head a couple of times until he realized what she was telling him.

"Will you marry me, Sera?" he asked, jerking her forward.

Serafina gasped. He was proposing?

Tears streamed down her face, and she couldn't decide if happiness or despair had brought them on. She knew, as she knew nothing else, that she wanted to be with Viktor, and as certainly, she would never give her magic up for him.

"Viktor," she croaked.

"Well, yes or no?"

"Give me time to think."

"Think? You need time to think?" he cried. He released her wrist like he had been burned. "We've been together our entire lives, and you have to think about whether or not you want to marry me."

"I do! I do, Viktor! I want to marry you, but..."

"But?" he roared. "The damn magic?"

"I can't give it up for you!" she screamed, collapsing to the ground at his feet. "I can't marry you. I can't. I want to, but I can't."

In disgust, he took a step back, and Serafina let sobs rack her body. Her trembling hands sank into the cellar floor. She tried to control her breathing, but too much was warring within her all at once.

Cyrene felt the buildup before she thought even Serafina was aware of it. Where before it had felt like a river, now, it felt like a dam had broken, and a tidal wave was about to flood the entire city.

"I thought you loved me," he cried.

"I do love you!"

"Maybe you never did."

"Don't say that. Please don't say that."

Viktor was silent for a second, listening to her sobs. He didn't even offer her a hand.

But Serafina was starting to realize what was happening. Whatever she had been trying to do to tamp the well did no more good than adding a pebble to the barrier. She quickly grew frantic.

A few minutes later, Viktor knelt down in front of her. He placed his fingers under her chin and forced her to look at him. "You won't marry me?"

She shook her head, unable to repeat the words.

"Very well."

"Viktor—"

"No, it's too late."

"I love you," she breathed.

"My father means to have me married by the end of the year," he admitted.

Serafina's mouth fell open. "Wh-what?"

"I wanted it to be you, but it must happen regardless. You're forcing me to marry someone else, Sera. This is your doing."

"No. Please don't."

He shrugged. "I have no other choice. Who would you have me choose? Tremlyn? Sauriel? Or should it be Margana?"

"How dare you ask me that! I will die if you marry someone else."

"And I am already dead without you!"

The words crashed over her, and everything she had been holding back released in an uncontrollable wave. It knocked both of them back in opposite directions against the walls. Viktor slammed his head into the stone. Serafina fell in a heap against the shelving in the pantry. The walls shook, and all the food and supplies crashed down to the ground, destroying their safe haven.

"Viktor!" she cried, crawling out of the rubble and rushing to his side. "Are you okay?"

He groaned and tried to sit up. She helped him, but when her hand came back sticky, she realized it was blood. If she'd had any ability in healing, she would have helped him. But she wasn't certain enough of her abilities as it was, and she had expelled so much power. She felt drained. She hadn't had an explosion like that since she had been presented to the Doma court.

"What did you do?" he asked.

"I don't know," she whispered.

She could hear footsteps coming toward them.

Cyrene knew that this was wrong. This was all a secret, and Serafina couldn't possibly get caught.

"You need to get out of here, Sera," he commanded. He pushed her away and tried to lie back down.

"I can't leave you here."

"What would they do if they found you?"

"Nothing. I'm Doma," she reminded him.

By the steely glint in his eyes, that was the last thing he'd wanted to hear. "You might get no punishment for using your powers here, but up in the castle, you might."

Serafina tried to put on a brave face, but Cyrene could tell there would be a serious penalty. She was to be better than the law to be able to uphold it. The sneaking out to see a man would be enough to get her in trouble, but the outburst would cost her even more.

"It's okay," she told him.

She needed to be here for him. He was losing blood. He needed a healer.

"Sera, go! I don't want to see you again."

"Viktor, please."

He turned his head away. "I'll be married in a matter of months, and then what will we do?"

She didn't have an answer for that, and Cyrene didn't like the way that made her feel. She had done enough with a married man—a married *king*—that she didn't want to think about repercussions.

"No answer," he said with a sigh. "You've chosen your life. Now, I'm choosing mine. Good-bye, Sera."

She swallowed hard. Tears were streaming down her face once more. "No matter what I am, I am always yours."

"What are you?" he asked desperately.

"What are you?"

Cyrene groaned incoherently.

"She's waking up!"

"Wha—"

"Child who walks in the Light," a voice whispered in her ear, "tell us, what are you?"

"I am yours."

"Mine?"

"Whatever I am, I am always yours."

"But what are you that can shine so bright?"

"Doma. I am Doma."

4

The
LEIF

"WAKE UP, CHILD. WAKE UP."

Cyrene's eyes fluttered open. The face of an angel—heart-shaped with large almond-shaped golden eyes and pouty pink lips—hovered over her. Her dark hair was long, to her waist. She was dressed in a floor-length white gown that shimmered and flowed effortlessly. She looked wise beyond her years.

"Farewell, child," she whispered as she stood. "Avoca!"

Another woman walked into the room, and Cyrene gasped. It was the woman from the woods. She was as beautiful as Cyrene had last seen with gold-spun hair and liquid blue eyes. She had an unmistakable innocence about her, despite the fact that Cyrene knew she was a fierce warrior.

"Yes, Healer," Avoca said. She touched her hand to her lips in a show of deference. She was dressed in leggings with a loose shirt and a jacket contoured to her shape in a camouflage of greens that matched the forest along with soft brown boots. Her clothes looked the worse for wear.

The healer nodded and then exited. She looked like she was floating more than walking.

Cyrene glanced around at her surroundings. Her room was a nondescript wooden structure with smooth, rounded walls and a green cloth covering the entrance. She was lying on a small bed with delicate white sheets. The room held little else for decoration besides a string of colorful glowing jars hanging from the ceiling. Everything smelled earthy and fresh.

"What's going on?" Cyrene asked. "Where am I?"

She tried to sit up but hissed as pain washed over her.

Avoca rushed to her side. "Take it slow. You've gone through quite an ordeal. You were lucky we got you here in time."

"Where am I? Where are my friends? Were you there with those…those things?"

"Your questions will be answered in time. You have an audience with the Queen."

"Queen?" Cyrene gasped.

"Yes. Now, up."

Avoca put an arm behind her back and slowly assisted Cyrene into a sitting position. The pain was there, but it did seem that her body was remembering how to function, lessening the impact. As a unit, she turned her body to the side, slid her feet to the floor, and stood. She was barefoot, and the floor was cool to the touch.

For the first time, Cyrene realized that she was no longer in her blue Byern gown but a loose-fitting white dress, similar to the healer's. It was more like a shift, and she blushed at the shape her figure took under the thin material.

"Where are my clothes?"

"Destroyed," Avoca said without emotion. "Now, let's go."

She disappeared through the door without further preamble, and Cyrene hurried after her. As soon as she stepped out of the room, her mouth fell open. *This* was unlike anything she had ever seen. She was currently in a forest village. Homes were carved into the giant trees surrounding her, bridges were strung among the branches, and vines dropped down to the ground where music drifted up toward her. From her vantage point, she could see people dancing and eating around a bonfire. She had walked right into some strange woodland festival.

"Come on," Avoca cried, exasperated. She grasped Cyrene's wrist and pulled her toward a bridge.

"Where am I?"

"The Queen will decide if you receive answers."

"You brought me all the way out here, and you're not willing to tell me where I am?"

"No."

"My companions—"

"Don't bother."

When they reached the other side of the bridge, Cyrene pulled up short. "Answer one question! I have to know where I am, how my friends are, what is going on."

Avoca barely batted an eye. "You are the mystery wrapped in light. When the Queen deems you worthy of answers, you shall receive them."

Cyrene huffed. "You were there…with the creatures. Were you the one who saved me?"

Her downcast eyes told the truth.

"How many died?" Cyrene asked.

Avoca took a deep breath and then met her eyes. "All of them."

Cyrene brought her hand to her mouth. But before she could get more of an explanation, Avoca was on the move again.

Cyrene wasn't sure she was prepared for more answers. She swallowed hard and kept her head held high as they meandered the twists and turns.

They went through a lush overhang of vines and into the outer chamber of an enormous tree. The room was full of beautifully colored objects with purposes that she had no clue of. In a kaleidoscope of colors, the same glowing jars hung from the ceiling, producing beautiful soft light.

With his back to them, a man stood in front of a large gold door intricately wrought with climbing vines, like the vines in Queen Kaliana's chambers back in the Nit Decus castle in Byern.

"What are you doing here?" Avoca demanded.

At her question, the man slowly turned around. He was as equally beautiful as Avoca and the healer. His face was roguishly handsome with impossibly high cheekbones, light hair, and eyes a vivid shade of gold. He wore the same type of green camouflage clothes as Avoca, but his looked brand-new.

"Hello, Ava," he said with a toothy grin.

Her eyes turned steely. "Ceis'f."

"I'm here to bear witness, of course."

Avoca ground her teeth together and tilted her head to the side. She looked like she would rather be dropped back into the woods with those monsters than standing before him.

"Witness to what?" Cyrene whispered.

Avoca sighed. "My unequivocal failure."

She was getting answers, but they were no more of use to her than Avoca's silence.

Ceis'f's eyes passed right over Cyrene, as if she didn't exist, before he turned back to the door. It opened a second later, and another man beckoned them into the inner chamber. The room was twice as large as the one they had just been in.

A small woman sat on a wooden throne at the front of the room. On her left, two other people sat at a table, speaking in hushed tones.

Their queen was beautiful and ageless with sweeping long blonde hair so fair that it was almost white with the lightest blue eyes. She wore a simple gown with no adornment, but she did not need it. The only embellishment was a crown of flowers atop her head.

When Cyrene met her eyes, she glimpsed nothing but wisdom and sharp intelligence.

"Avoca," the Queen said.

Avoca stepped forward and touched her hand to her lips. The Queen repeated the action, and Cyrene filed it away as some kind of greeting of their people.

"Queen Shira," Avoca murmured.

"Report."

"She's to report in front of *it?*" Ceis'f said.

"Are you questioning me, Ceis'f?"

"No. I was just unaware that we would be so freely opening our gates to their kind," he spat out.

"Now, you are aware," she said.

Her tone never changed from its neutral state, but Cyrene could feel the tension rolling off of Ceis'f. She was glad the Queen had put him in his place. Even if Cyrene had no idea where she was, at least no one else had called her an *it*.

"I responded to the Indres presence in the area with my team. We knew immediately that there were too many for a six team. Ceis'f came with backup. We attacked simultaneously. They were surrounding three humans—two girls and a boy. Our teams slaughtered close to forty Indres," Avoca told her.

Cyrene gasped. *Indres!* More creatures of myth had stood true before her eyes. Death wolves, they were sometimes called. Too scary, even for younger children, to hear the stories.

The Queen's eyebrows rose at the number. Her eyes flickered to Ceis'f for confirmation, and he nodded gravely.

"One was getting away, so I followed it to finish the job. I walked into an ambush and nearly died. The human called the

Indres off, nearly burning herself out, and then collapsed. Every Indres in the area lay dead."

Burned myself out? Is that what happened? And how does Avoca know that?

"How many died from the teams?" the Queen asked.

Avoca winced. "Four of mine and two of Ceis'f's."

"A whole team." The Queen seemed to consider that for a minute, and then her eyes turned to Cyrene. "Child."

Cyrene swallowed and then stepped forward. She had so many questions. But, for once, she held her tongue. She did not want to anger these people who could take on over forty Indres.

"What are you?" the Queen asked.

"My name is Cyrene Strohm."

The Queen thoughtfully tilted her head. "My healer said you used the word _Doma_."

Cyrene's hands sweat at the statement. _The Queen knew. Without a doubt._

Cyrene had used magic in that clearing. In fact, she was sure it had almost killed her. In part, that was why she had needed their healer. _But how could they have someone to heal her like that? How could they know about Indres? How could they know about magic?_

"Yes," Cyrene finally responded.

"And you used Doma power to destroy the Indres?" She didn't wait for Cyrene to confirm. "Where did you learn it?"

"I...I didn't. I don't know what I did."

"Untrained?" the Queen asked with a sigh.

Cyrene nodded slowly.

She was untrained. That was the whole point in leaving Byern. The traveling merchant Basille Selby had told her she needed to go to Eleysia to learn from Matilde and Vera, and that had been confirmed for her in her vision of Serafina. She didn't understand how they could be alive two thousand years later, but they were her only hope.

"I've never seen anyone hold so much power," Avoca interjected. "Even as she was burning herself out, she was still collecting more."

"You were half-dead, Ava," Ceis'f responded. "How do you even know that you actually saw this human use Doma power?"

"I know what I saw, Ceis'f! *Believe in those whose honor doth shine.* That was the Doma motto after all, and she looked like the sun before she released her powers and wiped out the Indres."

Cyrene's head was spinning. Those words, that motto, had gotten her out of a lot of bad situations in the last couple of months. She couldn't believe the words were related to the Doma. Not to mention, she was having a conversation about her magic with complete strangers, as if it were normal.

"Enough!" the Queen commanded. "You two will remain silent while I speak with the Doma."

"You truly believe her to be a Doma?" Ceis'f asked with a barely concealed scoff.

Queen Shira narrowed her eyes, and Ceis'f quickly closed his mouth.

"I believe she is Doma, yes. Not because I have seen her use her abilities, though I have no reason to doubt Avoca's story, but because of this."

Then, she slowly retrieved something from her side and held out Cyrene's book for all to see.

Cyrene gasped. "That is mine!"

"I'm quite aware. It was found when we searched your things."

"How dare you!" Cyrene snapped. "That is personal and classified."

The Queen gave her a wry smile. "And you can read its text?"

Cyrene opened her mouth and then snapped it shut. "Can you?"

"Only magical users have the ability to see the written text," the Queen said with a nod. "Anyone who attempted to read the book who had not passed a magical test would lose time—hours, days, years—due to the spell written into the text. A precaution to keep those who should not have access to the text from accessing it."

Cyrene tried not to show her surprise. That exact thing had happened to her when she first tried to read it.

"Are you actually saying, *that* book is the lost *Book of the Doma?*" Avoca asked in awe.

"Yes," she stately simply. "And you can read it, can't you?"

Cyrene nodded slowly. "But what exactly is the lost *Book of the Doma?*"

"A precious historical artifact of the Doma reign. Very few books chronicled their magical prowess, and *this* is one of them."

"The Circadian Prophecy stated that it would reappear with the Doma," Avoca said.

"Yes. If we have read it as intended, the lost *Book of the Doma* would be given to a new Doma, and so would begin the Rise of the Children of the Dawn."

"Rise?" Ceis'f snorted. "Even if this girl is a Doma, there is still only one. That isn't a rise."

The Queen smiled. "We will see."

Cyrene's head was spinning. The lost *Book of the Doma*. Circadian Prophecy. The Rise of the Children of the Dawn. She had thought, when she found out what the book meant, it would lead to answers…not more questions.

"Are Doma called the Children of the Dawn?" Cyrene asked.

That was the name that Basille Selby had used with her all those months ago. She had known even then that the man knew more than he let on.

"Yes, child. You know so little of your own people," the Queen said with a sad sigh. "I believe, at this time, it is best if the Doma remains in Eldora. We have to determine what our part is in the Rise of the Children of the Dawn. And, until she can protect herself, she is a danger to everyone she encounters."

"What?" Cyrene cried at the same time as Ceis'f said, "Never!"

"We cannot allow any individual to leave who could level a city without a way to control the current."

"What about my friends?" Cyrene asked. "I don't even know where I am or who you are or what you want with me, but they were out there with me last night. I cannot stay here while they are still alive."

"Friends?" the Queen asked Avoca.

"Captured by human soldiers and taken to Strat."

Cyrene's world tilted. "No."

"Are they Doma?" Queen Shira asked.

"No," she breathed. "They were to go with me on my mission. I must save them."

"Let her go," Ceis'f said. "We shouldn't have scum in our sacred halls."

"She saved my life!" Avoca protested.

"To your greatest shame, Ava."

"Enough!" Queen Shira cried, raising her voice for the first time. "You two are acting no better than children. Would you like me to strip you of your teams and return you to child status?"

Avoca and Ceis'f stood stiffly. Their shoulders were set back, and they shifted uncomfortably, back and forth, from one foot to the other. Cyrene wondered if they knew how similarly they acted in that moment.

"What is your mission, child?" Queen Shira asked her.

Cyrene ground her teeth together. "It's classified but of the utmost importance. I will stop at nothing to achieve it."

"I see. Does it have something to do with this?" She raised the book again.

Cyrene straightened herself up and nodded once. "Yes."

The Queen tapped her lips as she considered Cyrene. "I'm sorry. I can only grant you visitation rights. Avoca, you are to remain as her guide until I can decide on how to proceed."

"But I must find my friends!" Cyrene interjected.

"You are a danger to yourself as much as the rest of the world. We wouldn't let a newborn walk out of the nest. You may not leave the city until I say otherwise. Be gracious," she said lowly, "that I am permitting you this much."

5

The GIFT

"THIS WAY." AVOCA GRABBED CYRENE BY HER ARM AND hauled her out of the Queen's chamber. Ceis'f followed behind them, and Avoca threw him a derisive look over her shoulder. "I'll show you to your room."

Cyrene's mind was whirring with all the new information, but she still had so much more that she didn't understand. "Will you answer my questions now?"

"Go ahead," Ceis'f said as he passed. "Ava wants to tell her new pet about our people and bring destruction down on us all. Makes perfect sense."

Avoca faced him. "I'm sorry about the teams. I would never have gone in there with two six teams if I'd realized how many Indres there were. But every death isn't your parents."

"That's enough!" Ceis'f's eyes narrowed, and a wall seemed to shift in between them as he shut down. "Enjoy your pet." He stalked off, all broody and melancholy.

"He's pleasant," Cyrene said dryly.

"Come on." Avoca pushed forward.

When Cyrene exited the chamber, she noticed that the music had increased in volume, and voices were mixed with the instruments. People were dancing and twirling, unlike anything she had ever seen.

She had been to many dances in the Byern court that King Edric had thrown and even more during her childhood. Dancing was structured with specific steps that she'd had to perfect to get the fluidity of the movement. She had a natural knack for it.

But this dancing was nothing like that.

It was a fast-paced, joyous affair. People stomped and clapped and cheered along with the movements. Men and women danced with their bodies pressed together as they quick-stepped across the hard-packed ground. It was sensational and made her breathless just from watching it.

"Are you coming?" Avoca asked.

"What's going on?"

"The Harvest Moon Festival."

Cyrene looked up through the thick tree canopy and saw nothing but sunlight. "It lasts all day?"

"And all night, as the harvest moon presents itself as a blessing. Are these really the questions you want answered?" Avoca asked. She stood with her feet spaced apart and her arms crossed. She was clearly not happy to be working as an escort.

"No," Cyrene said. She took one last glance at the dancing and followed Avoca.

A few minutes later, they stopped in front of a door.

"What's this?"

The room she'd been in before only had a cloth to cover the entranceway.

"The visitor's living quarters, of course. You didn't think that you would be kept in the infirmary, did you?"

Cyrene hadn't even known that she had been in the infirmary. It certainly hadn't looked like the ones at home, which were blank sterile rooms full of medicinal tools, herbs, and treatments.

When Avoca realized Cyrene wasn't going to respond, she opened the door.

For visitor's quarters, the room was immaculate with the same curved wooden walls and hanging jars of light. A plush rug covered the floor, and the most impressively carved furniture took up the space. A giant bed with climbing vines cut into the frame was set against one wall, and a writing table sat across from it with fresh parchment and ink. The common area had a small dining table with flowers bursting from a vase.

"We weren't sure you would be staying, and we didn't have much time to arrange things for you, so we did what we could. A bath is being drawn in the adjacent room," Avoca told her. "We don't have many visitors."

"It's…it's wonderful," she admitted.

And it truly was. They had delicacies a plenty at home, but this place seemed special…magical. Not to mention, she had been on the road for weeks, and a proper bath had been nearly impossible.

"All right then," Avoca said as she turned to leave.

"You're not leaving me here, are you?" Cyrene asked frantically.

"I have things to do," she grumbled.

"I'm sorry about your team." Cyrene's voice was soft. She was in a different world without a way to escape and with people who knew about her magic. She needed a friend.

"Me, too," Avoca whispered. She paused and then sighed, as if resigned. "Thank you for saving me."

Cyrene cleared her throat. "You're welcome. Though I'm not sure what I did."

"I was bitten, and you called the Indres off me."

"But…how?"

"I'm not certain I understand your question."

"I just found out that I could…do this. Magic doesn't exist back home!"

Avoca laughed, actually laughed at her. Cyrene narrowed her eyes and waited for her to stop.

"You really do know nothing," she said when she seemed to realize Cyrene was serious. "How old are you?"

"Seventeen."

"You must have just manifested."

"I…what?" Cyrene asked.

"Manifested. Produced your abilities. If they don't come in by seventeen, then you'll never have them. Were you ever good at anything when you were growing up, particularly related to the elements? Anything with earth, water, wind, or fire?"

Cyrene considered the question and tried to think of where she performed well. "Like gardening?"

"Sure. Plant life listens to the call of your energies. Earth magic in particular."

The night of her Presenting ceremony came to her mind. *What had I said to King Edric that day?*

"My sister says I can predict the weather."

"Can…can people predict or alter the weather?" Cyrene asked.

Avoca stared at her. "Not in two millennia."

"Oh."

"Some minor changes can be made, usually with powerful water or air wielders, but weather is complicated, and much of our…your population was decimated in the War of the Light."

"The War of the…what?"

"The War of the Light," Avoca repeated, not giving Cyrene any further guidance. Avoca nodded to herself. "As it is the Harvest Moon Festival today, I have many things to prepare for, and now, I must take care of my fallen men. Stay here and get dressed. I will return to escort you to the festival as a guest, and we can discuss all of these questions at a later time."

Cyrene sighed in relief. "Thank you, Avoca. But who are your people, and why have I never heard of you?"

A true smile broke out on Avoca's face. "You have heard of us. Your world knows us only as Leifs."

She shook her head and laughed. "You're joking. Leifs don't exist. They're a fairy tale you sing to little children to warn them of the danger of the woods."

Avoca arched one eyebrow and then strode to the door. "And where do you think you are, Doma?"

The door closed behind her with a jarring bang, and fear crept through Cyrene's body.

Is every story true? Am I standing in the middle of a nightmare?

Leif, Leif, Leif Thief.
Don't get caught by a Leif Thief.
You must go in.
You can't come out.
Da-da, da, da-da, da, da.

The nursery rhyme played over and over in Cyrene's head as she stripped out of the Leif outfit, dipped fully into the heated bath, and waited for Avoca to return.

Leifs were real. She couldn't believe it. When she thought about Leifs she envisioned spritely creatures with glittery faces and pointed ears, who snatched children out of their beds at night. Instead, she was met with forest dwelling warriors. It seemed utterly impossible. But then again, she had thought Braj and Indres were made up, and she had encountered them, too.

All the while, she worried about her friends and whether she would ever be able to leave here to find them, but at least she was finally getting answers.

Cyrene finished her bath and returned to the bedroom to find a new Leif gown in royal blue waiting for her. She dressed quickly and pulled her hair up.

Night fell before Avoca returned to Cyrene's quarters. Avoca had changed out of her camouflage into a long blue dress that matched her eyes with braided gold sleeves and a matching band around her waist.

"Are you ready?" Avoca asked.

"Yes."

"As a guest, you will be seated at the royal table," Avoca explained as they circled back through the canopy to the floor.

"Why?" Cyrene asked in shock.

In Byern, guests in court were frequent enough, and while they were esteemed, they never sat with the king and queen.

Avoca scrutinized her and then responded, "Guests have the favor of the Queen, Doma."

"Oh, I see," Cyrene said, noting the differences between their cultures. "You can call me Cyrene, not Doma."

"As it is your title, I would prefer to address you as such, but I take your request and foreign customs for what they are."

"Thank you."

"Where exactly did you come from?"

"I'm from the capital city in Byern."

Avoca stopped in her tracks and turned to stare at Cyrene. Her nose was upturned, and she looked aghast. *"Byern?"*

"Yes."

"It is a good thing that Ceis'f does not know where you are from." Avoca controlled her facial features, but her voice still held disdain. "He might cut you down himself."

"And why would he do that?" Cyrene asked. She tilted her head up and held on to her pride for her homeland.

"You know too little about your people if you can defend them so easily," Avoca snapped before striding purposefully away.

Cyrene was left wondering what exactly she'd meant by that.

When they reached the ground floor, Avoca directed her into a spacious ballroom. Hundreds of Leifs were seated in high-backed chairs at artfully carved round tables. The floor had been formed from smoothed sparkling pebbles that reflected the dim lighting.

Cyrene's mouth watered as soon as she walked inside. The tables were piled high with the best-smelling food she had ever encountered. Gold goblets were placed before every individual, but no one was eating yet.

It wasn't until she was halfway across the room that she realized the voices were quieting and people were staring at her.

She heard someone whisper, "Human," and another said, "Six team," so she tried not to listen anymore.

Queen Shira was easy to pick out at the front of the room with a crown of climbing vines in her hair. That made Cyrene wish for her Affiliate pin, but if Avoca had been offended that she was from Byern, she was sure wearing it would have been dangerous.

"Queen Shira," Avoca whispered. She pressed her hand to her lips in deference.

The Queen returned the gesture.

Then, Avoca pointed at one of the empty chairs at the Queen's table. "Here."

"Where will you sit?" Cyrene asked without thinking.

She only knew three people in the entire place, and she didn't want Avoca to be far, especially since Ceis'f was seated at this table.

"Where I must."

And then, without ceremony, she strode around the table and took a seat at Queen Shira's right side.

Cyrene promptly took her seat. The right side was a sign of preference at home. Consort Daufina, the King's highest advisor, always sat to his right. It had to mean *something* that Avoca was seated in that position of favor.

"Let's begin," Queen Shira said.

Dinner tasted as good as it smelled. The feast was a merry gathering, and people spoke heartily at the tables as they ate. No one engaged Cyrene in conversation, so she remained silent.

Once the plates were cleared away, Queen Shira stood. Silence immediately followed, and all eyes turned toward her. Cyrene could feel the anticipation from everyone around her. It even made her lean forward as she waited to hear what the Queen had to say.

"Thank you for joining me for the Feast of the Harvest Moon. The Creator shines on us with her returning blessings. We have had much loss, but with each year, we are afforded a new beginning. Our harvest was plentiful, the sacrifices of a few have secured the whole, and we have among us a Doma and the sign of the Rise of the Children of the Dawn."

Whispers broke out across the room, and Cyrene felt her cheeks warm. She hadn't expected the Queen to mention her. The Queen might not feel so secure if she could see how many angry eyes turned toward Cyrene. A number of people appeared to agree with Ceis'f.

"Silence!" Queen Shira called. "Our honored guest tonight is Doma Cyrene, and she has been granted the rights of our people until she departs. I expect everyone to treat her with that same respect. Now, before we return outdoors to celebrate the Creator's blessing, my daughter has requested to be the first to give forth her gift of the new beginning."

Cyrene looked around the table and then out into the audience, wondering who the Queen's daughter was and what a gift of the new beginning entailed.

The Queen took her seat, and with her chin tilted up, Avoca stood gracefully from her seat. Cyrene narrowed her eyes, curious as to why she was standing.

"Thank you, Mother," Avoca said.

Cyrene's mouth fell open. *Avoca is the...princess?* That made no sense. She was sent on errands, like a servant, and forced to work in a military role, like someone in the Second Class. A princess should be learning her duties to better serve the country and eventually marry and become queen. It was reckless to risk her life as a soldier.

"I am glad that our new beginning starts tonight," Avoca began without preamble. "For this past evening, Ceis'f and I were out with two six teams and were attacked by a horde of Indres. As you have since heard, six of our warriors have fallen. Their lives lie heavily on my heart, and I will never forget their names or faces. However, I would not be standing here before you"—she stopped and gestured to Ceis'f and a table in the corner—"none of us would be standing here today, if not for a miracle."

Cyrene blinked. *Did Avoca just call me a miracle?*

"Doma, will you rise?" Avoca asked Cyrene.

She stood on shaky legs before a rapt audience. Avoca strode around the table and stood before her. Cyrene's heart hammered in her chest as she waited.

"I only have one thing to offer you as a gift of my new beginning, and that is my life."

And then Avoca knelt in front of Cyrene before the entire audience.

The room broke out into pandemonium. Cries and shouts echoed throughout the room. Chairs were knocked back to the ground as others exclaimed their distaste. Ceis'f jumped to his feet, grasped Cyrene, and pulled her back a few feet away from the Princess.

"Don't even think about it, *Doma*," he growled into her ear.

Cyrene stood, frozen, in shock. She didn't know what was happening, but it seemed like Avoca had just…forfeited her life.

The
CEREMONY

QUEEN SHIRA STOOD REGALLY, COMPLETELY UNPERTURBED BY
the fact that her daughter and heir to the throne had offered her
life to a stranger. She walked around the table to where Avoca
knelt, ready for a swift end to her existence.

"Stand," the Queen said. Her voice was firm but comforting.

Avoca's chest rose and fell heavily, and then she stood to face
her mother. A signal passed between them as they stared at each
other. Then, Queen Shira nodded softly. A smile played on Avoca's
features for a second and then was immediately wiped away. *She
doesn't actually expect me to kill her, does she?*

The Queen faced the frantic crowd and raised her hand, calling
for silence. It took longer than before as people were reluctant to
stop discussing Avoca's offering.

"Please return to the Festival celebrations and begin to
distribute gifts among yourselves."

Complaints rose from the crowd, but the Queen stopped them
with a sharp look in their direction.

"No harm will come to Princess Avoca. In fact, you are
disrespecting her gift to our visitor and the Creator herself by
speaking out against it."

That shut everyone up.

Though it didn't lessen Ceis'f's grip on Cyrene. He held her in
place the entire time as the rest of the Leif population filed out of
the room to go outside.

"Ceis'f, release our visitor," Queen Shira ordered.

"She's going to kill Avoca," Ceis'f protested.

"You are insulting our guest."

Ceis'f grumbled under his breath and then roughly released Cyrene. She staggered a few feet forward and then righted herself.

"What is going on?" Cyrene asked. "Why is Avoca offering herself to me?"

"You saved my life; thus, my life is forfeit," she whispered. She turned to face Ceis'f. "Surely, you can understand. My greatest shame—"

"Ava, I didn't mean…this," he said.

Cyrene put herself between Avoca and Ceis'f and shook her head. "I don't want your life, Avoca. There has been too much death already."

"You are rejecting my gift?" Avoca gasped.

"What good will your death bring?" Cyrene asked before anyone else could respond. "You are a crown princess. It would be a waste. I did not risk myself to save you so you could throw your life away so casually."

Queen Shira stepped forward then. "I must agree with the Doma on this."

Ceis'f breathed a sigh of relief at the words.

"Avoca, are you quite set on your gift to the Doma?" Queen Shira asked.

"Yes," she responded fiercely.

"No!" Ceis'f cried.

The Queen fixed him with her icy stare. "Do not believe that I cannot dismiss you, Ceis'f."

He ground his teeth but remained silent.

"Since you are set on your gift, might I make another suggestion?"

Avoca nodded her agreement.

"I have been around for a very long time. My mother and two older sisters were killed in the War of the Light nearly two thousand years ago. I was but a baby at the time. So much of their knowledge was lost when we did not win the war, but much has been handed down that I still have access to. At that time, we had more freedom between Leif and Doma. Many of us even chose to live among them, and they, among us.

"Magic has a certain consistency in the universe that draws in more of the same. Like calls to like. Magic calls to magic. And, at the time, Doma and Leif could be bound to one another for alliance, love, and even sometimes blood debt. Your magic would tie you to one another—weld it, increase it, intensify it. And, depending on the circumstances, the two people bound could not break the bond unless the bond had been satisfied. In your case, Avoca, until your debt has been repaid."

Cyrene shook her head. "No."

"Absolutely not." Ceis'f finally seemed to agree with her on something.

"It's perfect," Avoca said.

"It's hardly *perfect*! It means you're *bound* to me. I don't want to be tied to anyone. I'm my own person. I have my own life. And I have things I have to do. This is all well and good that you want to offer yourself up to me, but did you ever think I might not want that at all? You all are practically holding me hostage while my friends are in danger. Clearly, no one else sees the need for haste besides me!"

"I understand your need for haste," the Queen stated. "I understand a great deal more than that."

"Don't you see? I can help," Avoca said to Cyrene and then addressed her mother. "If my life belongs with her, then I would like to request to leave Eldora to go with her to help her friends."

"What?" Cyrene and Ceis'f said at the same time.

Avoca turned back to Cyrene with determination in her gaze.

"You do not know our customs, Doma. All I have is honor, and that was taken from me when I did not die a warrior's death. At first, I was angry with you for stealing away my right to die then and there. I thought it would be better if I forfeited my life to you, but now, I see what I did not consider before. My mother spoke of our part in the Circadian Prophecy. Why would the Doma appear to me in our very woods and save my life? There must be a reason. *This* is that reason."

Queen Shira smiled. "You believe this is how we fit into the Prophecy?"

"How could it be otherwise? It is right before our eyes."

"No one really knows how prophecies work," Ceis'f said. "You're grasping at thin air."

Avoca ignored him. "This is my choice. Whether we complete the official ceremony or not, I am bound to you. Without fulfilling my duty to you, I cannot properly accept my role in our society."

Avoca spoke with such conviction that Cyrene was no longer surprised that she had been groomed as a princess. No matter how backward their society was, it was clear that this really mattered to her.

Cyrene swallowed. "What does the ceremony entail exactly?"

"Come with me," the Queen said.

Ceis'f grasped Avoca's arm. "You can't actually mean to do this."

"I mean for you not to interfere." She withdrew from his grasp.

Queen Shira brought them into a giant domed library that made Cyrene smile with fond memories of Byern and Albion. It sent a pang through her chest as she thought about her best friend, Rhea, who had insisted on staying behind.

The Queen removed a book from a shelf and shuffled through the pages. "Here it is. Just as I thought, the magic is particular and requires three parts—acceptance of the ritual, a test of loyalty to check for compatibility, and an elemental binding."

"A test of loyalty?" Cyrene asked. *Why does that sound so familiar?*

"Yes. Not every person can be bound. In fact, even before the War of the Light, few did so."

"Why?" Avoca asked.

"Only magical users can be officially bound, and it is even rarer for people between races to be bound, for our magic differs slightly. Leif magic relies solely on the elements. We draw from things around us to increase our powers. Doma magic is able to do this as well, but there is always a component inherent to the user. You produce magic from within as well as draw from the outside world, which is why you need more training. But, to answer your question, some people feared sharing their powers and learning new abilities. They believed that it could weaken them."

"You mean, it could weaken your own daughter?" Ceis'f growled.

"It makes you weak in that you are loyal to someone other than yourself, Ceis'f. It takes a certain kind of person to share yourself and your magic with another. I, myself, do not think that is weakness but strength. Now, are you willing to try to see if you are compatible?"

"I am," Avoca said immediately.

Cyrene mulled over the situation. Avoca was her best bet of getting out of here. As far as Cyrene saw it though, her gift had already been paid. Cyrene had saved Avoca from the Indres, but someone had had to bring her back to Eldora to be healed. Cyrene could have easily died out there, alone in the woods.

Just that thought alone dredged up feelings of gratitude and loyalty to Avoca. And, while the thought of sharing her powers terrified her, it also excited her. She didn't feel the same fears that the Queen had discussed. She wasn't afraid to weaken herself. Having someone to guide her, to share her frustrations, to maybe even tap into the floodgates would be a comfort.

"What happens if we're not compatible?" Cyrene asked finally.

"The loyalty portion can effect people in different ways. Some have felt nothing, some have felt a lingering feeling of attachment to the person, and some have died."

Cyrene sucked in a breath.

"Think on it. I am going to mix the ingredients required in the instructions, and then I will need your answer."

The Queen stepped out of the library, leaving the three of them alone. Cyrene paced as she thought about how she had gotten herself into this mess. Avoca and Ceis'f argued quietly across the room. Ceis'f was likely trying to talk Avoca out of this foolishness.

The thing was, if Avoca wanted to follow her around on her mission, she could do that, and there wasn't much Cyrene could do to stop her. She couldn't even touch her powers. She liked to believe that she was a good judge of character and that she followed her gut when it told her to believe in people. Ahlvie had seemed like a dirty, drunk scoundrel, but she had put her faith in him when no one else would. And he had helped her, blind of her reasons. This had the same nagging tug.

She *should* trust Avoca.

She *should* be loyal to these people.

She *should* be bound.

"I'll do it," Cyrene said.

Avoca nodded in satisfaction, but Ceis'f seethed next to her.

"Neither of you has any idea what you're getting into. It's reckless. Avoca. Will you not see reason? You are risking your life and the safety of all Leifs by abandoning us to run away with *it*."

"I've had about enough of you," Cyrene cried. "You were out there yesterday. You saw the Indres. I saved your life, too. At best, you would have run away as a coward. At worst, you would be dead. If *you* had any honor, you would allow the Princess to make decisions for herself. Certainly, she is capable of doing something without you breathing down her neck."

"You are mistaken," he growled. "I have no honor. Your kind robbed me of it."

"Ceis'f," Avoca whispered. She placed her hand on his arm. "That is a tale for another day."

"I will not idly sit by and watch you throw your life away," he said, wrenching his arm free and storming toward the door.

The Queen returned at that moment. She raised a questioning eye at Ceis'f as he hurried past her but did not object when he left the room. "Have we come to a decision?"

"Let's do it," Cyrene said.

Cyrene and Avoca each took a glass that Queen Shira had handed to them. Cyrene had a sense of déjà vu settle over her, but she couldn't place it exactly. She glanced over at Avoca, who seemed entirely resolute about her decision.

"Please grasp arms." The Queen clutched the book in her hand and faced the girls.

They looked at each other. Cyrene swallowed back her fear. She stretched out her right hand, and they locked forearms in a tight embrace.

The Queen began to read directly from the book. "*The Bound ceremony is a sacred act, set up to strengthen and combine the magical properties from the originators. Three qualities above all link you together—loyalty, trust, and acceptance.*"

Cyrene gasped and felt a tingle shoot up her arm. Avoca seemed to have felt the same thing.

As disconcerting as the strange feeling in her arm was, it was stranger still to realize that she had heard these words before at her Ring of Gardens ceremony back in Byern. The Byern royalty had stood before her and made her drink a vial. Then, she had seen a series of possibilities for her life—Third Class, leaving the man she loved, giving up her baby, and bowing to Kael Dremylon as king. She had chosen to put her country above all else in every instance, and thus passed the test. *But how could that be similar to this if magic did not exist there?*

"The circumstances of your binding will test for loyalty, trust, and acceptance between the hosts. Avoca and Cyrene, do you wish to be tested for the Bound ceremony?"

Both girls nodded and squeaked out, "Yes."

The tingle in her arm had broken out into a dull throb.

"Know that the trials might be difficult, and once you start, there is no going back," Queen Shira said gravely.

Cyrene's powers seemed to have awakened for the first time when she wasn't in mortal danger...or perhaps she was.

"Do you accept the circumstances?"

"Yes," they whispered.

"Then, you may begin."

Cyrene stared down at her glass and then up at Avoca. Finally, an ounce of fear crept up into Avoca's features that mirrored Cyrene's trepidation.

As they lifted the glasses to their lips, a tremor shot up to their shoulders, threatening to pull them apart. Cyrene didn't know if it was a sign that they should stop. Their blue eyes met across the distance. For a second, it felt like she had known Avoca all her life. Mutual understanding crashed between them, and then they tilted the glasses all the way back and downed the drink.

As soon as the potion settled in Cyrene's stomach, fire lashed out at her from the inside out. She thought she might vomit up the contents just to rid herself of the terrible pain wrenching through her.

The girls collapsed to the ground at the same time.

Queen Shira reached out for them, but she could do nothing at this point. They were in it, no matter what happened.

Tears streamed down Cyrene's face. It felt like her skin was melting off, her bones were turning to molten lava, and her head was going to explode. Just when she thought she couldn't hold on any longer, numbness set in, and she blacked out.

1

The BOUND

CYRENE WAS JOSTLED HARD ON HER HORSE. SHE HAD BEEN IN the saddle for days, riding at breakneck speed, with nothing but stale bread and hard cheese. Her stomach protested even more than her thighs, which were bruised from the saddle, and her back that ached from galloping all day.

She didn't remember how she had gotten here. *Did that potion completely knock out my memory from the last couple of days?* She glanced down at her outfit and nearly pulled the beautiful black stallion up short.

She was in…pants.

Men's pants.

She stared, aghast at the indecency of walking around with the outline of her legs completely visible to anyone she rode past. She didn't care that they seemed to be a fine black leather that made it much easier to ride in than her dresses and skirts. She just wasn't someone who wore men's clothing.

What was almost more surprising was that she had some kind of armor over her chest that sat heavily against her. *What could I possibly need armor for?*

As soon as that thought flittered into her mind, it disappeared. Of course she needed armor. They were in the middle of a war of the ages. She wasn't safe to walk around in petticoats and silk gowns when she needed to be on the battlefront, commanding a legion. The final battle was drawing near, and this interruption was unfortunate but necessary for Avoca. Cyrene could never deny her anything…even in the midst of the hardest battle of the last two millennia.

Cyrene felt her skin prickle and recognized it as a directional shift from Avoca. Cyrene veered left and ran into a pack of Indres prowling near the path that led to Eldora. A glance from Avoca told Cyrene all she needed to know.

Avoca and Cyrene broke formation and darted around the pack. As expected, they split, and six rushed toward Avoca while three followed Cyrene. They had identified the Leif as the more viable threat than a traveling human. She preferred having the tactical advantage in times like this.

She and Avoca reached for their powers at the same time. Working as one, they never faltered. Years together had fused their powers, so when their powers were used separately, a supreme lack would race over Cyrene as if part of her was missing.

Avoca raised her hand, and the ground trembled beneath the Indres's paws. Cyrene grasped her sword and cut through the first Indres as it was incapacitated by Avoca's distraction. The second leaped at Cyrene's horse, but she caught it in the face with her sword. It backed up and growled a command to the Indres facing Avoca. They reassessed their situation and were drawing more toward Cyrene.

Time to end this.

Cyrene pulled in sharply on the well of energy that always bubbled under the surface. It swirled around her core, like a living, breathing life force. She reveled in the ecstasy of it all. Touching her magic was addictive and intoxicating.

Avoca had removed her own weapon from the sheath and attacked an Indres. She killed two before Cyrene let loose a burst of energy at the remaining six. Two scattered before it reached them, but the other four went down at her targeted hit. With their brothers on the ground, the remaining two tried to flee, but Avoca had her bow off her back and arrows through their foreheads before Cyrene could blink.

"Don't draw so much," Avoca snapped.

"Sorry."

"What if a Braj had been nearby or worse?"

"You're right," Cyrene agreed.

It was a reprimand, but from Avoca, it didn't feel like it. It was just a reminder. Cyrene had always had a problem with controlling how much energy she drew from her source. She just had so much power.

"Let's go," Avoca said, nodding toward the woods.

They broke through the tree line and down the secret passage that led to the gate of Eldora. Two Leifs stood guard with their bows ready to slice down any intruders.

Avoca pulled back her headdress that had been hiding her revealing golden blonde hair. "Open the gates!" she called.

"Princess Avoca," one of the men called in greeting.

"Open the gates," the second called down to the ground level.

As soon as the doors were open, Avoca and Cyrene trotted through the narrow opening and into Eldora. When they reached their destination, they dismounted and threw the reins to the nearest bystanders.

Avoca led the way into the Queen's chamber and bypassed the guards at the door.

They tried to block Cyrene's entrance, but Avoca hissed at them, "She is family."

"Pardon, Princess, but we have orders."

"And your orders are to stand down, soldier," she growled.

The soldier stepped out of the way, and Cyrene followed Avoca inside.

Queen Shira lay on her bed. Cyrene had always thought she was a beautiful, strong woman, but lying there, she appeared so weak. Death hung over her.

Then, she opened her eyes, and those same wise eyes focused on the two girls. "You came," Queen Shira said.

"As fast as we could," Avoca said. She sat next to her mother and took her hand.

"I can pass now, child," Queen Shira murmured. "You will take the throne and lead our people, as you were always meant to."

Cyrene could feel the turmoil roiling through Avoca. Cyrene had tried to talk Avoca out of her decision so many times. She was to stay and rule. That was her destiny. They'd done much together, but this was Avoca's time. Cyrene would give her up.

"No, Mother," Avoca said. She brushed back the Queen's hair. "I am bound. I will pass the crown." She choked on the last word, and tears streamed down her face.

Cyrene wasn't sure if she had ever seen Avoca cry in all these years.

"My child, please. Please, you must."

"I'm sorry, Mother. I love you." She kissed the Queen's frail cheek. "My place is with Cyrene."

Avoca's eyes locked on Cyrene, and she felt the power rise between them, as it always did when the other was emotional.

"Avoca," Cyrene whispered.

She shook her head and then smiled down at her mother. "I will visit you soon," she whispered morbidly. Then, she strode from the room.

Cyrene stared down at the dying Queen, brought her fingers to her lips, and showed her deference to a majestic ruler.

"Take care of her," the Queen said with her last breath.

Cyrene wrapped an arm around Avoca's shoulders until her tears halted. Neither of them had been able to hold back their sorrow for the lost Queen.

Cyrene couldn't believe that Avoca had given up the throne. She had been preparing her whole life for this opportunity, and now, she would have to give the responsibility to someone else. It was unfathomable that she would do that all because of the war.

She glanced up to say another word of comfort to Avoca, and then her heart stopped.

She stared up at the Nit Decus castle in Byern. Her home. The majestic construction jutted out of the side of the Taken Mountains. The Keylani River gleamed from the mountain pass, and the giant gate that separated the castle from the city beyond was closed tight.

Byern would always be her home. Though she had traveled far and wide with Avoca, she never felt entirely whole until she was back in the city or walking the palace grounds. Her clothes had changed back into a vibrant silky red, and her toes wiggled in slippers.

Why did I think I would wear anything else? Of course she would be wearing her finery.

As soon as she had gotten back into town, she had been summoned to court, and they had changed promptly. Now, they were in the carriage and on the way to the castle.

"What do you think he wants?" Avoca asked.

"Oh, who knows with Edric?" Cyrene fluttered her fingers in an impatient gesture and sighed. "It's hard to read him."

"That's because you're still in love with him," Avoca said as a matter-of-fact.

Cyrene felt her cheeks heat, and she glared at Avoca. "I am not, nor have I ever been, in love with him. He's married."

Avoca shrugged, and a small smirk touched her lips. "You play a dangerous game, Doma."

"Careful with that title."

"What am I but careful in this Creator-forsaken country?"

"Why must you torment me?" Cyrene grasped Avoca's hand, and a current of magic coursed between them. "The Creator is alive and well in Byern. She breathes through me, through you, through the land."

"Yes," she finally agreed. "Your desert drains me. It is harder to feel the connection to the land with it pressing in on all sides. If it continues, it will drain your river and take over the city as well."

"But not today."

Avoca stared out at the road as they approached the formidable gate and nodded. "Do you love the other one, too?"

"I don't know who you mean." But Cyrene did.

"Prince Kael," Avoca breathed.

Cyrene didn't respond.

"How can you feel this compulsion to both of them?"

Their eyes met across the short distance. Cyrene had no answers for her. She had always been like this with them. It wasn't…love but something different. She didn't understand it.

"And will you marry the Prince and then become the Crown Princess of Byern, Duchess of Albion, Doma? For you know, he will ask. Perhaps that is why we're here."

Cyrene was saved from answering as their carriage rumbled to a stop. She stepped out onto the castle grounds. They were escorted into the throne room where Edric sat with Queen Kaliana, Consort Daufina, and Prince Kael.

Cyrene's eyes swept to Edric. A pull greater than the source of her magic tugged at her, as she was lost in the depths of those blue-gray eyes. With great difficulty, she averted her eyes and found she was instantly swept up in Kael. The desire was clearly written on his face. He had never masked it, and the same compulsion hit her fresh.

She didn't want either of them, yet she couldn't stop this obsession either.

"Leave us," Edric barked.

The Queen and Consort looked at him, appalled, but they could not refuse a direct request. Kaliana bit out a smart remark to him, which he ignored, and then she sauntered out.

Kael never moved.

"You, too, brother."

Kael sent him an icy glare. He walked directly to Cyrene, grasped one of her hands, and whispered none too quietly, "Find me after," before he kissed her hand.

Cyrene never took her eyes from the throne as he passed her.

"Are you going to release her?" Edric asked, gesturing to Avoca.

"She is not mine to release, and anything you have to say may be said in front of her."

His eyebrows rose at her defiance.

"You knew this day might come, Affiliate. You swore fealty to the throne and loyalty to Byern. Dissension has been brewing ever since these…Leifs were introduced into our society. I thought I was doing the right thing by making you an Affiliate Ambassador to their people, but that time is over." His eyes slid to Avoca with a deep-set hatred in them before returning to Cyrene. "You need to come home and sever ties with their…kind."

Cyrene gasped at the insinuation, and Avoca straightened at the insult.

"Excuse me? Do you find something wrong with diplomacy between our two races?" Avoca spat.

"I didn't ask her to bring you, Leif. You may speak when spoken to."

"I am the Crown Princess of Eldora," Avoca said. "You will learn propriety, or I will be happy to teach it to you."

Cyrene grasped her arm before she could send the wave of energy building inside of her. She didn't like this any more than Avoca, but giving away the fact that they harbored magic was the worst thing they could do.

"Edric, please. You're mistaken. Their people are good. We should want them as allies."

"I've made my decision, Cyrene. Come home. Take your seat at my side."

"You already have a queen, Edric." Cyrene rushed forward. "Do not make me choose between my country and what I know is right."

"That should not be a choice you have to make. Byern is where you belong."

Cyrene shook her head. "I am sorry. Are you sure you cannot reconsider?"

"The decision is made."

Cyrene swallowed hard, unable to believe what she was about to do. "So is mine."

She turned on her heels and strode from the ballroom with Avoca on her heels. Avoca clasped her hand in Cyrene's as they exited.

Cyrene heard Edric call her name behind her, but she didn't stop, and she didn't look back.

Cyrene kept walking until she felt Avoca pull her to a standstill. She had just walked out on Edric. On Byern. All of this, for her loyalty to Avoca. Giving up her homeland was something she had never considered, never been willing to consider. Byern was her real love, and now, she had to leave…forever.

"You're back!" a voice called from down the hall.

Cyrene brushed the tears from her face. A whisper of regret fluttered through her mind and then was gone. She didn't know why she had been thinking about leaving her country. Byern was not her present concern. She and Avoca had been too busy with traveling the countryside, looking for others who might be like her.

"Ceis'f," Avoca whispered when he rounded the corner.

"They said you weren't coming back, Ava," Ceis'f said. He jogged down to meet them, never taking his eyes from Avoca.

"I never said that I wasn't."

"Tell me you're back for good." He reached out for her hand.

Cyrene didn't want to be here for this. It was so clear that Ceis'f loved Avoca. It was almost painful to witness.

"I—" Avoca began.

He cut her off as he pulled her hard against him.

"Are you…okay?" Avoca asked.

"I am now," he whispered.

Cyrene felt the swell of Avoca's powers as her emotions hit her head-on.

Avoca hadn't known that he loved her. She hadn't even thought that he would have missed her.

"I'll, uh…give you two a minute," Cyrene said.

She tried to slip by them, but Avoca grasped her arm.

"Wait…" Avoca looked at Ceis'f and then back at Cyrene, torn. "Just a minute."

Cyrene nodded and then darted down the hallway. She turned the corner and pressed her back against the wall, breathing heavily. They had a lead on a possible Doma in Aurum, but the last thing she wanted to do was pull those two apart. She cared too much about Avoca to do that to her.

A part of her thought about slipping out the back while they had their moment, but the way their powers were connected, Avoca would know. She would be able to track Cyrene. It had come in handy when they were separated on a mission, but now, it felt intrusive. She felt intrusive.

Avoca's and Ceis'f's voices carried down the hall, and Cyrene peeked around the corner. Ceis'f's arms were in the air, and he seemed to be trying to make his point. Avoca pointed down the hallway, and Cyrene heard his reaction to whatever Avoca had said about Cyrene.

"You're choosing her over me?"

"It's not a choice!" Avoca yelled back.

"So, it was never me?"

"Why does this have to be an argument?"

"Because I've loved you my entire life, and watching you walk away nearly killed me!"

Avoca took a step back, shocked by his honesty. Leifs weren't a particularly affectionate bunch. It made this all the more difficult for Avoca.

"Tell me you feel the same, Ava."

Avoca sighed and cast her eyes toward Cyrene. Avoca's eyes pleaded with her for an answer that Cyrene didn't have. Avoca would have to decide for herself.

"Matters of the heart cannot interfere when you have a higher calling."

Ceis'f balked at her clipped tone. His eyes shot down the hallway where Avoca was still looking, unable to meet his eyes. And then he was barreling toward Cyrene. She stepped out from behind the wall and awaited his anger. He engaged her, but she sidestepped him.

She didn't want to hurt Ceis'f. Avoca was already hurting him.

He rounded on her and came at her again, but Avoca was there to block his attack. She grasped his arm and twisted it behind his back in a painful hold.

"You dishonor me," she spat.

Avoca released him and shoved him back. Her insult crumpled his features. Honor was all they had.

"We have no future," Avoca continued. Her voice trembled on the last word, and Cyrene reached out for her. "You choose to cower behind these walls, like everyone else, when we are needed out there. I have no place here. No place with you."

Cyrene looked up just in time to raise her sword to block the assault from her attacker. She didn't know what had made her think of Ceis'f, but she needed to keep her head in the present.

Steel screeched in the night air as she met her opponent over and over. Her foe was fierce, well trained, and deadly. She could already feel how sluggish her movements were and wondered where Avoca was. She always flanked Cyrene's right side, but they had been separated.

Cyrene could use the bond to find out where she was, but even that amount of magic would be painful to conjure up at this point. She needed to conserve her energy. That might be the only thing to stop the enemy from getting through the front line.

Cyrene feinted right, rolled to the ground, and popped back up to slash at the man again. He parried her advance, and with his extra strength, he shoved her backward. She stumbled over a fallen body and toppled over. Her shoulder hit the ground with a disgusting crunch. She released a high-pitched scream.

Another time, when her magic was not depleted, her injuries would have healed unbelievably fast, but now, she couldn't even count that her shattered shoulder would mend enough for her to hold her weapon.

The man thrust forward for a death kill, and with her last whisper of energy, she batted the blade aside with her powers. That was it. That was all she'd had.

His eyes enlarged, and she used his hesitation to move back to her feet. She switched the blade to her left hand. She was glad for the hours of practice she'd had with it. She would never be a master, but at least she was proficient.

He assessed her with fear that she might be able to produce more magic to stop him. Lucky for him, she was out. Her best chance would be to turn and run, like a coward. Or maybe she had a will to live rather than to be run through by her enemy.

Cyrene heard her name being carried on the wind, and then Avoca jumped in front of her, as if appearing from thin air. A loud thwack sounded. Avoca collapsed to the ground an arrow protruding from her chest.

"No!" Cyrene screamed.

Cyrene dropped to her knees by Avoca. Blood was bubbling up between her lips, and she coughed.

"No. No. No. You can't do this to me, Avoca," Cyrene commanded.

Tears welled in Cyrene's eyes, and her hands trembled as she tried to stop the blood from pooling around at the chest wound. It hadn't hit her heart, but it was doing enough damage with internal bleeding that it couldn't be stopped.

Cyrene reached futilely for her magic, but it wasn't there. She wasn't skilled enough in healing to mend the wound anyway, but her uselessness was debilitating.

"You're not supposed to go this way!"

"Cyrene," she garbled, "I have fulfilled my destiny."

"No. Don't even say that!"

"A life for a life."

"Stop! Stop!" Cyrene screamed. Tears splashed down her cheeks, and she pressed her face onto Avoca's chest. *This can't be happening.* "You think that you've fulfilled your destiny, but your destiny is to live."

"I love you," Avoca whispered.

"I love you, too." Cyrene's voice shook.

Avoca's eyes fluttered closed, and then she went still.

Cyrene opened her tear-filled eyes and stared at Avoca, where they sat crumpled in a heap on the floor. It was as if they had gone through a lifetime together all in a matter of hours. Avoca nodded in understanding of what had passed between them. They were both still shaking, but their arms were linked.

Loyalty. They had sure proven their loyalty to each other.

The crown, home, love, and death.

They were cruel challenges, but Cyrene already felt closer to Avoca. Her soul had been stripped bare for another to witness.

"You completed the task," Queen Shira said in awe. "Let me perform the final binding. I suspect you would like to finish?"

"Yes," they said in unison.

There was no longer fear. Just determination.

A smile crept onto Avoca's face, and Cyrene's eyes crinkled at the corner. They stood uneasily, holding on to each other on unsteady feet.

Queen Shira dropped her hand onto their clasped hands and breathed in deeply. Energy passed from the Queen to the joined hands. The Queen spoke a few words in a language Cyrene did not understand. Then, a jolt zapped through both of them, and she released them.

When she next looked up at Avoca, Cyrene gasped. A gold nimbus hovered all around herself and Avoca, like they were shining beacons of light. The magic coursed through them, and when it had finished, the light disappeared. It embedded itself into their wrists, leaving a shimmering gold tattoo in the shape of a dragon making a figure eight, and then vanished entirely.

They released each other and took a step back.

For the first time, Cyrene's mind was filled with the sense of another. She could feel Avoca's presence.

They were bound.

8

The
SECRET

Rhea

"Excuse me," a voice said from the entrance to Rhea's office in Master Caro Barca's home where she lived in Albion. His fingers wrapped softly on the wooden door.

Her head snapped up. "High Order Eren!"

"Hello, Rhea."

"How can I help you?" she asked, standing quickly.

"King Edric has requested your presence at court. We should have a report in from Aurum," Eren said.

"Wonderful. We should go swiftly then." She grabbed her bag and hurried with him out of her home.

Ever since Cyrene had left, Rhea's life had been turned upside down. In truth, the kingdom had been turned upside down.

High Order Eren had been in charge of the investigation regarding the deaths of the Affiliates and High Order when they traveled on procession to Albion. It had turned out that the deaths were linked to Cyrene. After discovering that she had magic, she had confided in Rhea and told her that she was fleeing the country to discover how to use her abilities.

While that was great news for Cyrene, it'd left Rhea in a terrible place. She was the only one who knew the truth, and as much as she hated lying, she had promised to hold Cyrene's secret.

"Do you think they've located Cyrene?" Rhea asked.

High Order Eren sighed and let his guard down. He didn't do it often. "I'm not sure. King Edric sent the remaining Affiliates back to Byern this morning. I fear he is losing hope on her rescue."

"It has been weeks since she disappeared without a sign." Rhea wished the King would call the entire thing off, but she couldn't sound too eager about it either. "I just hope she's okay."

"I'm sure she will be," High Order Eren said, dropping his hand down on hers.

She stared at their hands between them. Their eyes met, and then he quickly pulled away.

"She's a fighter, and as far as we know, she has Affiliate Maelia with her. Born with two Captains as her parents, I'm sure Maelia will defend Cyrene. I can't think she was involved," he said.

"Oh, yes…Affiliate Maelia." Rhea heard the bitterness in her own tone but couldn't seem to stamp it out.

Maelia and Eren had had some kind of relationship while on procession together, and every time Maelia's name was brought up, Rhea would feel guilty, for she could not stop the growing feelings she felt for Eren.

Their trip to the palace was thankfully a short one. Albion had been built up around Krisana, the great white castle, which gleamed like a whitewashed pearl at all times. Surrounding the castle were the various neighborhoods called Vedas. Her master lived in the wealthiest of all the Vedas, and his estate spanned an entire city block.

The Royal Guard posted at the gate bowed to High Order Eren as he walked through the door. She knew their respect ran deeper than just the fact that he was High Order. He'd frequently train with the guards in his spare time and consult their strategists for the best way to initiate his plans and even change them based on their suggestions.

Krisana's mother-of-pearl doors stood open, and they walked across the beautiful foyer to the doors of the throne room. The new Royal Guards Edric had created after Cyrene's disappearance—the first such group in two hundred years—were posted at every corner. It was an elite small group that had been handpicked by Captain Merrick, Edric's personal Royal Captain of the Guard.

Eren lightly placed his hand on her back to usher her forward. Butterflies hit her stomach at his touch, and she immediately felt foolish.

"It's going to be winter soon, Edric. There is so much to do to prepare for the Eos holiday. You know it's the biggest holiday of the year, and we host the entire country in Byern. Why must we continue to be away from our home?" Queen Kaliana nagged.

Rhea ducked her head and pretended not to hear. Since day one, Queen Kaliana had been arguing with King Edric about his plans, but she hadn't yet convinced him to give up.

"This way," High Order Eren said.

Rhea followed him to the side of the room to observe the court and wait for the messenger from Aurum to arrive.

"Kaliana," King Edric said sharply, "enough."

Consort Daufina whispered something in his ear that Rhea couldn't hear, and he smiled up at his Consort. Queen Kaliana fumed even more at the display, but the King wasn't paying attention. He was playing a dangerous game, one only he could get away with. *For who would challenge the King?*

"You could always return to Byern to begin your festival preparations alone," Prince Kael suggested to the Queen.

Kaliana openly scowled at him.

A mischievous glint was in his eye.

Rhea was certain he was only around to badger everyone. He never offered any real insight and infuriated the whole lot of them.

Queen Kaliana opened her mouth to respond, but King Edric stood and sliced his hand through the air.

"I'm tired of hearing both of you speak. Do not say another word until we have news! Do not forget that Affiliate Jardana was recently found dead. The threat is not past us yet, and this is the most pressing matter to the country."

Everyone fell silent at that proclamation.

King Edric wasn't easily angered, but weeks without news had him on edge. Not to mention, there was the gruesome death of Affiliate Jardana. That had even shaken Her Majesty, who had been close to the Affiliate. Rhea hadn't liked Jardana much. She had thought Jardana was a simpering idiot, either trailing the Queen or Prince Kael at all times. Prince Kael was the only one who didn't seem too terribly upset by her death. He clearly took everything in stride.

The silence chilled Rhea, and she turned to High Order Eren. Words stuck in her throat as she took in his handsome dark features. She spat out the first thing she could think of, "What do you think of this weather, High Order Eren?"

"The weather?" Eren asked, looking down at her. "And, please, Rhea, no official titles."

Her face burned, and she pulled away from his warm brown eyes. "Of course, Eren. I simply mean that, in the last couple of weeks, we've gone without rain. It's so dry."

"And it's the rainy season," Eren finished.

"A rainy season with no rain."

"Odd indeed."

Just then, a messenger ran in through the double doors. The woman was small, only just over five feet tall, with a wiry frame that probably suited her well for a long day on horseback. Her clothes were travel-worn, but Rhea was too excited to hear the news to pay attention to much else.

The woman bowed at the waist and crossed her arm over her chest in a formal military greeting. "Your Highness," she said stiffly, "I bring news."

"Speak freely," King Edric commanded.

"As I was about to leave, two of the kidnapped were apprehended in the Aurumian Hidden Forest and brought into river town of Strat."

"Two?" King Edric asked curiously.

Thus far, they had only discovered that Maelia was missing. Rhea knew that Ahlvie and Orden were going to be the likely suspects of the kidnapping, but she didn't know how to stop their arrests.

"Affiliate Maelia and High Order Ahlvie. Before I left, neither had confessed to participating in the kidnapping, Your Highness."

"And the kidnapper and Cyrene...Affiliate Cyrene?" he asked.

"We have men tracking the kidnapper who had abandoned them in the midst of a wolf attack. The target eluded capture and was not found after the attack had ended. We lost Affiliate Cyrene, Your Majesty."

The room was silent.

Then, King Edric erupted. "You mean, you finally tracked her down, and neither apprehended the kidnapper nor located Cyrene!"

The messenger's eyes dropped to the floor and then met the King once more. "Yes, Your Highness. We have High Order Ahlvie and Affiliate Maelia in custody. The guards are waiting for your decision before returning them to Byern for questioning."

Rhea felt light-headed with the news. She was equal parts relieved that Cyrene had not been caught, worried about the wolf attack, and terrified that Ahlvie and Maelia might give away the entire thing that Rhea had been protecting all along.

"No," King Edric said. "I'll go to Strat myself!"

"What?" Queen Kaliana shrieked.

"Edric!" Consort Daufina chided.

Prince Kael just looked smug.

"Nothing seems to get done around here unless I do it myself. I'm on my way to Strat now to sort this whole thing out!" King Edric said.

"You can't go into Aurum, Edric," the Consort said. Her voice was shaking, and she tried to regain control.

"I am the King of Byern. I can do as I please."

"Your Highness," a man said off to his left.

The King whirled on who had spoken. "Yes, Merrick?"

Rhea shivered. She detested the King's new Captain of the Royal Guard. King Edric had chosen him because he was the very best at what he did, but something was off about him. He never smiled, and his features were so severe. It was like he cast a shadow over the court.

"If you entered Aurum, it would not only look like a direct proclamation of war that we could not get your sister, Queen Jesalyn, to fix. It would also look like a dire situation for the country. You are needed here, Your Highness." Merrick slapped his hand to his chest and bowed after giving his advice.

Consort Daufina glared at him. She didn't like that Captain Merrick was overstepping his bounds into her advisement territory. And he had done it without blinking an eye in her direction.

"I could go in your stead," Prince Kael said nonchalantly. He raised an eyebrow at the King, as if awaiting his outburst.

Tension rose in the room, and Rhea felt like she needed to do something to defuse the situation. She couldn't have the King or the Prince gallivanting through Aurum and bringing war onto her homeland.

By the Creator, Cyrene! Look at what you have done!

"Your Highness," Rhea said, boldly stepping forward. She curtsied low and waited for him to acknowledge her.

"Ah, yes, Rhea. What is it?" King Edric said.

"I thought I would provide some insight into Cyrene, as you would still need to find her."

"Go on."

"If I know anything about Cyrene—and I do since I've known her my entire life—she would go after her friends at all cost. I doubt she would cooperate with her kidnapper if her friends had been taken away, and she can be quite convincing under any conditions."

Rhea looked up into King Edric's blue-gray eyes and then quickly dropped his gaze. She hoped he hadn't read too much into her words.

"I am not a military strategist, but there is nowhere else other than Strat to safely cross the Huyek River. I would concentrate your guards at the crossing with the acquired Affiliate and High Order. She will turn up. I would count on it."

9

The DUNGEONS

Ahlvie

"ARE YOU ACTUALLY INCOMPETENT OR JUST DEAF?"

"Why you little…" The Aurumian guard stood, thrusting his chair back against the wall, and towered over Ahlvie, as if meaning to hit him.

Ahlvie blankly stared back.

"You will answer the question!"

He sighed. This was all so very tiresome. "I don't know how many times I have to tell you. I don't know where Cyrene is. I wasn't involved in her kidnapping."

"We'll see about that," the man said.

Ahlvie groaned. "How do I always end up in these situations?" he mumbled under his breath.

Ahlvie and Maelia had managed to escape from those murderous beasts through the woods, only to run headfirst into a Byern raiding party on the search for them. The guards had trussed them up like prized turkeys and brought them straight to Strat. The pair had been in the dungeons ever since.

Yet only Ahlvie had been the one under interrogation. Ahlvie knew that it was because of Aurumian beliefs about women. He'd read enough about it back home to understand why it was happening, but he didn't think it was smart. However, considering

Maelia had been raised by two Captains of the Guard, he doubted they would get any information from her either.

At least they weren't torturing him or anything. Since they were Byern aristocracy, the Aurumians wouldn't risk too much. They wanted all of the Byern soldiers out of their country enough to leave them buried in the dungeons but not enough to do any real damage. It didn't make the questions any less annoying.

"I think that's enough for today," said a man Ahlvie knew to be General Wingra.

He was a fearsome giant that Ahlvie had no intention of crossing. A few inches taller than Ahlvie with massively wide shoulders, he seemed to take up the small room they'd dragged Ahlvie into a few hours ago.

"Yes, sir." The man knuckled a salute. "Come on, you."

Ahlvie lumbered back down the narrow hallway, as if it were the last thing he wanted to do. He really didn't care either way, but giving the guard a hard time was the only thing he had to look forward to.

The guard shoved him against the metal bars, and Ahlvie grunted. He hated acting pathetic around this man. He could have taken him down and gotten out of this prison in a matter of minutes, if he'd wanted to.

But one, he couldn't leave Maelia, and the idiot guard didn't keep the keys on him. So, it would take more strategy than that. And two, Cyrene would come for them. This was the only logical place for them to be taken so this was where he needed to be. He'd plot their exit strategy and wait for her signal.

"Get in there," the guard said. He wrenched Ahlvie forward by his arm and slammed the door in his face.

Yeah, Ahlvie hadn't made any friends.

"See you again soon," Ahlvie called cheerfully.

The guard glared at him and strolled away.

"Why must you irritate him?" Maelia asked him.

She was seated on the wooden bed in the cell next to him. Her forest-green dress was tattered from the fight with the beasts, but she managed to look demure and important. The guards underestimated her. He knew the ruthless killer that lurked under that facade. She'd taken down enough beasts with her sword that he was glad she was not against him.

"I have so little amusement in here," Ahlvie said with a wink.

Maelia blushed, which was why he kept doing it. Though he was pretty sure she still didn't like him.

"You should focus on more important things."

Ahlvie prowled over to the bars that separated them and lowered his voice. "What do you have in mind?"

She raised her eyes to him. "I'm sure you've been so busy with bothering the guards that you haven't even thought about escaping here."

"You know, I find you very entertaining." Ahlvie leaned against the bars and stared down at her.

Maelia glared. "Can't you take this seriously?"

"Why does everyone keep asking me that?"

"Because we're in jail!" she said, raising her voice. She clapped her hand over her mouth and looked down.

He could see the panic on her face. Despite the front she was putting up, she was clearly terrified.

"And we'll get out." He shrugged his shoulders.

"Perhaps we should be here."

"We didn't kidnap Cyrene."

"Why don't you tell them that then?"

Ahlvie laughed. "You don't think I've tried? No one cares. They're waiting for her to either show up or for the word to come with what to do with us."

"Do you think she'll show?" Maelia asked softly.

"Course she will. She's *Cyrene.*"

"You have a lot of faith in her for someone who hasn't known her very long."

"You have so little faith for someone who claims to be her best friend," Ahlvie countered. "I've known her nearly as long as you and imagine what I've seen in that time. Cyrene is a force to be reckoned with. She shines brighter than everyone else, moves with purpose, and follows her heart. She is worth believing in."

Maelia's eyes widened. "That might be the most straightforward thing you've ever said to me."

Ahlvie nearly cursed, but then he let a lazy smile grace his features. "Needed to say something to get you to agree, and you do, don't you?"

"Yes," she peeped. "But how are we going to get out of here?"

His eyes flickered to life. "I have a few ideas."

10

The
RESCUE

CYRENE WAS RECONSIDERING HER PART IN THIS WHOLE scheme. Waiting was not her specialty, and she had been waiting an awfully long time for her part in the plan to rescue Ahlvie and Maelia in Strat.

As soon as Cyrene and Avoca had completed the Bound ceremony, Queen Shira had permitted them to leave Eldora. Avoca and Cyrene had gotten as many supplies together as possible and had been working out a plan when Ceis'f butted in. Despite their best efforts, he had insisted on coming with them, and the Queen had agreed that it wasn't a bad idea.

Cyrene had left Avoca alone with him then to saddle up her prized dapple, Ceffy, and retrieved the *Book of the Doma* from the Queen.

The Queen had handed back the tome with a sad smile. "When your mission is complete, I implore you to return to me. I'm one of the few creatures still alive that remembers things that can be of use to you. I will help how I can."

"Thank you," she'd replied.

And then they had been off.

Their plan was simple. Avoca would create a diversion, using the Byern and Aurum guards as bait, and then Ceis'f would give a signal to Cyrene to steal the keys from the prison and break her friends out.

Simple.

Except nothing was going as planned.

No diversion had happened. No signal from Ceis'f. If they didn't do it quickly, Cyrene would never make it to the jail for the shift change.

Cyrene frowned. Ceis'f was supposed to have given the signal. The guards would be changing without him there to distract them as she walked by. She needed an escort, or everything would fall apart, and she would end up in prison for being without one. *Stupid backward Aurumian customs.*

The second watch approached the prison door. She looked furtively around for Ceis'f, but he wasn't there.

The guards laughed to each other, and as Ceis'f had said, a set of keys passed from one man to the other before they departed. He'd said another set of keys was inside the prison. Though how he had determined that, she didn't know.

As always, Cyrene would have to rely on herself. She couldn't wait here and let her chance pass.

A steady stream of people moved in front of her, and she casually joined them. Cyrene kept her steps timid and controlled as her hands shook.

As she reached the guard on duty, she took a deep breath and then purposely tripped over her own feet. She went sprawling to the ground and cried out as her knee jerked underneath her. One hand grabbed for her hood to keep it in place and the other scuffed the boot of the man standing guard.

"I apologize. So sorry," she murmured under her breath. She coughed and tried to stand with difficulty.

Several people stopped to ogle her fall.

The guard stooped low and roughly grasped her by the arm. "Get up, peasant. Where is your husband?"

Cyrene cast her eyes down and hid under her deep hood, thankful for the itchy, disgusting thing. "I-I must have lo-lost him in the crowd," she stammered.

"Lost him in the crowd, eh? Or left him behind at home?" the guard growled. He eyed the state of her cloak with distaste but thankfully didn't see the good sturdy dress underneath the tatters. People saw what they wanted to see.

"He was ri-right...right here," she warbled.

"I've heard that story before. I'll get another soldier over here to take you to the square."

Cyrene crushed herself against the soldier and wailed. "No. No. Please. He was right here. Please don't take me to the square." She was nearly as frantic as she was acting. She could *not* go to the square. She would certainly be recognized.

Then, the distinctive sounds of fighting rang out from the direction of the square. *Finally, a sign.*

"What in the bloody Creator's name is going on?" the guard who was still holding her arm cried out.

Four Aurumian guardsmen rounded the corner.

One cried out, "All able-bodied soldiers to a defensive position in the square. Now."

When he was distracted, Cyrene slid her hand through the loop on his belt, plucked the keys to the jail right out from under his nose, and added them to her pouch at her waist.

"Moor, stand guard while I take this girl to the square and find out what all the commotion is about," the guard snapped at a man standing inside the doorway.

The man knuckled a salute and took up the place at the door.

Cyrene was visibly shaking at this point. She had the keys to the prison, but it would do her no good if she became a prisoner herself and had the keys confiscated.

As the guard tried to drag her toward the square, a hand grasped on to her, bringing the guard up short.

"There you are, darling," a man said. "I thought you were with me the whole time. You gave me quite a fright."

"And who are you?" the guard asked. He puffed his chest out.

Cyrene didn't dare look up at her savior. The man had a smooth voice but with an edge to it that made him sound superior.

"Her husband," the man answered in a mockingly self-righteous tone.

The guard huffed in disbelief. "Keep better control of your wife." Then, he tossed Cyrene away from him in a hurry.

Her pretend husband swiftly guided her away from the man.

Cyrene sneaked a peek up at the man and gasped outright. "Orden!"

"Shh," he said. "Keep your head down and your hood up. You shouldn't even be in the city. Your face is in every inn and pub. The last thing we want is to have come all this way for nothing."

He abruptly pushed her through an open doorway. They were standing in a small merchant's storage room.

"How did you find me?" Cyrene asked.

"Everyone has been expecting you to show your face since the other two were brought in. You shouldn't have come alone."

"I didn't. I have two companions helping me. I trust them, Orden, but there is no time to explain," Cyrene told him. She produced the keys to the prison. "I collected these."

"Girl," Orden said with a soft shake of his head, "you have some unfounded plans for someone so young."

"Are you sure you know what you're doing?" Orden asked Cyrene for the third time.

She didn't have time to keep explaining this to him. They needed to be in and out of that prison and then down to the dock as soon as possible. They couldn't delay another minute.

"Yes, I'm sure," she replied impatiently.

Orden nodded. He would do as she'd asked because he had asked to come along for this adventure, but he didn't like it. She could tell that for sure. But he hadn't come up with an alternative that she could agree on, so they were going ahead with her plan.

Cyrene pulled her hood up to hide her face from view before following Orden out onto the busy street. He walked with an exaggerated gait that seemed to take up the road. People hurried out of his way even though he wasn't wearing anything that showed he was distinguished.

She allowed him to lead the way back to the prison and focused instead on listening to the bustle around them. Clearly, something had happened in the square. Perhaps it was what had kept Ceis'f from getting to her in time. Though she suspected he had ditched her at the first chance.

Cyrene caught only parts of hurried conversations as they passed, but they were enough to raise her interest.

"A Byern noble in the square…"

"A guard assaulted the General…"

"The merchant was thrown to the ground. He was killed…"

"Bloody prisoners were taken away and transferred to the inn from a bloody royal command. He thinks he has authority here…"

Her head popped up, and she stared at two Aurumian soldiers walking away from the square.

"Orden"—she tugged on his cloak—"ask them about the prisoners."

But Orden was a step ahead of her, already turning in their direction. "Good sirs," he said, offering them a stiff, short bow, "did you say the prisoners were relocated to an inn? All of your hard work, and they've already been transported. Did you find the woman you were looking for?"

The soldiers looked back and forth between each other. Their expressions gave away that they were trying to place Orden but drawing a blank.

"Speak quick, soldier. I'm on my way to speak with General Wingra at present, and I need some answers." Orden was over a handbreadth taller than both men, and without his oversize floppy hat, he even appeared dignified.

Mention of the General got their tongues wagging.

"Yes, sir. The prisoners were relocated to the Huntress and Eagle Inn and put in custody of a Byern royal. I've not heard about the other girl."

Orden tossed each man a silver coin from his purse, and they disappeared without another word.

"Good lads there," Orden said, shaking his head. "To the inn then?"

She followed him without complaint. Thankfully, they had gotten the information they needed and avoided a blunder in the prison.

With Orden at the lead, they took a strategic path around the square to the Huntress and Eagle Inn. Cyrene could just see out of the corner of her eye that the square was a mess of soldiers and citizens brawling in the center. Tensions seemed to have come to a peak between Byern and Aurum. It was pandemonium.

They slipped through the front doors without being harassed, and Cyrene was shocked to see the disarray inside. The common room was as bad as the fight outside. A man was in the thick of it, swinging at another man in front of him and yelling insults. The crowd was growing, drawing in more people from outside. It was likely how she and Orden had slipped inside so easily.

With a start, she realized that the instigator in the fight was…Ceis'f.

"Creator!" Cyrene cried.

He must have found out that Maelia and Ahlvie had been transferred here.

Orden nudged her toward the now abandoned stairs leading up to the rooms. She and Orden hurried up the steps.

"We should split up," Cyrene said. "We'll cover more ground. You take the next flight."

"I can't leave you here alone. If you get caught, it'll be your neck."

Cyrene opened her mouth to argue, but he just bullied his way past her and down the hall.

"All right," she grumbled.

They checked the first three rooms but to no avail. They were completely empty. As they were moving toward the next room, she heard steps from the far stairwell. She and Orden hurried into the room, but she left the door cracked open and peeked out into the hallway. Her heart beat heavily in her throat as she waited.

Two figures appeared at the base of the staircase. "Come on, Affiliate."

Cyrene's eyes widened, and her stomach dropped clear out of her body.

Kael Dremylon.

By the Creator! What is Kael Dremylon doing in Strat? And why is Maelia with him?

Cyrene had thought that the townspeople were exaggerating by calling a Byern noble a royal. But it actually was the Crown Prince. Her heart fluttered as she got a good look at him for the first time. He had roguish good looks with dark hair and blue-gray eyes that held only mischief. Blood coated the sleeve of his white shirt, and he seemed to be favoring his right arm.

"If she doesn't turn up," he said, looking at Maelia, "then I'll have to take you with me to the Aurum capital. We can let this..." Kael's voice trailed off as he escorted Maelia into a room and shut the door.

Cyrene's hands shook but with fear or anger, she wasn't sure.

Kael wants to take Maelia all the way to the capital of Aurum? No, I need to take Maelia with me. This is not a part of my plan!

"We have to get her out of there," Cyrene said.

Orden grabbed her arm before she could do anything rash.

"You can't just barge in there. If the Prince gets one look at you, there will be hundreds of guards on our heads before we can get ten paces away from this inn. Do you want to jeopardize everyone?"

"I can't leave her behind," she insisted.

"She would want you to be safe before compromising everyone."

Cyrene furrowed her brows, and Orden released his hold on her with a sigh.

"Didn't you hear what he said? If you don't show up, then he's taking her to Aurum. Let's get Ahlvie and then come back for her. At least we have the advantage of knowing where she's headed if we can't get her out."

Cyrene nodded. She didn't like this, not one bit, but the last thing she wanted was to barge in on Kael Dremylon and ruin everything.

Orden hurried back out into the empty hallway. They were halfway up the third flight of stairs when they heard a series of loud thumps. Cyrene met Orden's eyes, and they rushed up the last few stairs to find four guards crumpled on the ground. Avoca was standing over them in a plum cloak with gold stitching. Her blonde hair fell loose over one shoulder, and she looked both beautiful and deadly.

Ahlvie stood behind her with his eyes nearly popping out of his face. Then, his expression softened into something just short of adoration. A second later, he noticed Cyrene standing on the threshold and broke out into a smile. "You're alive!"

"I'm all for the heartfelt reunions," Avoca said, "but this place is crawling with soldiers. I suggest we make a hasty exit."

"I have to agree with the woman," Orden said.

"What about Maelia?" Cyrene asked. She looked back down the stairs with regret. The sounds of feet stomping up the stairs behind her made her jump forward. "Guards."

"Another day for Maelia," Orden advised.

"Yes, I think so," Avoca agreed.

"This way," Orden said.

They hurried after Orden, who revealed a side staircase as a group of guards appeared on the landing. She heard shouting behind her, but she didn't stop to ask questions.

A minute later, they landed in the kitchen, which was bustling with people. She could hear the guards coming down the stairs after them.

"What do you think you're doing?" a large woman in a cook's dress asked.

"Just passing through, my lady," Orden said. He dropped a gold piece into her hand, and then as the rest of the group ran past, he dropped two more into her palm.

They had made it out onto the street when Cyrene heard the greedy woman giving the soldiers instructions on where they had gone. Their group rounded a corner away from the square and took off at a dead sprint.

"Avoca and Ahlvie, go east. Orden and I will head west. We'll loop back around and meet you at the docks. We'll have a better chance if we are separated," Cyrene instructed through breathless pants.

Avoca nodded without question, taking instructions like a soldier, and disappeared behind the next bend with Ahlvie. Cyrene and Orden went the opposite direction at the next fork.

After another minute of jogging, Orden put his hand on her shoulder. "Try to act natural. We need to blend in."

Despite her shaking hands and rapidly rising chest, she slowed her steps and tried to follow Orden's lead. She had given him directions to the boat earlier in case they were separated.

Now, they just had to get there.

11

The
DOCK

CYRENE CAUGHT HER BREATH WHEN THEIR BOAT CAME INTO sight, bobbing softly on the rushing Huyek River. Ceis'f was impatiently pacing the docks, and Orden and Cyrene hurried to reach him. The captain and crew of their vessel were already setting up the rigging for the destination, and now, all they needed was Avoca and Ahlvie to set sail.

Ceis'f stalked over to Cyrene and growled in her face, "What's taking her so long?"

"Soldiers followed us after we got Ahlvie out. I'm sure they're just dodging patrols. What happened out there? You weren't in your position, and I barely made it out alive."

"That would have been all the better for me," he snarled.

Cyrene fixed him with a pointed stare.

"That Byern royal showed up and messed everything up. Avoca ended up shooting an arrow at him. He shifted at the last second, and it only grazed his arm. I don't even know how he moved that quickly or how he heard the arrow coming. It caused chaos after that, which was the distraction, but by then, I was engaged and couldn't get to you."

Cyrene's mouth hung open. "Avoca shot an arrow at Kael?"

"That's what I said. What about your other human?"

"We…we had to leave her behind."

"All this work, and you couldn't even manage to get both. Then, you leave Avoca," he accused.

Cyrene ground her teeth and almost left, but she couldn't just walk away. She knew what Ceis'f was feeling right now. Even if he hated her and treated her terribly, he had helped her.

"Thank you for helping today. I know how you feel about me—"

"You know nothing," he snapped viciously. "And, until you do, you can keep your mouth closed."

Cyrene sighed. *So much for trying to be nice.* She strode aboard the ferryboat that Avoca had secured for them. As she waited, she tried not to think about the sidelong glances from the crew or the large sum of money she had seen Orden hand over to the captain for his silence. Instead, her thoughts strayed to more dangerous territory. She worried that war between Byern and Aurum was imminent, because of the brawling in the streets and the number of guards on foreign soil. It would be in Byern's best interest to send Kael on to the capital city in Aurum to smooth things over with his sister, Queen Jesalyn.

But Edric would never have sent him in the first place. That made her think that Kael had come of his own volition. *But to what end?*

Her history with Kael was rocky at best. They had wavered between lust and hatred and revulsion and sometimes even friendship. His obsession with her only infuriated her more because of the uncanny pull she felt for him, even when she did not want to.

Just like with Edric.

No. She shouldn't think about Edric right now.

She closed her eyes and remembered their shared kisses and the stolen moments away from the prying eyes of court. She had been willing to give herself over to him, and she would have if she had not fled Byern. In the end, nothing could change the fact that Edric had all the power, and he already had his Queen.

"Cyrene," Ceis'f called from the dock.

She turned around, ready to reprimand him for using her name. They were so close to getting across this river and out of trouble. She couldn't have the captain or crew recognize her now.

"Ceis'f, watch what you say!" she snapped, storming to the railing.

"You might want to see this."

Her eyes widened as she took in the scene before her. Two figures were racing down the dirt road that led from Strat. Farther back, just visible, coming out of the city gate, were more than a dozen Byern guards running after them.

"Orden!" she shrieked. She could just start to make out Avoca and Ahlvie in the lead.

"Cast off!" Orden cried. "Captain Iscoe, let's get this ship moving. We leave now."

"What have you gotten me involved in?" he growled.

"If you cast off now, get us safely to the other side of the river, and ask no questions, I'll double the sum that has already been paid to you. But we leave *now*."

"Blood and bloody ashes," he cursed under his breath. "Let's get moving, men. What do you think I'm paying you for? Cast off!"

The crew burst into action. Cyrene watched with a fearful eye as her friends sprinted toward her, and the sailors worked to get the boat out of port.

Her friends were outpacing the soldiers on foot, but Cyrene saw two men step out of line and draw their bows. Her stomach dropped to her feet.

Cyrene zeroed in on the two guards who were aiming at Avoca's back, and she reached for her powers. She knew she had the strength to stop them from doing this. If she could kill a Braj and take out a pack of Indres, then surely, she could stop a few arrows from killing someone she desperately needed alive.

But her powers never came. A flicker. There and then gone. It was like she had some kind of block that kept her from accessing them. She gasped at the effort she was exerting and held on to the rail as her knees nearly buckled underneath her.

Avoca and Ahlvie were almost on the dock when the arrow flew true and straight. Cyrene cried out Avoca's name, but by her estimation, it was going to be too late.

At the sound of Cyrene's voice, Avoca ducked and rolled to the right, just missing the first arrow. Cyrene felt Avoca latch on to her powers, like a fist to the gut. She coughed and sputtered at the feel of their connection in action. And then the ground began to tremble. Just lightly at first and then rockier until the guards were jumping around under the quake.

The boat heaved forward, and Cyrene fell to her knees with a lurch. She scrambled back up in time to see Avoca miss the second loosed arrow, and she ran back toward the dock.

Ahlvie was ahead of Avoca and took a large leap onto the boat. He collapsed to the ground, heaving big breaths. But Avoca was still too far away. The gap was widening further, and though she had outpaced the threat, she now had to vault herself off the dock and hope to make the leap or brave the current.

"Come on, Avoca," Cyrene whispered.

They all watched her pick up speed as she reached the dock. Cyrene could see it now. Avoca wasn't going to make it. There was no way. The boat was thirty feet out, moving toward forty feet. They were past the point of where any human could make that jump.

But Avoca wasn't slowing down. She was going to try the jump anyway. There was no other option in her eyes as she ran. Just a clear determination to get away.

Her feet left the ground, and she was sailing through the air. Her body arced as she reached out toward the boat, but she was quickly losing ground. Soon, she would plummet into the river, and they might not be able to get her on board. Cyrene held her breath, and her knuckles turned white where she gripped the railing.

More than halfway across the distance, Cyrene felt a small tug in her chest. Her eyes widened when she realized what Avoca meant to do.

Suddenly, the water lifted under Avoca and careened her forward. The water pushed her the last ten feet with the force of a tidal wave propelling her onto the boat. The wave crashed wildly over Avoca's head just as she reached the deck. The water sloshed onboard and threw everyone off their feet as it ferociously threw Avoca down. She rolled the length of the deck before smashing into the railing and lying still.

Ceis'f beat everyone to Avoca. He dropped to the ground at her feet and carefully rolled her onto her back. He placed his ear on her chest, but Avoca didn't move. He cursed loudly, tilted her head up, and started pumping her chest. Three quick pumps to her chest and then a deep exhale into Avoca's lungs. He repeated the movement. Cyrene watched Avoca's chest expand.

After the second breath, Avoca coughed suddenly and spewed water out of her lungs. She leaned over and coughed until there was nothing left.

Cyrene sighed in relief, and Ceis'f sat back on his heels.

"You're all right," he said, reaching for her.

"Get off of me," Avoca groaned.

She pushed Ceis'f away from her with one last sputtering cough and then rose to her feet, as if she hadn't just inhaled half of the river.

Ceis'f sighed and followed her lead. Avoca crossed her arms. Besides being soaking wet, she looked better than most of the rest of them.

"What?" she demanded.

Ceis'f's expression hardened. "Air would have been easier."

Avoca shrugged and brushed past him. "Water worked."

"Nothing to see here," Captain Iscoe called out to his crew, who had finally righted themselves and were staring around in shock. "Get back to work. We've already lost too much time."

"Perhaps we should all convene elsewhere," Orden suggested.

He gestured toward the front railing where less people were around for eavesdropping, and the group followed him.

He plopped his big, floppy hat down on his head and then turned to face them. "We're sure to have guards on our trail after all of that. So, we're moving as fast as possible down the river. The captain said that no other ferries or boats would be equipped to make the trip until late this afternoon, and any that might follow us would be several hours behind us. With our luck, we'll have a half day head start on our pursuers by the time we dock, and then we can lose them in the countryside."

"That's a relief?" Ahlvie asked.

"Unfortunately, we only have three horses on board for the five of us, which will slow us down considerably. That's time wasted we can't afford. So, we'll need to…"

"And who are you?" Avoca asked with raised eyebrows.

"My apologies. I am Orden Dain."

"He was traveling with us," Cyrene said.

"You made no mention of him," Avoca accused.

"He was scouting when the Indres attacked, and Ahlvie and Maelia were captured. I had no way of knowing where he was," Cyrene explained. "We had to go where I knew to find people. He found me in the streets in Strat, but he's been traveling with me since Albion."

Orden's eyes widened. "Did you say Indres?"

"Yes," answered Cyrene stiffly.

"That's not something to bypass lightly," Orden said.

"Is that what they were?" Ahlvie asked shakily. "Maelia and I thought they were wolves."

"It seems folktales are truer than we could have ever imagined," Cyrene said.

Orden nodded and then glanced purposefully at Avoca and Ceis'f. "It seems that way," he said, as if he knew that Avoca and Ceis'f were Leifs. "Where did you pick up your rogue companions?"

Avoca and Ceis'f stiffened.

Cyrene spoke up, "They saved me from the attack and offered their help. Let's just get somewhere safe, and then we can all catch up on where we have been the last couple of days. What's the plan, Orden?"

"Ah, yes. There's a small town called Gildan just north of where I've asked the captain to let us off. We can procure horses and supplies there before getting on the road to Aurum."

"You plan to go into the capital city?" Ceis'f asked in disbelief and revulsion.

"You don't have to come," Avoca told him.

"How can you even bear it, Ava? Surrounded like that, without the trees—"

"I am not you, Ceis'f. And I will do as Cyrene guides."

"What happened to Maelia?" Ahlvie interjected.

"We had to leave her behind," Orden told him.

Ahlvie arched his eyebrows and then turned to face Cyrene. "What happened?"

Cyrene swallowed. She hated that, after all that effort, she had only been able to get Ahlvie out. It was a bonus that they had Orden to guide them through Aurum even though Avoca and Ceis'f could have probably gotten them there, but Maelia was a terrible loss. Cyrene would have done anything to get her to be here with them right now, but there just hadn't been any other option. They had barely made it out of there as it was.

"Let's walk a bit, and I'll tell you about it," Cyrene said, taking Ahlvie's arm and guiding him away from the others.

Avoca and Ceis'f stormed off together, already deep in conversation. Orden remained, contemplatively staring out across the Huyek River.

"I'm sorry about Maelia," Cyrene said at the exact same time as Ahlvie said, "I'm sorry we lost you."

They both laughed softly and then kept up their slow strolling pace around the deck.

"You first," Cyrene told him. "What happened?"

"There were too many of those things—Indres. I never thought I'd hear that word spoken so seriously again."

"What do you mean?"

"When I was growing up, the elders in my village spoke of them. Rumor had it that Indres along with some other creature that they refused to put a name to attacked a forest village near my home, Fen, and slaughtered every man, woman, and child. It left the village decimated."

Cyrene gasped.

"I was so young at the time, only four years old, but I remember my mother crying for weeks afterward. Most of her life, she had been friends with a man from the village. It was a great loss." He sighed at the painful memory and continued, "But something stopped the Indres in the Hidden Forest. Maelia and I were fighting them off as best we could. Then, the guards showed up from across the river. They were helping, but when all the Indres died, the remaining guardsmen apprehended us and brought us to Strat. They interrogated me about you, but after a couple of days in prison, Prince Kael showed up and moved us to the inn."

"I can't believe he showed up," Cyrene said in disbelief.

"I never liked the guy, but he took an arrow to the arm and kept going, like it didn't matter."

Cyrene shook her head. "Only Kael Dremylon."

After a few minutes of silence, he said, "But you know the craziest thing out of all of this is seeing all of the Indres dropping dead. It came out of nowhere. I felt that same blast, like when the Braj was killed."

Cyrene sighed and closed her eyes. "It felt the same because it *was* the same."

"What do you mean?"

"You know when we were in Albion and I said that I somehow killed...the Braj?" she whispered.

"Yes," he said, his voice dipping to match hers.

"I know now what happened where I wasn't sure before." She opened her eyes to meet his dark eyes. "I killed them with...powers. I have magical powers."

"Magical powers?" Ahlvie skeptically eyed her.

"Yes. I know it sounds insane."

"Yeah," he agreed. "It does."

She laughed hesitantly. "I know. I wish I could show you, but I can't because I don't really have access to my powers. They only show up under life-or-death situations—or at least that's when they have so far. That was the energy rush that you felt when I killed the Braj and Indres."

"The energy was you."

Cyrene sighed. "I know it might be hard to believe. I didn't even believe it at first."

"That's because magic is a myth, like the Braj and Indres."

"Yes. But it's real, and that's the full reason I'm going to Eleysia. I need to find someone who can help me control it," she said in a rush.

"This Matilde and Vera?"

"Yes."

"How do you know we'll find them or that they'll even help?"

Cyrene shrugged. "Honestly, I don't."

"Look...I trust you. I've trusted you from the beginning, but we've risked our lives for this. Are you sure it's...magic?"

"Absolutely." She wished that she could explain it better.

"Okay."

"Okay?"

"Yep. Okay."

"How are you always so okay with everything?" she asked in disbelief.

He laughed thoughtfully. "I've learned to just go along with the flow. I've seen and heard things in my village that no one else would believe, and since we've been together, I think I've seen enough to know when you're telling the truth."

"Okay," she said.

She thanked the Creator every day for sending her someone like Ahlvie who never questioned her motives.

Ahlvie smiled that devious smile that was always on his face and glanced across the boat. "Now, tell me about Avoca."

Cyrene laughed lightly and shook her head. Only Ahlvie would dismiss her information about having magical powers that allowed her to kill the most dangerous creatures in the world when a pretty girl caught his eye.

"Leave Avoca alone, Ahlvie. She and Ceis'f are involved."

Ahlvie shrugged nonchalantly. "That's not the part I wanted to know."

"She's not one of your girls that you can drunkenly find at a tavern."

"I didn't find her in a tavern, did I? I found her when she broke me out of prison, took out four Byern guards single-handedly, and then helped orchestrate my escape."

"I orchestrated your escape," Cyrene grumbled.

"Yeah, but you're…you."

"Why, thank you, Ahlvie. You have quite a way with words."

He continued, ignoring her, "Plus, she's beautiful."

Cyrene rolled her eyes. Just what she needed on this already complicated trip—to have Ahlvie and Ceis'f kill each other. She generally thought Ahlvie was smarter than that. In fact, many considered him to be a genius, which is why he had been promoted to First Class and made a High Order even though his entire family was Third Class. At times like this, she wasn't so sure about his supposed genius status.

"Let's concentrate on what's important here," Cyrene said. "We're being chased by the entire Byern Guard, we almost sparked a war between Byern and Aurum, and we still need to get to the capital and procure a ship to take us to Eleysia. Not to mention, we need to locate Matilde and Vera in Eleysia."

"You'll work out the details," he said, clapping her on the back. His eyes were distant as he stared across the boat at Avoca. "I have faith in you."

12

The OUTBURST

Rhea

"So, where do you think Cyrene will go from here?" Eren asked Rhea.

He was hunched over a map in the study attached to the war room in Krisana. He had taken it over, despite the complaints from Captain Merrick, King Edric's personal Royal Captain of the Guard, that the King's guards would find more use for it.

Rhea was under the impression that Captain Merrick had no interest in Cyrene's rescue even though, more than a month later, it was still King Edric's top priority. Captain Merrick was a man who, first and foremost, looked after his job. That job just didn't always coincide with what anyone wanted, the King included. Rhea was starting to despise any time she had to be around the man.

"Oh, it's hard to know where the kidnapper will take her," Rhea said. She had been staring at Eren's profile while he worked, and she needed to focus. "Perhaps the capital. They have the largest seaport on this side of Emporia. He could take her anywhere from there."

"Yes, but so many pieces don't add up. Why not get a ship out of the Albion port? It's not as big as Aurum but not insubstantial either. Why take Cyrene across Aurum? Where is the kidnapper headed?"

"I doubt he thought he would be pursued." She cast her eyes over his sharp cheekbones and up to his focused eyes. When he met her gaze, she glanced away. Her cheeks flamed at his attention.

"He must not have. I've never seen anything of this magnitude for the rescue of one Affiliate, but with all the First Class deaths lately…"

He cringed, as he surely must have thought about Zorian, his brother and another member of the High Order. He had died earlier this year on his way to Cyrene's Presenting, and Eren had taken it hard. Rhea was certain it was part of the reason he had agreed to search for Cyrene.

"We have to keep searching after all the loss."

"It's a necessity," she said, gently placing her hand over his.

His eyes shot up to hers.

She quickly retrieved her hand. "So long as they don't get a ship out of Aurum."

"She would be impossible to track," he agreed. After a pause, he reached out and placed his hand on her shoulder. "I won't let that happen to her."

She shifted in her seat and wished away the warmth touching her cheeks. "Or Maelia?"

His face fell, and he stepped away. *Creator, why do I keep doing this?* She could have just let it be. Every time she thought she saw affection between them, she would wedge the block in.

"Yes, Maelia, too, of course."

"So, Aurum then," she added softly.

"Rhea, I—"

The door crashed inward, and Rhea jumped up. Eren reached for his sword and threw himself in front of her. In walked King Edric. Rhea immediately felt foolish for being so terrified and dropped into a respectable curtsy. Eren bowed low next to her.

"Rise," he said curtly.

When she glanced up at the King, she noticed that he was a bundle of tension. His shoulders were high, his face set in a stern scowl, and his hands clenched into fists at his sides. Captain Merrick walked in after him.

"I've news that the kidnappers recaptured High Order Ahlvie and left the city with Cyrene in tow. They were pursued, but the guards lost them after they took a ferryboat from the docks on the Huyek River," the King growled.

Rhea put her hand to her mouth. They had gotten away. She tried not to look relieved in front of the King and Eren, who knew her so well.

"What of Maelia?" Eren asked.

"Safe," the King said. "Prince Kael managed to do one thing right in all of this."

He unclenched and clenched his fists. He was at the boiling point, ready to explode at any moment. She would not want to be the one on that end of the tether.

Eren visibly relaxed at the news. He had been worried. Guilt ate at her.

"My idiot brother has decided to go on to the capital to try to sniff out the kidnapper. He believes that is their destination and paid no heed to how it would appear to ride into the capital city with a battalion of the Royal Guard. Even though our sister is there, she cannot stop war if it comes to her doorstep. She was always a weak child, and I suspect nothing less. The fact that she could stave King Iolair off from retaliation for our forces in their country for this long is a welcome surprise."

"What would you have me work on, Your Majesty?" Eren asked dutifully.

Captain Merrick stepped forward. "His Majesty feels as if this mission is coming to a close for you." His sharp eyes took one glance at Rhea, and then he added, "For you both."

"A close?" Eren asked in surprise. "They haven't even reached Aurum. We still have hope," he pleaded with the King, a man he considered his friend.

Rhea could already see the King was lost. He felt something for Cyrene. Her absence and the chase of trying to rescue her had turned to an obsession. Everyone always loved Cyrene, but this…to make the King fall victim to her, both amazed and terrified her.

King Edric turned from Eren, as if to walk out, but then added at the door, "Listen to Captain Merrick. He is a good man. He has your new assignments."

"Edric," Eren protested.

"What more would you have your King do?" Captain Merrick asked, stepping in his path. "Byern is vulnerable with a sizable number of our guards on foreign soil. The possibility of war is imminent. Sending any more to retrieve the Affiliate while Crown

Prince Kael, second in line for the Dremylon throne, is in the country would be sending him to his death."

King Edric rested his hand on the doorframe before he spoke again, "If Kael cannot bring her back from Aurum with the guards already in the field, I will consider it a lost cause. A number to add to the death toll."

And, with that, he walked out, leaving them alone with Captain Merrick, who looked much too satisfied for such an ominous exit.

"High Order Eren, you will return from procession to the capital city to resume your work henceforth."

Eren didn't flinch, but Rhea could see his irritation in the set of his jaw. "Thank you, Captain."

Rhea wanted to reach out and comfort Eren. He was to leave to go back to Byern, and she might never see him again. She should have known that it was too good to be true to be in his company all this time. He was First Class, returning to Byern, and she was a Second, forever to remain in Albion where Master Barca's home was. It had always been an impossibility.

"Rhea Gramm," Captain Merrick said, drawing her attention.

"Yes, sir," she said timidly.

"Master Barca has agreed to accompany the court back to Byern for the Eos holiday festivities. You are to travel with him and report to court on his progress."

Rhea's eyes bulged. "Master Barca is…moving?"

"He was persuaded to take up a new residence during the holiday season and while we have a military threat at our backs."

She assumed *persuaded* meant that they were physically removing him from his house because she never saw the man leaving otherwise. He was a recluse, brilliantly mad, and a bit superstitious.

"Do you know what progress he has made with militarizing his Bursts?" Captain Merrick asked suspiciously.

The damn Bursts. Master Barca spent more time on his fireworks for his own amusement than on using them to build a military device, but she wasn't about to tell the Captain that. If he wanted it military ready, then he was going to need someone other than a genius scientist to engineer it.

"It's going quite well. Almost ready to be fully tested," she lied.

"Good. See that it is," he said. Then, he turned on his heel and walked out of the war room.

"I guess I'm going back to Byern," Rhea said, turning to Eren.

Despite everything that had happened, the smile on his face seemed to right everything in the world. She was to go home. Eren would be there as well. She prayed to the Creator for Cyrene's safety and secretly for Maelia not to return.

13

The
ROYAL GUARD

Daufina

THE DOOR CRASHED INWARD WITH A FORCE THAT RATTLED THE hinges. Consort Daufina jumped backward, uncharacteristically terrified. She landed on the cushioned divan in front of her wooden bed. The room was dimly lit, and a part of her held still to wonder who would disturb her.

But when Edric stormed into her bedchamber, she relaxed.

"What an entrance," she said.

"Don't," he snapped. "Not now, Daufina."

He slammed the door with vigor and strode toward her. Edric's blue eyes were storm clouds. He looked stiff and tense and irritated beyond belief. No, furious. If she didn't know him so well, she wouldn't have seen the fury buried under it all.

Before he had arrived, unannounced, she had been in the process of undressing for bed. She was still in her silk shift and reached instinctually for a dressing gown to cover herself before the King. Not that Edric hadn't seen her in less before, but…well, things were different now. They were not together like that, nor had they been for a long time. She was an advisor, his best friend, and confidant, not a lover. She took the pink gown from the end of the bed, slipped it on, and began to tie it into place.

"Leave it off," he said forcefully.

Her eyes rose to meet his. She was sure that they mirrored the shock in her expression. "Excuse me?"

"I'm your king. You'll do as I say."

She narrowed her eyes but let the dress fall from her shoulders into a pool on the floor. She was still completely covered in her white shift, but she felt naked in that moment, exposed in a way she hadn't felt around Edric in a long time. He held the power, but he treated her like a partner. He must be irritated indeed to command her.

She dropped a regal curtsy and downcast her eyes. If he wanted to be above her, then she would hold to his station.

"As you command, Your Majesty."

"Rise, Daufina," he growled. "I've no time for it."

"Of course, Highness."

He cleared the distance between them, took her by the shoulders, and firmly planted a kiss on her rosy lips. She stood, frozen in plain shock for a moment, before reminding herself that this was the King of Byern, and she relaxed into his hold.

He stopped abruptly, only seconds after starting, and stared down into her eyes, searching. She had no clue as to what he was searching for.

"It's not there," he said dismally.

"What's not there, Highness?" She was a little woozy and was glad that he was holding her up. She wasn't sure he'd ever kissed her like that before. Perhaps if he had, she would have fallen in love with the man and not the crown after all.

"The energy. The current. The passion. That blasted...zap that tethers me to her," he said miserably.

Cyrene. He was talking about Cyrene.

She wasn't sure why she deflated, but it felt like a blow. He'd kissed her to see if he'd feel something...anything for someone else.

Daufina's gaze hardened, and she straightened up. She was not some wanton woman he could just throw his fancies at. She was near his equal and had risen to it by her intelligence, *not* birth. She was the highest-ranked woman in the land, and she would never again fall prey to the King's whims.

"What is troubling you, Edric?" she said, dropping the formality now that she knew where this was all leading.

"You know. Of course you know."

"The entire kingdom knows by now."

He turned away from her, staring at her empty bed. "I'm calling it off."

"The search?"

"Yes. Kael has gone on to the capital city, and if he cannot bring her home, then she is lost to me." He sounded bitter, like a broken man.

"You love her." It was not a question.

"Yes."

"You should go see your wife."

Edric whipped around to face her. He looked aghast at the suggestion. "How do you think that would possibly fix anything?"

"It would fix one thing."

"No. It would not fix that either. She has miscarried three times now, Daufina. How many more before we realize that she is unfit?"

"And what will you do if she is?" Daufina asked. "Would you turn her aside and remarry? Could you?"

Edric ground his teeth. Only with Daufina would he allow so much loss of control. "Merrick already believes that I should."

"Merrick," she snarled.

She hated that man. Usurping her authority, looking down on women, shadowing the King like a watchdog. He was dangerous, and the King didn't even see it.

He ignored her distaste. "I don't know," he finally said. "My father's dying wish was for an heir. If I can't get one with Kaliana, then what? I let the Dremylons die out after nearly two thousand years of rule? I allow Kael's children—Creator help us all—inherit the throne? If it comes down to it and it's the only way, I would have to."

Daufina reached out and placed her hand on Edric's shoulder. "Then, make certain that it is not the only way. You have not been to her quarters since Cyrene left…since before that."

"How can I when I am so in love with someone else?"

"Tell me," she said, reaching out and bringing his chin to face her, "do you love her more than your country? Would you give it all up for her?"

What she saw in his eyes scared her witless. Because she knew…deep down, the answer could be yes, if only Cyrene asked.

"Don't even think it," she breathed. "Make your country whole again."

Edric nodded, resigned to his task, and left her chambers.

She swallowed hard in his absence. *What kind of spell had Cyrene Strohm cast that could corrupt him so?*

The
JOURNEY

A FEW HOURS LATER, THE BOAT DOCKED ON THE OUTSKIRTS OF a large estate that Cyrene could just barely make out over the horizon. A dirt path disappeared into a thicket of woods, and it all appeared so calm and serene from the water.

Once the boat was tied down, the crew lowered the gangway and began hoisting the horses from below deck back onto solid ground. Orden paid the Captain a fat sum for his worries, and their group disembarked shortly after. Then, the captain and his crew untied the boat and were careening back down the Huyek River.

"Gildan then?" Ahlvie asked.

Orden's gaze rose to the property on the hill and then frowned. "Yes. We'll head northeast until we reach the trail that leads into town. A day-and-a-half ride if we set out now. Who will take the horses?"

Ceis'f spoke up, "Avoca and I will scout ahead. We are familiar with the woods and twice as fast."

Avoca pursed her lips but didn't disagree.

"No," Cyrene said. "Ceis'f, you will go with Orden. He already knows this land and is an excellent scout. Avoca will stay with Ahlvie and me with the horses." She turned her attention away from Ceis'f before he had a chance to disagree. "Is there anything else we need to know?"

Orden sent her an amused look but didn't comment on her taking charge. "Just stay away from the property. That house belongs to Lord Barkeley, and he doesn't take kindly to strangers, so step lightly."

With that, Orden and Ceis'f gathered small packs from the supplies provided in Eldora and set off. Ceis'f glanced back once at their party, but he left albeit reluctantly. Avoca gave Cyrene a curt nod. Whether for getting Ceis'f to go or for taking charge once more, she wasn't sure.

The rest of them finished tending to the horses and then cut a wide path around the plantation home. If this Lord was half as bad as Orden had made him seem, she didn't want to have a run-in with him.

The three of them set an easy pace, and by the time the sun was setting low on the horizon, they had put the Lord's manor behind them. Soon, they caught up with Orden and Ceis'f, who had prepared a fire in a clearing. They sat on opposite sides of the fire without speaking or looking at each other. It must have been a long afternoon if even Orden was testy.

After setting up a rotating watch schedule, Avoca let the men cook a small dinner with what they had caught during the day and then insisted she and Cyrene had work to do. She forced Cyrene to hand over the *Book of the Doma* and dragged her off into the woods. After a short trek, Avoca found what she had been looking for—a rivulet that barely trickled water.

Avoca turned to face Cyrene and contemplatively stared at her before speaking, "You have not touched your powers since we were bound. Why?"

Cyrene should have known this was coming. Of course, Avoca would notice that she hadn't used her magic. There was so much to discuss between them, but the magic was the most obvious. Cyrene wavered on what to say and then final blurted out, "I…I can't."

"What do you mean, you can't? I watched you kill all those Indres."

"I know, but I can only feel my magic in life-or-death situations. I reach for it, like I did with the Indres, but it's just a flutter, like a butterfly in my stomach. Then, it's gone."

Avoca stared at her with wide eyes. "Have you ever been able to reach them without your life being in danger?"

"No," she admitted.

"Well then, this will not be of much use," Avoca grumbled with a sigh. She sank to the moss-carpeted forest floor and set the book down next to her. "Sit."

Cyrene did as instructed. "Why won't the book help me?"

"Because you are blocked."

"Oh," Cyrene whispered. "But how do you know it won't help with that?"

"Because, when Doma ruled the world in our distant past, they did not have blocks. It was not heard of, just as it is not presently heard of in Leif society. I fear your block comes from the corruption of Byern."

Cyrene furrowed her brow. "What exactly does that mean?"

"The history lesson will be for another day, but I suspect it is because you grew up in a world without magic and in a world that does not believe in magic. If you do not believe you can do magic, Cyrene, then you will never truly harness your powers."

"Okay. So…I just have to believe in myself, and then it'll happen?"

Avoca smiled. "Let's hope that will suffice. First, let's do some basic meditation lessons to get yourself in tune with the elements. While Doma magic is more inherent, as you are drawing from your own body, you can access the elements, and in fact, it will help you when you feel your own core running on empty. You never want to weaken yourself beyond what you are capable of holding."

"And how will I know that?"

"With a lot of time, practice, and patience."

"Great," she grumbled. "My specialties."

"Now, enough talking. Close your eyes, and clear your mind. Think about your breathing. In through your nose, out through your mouth. In through your nose, out through your mouth."

Cyrene breathed deeply as Avoca spoke to her, "Yes, that's good. Now, empty your mind of all your worries and concerns, of your mission, of your friends and your home. You are one."

Her voice was gentle and soothing, and Cyrene found herself drifting in the emptiness of her being.

"Now, sense the river beside you."

Cyrene started out of her trance and opened her eyes. "What do you mean, *sense* the river?"

Avoca sighed heavily. "Everything in existence has a pulse. You and I have a pulse. The forest has a pulse. The river has a pulse. Each of us Leifs has an element that calls to us more strongly than the others, but we can feel the pulse of each of the other three elements. I am strongest in earth and then water, as is common with my people in Eldora. Ceis'f senses air and then fire, as was common with his people in Aonia. We balance each other out in that regard." Avoca smiled fondly.

"Wait…Aonia?" Cyrene asked.

Avoca cringed. "The Leif village Ceis'f is from."

"He's not from Eldora."

"Cyrene," Avoca reprimanded lightly. "Let's concentrate on your powers. Ceis'f's story is his own."

"Okay," Cyrene said. "What element am I strongest in?"

"I am going to attempt to find that out," Avoca told her. "Now, start again. Shut your eyes, empty your mind, and remember your breathing. Now, I want you to reach out with your powers. Don't try and well them inside you, as you last did. Just let that flutter of butterflies brush against you. Don't try to guide it. Let it guide you. Just reach out and sense the pulse of the river."

Cyrene emptied herself of everything, fully giving herself over to her meditation. Then, she felt for her powers buried deep within her. She let it guide her instead of forcing the magic to the surface. She tried reaching out with it and sensing the pulse of the river. But it just didn't work.

She opened her eyes again in frustration. "Nothing is happening."

"Try a different element. Find the one that calls to you. It will make itself known." Avoca dug her fingers into the earth with pleasure. "Let me try to explain. Earth sounds like a drumbeat, low and distant but constant. Water sounds like a wave crashing, rhythmic and enticing. Air sounds like a whistle, harmonic like a bird's song. Fire is the hardest for most. Its pulse is a heartbeat that practically sizzles with the force of the flame. Now, try once more and let the energy find you."

Cyrene got to work again. She reached her meditative state quicker, and instead of concentrating on water, she reached for earth. Her fingers were buried in it. The slightest flicker of power washed through her and then disappeared as quickly.

By the time she focused on air, she was too frustrated to concentrate.

Avoca made her release all her anger and try again.

And again.

They tried until the sun had completely disappeared, and they had to precariously pick their way back to camp through the woods by moonlight.

Cyrene felt defeated. She'd had no luck. Her powers never surfaced, and the energy never flowed through her. She certainly hadn't heard any pulse, other than the one signaling she was getting a headache.

"Still nothing," Cyrene said. "I can't hear anything."

"You are very strong. You would not have been able to kill the Indres with the force-field burst otherwise. You just need more practice."

"A force-field what?"

Avoca sighed. "You used a force-field burst, which harnesses energy into an offensive blast that can be powerful enough to take out your enemy or tear down a mountain. It's very powerful, very difficult magic. Can you think about how you did it?"

Cyrene felt helpless. "It was either I died or they did, so my body just reacted. It happened when I killed a Braj in Albion."

"A Braj?" Avoca asked, her voice raising an octave. "Why did you not tell me of a Braj? They are deadly assassins. More will come after you. We should have been on the lookout this entire time."

"I know. Orden told me about them."

"That man seems to know an awful lot about everything," Avoca said.

"Indeed. He is a mystery."

The pair made it back to the camp and stopped before entering. Avoca stayed silent for a minute as she stared at the ever-darkening sky. "Let me worry about the Braj. You focus on releasing the block from your powers. We will continue to do this every night until you get past it and find your elemental pulse." She turned her gaze back to Cyrene and smiled a rare beautiful smile. "Just try to find it in yourself to accept the power. It is the life force of the world, and the Creator has entrusted us with it. The least you can do is use it."

And so Cyrene spent the next day in her saddle, reaching for her powers. By midday, she was exhausted, had a terrible headache, and was beyond irritated. She snapped at everyone who spoke to her. All she wanted to do was find a way to reach her magic. *If I can*

make this force-field burst that Avoca had talked about, how come I can't duplicate it? How come I can't even feel my magic?

They reached Gildan at nightfall. Orden got them two rooms at an inn on the outskirts of town. They would buy and trade for supplies in the morning, but until then, Avoca wanted to work with Cyrene to find a way to get past her block.

They spent half the night in the woods but to no avail. When they made it back to the inn, Cyrene could do nothing but collapse into a fitful slumber where she dreamed of Indres and Braj attacking her, which only forced her awake repeatedly.

Orden and Ahlvie completed the shopping before mid-morning. After waking, Cyrene took her time in a long bath, knowing she would not have another for a while, and she tried to listen to the pulse of the water. All she felt was it getting colder and colder.

She dried off and returned to her chamber to find new Aurumian dresses in a cheap itchy wool. Both were brown, and while they were of lighter material than the dresses she had packed, they would have to do if she wanted to fit in. The skirts were fuller, the waistline tighter, and the sleeves were large and voluminous at the shoulders before tightening around her wrists.

Aurum was a three-week ride from the northern town of Gildan. Orden and Ceis'f alternated with scouting shifts, and they continued their routine for watches at night.

Most nights, Avoca would haul Cyrene away from camp and spend an hour or two thinking of ways for her to figure out her powers. But, if they were still there, neither girl could find a way to access them.

On nights when they were most annoyed with the fact that they weren't getting anywhere, they would return to the men. Nearly two weeks into their journey, Cyrene and Avoca came back early to camp to find Ahlvie instructing Ceis'f on a dice game.

Cyrene warily eyed him. "Dice? What are you wagering?"

When they had been in Albion, Ahlvie had gotten them into trouble by wagering Cyrene as his wife in a dice game with a tavern owner, who hadn't taken too kindly to losing.

"No worries, Cyrene. Just coin," he said with a wink. "We're playing All the King's Men."

"Don't let him steal all your money, Ceis'f," Cyrene warned. "He's a dirty cheat."

Ceis'f laughed callously. "I'd like to see him try. Besides, I've played this game before many years ago. It was called by a different name in my village—the Serpent's Luck."

And, to Cyrene's shock, the game was evenly matched. By the end of the first game, the two men were playing jovially together. Ahlvie was reminiscing about stealing a man's money right out from under his nose at a tavern, and Ceis'f seemed to forget that he was enjoying himself with humans for a time. Orden even joined in on the game and lost some coins to the two of them.

Cyrene just hoped the good cheer of their journey would last once they reached Aurum. Much depended on what happened once they arrived in the capital city.

THE LIVELY DAGGER

ALL DAY, ON THE LAST LEG OF THEIR CROSS-COUNTRY JOURNEY, Aurum stood out like a beacon on the horizon. The giant stone castle stood atop a hill, overlooking the red, cream, and brown buildings of the seaside city. Five large lanes cut into the city and went down to the central port, which was filled, day and night, with hundreds of ships of various shapes and sizes from all around the world.

Halfway through the day, Orden and Ceis'f returned from scouting and informed the rest of the party that the road seemed to be clear of Royal Guard. Cyrene was glad for that, but she didn't think it put them out of harm's way. If Kael hadn't made it to Aurum yet, there was still time for him to get there.

By mutual assent, they split the group up when they entered and then reconvened at The Lively Dagger, an inn that Orden swore had higher repute than the name suggested. Orden disappeared first, and after an hour, Cyrene set out with Ceis'f. She wished that she could have been paired with Ahlvie or Avoca, but she and Ahlvie couldn't be seen together, and law dictated that she had to be with a man.

A cool breeze was blowing in from the Lakonia Ocean, shepherding in the first cold weather of the season. In Byern, snow would already be blanketing the mountains, and in a few weeks, it would be down in the city. It would be another month before the temperature dropped that low in Aurum.

Cyrene tried not to stare too obviously at the beautiful new city she was in. She felt more at home in a burgeoning metropolis than in the country, but this was so very different than her home. In fact, she was surprised to discover that the city itself was larger than the Byern capital. Byern was sequestered between the Taken Mountains and the Keylani River, which halted outward growth. Aurum had no such limitations and had grown up and out around the marina and the castle.

The streets were packed with people and bustling with trade merchants. She caught a glimpse of three different men in traditional Eleysian garb as well as a pair scantily clad in Biencan silks, a Carharan fur trader, and even a Tiekan man in a tight-fit hat that flopped off one side of his head.

Finally, Ceis'f turned down a street and stood face-to-face with The Lively Dagger, a run-down inn that looked every bit as awful as Cyrene had imagined. She wasn't sure how Orden had thought that this was a reputable location.

"Perhaps we should find another inn. One a bit more refined," Cyrene suggested.

"Is that an order…my lady?" Ceis'f asked with a bite to his tone.

"No." Cyrene sighed. "We'll stay here."

Cyrene entered the inn with Ceis'f on her heels. It was mostly empty, save for a few foul-looking men at one table and a handful of busty serving girls. A large woman in an oversize dress with puffy sleeves and an apron over top strode right up to them. Her brown hair was pulled loosely off of her sweaty red face. She gave Cyrene a once-over, seemed to deem her unworthy, and then turned to Ceis'f, as if Cyrene wasn't standing right in front of him.

"Can I help you, good sir?" she asked. She dabbed at her forehead with a handkerchief and gave him a toothy smile.

"Yes. We're here for a room," Ceis'f said.

Somehow, every word out of his mouth sounded like he was trying to snap her head off. She looked affronted by it, and Ceis'f didn't even seem to notice.

"Madam LaRoux, at your service," she said, suspiciously eyeing the pair.

"I'm Haenah, and this is Roran," Cyrene told her when Ceis'f didn't speak up. "We're just here for a couple of weeks before the cold sets in."

It was the set answer that Orden had instructed them to give. He had said that the madam of the inn would understand.

Madam LaRoux gave them a knowing smile with a wicked glint in her eye. "Perfect timing then. We have a lot of travelers coming in for the festival season. Come this way, and I'll show you to your rooms."

They were whisked up to the second floor and to the last room on the left. Madam LaRoux knocked twice, paused, and then a third time before opening the door and ushering them inside. Once they were inside, she shut the door in a hurry, turned to face the room, and planted her hands on her hips.

"Master Dain!" she said in a scolding tone. "You did not tell me that you were harboring fugitives. You mean to keep this girl in my inn?"

"Laurel, Laurel, Laurel," Orden said. He stood up from a hard wooden chair where he had been gazing out the window, smoking his pipe. "This girl is not a fugitive. She is a guest."

"I have been around long enough to know when you are weaving a story, and I'll not fall for it. We've worked together for too long. She has to go."

"Laurel, you know how the Affiliate program is in Byern," Orden said encouragingly.

Cyrene bristled at the comment.

"I know. I know you said that, but I didn't think you meant...her," Madam LaRoux said, glancing anxiously at Cyrene.

"We won't be staying too long, and we'll keep your establishment out of trouble. I assure you, Laurel," Orden said. "She is fleeing injustice, and you would be doing us all a great service by helping."

Madam LaRoux sighed heavily and then nodded. "All right, all right. You'll owe me though, Dain."

"I am in your debt."

She seemed to accept this before leaving just as quickly as she'd come.

"Injustice?" Cyrene asked at the same time as Ceis'f asked, "You trust her?"

Orden folded his arms. "I trust her wholeheartedly. I've been working with her for over fifteen years, and she would never tell anyone that you are here. As for the injustice," he said, turning his eyes on Cyrene, "surely, you know that the conditions in Byern are not highly favored in the rest of the world."

"Not highly favored?" Ceis'f asked in disgust. "They're despicable."

"I don't understand why there are such problems with how Byern runs its affairs," she said stiffly. "Aurum women cannot even walk around the city by themselves without getting manhandled and arrested."

"You see what you were raised to see," Orden said. "Affiliates and High Order are sent to other countries as ambassadors—not to learn about foreign cultures, but to force an unwanted Class system on other rulers. Eleysia has banned all trade with Byern and refuses access to Affiliates and High Order who wish to come to their lands seeking change.

"And, while we're on the matter, Aurum is far from degrading to women. Men and women work together, especially here in the capital. The wives make nearly all of the decisions for the household and hold significant power. Madam LaRoux is a supreme example, but I've been told that even Queen Jesalyn is effectively ruling over her husband, King Creighton Iolair. Just because it is different than what you know does not make it wrong."

"I…I didn't know about all of that," Cyrene said. Uncertainty hit her head-on for the first time.

She remembered the conversation she, Maelia, and Ahlvie had had with Captain De la Mora when attempting to escape Albion. He had refused them passage onto his ship.

"I have no room for First Class passengers seeking to infiltrate my beloved country."

Is this what he had meant? Had other Affiliates and High Order been trying to infiltrate Eleysia and enact change?

"But how exactly was I supposed to know all of this? No one told me about the problems with Eleysia. The only problem I realized was that Eleysian vessels wouldn't take me on their ship, so I walked halfway across the world to try to get there. As for Aurum, I was apprehended in Strat and almost arrested in public for *falling*. You two were the ones who said how dangerous it was for women to be out, alone, in public. I'm not sure what other assumption I was to draw from that."

"Well, now, you know," Orden said. He shifted past her and to the door. "Ceis'f, we're in the room next door."

Orden yanked open the door and strode out of the room with Ceis'f on his heels.

"What is going on here?" Avoca asked, striding purposely down the hall in front of Madam LaRoux.

Orden just kept walking without a word.

"Nothing," Cyrene said finally.

Avoca's lips thinned out as she stared at Cyrene with all-knowing blue eyes.

"Then, let's settle into our rooms." Avoca entered the room she would be sharing with Cyrene and dropped her bags on the floor next to her small bed. "You were arguing with Orden, weren't you?"

"You could say that."

"You push him too much," Avoca said.

Cyrene shrugged. "Some people need to be pushed."

"Men need to be handled differently. Ceis'f needs a tight leash, and Orden needs a long one, but they both require a leash."

"And Ahlvie?" Cyrene asked.

Avoca smiled softly, and then it disappeared. "He is a man of his own choosing. I believe he will follow you to the ends of the earth if you but ask him."

"You think too highly of him. You've never seen him dicing in a tavern with your life on the line."

"He is loyal. That is a good quality in a man. You should hold on to him."

Cyrene nodded. "Well, I don't intend to let him go."

"Let who go?" Ahlvie asked, peeking his head in the door. "Did you say my name?" He winked at Cyrene and then walked inside without an invitation.

"Ahlvie! Knock next time. We could have been undressing," Cyrene chided.

"Is this supposed to convince me to knock?"

Cyrene rolled her eyes to the ceiling. "Insufferable."

"Alas, you aren't undressing, so I assumed it was safe for me to enter."

"Just shut the door," Cyrene commanded.

Ceis'f slunk in behind him and leaned against the wardrobe in the corner. Ahlvie walked right over and plopped down on Cyrene's bed. She didn't know how he always seemed so completely carefree. Orden entered a few minutes later, and they set out a plan for the next couple of days.

Ahlvie was set to wander the pubs to seek out any information he could find that would help them. Ceis'f and Avoca were employed to go to the docks to look for a boat setting sail to Eleysia, while Orden was going to check in with the contacts he had in the city.

"And where does that leave me?" Cyrene asked the quiet room.

Orden gave her a stern look, but it was Ahlvie who spoke up, "We want you to stay safe. You're the reason we're here. We can't lose you. With guards still on our tail, I'd feel better if I knew you were here while we were out." Clearly, they had already discussed this without her.

His pleading look did her in, and eventually, she agreed, "Fine. I'll be right here. Waiting."

Ahlvie kissed the top of her head on his way out and whispered, "Thanks," into her hair.

Sometimes, he reminded her too much of her brother, Reeve. Not that Reeve would have ever approved of this plan.

Cyrene grabbed Avoca by the arm before she left. "If you're in any sort of trouble, please reach for your power, so I know."

Avoca nodded her head, relenting. "I will give a hard tug like this," she said.

A sharp jolt snapped through Cyrene, and she nearly sank to her knees. She had not been prepared for that.

"You will not confuse that for everyday use, I think."

"No," Cyrene agreed.

"Good." Avoca placed her fingers on her lips and then raised her hand to Cyrene in a sign of deference she had not seen since leaving Eldora.

Cyrene returned the gesture, and then Avoca was gone.

Cyrene peered around the empty room with a heavy sigh. Now, she must do the hardest part of her entire mission.

Wait.

Four days.

Cyrene spent four days holed up inside that room before someone returned with good news.

The door burst open unexpectedly, and Cyrene jumped out of the chair she had been attempting to meditate in.

She glared at Ahlvie as he sauntered in, and she threw a pillow at his head. "Will you knock? I was in the middle of something!"

He caught the pillow midair. "Good to see you, too."

"Well, have you found anything?"

"A rather attractive redhead."

Cyrene groaned. "You're disgusting. I don't want to know about any of that."

"The little redhead's father is a wine vendor for the Royal Court, and she let it slip that he has been asked to procure a striking number of barrels of wine for a ball for a royal visitor next Saturday. Now, who do we know that might elicit such a celebration?" Ahlvie asked.

Cyrene sank back into her seat. "Kael."

"That's what I assumed, and where Kael is, so is Maelia. We need to get into that castle before we get on a boat."

They had been waiting for Kael to show up in Aurum since they arrived. Based on the conversation she had overheard in Strat, they knew that Kael would be coming into the city, but this was the first real piece of news they had.

Avoca and Ceis'f had come back the first day with grim news about Eleysian boating. Due to the festival season, which was a monthlong affair leading up to the Eos holiday, travel had stilted between Aurum and Eleysia. A boat carrying travelers had left two days before they had arrived, and several Eleysian fishing boats had decided to stay for the entire season. They hadn't seen or heard of anyone going to Eleysia, other than a mysterious large ship flying Eleysian flags that had apparently been in port for over a month. No one who they'd asked claimed to know whom it belonged to or when it intended to depart.

When the others returned that night, Ahlvie and Cyrene filled them in on what he had found out, and they set about trying to find a way to get into the ball.

"We're going to need to hire a boat to take us out of the harbor. Even if it won't take us all the way to Eleysia because of the festival season, it won't be safe for us to be in Aurum after we break Maelia out," Cyrene said.

"We'll look into vessels leaving for other destinations," Avoca said. "See if we can manage something that won't be noticed."

With their assignments divvied up, the crew returned to their rooms to pass out after another long day. Avoca never seemed to tire, and after changing, she was ready to begin Cyrene's training once more. It was the only part of the day that Cyrene looked forward to even though she'd had no success locating her magic.

They spent the next two hours dutifully reaching a state of calm and then trying to sense one of the four elements. It didn't matter that Cyrene had worked all day doing the same thing. Avoca demanded more from her. She always came full of new theories to break Cyrene's block that she had thought of when she was out working with Ceis'f during the day.

Today, Avoca thought that since they were Bound, Cyrene might have an affinity for earth, like herself. For a solid hour Cyrene reached inward, touched the knot in her chest, and tried to focus it on earth matter. Avoca had even brought a pot of dirt into the room so that Cyrene could feel closer to it. It didn't help.

"You know, I was thinking," Avoca said after another failed attempt, "maybe you are more like Ceis'f."

Cyrene snorted. "I highly doubt that. And, dear Creator, do not let him hear you say that."

"I just mean, what if our magic complements one another? Ceis'f is better with air and fire. Perhaps you are, too."

And so their training went on endlessly. Cyrene was no better with air or fire, but Avoca kept coming up with other possibilities that would lead them to more dead ends.

Cyrene had never been good at remaining calm and doing nothing. Now, those were her only tasks until they got out of this Creator-forsaken city. Her anger started bubbling up, which usually brought their sessions to a screeching halt.

"There's nothing there!" Cyrene cried. "I'm sitting around all day, meditating and trying to find these elusive pulses that you claim exist, but I can't even come close to sensing any of them! Are you sure you know what you're doing?"

In truth, Cyrene didn't like being bad at anything. She had always been an exemplary student, and having something that was completely beyond her control was more irritating than disappointing a tutor.

Avoca just pursed her lips at Cyrene's outburst.

"Okay. I'm sure you know what you're doing, but maybe I just can't do it," Cyrene offered.

"I don't believe that." Avoca stood and began pacing the room. "I admit, I'd be surprised if you could sense anything in this city if you weren't able to do it out in the woods. I can barely sense the earth in this place. It's been so trampled and forgotten that the pulse is just a distant hum. Even *this* earth is…lost." She toed the pot of dirt.

"If even you can't find it, then how am I supposed to?" Cyrene asked in frustration. "You've set an impossible task for me."

"I've not been in a city in nearly fifty years, Cyrene," Avoca said. "It is easy to forget in that time."

"Fifty years?" Cyrene asked, her eyes bulging.

"Yes. Leifs have exceptionally long lives, and at our hundredth birthday, we are given a year abroad with an elder. Most do not even take that year, but I did."

"So…you're a hundred and fifty?" Cyrene gasped.

"A hundred and forty-nine," Avoca corrected.

"Where did you go? What did you see when you left?"

Avoca sighed. "That is neither here nor there. A story for another time. I have no more patience for training tonight. Soon enough, we will be out of this city and in a place more conducive for training."

"Maybe I should go into the woods tomorrow then."

Avoca gave her a sharp look and shook her head. "No. We're very close to getting you out of here."

Cyrene grumbled under her breath, but Avoca just ignored her and crawled into bed. She was an incredibly light sleeper and seemed able to pass out as soon as she closed her eyes. Cyrene heavily lay back in bed, and for the next two hours, she wished she'd had that talent of Avoca's as well.

16

The
HEARTBEAT

EVERYONE LEFT EXTRA EARLY THE NEXT MORNING, rejuvenated with a sense of purpose from the news that Maelia would be in the palace soon. Cyrene was alone, eating a small breakfast, when there was a knock on the door.

"Your laundry, Lady Haenah," a girl called from the hallway.

"Yes. Come in, Elzie."

Elzie entered the room and set down a bundle of laundry on the trunk at the foot of Cyrene's bed. "I had your cloak mended and washed three times, as instructed."

She stood and plucked the cloak off the top of the stack.

It was the disgusting thing Ceis'f had gotten for her on short notice when outside of Strat. Her own cloak had gone missing, and she was glad that she had not brought the ermine-lined red one Edric had given to her as a present.

Thankfully, after a few good washes, this cloak looked to be in much better condition—not anything she would have worn at home, but nothing that would make her stand out in a crowd.

"Very good," Cyrene said. She dropped a silver Aurumian trinket into Elzie's hand and then dismissed her.

As soon as the door closed, Cyrene threw the cloak around her shoulders. She tucked her dark brown hair up into a cap that she had taken from Ahlvie's belongings and then threw the hood over her head. Her own blue dress from Byern fit snug to her body, and without the added bulk of the Aurumian dresses, she felt like she could walk freely for the first time in weeks. As long as she kept her head down and returned quickly, no one would be any wiser that she had left The Lively Dagger.

Cyrene had memorized the comings and goings of Madam
LaRoux by the distinctive sound of her gait. Every morning, she
would meet with the gentleman across the hall for a half hour and
wouldn't return upstairs until lunch. She never bothered Cyrene. In
fact, Elzie was the only person Cyrene ever spoke to in the inn. She
wanted to keep it that way.

The familiar *clunk, clunk* of Madam LaRoux's steps sounded on
the second-floor landing. Cyrene pressed her ear to the door and
waited. Like clockwork, Madam LaRoux knocked on the door
across the hall. A man welcomed her inside and then shut the door.

Cyrene would have thirty minutes to get out of the building
without Madam LaRoux knowing, and then she had the rest of the
afternoon to herself before anyone else returned to the inn.

Cyrene slung a bag over her shoulder and slunk out of her
room. The hallway was empty, but she encountered a man walking
up the stairs. She kept her head low and hoped he'd just walk
right by.

"Where ya goin', missy?" he asked, stopping her in her tracks.

"To collect a tray for Madam LaRoux," she warbled meekly.

"Well, tell the old hag to bring me some more of those
breakfast rolls." He strode past her and smacked her on the bottom
as he passed.

She took a few deep breaths in and out before continuing
down the stairs. All she wanted to do was turn around, throw the
man back down the stairs, and teach him a real lesson about how
to treat a woman. But she couldn't afford that complication at the
moment. So, she forced herself to put one foot in front of the
other.

Elzie was helping another man, who kept trying to get her to
sit on his lap. Cyrene was grateful for the distraction, but it did
nothing but fuel her anger. She hurried out of the open front doors
and onto the busy streets of Aurum.

It took her a while to regain her bearings in the foreign city.
Back home, she had always had the mountains to guide her. Now,
she had only the sea at her back and the looming castle on the hill.
She located a street that she had taken on the first day, and the map
came back into her mind. She retraced her steps, but without Ceis'f
there for comfort, she saw what she had missed the first time.

Dirty faces. Hunger. Poverty that clogged the streets. Women
and children left out to starve.

She swallowed and kept moving forward. These things didn't exist in Byern. There was always plenty. That was what the Class system was for. At least, that was what she had always thought before.

Have I been blind to this in my own city?

Either way, she didn't understand how the King Iolair could rule over people he allowed to suffer while he looked down on them from up high.

It made her stomach twist as she veered through the streets. She didn't feel safe again until she was out of the winding streets and in the woods. She took a deep cleansing breath. It surprised her how at home she felt out here, considering she had lived her entire life in a big city and only the last couple of months in the woods.

But Aurum wasn't Byern.

With the city behind her, Cyrene headed deeper into the woods at a brisk pace. If Avoca couldn't sense the elements pulsing in the city, then Cyrene wanted to be as far away from the city as she could get. Avoca had told her that, once she could sense the pulse of the elements, then she could start manipulating them with more ease. It was the reason Avoca could still use her magic, even in the city. But Cyrene saw little hope for herself in that environment. It would hurt nothing to sit outside and meditate all day. She did the same thing in the room, and she couldn't spend any more time in it.

She walked until she could no longer hear the sounds of the city and then found a small clearing in the woods. She took off her cloak, removed the cap, and let her long locks fall down nearly to her waist.

Taking a seat on a section of soft grass, Cyrene closed her eyes and opened her mind.

She could immediately tell the difference between the city and the woods, not that she found a pulse. But it was definitely quieter out here alone. Since she was closer to the elements she was attempting to tap into the meditative state came much quicker.

She went through the exercises—earth, air, water, fire.

Each one came back blank.

No pulse. No magic. Nothing.

By lunch, she was starving. She took a short break to eat the bread and fruit that she had brought with her in her pack, and then she got back to work. She only had a precious few hours left before she'd need to return, and she didn't want to waste any of it.

Cyrene rearranged her skirt and then closed her eyes again to try to reach for her powers. Almost as soon as she reached her meditative state and opened herself up to her magic, she felt something stir within her chest. Her eyes flew open in shock, and she lost whatever had been happening. Her breath came out in short gasps.

"What was that?" she wondered aloud.

It certainly wasn't the soft flutter she had been feeling all this time. That was like hitting a wall. It definitely was not like the well of energy she'd used to create the force-field pulse. But it wasn't like any of the pulses that Avoca had said she would feel.

But Cyrene couldn't just ignore it. If it meant she could feel anything, then it was worth it.

Wiping the worry off her face, she waited until her heart rate slowed again, and then she reached back out for her calm state. It hit her full-on.

A heartbeat. A crescendo.

Not a pulse. A coursing boom that could have burst her eardrums if she had been listening to it outside of this state. She resisted the urge to clutch her head to stop the noise. She *wanted* the noise.

As she peeled back the layers of what she was listening to, she realized that she had intentionally grasped her magic for the first time. She fumbled with it and then felt it drifting away.

Then, she remembered all of Avoca's lessons. Instead of trying to direct the magic, she let it direct her. She stopped trying to work with it and just let it set the pulse.

The noise picked up pace, and everything steadied out.

It was a pulse.

A real pulse.

A heartbeat.

Fire.

She was fire!

Yet it all felt so different than how Avoca had described fire. No sizzle intensified with the flame. In fact, there was no flame. The pulse felt like a jumbled mass of confusion. Like the heartbeat was running. Like it was *something*.

She quickly grabbed her bag, cloak, and cap and then ran toward the pulse that still echoed in her mind. She never released her magic in fear that she would never be able to find it again. Her legs pumped beneath her as she followed the feeling inside her. When she sprinted into a clearing, the heartbeat she had been following started to fade.

"No!" she cried.

She couldn't let this slip away. She had come all this way. She had to discover what it all meant.

Then, she saw the most beautiful white-tailed deer stride into the clearing. It was a massive buck with enormous antlers. The deer turned in her direction and looked directly at her. She watched with bated breath as the fading heartbeat continued to hum in the background.

The deer inclined his head in her direction. It was the deer. He could sense her, too.

They shared a moment where she could feel every heartbeat from the magnificent creature. If this was fire, it was incredible. Her magic felt full and whole, not overwhelming, not like it was going to make her collapse.

She was one with the deer before her.

Then, he stumbled forward, and that was when she saw the arrow protruding from his side.

Her hand flew to her mouth. She had seen hunting expeditions while growing up. It was basic survival methods to hunt deer from the mountainsides. She understood why this was happening, but it didn't make it any easier to watch the magnificent animal die. Not when she could feel everything.

A second arrow whizzed through the air and thumped heavily into the creature's neck. The fire went out. The heartbeat quieted. All was still once more.

Even though she knew it was pointless, she dropped her things, rushed to the animal, and fell at its side. Tears immediately hit her eyes, fresh and hot, and she released her magic in a rush. No magic could bring back the life of this animal. And if that kind of magic existed out there, it was not something she was interested in.

She realized then, quite plainly, that what she had heard wasn't fire at all. It was the actual heartbeat of the buck. She had never been surer of anything in her life. She felt like she owed him something for surrendering his life and for inevitably giving her the key to her magic for the very first time. But the creature was dead, and she could never thank him for his deed.

17

The
HUNTER

"YOU THERE," A MAN CALLED OUT.

Cyrene stumbled back from the animal. *How could I be so careless? Of course there are men in the woods. Who did I think had shot the beast?*

But she hadn't been thinking. All she could do was rush toward the animal that had given himself for a greater purpose.

A man came galloping into the clearing on a brown steed. The horse looked as beautiful as any her father would have kept in the stables, but the man riding it was not in nobleman's attire. He had on brown pants, tucked into nearly destroyed riding boots, and a drab green shirt with the laces open in the front, so she could see his tan chest beneath.

Her eyes snapped upward to his face. He was blindingly attractive with light hair and intense brown eyes. He carried himself on the horse as well as King Edric himself. She swallowed back her fear and tried to ignore how attractive he was.

She had to find a way out of this. All she had done so far was stare at him.

Once he got a good look at her, he vaulted off his horse and reached his hand out to help her up. "My lady, allow me to assist you. I thought you were…well, I wasn't sure what you were doing. What *are* you doing out in the woods?"

He effortlessly helped her to her feet.

What could she say to him to convince him to leave her alone? The last thing she needed was to be recognized by some strange man. She was wearing Byern clothing with neither hat nor cape to hide her features, and she was alone in a country that forbade such behavior while the Prince of her own country was in the city, looking for her.

She couldn't even bring herself to play the meek, submissive role and break out the I-got-lost routine.

"I was just in the area."

"There's nothing in the area."

"There are trees."

"Yes. Yes, there are," he agreed. "Do you talk to the trees?"

He wasn't laughing at her, but she could tell she amused him.

"Of course not. Are you finished mocking me? I have more important matters to attend to." She raised her chin and stormed away from the man, hoping he wouldn't follow her and ask more questions.

"Stay, Raeder," the man said to his horse.

Then, she heard him following after her.

"I didn't mean to offend you. I was merely curious. I seek solace in the trees to escape the city. It is quieter out here, and I'm able to think. I would never judge someone who also loved the trees."

"You might love the trees but not the animals in it," she said. The heat of the moment was still wrapped around her after the death of the buck. "You took down that buck, but you hardly look as if you are starving. For sport then?" She whirled on him and planted a finger in his chest. "Did you never think of what its death would mean?"

"A hunter rarely considers its prey," he said, stepping into her finger.

"A hunter who does not consider its prey is destined to become prey himself."

His eyebrows rose high, and then he smiled, lighting up his entire face. The force of it seemed to knock the breath out of her. All she could do in return was stand there and smile back.

He cocked his head to the side. "You are very different than the rest of the women in this country."

"Yes…well…" she said with a soft shrug.

"You act as if that is not the first time you have heard that."

It wasn't. Far from it.

"So, what would you have me do with the prey the hunter killed for sport?"

Even though something in her mind was buzzing around, telling her to leave, to get out of this situation immediately, she didn't back down from his challenge. "Give it to the hungry. There are too many in the streets."

"A kindred spirit," he whispered. "A woman who stands up to a stranger she meets while all alone, who prefers the solitude of the woods, and who recognizes the needs of others. Pray tell, where did the Creator send you from, and why is this the first time we have met?"

Cyrene flushed and took a step away from him. When he put it that way, she realized how very alone she was out in the woods here with this strange man.

"I...I should probably go," she said softly.

"Now?"

"Yes. I just remembered I have somewhere to be."

"Allow me to take you," he said, gesturing back to his horse.

"Oh no, that's not necessary."

Cyrene retrieved her bag and cloak, threw it back over her shoulders, and turned to flee. He grasped her hand to keep her from leaving.

"Please," he said, bringing her hand to his mouth and softly kissing it. "After I've offended you so, please allow me to do this. I have eleven sisters. They would have my hide if they knew that I had made such a fool of myself."

Just then, three men galloped into the clearing.

"Dean! Dean!"

The man before her shifted so that she was completely blocked from their view, and then he waved his hands at the men. "I'm over here."

A man on a chestnut-colored horse pulled into the lead. He had dark hair past his shoulders and a full beard. "Bloody hell, Dean, we didn't know where you had gone. If your father heard about this..."

"Well, he won't," Dean said stiffly. "Just a friendly hunting excursion. I took down a buck."

"Fantastic," a second man said. He looked younger than the other man with sandy-blond hair and a lean, almost stringy, build. "We'll get him cleaned up."

The second man dismounted and strode over to the fallen deer. A third followed behind him.

129

Cyrene knew, if she would ever have an opportunity to escape, this would be the time. Dean was hiding her from sight from the other men for some purpose, and maybe it would be easier for both of them if she just disappeared.

She bit her lip and contemplated her options. But Dean seemed to have another idea.

"I've picked up a young maiden walking in the woods and agreed to take her back to her home."

All three men snapped their heads over to Dean, who stepped aside so that they could get a look at Cyrene.

"If you three would bring the buck into the city and deposit it with the butcher to be distributed at the shelter, I will be on my way."

Cyrene's eyes went wide at his statement. *He is actually going to give it away, as I had suggested?*

The other men seemed to find this strange as well, and she could hardly blame them.

"You can't go gallivanting off alone," the first man said.

"What would your father say?" the second asked.

"Now, wait one minute!" the third cried indignantly.

"I will hardly be in harm's way by escorting her back into the city," Dean said.

Cyrene glared at all of them. "I do not need to be escorted anywhere. I am perfectly capable of walking around on my own two legs."

All the men stared at her.

Oh, right. Aurum women never speak this way.

"Now, if you'll excuse me," she said, backing up. Dean reached for her again, but she avoided him. "I'm going."

"I just want to help."

His eyes were so earnest and sincere that she actually felt her walls crumbling. She had a hard time trusting anyone, but in that moment, she trusted her gut to get her through this, as she had so many other times.

"Okay."

At her acceptance, he nodded firmly with a small smile creeping onto his features.

Dean whistled and his horse trotted over to him, like a properly trained steed. Cyrene stepped up to the side of the horse, and Dean lifted her into the saddle. He did it so easily that she might as well have weighed nothing. Dean swung up into the seat behind her, and she tensed as he slid his hands on either side of her waist to grip the reins.

"Dean," the first man said. His voice was both irritated and coercive.

"Not now, Darmian." Dean wheeled the horse around, and Cyrene had to tighten her grip at the sharp turn.

"Faylon and Clym can bring back the animal," Darmian said. His point was clear—that he should go with Dean.

"Are you going to insist?"

"I'm afraid I must," Darmian said.

"Come along then."

Dean set out, whipping past Darmian to take the lead. "Am I right in believing that you are staying in the city?" he asked.

"Yes, at the present moment."

They trotted along for a few moments before Dean spoke again, "I thought there was an elaborate celebration for the Eos holiday in Byern. Is it not the day of your independence?"

Cyrene nearly choked out a gasp. So, he had known all along that she was not Aurumian.

"It is," she said, deciding to go along with it, "but I've been out of Byern for some time now. I will be spending the Eos holiday elsewhere this year."

"Here in Aurum?"

"Perhaps."

"I heard a rumor that there is a grand ball to be held at the end of this week for a Byern Prince who is in town, visiting his sister. Are you to attend?"

Cyrene laughed. "Do you take me for First Class? I had not even heard there was to be a ball."

She was glad that he could not see her face. She was not sure she could lie so easily to his face.

"My apologies. I do not always understand how your Class system works."

It was quite simple, but she had grown up with the Class system. As Orden had said, Aurum customs seemed foreign to her because she was a foreigner. Byern's customs must feel the same way to others who were not from there. She just hoped that not everyone thought so little of Byern citizens. Dean, at least, didn't seem opposed to speaking with her just because of her background. Maybe he would treat her differently if he knew she was an Affiliate.

When she didn't respond, Dean continued, "I do not have plans to be in Aurum for much longer. I am here, visiting a friend of my father's, for a short time, but I must return home soon. The family business is in need of me. I'm sure you understand."

"Of course," she said simply.

She wondered what his father did. His friends had acted as if his father would wring his neck for wandering off alone.

"Can I call on you while I'm still here?" he asked, interrupting her thoughts.

"Call on me?" Surely, she had heard him wrong.

"Yes. I'd like to see you again. Court you," he clarified so that she couldn't mistake his intentions.

"I-I'm sorry. I don't even know you."

"But I'd like to get to know you."

It was too bad that all the circumstances were wrong. He likely thought she was some Third Class merchant's daughter, out for the holiday season. And she could never tell him the truth—that she was an Affiliate with magical powers, on the run from her country to seek two women, who each had to be two thousand years old, to answer her questions. Courting seemed like the absolute worst thing that could happen right now.

"I'm not sure that is a good idea," she said softly. "How long are you even going to be in the city?"

"My ship departs in a week."

"We're from different worlds, in different places, and in a week's time, we'll likely never see each other again. You are offering something that can never be. Now, please, stop. This is far enough. I can walk the rest of the way myself."

"We're almost to the city..."

Cyrene rolled her eyes. *Men! Creator, I miss Byern.*

Well, she had been raised on Ceffy and Astral and her father's unbroken stallions. She twisted in her seat, judged the distance and speed they were going, and then hopped effortlessly off the saddle.

"What are you doing?" he called as she turned and walked away. He galloped after her. "That was a clever trick. Where did you learn to ride like that?"

"My father. Now, please, leave me be."

"I was forward. I apologize again, but I cannot simply let you walk away."

"The answer is no. Now, leave me." She kept her pace hurried as she strode away, but he didn't seem to care what she had said.

Just then, a figure came sprinting down the center lane and collided with Cyrene.

"What are you doing?" Avoca yelled, pulling back and grasping her shoulders. "You could have died! How was I to know where you had gone or what you were doing?"

"Ava, I'm sorry," Cyrene said.

She hadn't even thought about the fact that Avoca would be able to feel that she had grasped her magic. Avoca had probably panicked when it happened, just like Cyrene would have done if Avoca had tugged on hers.

"You nearly knocked the wind out of me. I had to leave Ceis'f at the docks—"

"Ava!" she snapped.

They were supposed to be in disguise. No one should know their real names.

"Don't *Ava* me!"

"We have a guest," Cyrene said, pointing up at Dean. "He helped me out of the woods."

"What were you doing in the woods in the first place?" she asked through gritted teeth.

"Communing with nature."

Avoca put her fingers on the bridge of her nose, closed her eyes, and breathed out heavily. When she opened her eyes again, she managed a smile for the man. "Thank you for looking after her for me. We have to go now though. I think I have a silver trinket here somewhere," she said, fumbling in her gown for some money.

Dean laughed lightly at the gesture and shook his head. "No need. But please allow me to walk you two ladies back to your inn. Two unescorted women are not always safe in Aurum."

"We can manage," Avoca said testily. "Let's go."

Dean trotted after them and called out to Cyrene, "Please, I don't even know your name."

"What's in a name?"

"Everything," Dean answered. He vaulted off his horse and grasped her hand. "Please, just your name."

"Then, will you leave?" she asked.

"Yes."

His face was so open to her in that moment that she felt almost compelled to give him her real name. She didn't want him to know her as Haenah. She was not some fairy-tale princess, long forgotten, who was only remembered in the slow steps of the Haenah de'Lorlah dance, the one she had waltzed with Prince Kael during what felt like a lifetime ago. She wanted to be herself...the person Dean was obviously falling for.

"Haenah," Avoca said. "Her name is Haenah."

Cyrene swallowed with a sigh and then nodded in confirmation.

"Haenah," he said with a smile. "Perhaps you are a princess then."

She laughed. "Hardly."

Dean let her be dragged away by Avoca then. He put his foot in the stirrup and easily hoisted himself up into the saddle once more. Then, he called out to Cyrene, "I will find you again, Haenah de'Lorlah."

18

The
SUMMONS

"WHAT IN THE CREATOR'S NAME WERE YOU THINKING?" AVOCA asked as she pulled Cyrene away from Dean and back toward The Lively Dagger. "You could have been captured or killed or worse! We are bound, Cyrene. I've traveled very far from my homeland, from my family, to fulfill a debt to you, but how can I protect you if you will not let me? Does that mean anything to you?"

"You said yourself that you couldn't feel a pulse in the city. How did you expect me to?" Cyrene countered.

"That wasn't an open invitation to leave the city, alone, with no means to protect yourself. I said that we would work harder once we were out of the city. You shouldn't have left."

"I couldn't stay inside any longer, and I didn't think that I would actually find a pulse anyway!"

"But you did! Or at least you touched your magic. Since the only way you'd done that was when you were in life-or-death situations, I had to assume the worst."

Avoca dodged a man who looked like he wanted to say something about them walking alone. She gave him a venomous glare, which actually was pretty fearsome, and he kept walking.

"I know. I didn't think about that."

"Obviously! Sometimes, I wonder if Ceis'f is right about humans. You're so selfish."

"And he isn't selfish?" Cyrene demanded.

Avoca's lips thinned, and she picked up her pace. "Fine. Yes, he is. But you scared me, Cyrene. I am glad to find you all in one piece. Imagine if you were not! What you did was careless and inconsiderate. We have all been working to get out of here, and then you disappear." She shook her head, like she couldn't even form the words for her frustration. "Not to mention, I found you with a strange man. Who was he?"

"I don't know. No one. He found me in the woods."

"He *found* you in the woods?" Avoca breathed out heavily. "I'm going to have to stay in the room with you, aren't I?"

"What? No. I'm not going to go back out there. Avoca, don't you know what happened? I found a pulse." Cyrene looked around to see if anyone was listening. "Fire."

"Fire?" Avoca asked in surprise. "Your first element was fire?"

"Yes, it was a heartbeat."

"There hasn't been a Leif with their first element as fire for two thousand years," Avoca said. "Are you sure? What did it feel like?"

"It's a strange story," Cyrene said. Then, she recounted what had happened in the woods up until Dean had wandered in to retrieve his fallen buck.

Avoca stopped dead in her tracks. "You felt the *actual* heartbeat of the buck?"

"Yes. I think I picked up the pulse because it was so frantic. It drew me to him, and then I felt the pulse weaken and die just as he did," Cyrene explained. "It was wonderful and painful. I've never cried like that before."

Even thinking about it still hit her head-on. She had felt the life drain out of the buck. It was something she would never forget.

"No, no, no. That's not fire," Avoca said contemplatively. "I mean, it's partially fire because there is a spark of fire in life. But it's also water and air and earth. If you were strong in just one element, you would be able to feel them individually, but you've not mastered any. And you said it was overwhelming." By this point, Avoca was speaking fast, as if trying to get all her thoughts out at once. "I've read about this. I've heard about things like this before. Things Leifs aren't able to feel. Things long forgotten, long lost with the death of the Doma. So much loss."

Cyrene put her hand on Avoca's shoulder. "Slow down. What are you saying? I didn't feel fire? That wasn't the pulse?"

"No. I believe you felt spirit, the fifth element though not an element at all. I've not done enough research in the area to know for certain. I never thought I'd encounter a Doma, after all. But spirit is the essence of a thing. You effectively touched the deer, the essence of the deer."

"That can't be right. Can it?"

"I don't know," Avoca admitted. "Spirit users are rumored to be able to touch all four elements equally, as strongly as a normal user. I don't know if that's true. It is an inborn ability, an old ability, something I could never touch."

"I don't know what any of that means."

"Neither do I," Avoca said softly. "It gives me something to think about though."

Avoca continued down the street, muttering to herself. At least she wasn't yelling at Cyrene anymore, but Cyrene didn't know what to think about this spirit thing. All she felt now was a renewed need to get to Eleysia and find Matilde and Vera. They had to be there. They had to know how to help.

Avoca and Cyrene rounded the corner to the inn and walked in the front door to complete and utter chaos. Orden, Ahlvie, and Ceis'f were standing there with their swords drawn, facing off with half a dozen Aurumian soldiers. Madam LaRoux was fluttering her hands about and shrieking. The serving girls were all huddled in a corner, crying.

Avoca quickly obscured Cyrene from view of the guards in case they were here for her.

"What in the Creator's name?" Avoca whispered.

"Put down your swords," a soldier commanded.

"You storm in here with swords drawn and expect us to lower ours?" Ahlvie asked. He snorted and cocked his head to the side, as if they were stupid.

"What is the meaning of all of this?" Orden demanded.

"We have a summons from King Iolair himself," one man said. He took a step back from the other soldiers and sheathed his sword. He pulled a rolled parchment from a pouch at his waist. "I, Creighton Lanett Cavel Iolair, King of Aurum, Arrow of the Huntress, Guardian of the Eagle, do request the presence of Lord Barkeley Iolair of the Asheland Moors and keeper of the Halstedt provinces and his companions in the Draydon castle upon receipt of this summons."

Lord Barkeley. Why did that name sound familiar? It was the estate they had first traversed when they left the boat from Strat. Orden had claimed he was not to be messed with. *Why on earth would these men be looking for him?*

"We don't know of any Lord Barkeley," Ahlvie cried. "So, you can all withdraw immediately."

"Actually," Orden said, lowering his sword and stepping forward, "we do."

"What?" Ahlvie asked.

"I am Lord Barkeley," Orden said. "Put away your weapons at once. You are causing a scene."

The shock on Ahlvie's face perfectly matched what was written on everyone else's in the room.

Orden is a Lord? And not just a Lord...an Iolair? Related to the King? What alternative world did I just step into? This surely had to be a joke.

"A Prince?" Ahlvie spat. "You're a Prince?"

Cyrene couldn't believe this. This man had helped her when she had passed out from a Braj, trekked across Aurum with her, saved her from arrest, broken out a prisoner, bribed a sailor, and all the while, harbored a wanted fugitive and allowed himself to be seen as a kidnapper. This man was a Prince!

"We're ready to head out," the soldier said. "You will bring the rest of your party with you."

"No. They will stay," he said.

"The summons requests your party as well," the soldier said.

"They're not necessary. Just some people I traveled into the city with," Orden said.

"A summons from the King is a summons. I cannot leave without the party as well."

Orden ground his teeth and then nodded. He turned toward Cyrene and Avoca. "Perhaps the women should freshen up first."

Avoca grabbed Cyrene's arm and hurried her toward the stairs. "We'll only be a minute."

Cyrene waited until they were upstairs before unleashing. "A Prince! By the Creator, how did I not see it before? The man is the most infuriating person I've ever encountered, and I thought Ceis'f and Kael were high up on that list. Now, he is dragging me into the castle to meet the King while Kael is up there!"

"Would you be quiet?" Avoca said. "I want to slaughter him as much as the next person, but we have got to get you out of these Byern clothes and do something about your hair. You can't stroll into a castle, looking like a fugitive. When my mother issues the equivalent to a summons, she never sees the whole party unless it's for a specific reason. So, let's just use this opportunity to scope out the area for Maelia and try not to be seen."

"If I get the opportunity, I'm going to punch him in the face," Cyrene grumbled.

"Allow me to do it for you."

Cyrene acquiesced, and then they went to work, changing her clothes into proper Aurumian clothing—a dark green dress with huge overlapping skirts and enormous long sleeves that tightened around her biceps. Avoca plaited Cyrene's hair and then hastily pinned it up into a bun.

"That's going to have to do. Look at me quick." She used her earth skills to paint Cyrene's face.

Cyrene's lips turned a fuller red, her eyes changed from their vivid blue to a dull brown, her cheeks tinged with red rouge, her nose appeared thinner by the makeup, and her cheekbones were severely accentuated. She hardly even recognized herself.

Cyrene touched her cheek in awe. "You will teach me how to do that?"

"Eventually," Avoca said. "It won't last forever. I'll have to touch you up, but it should last through the summons. If I had more time, I could change your hair color, but we have to go." She produced an Aurumian hood, which was in fashion at the time. It was rounded at the top with a dark veil to cover her bun, obscuring most of her hair from view. After securing it in place, Avoca nodded. "Let's hope that's enough."

"Ladies," Madam LaRoux called from the other side of the door as she banged on it. "You have an appointment with the King. You should not keep him waiting."

Avoca swung the door open and walked briskly past Madam LaRoux without saying a word. Cyrene grasped her cloak in her hand and followed after Avoca.

The soldiers ushered them outside. Their horses had been saddled while the girls were upstairs.

As Cyrene looked around for Ceffy, Orden walked right up to her.

"This is yours," he said quietly. "Your dapple is too recognizable in the city."

She nearly cursed but nodded. "You lied to me…to all of us," she said softly.

"And you were always so forthcoming?" Orden asked. "My past is my past. Lord Barkeley is as much me as the meek girl who tripped over the soldier's boots in Strat is you. It is a part I play. Now, the most important part that you will play is an invisible one. Your disguise is good but not perfect. Do not, under any circumstances, draw King Creighton's attention. He has a habit of keeping pets around."

Cyrene arched an eyebrow. "Pets?"

"Beautiful young women. He goes through them weekly. We cannot afford the delay that would bring or the chance that you would run into Prince Kael while there."

"No, we cannot."

"Up you go," he said.

He hoisted her up into the saddle, and she adjusted her skirts to fit on her perch. She would have killed for her divided riding skirts from back home.

Orden hurried into his saddle and then rounded on Avoca, sitting on her horse. She glared at him while he spoke but eventually nodded. Clearly, he had gotten the same information into her head because she kept shooting furtive looks back at her.

"Formation," the soldier called.

Then, the men formed up around them.

Cyrene heeled her horse into line next to Ahlvie. He gave her an easygoing smile that he always had plastered on his face. She could tell, underneath it all, he was anxious for her, but he kept up a stream of jokes the entire way through the city and up to the royal castle.

"So," he asked, leaning over toward her, "has she asked about me?"

"Who?"

Ahlvie gave her an exasperated look.

She returned his look with a coy wink. "Oh. I think I know who you mean. Didn't I tell you to steer clear of her?"

"Do I ever listen?"

"No."

"And you said that our good friend Roran would kill me if he knew my intentions. There have been no deaths."

Cyrene rolled her eyes. "Don't think I'm dense. I'm sure it is only because our good friend Roran has not learned of your intentions yet."

"You never show your hand to your opponent," Ahlvie said with a smirk.

"Of course not. You just cheat."

"Now, you're getting it."

She shook her head and tried to put thoughts of Ahlvie, Avoca, and Ceis'f out of her mind. She had too much else to focus on as they trotted up the massive hill to Draydon Castle.

19

The
CASTLE

DRAYDON CASTLE WAS AN UGLY BLEMISH ON A HILL OF AN otherwise perfectly acceptable-looking city. It was like a black box that jutted out of the ground without even a fortress to protect it from attack. Its only advantage was high ground. The city itself had switched hands with so many rulers in history that Cyrene, even with her affinity for history, couldn't remember past the last five hundred years. The current King held the land tenuously at best.

They stopped in front of the large wooden door branded with the Aurum symbol—an eagle wearing a crown of oak leaves, the symbol of the Huntress.

"Wood," Cyrene said softly, shaking her head.

They dismounted, and Cyrene's horse was shepherded away.

"This way," a soldier said as the doors creaked open.

Cyrene's mouth dropped open at the interior of the castle. It was night and day from the ugly exterior. The walls were a soft blue color with intricate molding. The floors were covered in the most elaborate Aurumian carpets that she had ever seen. Her parents had Aurumian rugs in their foyer, but they looked paltry into comparison to what she was sinking her booted feet into. Framed portraits lined the walls, and Cyrene had a hard time believing all of the beauty before her.

After a few turns, a man opened a door into a large room and stepped through. He bowed formally. "Announcing Lord Barkeley Iolair and his traveling companions—Master Haille Mardas, Madam Haenah Mardas, Master Roran Rourke, Madam Ava Rourke."

Cyrene nearly rolled her eyes. The last time she had pretended to be Ahlvie's wife, they had nearly been killed. She wasn't looking forward to that cover story, but if being married kept the King at bay, then so be it.

They were ushered into the room. Cyrene lowered her face, but she kept her eyes trained on the throne room they had entered. It wasn't half as elaborate as the one in Byern, but it was still gorgeous, set in Aurum reds and blues.

The King sat in the Iolair eagle throne. He was a red-faced, overweight man in layer upon layer of fine silks and a long fur cape that hung past his feet when he sat. He had straggly red hair and seemed to be balding at the crown of his head.

They all dipped into demure bows and curtsies befitting the royalty before them.

"Lord Barkeley!" the King crooned.

He stood from the throne, wobbled considerably, and then paraded down the small set of stairs. A group of attendants jumped forward to help him.

Cyrene nearly grunted in disgust at the drunk pig. *What a way to hold court.*

"Rise, rise, of course," King Creighton said dismissively. He finally reached Orden, who stood and towered nearly a head taller than the man. The King clapped him on the back. "Barkeley, my old friend. It has been a long time, cousin."

"Indeed it has," Orden said.

"Years in fact. When I heard that you were in the city, I just had to see you! Couldn't miss the chance to see my favorite cousin."

Cyrene narrowed her eyes and waited for the punch line. The guy sounded like he was telling a joke, but she didn't quite understand the humor in his words.

"Yes, of course, King Creighton. I am your humble servant," Orden said sardonically.

The King didn't catch the difference.

"Enough with the formalities, Barkeley! We've known each other since we were children."

"As you wish, King Creighton."

The King's smile wavered, and then it returned just as quickly. "So, tell me everything. Where have you been all of these years? And who are your mysterious traveling companions?" He glanced over at them, his eyes lingering on Cyrene and Avoca just a touch longer than everyone else.

"As I told your commander, they were just people I happened to pick up along the road. I hardly know them," Orden lied.

"How long will you be staying? Long enough for the ball, I hope! I know how you love a ball."

"You're throwing a ball? For the Eos?" he asked, acting coy.

"We have visitors!" he cried, clapping his hands together. "For the first time in the-Creator-knows-how-long, three royal houses are under one roof, Barkeley. It will be a splendid occasion. You and your friends can stay here until then, of course. That will give us all the time we will need to catch up."

Orden tried not to look panicked, but if Cyrene could see it on his face, then surely, someone who had known him his whole life might be able to see it. Of course, the King *was* intoxicated.

"We already have rooms. Paid in advance, Creighton. All our belongings are there."

"Nonsense. At The Lively Dagger? No Lord of mine is going to be staying at a dastardly inn. Since your Lordship accommodations in the city have gone out of use, you can stay here with me and my little Jesi flower." His eyes sharpened for a second as he waited for Orden to disagree with him.

Cyrene nearly opened her mouth to do it herself. *We can't stay here in the castle!* Kael was here in these walls, and there would be no way to escape then.

Ahlvie nudged her when he saw that she looked ready to speak up, and she ducked her head again. She needed to get herself under control. Orden had said to remain invisible.

"What a wonderful suggestion," Orden said smoothly. "I'm sure Queen Jesalyn would love to have two new female attendants who are so reserved, soft-spoken, and altogether well-rounded ladies."

Cyrene didn't dare look at him. She plainly understood his suggestion.

"Yes, I believe my wife would love some new attendants. We should keep them close by," he said, eyeing them carefully. "Schumle, please escort these women to the Queen and let her know that I have given her these ladies-in-waiting as a gift with my blessing."

One of his female attendants dipped a curtsy to the King, her bosom nearly falling out of her corset. "This way," she said to the girls.

Avoca shared a glance with Cyrene before following. She was glad to be leaving the heinous King behind them, but she was not looking forward to meeting Kael's sister.

Cyrene straightened out her shoulders and held her head high. This was no time to panic. She couldn't change anything that was about to happen.

Schumle stopped in front of a huge gilded door. Music was playing on the other side, and they could hear laughter. Schumle didn't look pleased about entering these quarters.

Schumle entered the room and announced them. "Your Highness, gifts from your husband, the King. Two ladies-in-waiting, Madam Mardas and Madam Rourke."

Cyrene and Avoca curtsied lowly before Queen Jesalyn. The music stopped playing, and all around them was silence.

The room was filled with over a dozen women in extravagant clothing with their hair piled high on their heads in extreme curls and their fingers dripping in jewels. The room itself was plush and lavish. The divans were all a soft cream, blush, and champagne-coloring and heavy on the lace with excessively gaudy trim.

The Queen sat among her ladies on a large circular cushion covered in cream silk. She wore a pink dress in the highest of Aurumian fashion with skirts that bunched around her hips to reveal several layers of darker pink and a corset that accented her tiny waist. It seemed the trend in court hadn't yet trickled down to the commoners for the billowy sleeves had been replaced with a tight fit to her elbows and lace trim on the sleeves and the neckline. Her dark hair was in the same enormous curls with a long white feather pinned in, attached to a brooch of diamonds.

But it was the blue-gray eyes that made Cyrene stop. Those ran in the family.

"Well, what do we have here?" Queen Jesalyn asked. "Gifts from my husband. Oh, how I love gifts. You may rise."

They rose and waited, praying that Cyrene's disguise was enough.

"And what...lovely gifts they are." Jesalyn choked on her laughter.

Her other ladies couldn't hold it together.

"Why, I'm not sure what to do with commoners in such…clothing and without a single trace of makeup. Why, I still think I'm the only one who can wear my face natural, but that is the Dremylon grace."

Cyrene nearly sighed with relief. If Jesalyn thought her face was unadorned, then her mask had worked. That was all that mattered. Not Jesalyn's catty behavior or rude comments.

"Where did you get such…pretty garments and in such beautiful colors?" Jesalyn asked.

Her ladies snickered behind their hands as they exchanged glances with each other.

Cyrene sighed. It was hard enough, keeping two Dremylons in line, and she didn't want to have to deal with a third.

"Our apologies, Your Majesty," Cyrene said, offering a second curtsy. She wanted Jesalyn to think she was obedient. "We're from the Western banks of Aurum, near the Byern border at Albion. The styles of Queen Kaliana permeate into our city." Cyrene stepped forward, seeing that she had gotten Jesalyn's attention. "When we traveled here for the festival season, we had commissioned dozens of gowns for the journey, and we each carried three trunks with us, only to discover that the gorgeous silks and humble slim-fitting gowns hadn't *yet* traveled this far east."

Jesalyn turned up her nose at the slight insult. To say that the Queen of Byern had a style that had not yet reached Aurum would surely put Jesalyn in a tizzy for new gowns, if she were the type of person that Cyrene suspected she was.

"We bought new attire in the city when we arrived so that the citizens wouldn't keep marveling at our gowns and asking about the patterns," Cyrene continued. "It was quite wearisome, as you can imagine. We were just unaware that we would receive a summons on such short notice or else we would have made ourselves more presentable for Your Majesty." Cyrene kept her smile as sugary sweet as possible.

Avoca idly stood by. At least she didn't glare at Jesalyn.

"Well, I am always interested in new fashions. Aren't I, girls?" Jesalyn asked her ladies. "Perhaps you will offer your trunks of gowns to my husband as a gift to me, as he has so graciously offered you hospitality."

Avoca tensed next to Cyrene.

"I would have, of course, Your Highness, but we already sold most of the gowns to have new ones commissioned in your style while we were here."

"How unfortunate," Jesalyn said with false sympathy.

Just then, a woman scurried into Jesalyn's quarters, bumping into Avoca. She quickly strode around Avoca and ducked her chin to her chest. "Queen Jesalyn." She dipped into a curtsy. "I apologize for my tardiness."

Cyrene turned to gaze at the intruder, and her mouth nearly fell open.

Maelia!

"Affiliate Maelia," Jesalyn said with a keen smile. "How nice of you to join us. How does my devious brother fare?"

"He has gone into the city, Your Majesty," Maelia said meekly.

"Again?" she grumbled. "It's as if he didn't come all this way to see me!" Everyone shifted uncomfortably. "He's so obsessed with finding this Affiliate for Edric. You'd think they were both sleeping with her."

"Oh, Jesalyn, you are so bad," a lady seated to her right said.

"What? As if the Byern court is any more pious than our own," she countered with arched eyebrows. "Dremylon men are notorious."

Cyrene stiffened at the comment, and Avoca nudged her to remind her to remain calm.

The lady on Jesalyn's left giggled into her white feather fan and whispered something under her breath.

"Speak up, Salissa," Jesalyn commanded.

"Sorry. I only said that perhaps it isn't just the Dremylon men."

"Salissa! I'm scandalized." Jesalyn put her hands over her heart, but she was smiling, despite the supposed insult. "Anyway, Affiliate Maelia, please welcome our new guests. They are from the Western banks near Albion. A generous *gift* from my husband."

Maelia turned to face them and struggled to keep her face blank.

Finally…finally, they were back together.

It had been so long since Cyrene had seen her friend, and all she wanted to do was run to her and give her a hug. The separation had been more difficult than she had even realized now that she was looking at Maelia. She had left Rhea behind and acquired

Avoca along the way, but Maelia really knew what Cyrene had gone through as an Affiliate. They were bonded in their own way because of that.

"Affiliate," Cyrene said, dropping a curtsy to Maelia that Avoca mirrored.

"Welcome to Court," Maelia said demurely.

"All three of you, find a seat," Jesalyn commanded. "We will outfit our guests better for the next time you are in my presence. But, first, I would like Emari to finish her story about Lord Wimberely."

All the ladies broke out into giggles while Cyrene, Avoca, and Maelia quickly sequestered themselves at the back of the room.

The
QUEEN

HOURS LATER, JESALYN FINALLY DECIDED TO BREAK TO GET dressed for dinner, and the girls were free of her for a short time. Maelia lowered her eyes to the ground and then walked out behind the Queen.

Cyrene and Avoca waited for everyone else to leave before they stood and left the Queen's chambers. The hall was mostly deserted when they emerged, but they kept their heads together and mimicked the indulgent way the other ladies-in-waiting conversed. They followed Maelia back to her room.

Maelia firmly closed the door and then threw her arms around Cyrene. Her cheeks were wet when she pulled back. "I never thought I'd see you again," she gasped.

"Of course you'd see me again," Cyrene said. "I could never leave you behind."

"What happened in the woods and then Strat?" She wiped the tears from her face. "You were there, and then you were gone. The Royal Guard captured Ahlvie and me. Then, they wouldn't tell me what happened to him."

"He's with us," Cyrene told her. "We got him out, but you were meeting with Kael at the time. There was no way for us to get to you without everyone getting captured."

Maelia nodded. "I understand. In combat, you always sacrifice one for the sake of many."

Avoca visibly brightened. "Finally, someone who understands."

"I'm sorry. I don't think we were introduced."

"Oh. Right," Cyrene said. "This is Avoca. She helped me escape the attack by the Indres and brought me to safety. She and her friend have been with us since Strat."

Maelia frowned at that news. It had taken her a long time to trust Ahlvie. She had never adjusted to the addition of Orden, and she would surely doubt him even more after finding out what he had hidden from them.

"I'm not sure about bringing on new people, but did you say Indres?" Maelia asked with wide eyes.

"Yes. Turns out myth is coming to be reality," Cyrene told her.

Maelia shook her head. "This is a lot to take in. Indres and then other people saving you...us."

"Avoca is a friend," Cyrene confidently told her. "She knows our mission and has agreed to help."

"I know that I do not trust easily, but do you not find it convenient that she showed up to help and then brought you to safety?" Maelia asked.

Avoca crossed her arms. "My people live separate from Aurum. We reacted to the threat and got your friend out as fast as we could. We had a military force. I am a soldier. That was my charge, and I completed it. But I will fight for Cyrene, no matter what. Do not insult my honor."

Maelia stared at her for a moment and then nodded. "I, too, come from a military family. I understand the conviction." She turned back to Cyrene and looked once more like the lost girl who had helped Cyrene on her first day as an Affiliate. "So, what is the plan?"

"The plan is the same. Get to Eleysia. We have a bit of planning to do beforehand, but we want to make our getaway at the ball."

"Prince Kael is in the castle. He's been desperate, looking for you. If he finds out that you're here, he'll tear the castle apart, stone by stone, to get to you."

"Well, we're not going to give him that opportunity," Cyrene told her.

"Wait...how did you get into the castle in the first place?"

Cyrene sighed and rolled her eyes. "Orden."

"Did he commit high treason or something?"

"No. Lord Barkeley Iolair received a summons to appear in Court from King Creighton."

Maelia furrowed her brows.

"Apparently, that is Orden's real name, and he is cousin to the King."

"I knew something was off about him!" Maelia cried.

"Yes. Well, we'll have to deal with that another day. In the meantime, we need to find a suitable exit strategy for the ball, find a boat to take us to Eleysia, and"—Cyrene couldn't hold back her giggle—"suitable clothes that will knock Jesalyn speechless."

Maelia smiled. "I think I know just the thing."

Maelia figured out where Orden and his guests had been given rooms and then started out in that direction with Cyrene and Avoca in tow.

"I've been here a week. Of course, I wasn't allowed to leave the castle or venture onto the grounds, so when I wasn't with Kael or Jesalyn, I searched for an exit."

"And did you find one?" Cyrene asked hopefully.

Maelia looked grim. "Nothing that isn't heavily guarded."

Once they reached the rooms, Avoca made them keep walking past the door that Maelia had pointed out. They stopped a safe distance away.

"I'm going to go in first, see if the coast is clear, and then give you the signal to come in. I don't want anyone to recognize you."

They waited impatiently while Avoca disappeared back down the hallway. It was the first time Cyrene and Maelia had been alone since the night they were separated.

"Maelia, I'm so sorry I left you," she whispered. "I should never have done that. I should have fought at your side."

"No. Don't apologize. We told you to go, and if you had stayed, then we all would have been captured. Where would we be then?" Maelia asked. "Back in Byern."

"And then I couldn't get you out in Strat."

"You're here now," Maelia said, grasping her hand and smiling. "We'll get out this time."

Cyrene threw her arms around Maelia one more time and sighed.

Avoca whistled softly down the hallway, which was their signal. The girls broke apart and walked briskly to the door.

"You're not going to like this," Avoca said. Her nose was wrinkled in disgust.

"Like what?" Cyrene asked.

She found out as soon as she entered the massive quarters that Orden had been given by the King. They dwarfed Maelia's rooms threefold and were swathed in deep blue and gold. But the smell was undeniable.

"You're all drunk!" Cyrene cried.

Orden, Ahlvie, and even Ceis'f sat around a couple of clear crystal bottles with dark amber liquor. Their clothing was disheveled, their eyes were glossed over, and they were taking turns in laughing boisterously.

"What in the Creator's name?" Maelia whispered, shaking her head.

"You found her!" Orden cried in triumph.

Ahlvie staggered to his feet and then stumbled toward Maelia. "So...so glad you're ba-back," he said before breaking out into laughter.

"That is quite enough," Cyrene said.

She stormed across the room and snatched the bottles off the table before they could stop her. Avoca took them out of her hands and went to place them out of reach.

"What exactly is the meaning of all of this?" Cyrene demanded.

Maelia sighed. "I should have guessed they would be in this condition. The King drinks day and night. The first night we were here, Prince Kael returned to the rooms in a worse state than this." Her cheeks colored lightly, and she looked away.

Cyrene's jaw tightened. She had seen Kael drunk before. The night he had propositioned her in the castle. The thoughts made her blood run cold.

"Just lay off, Cyrene. We were just having a bit of fun," Ceis'f said. He looked the least intoxicated of all the guys, but if he was addressing her without biting her head off, maybe she should keep him drunk.

"We're not going to get anything accomplished with you three drunk," Avoca spat. "We have a mission. Soldiers shouldn't drink on the job."

"We're not soldiers here, Ava," Ceis'f said.

It was the wrong thing to say.

She glared at him. "We are always soldiers until our mission is completed. Has your training left your head this quickly? We are not safe in here. We are trapped like mice. And the King purposely got you intoxicated to let your guard down. How can you trust him?"

"We can't bloody trust him!" Orden bellowed, rising to his unsteady feet and glowering at the lot of them. "And he didn't purposely get us intoxicated. We purposely got *him* intoxicated. Do you know the kinds of leading questions he was asking to try to get to me? You don't. You don't know anything!"

Everyone stared back at Orden in utter silence. Orden was known to have a temper, but only when Cyrene pushed him past his limit. Otherwise he was a mild tempered man with a flair for adventure.

Cyrene had always wondered why he had agreed so easily to help them and why he had insisted on coming along. But she had been thankful for his help at the time. Now, it seemed there was much more to his story.

"What sort of leading questions?" Cyrene asked carefully.

"None of your ruddy business." Orden pushed past the lot of them and grabbed a bottle from where Avoca had deposited it. No one moved a muscle.

"Truly, I think it is our business. You led us straight to the capital knowing that you were cousin to the King. You must have known he would call on you," Cyrene insisted.

"I haven't seen my cousin in nearly fifteen years," he spat. "I'm no longer an Iolair. I gave up that name a long time ago."

"But why?" Cyrene asked. "I know that we all have our secrets, but we're in the thick of it with you now."

Orden tipped back the bottle and took a long swallow before addressing the room. He looked grim. "Aurum has a hard fought history to say the least. The throne is won through force more often than bloodline. There's no guarantee that if Queen Jesalyn gives Creighton a son that he will be king one day. He may not look like it now, but twenty years ago Creighton was formidable. I regret to say that I idolized the pig, but I was just a boy at the time. I was there at his side when he murdered the reigning monarchs and took the throne for his own. When he finally had the throne secure as his own, he let it known that he had married in secret during the war, and his new bride was my sister, Lissa."

Cyrene flinched. "He married his cousin?"

"It's not unheard of, but generally frowned upon. But who would challenge him?" Orden asked. "I tried, of course. Tried and failed. But Lissa stepped in for me and had me sent away for a time instead."

"And this is the first you've been back since then?" Cyrene asked.

"No, I came back a few years after that. Lissa was about to have her child. By then, Creighton was taking up with at least three other women at court. We parted on…less than pleasant terms, and I decided that this was not the life I had chosen."

There was a deafening silence when it seemed Orden had finished his sad tale.

Ahlvie cleared his throat. "What happened to Lissa?"

"She died," he said bluntly without explanation and no one could bear to ask how. "So, you see, I would never have brought you here if I'd had another choice. Creighton is doing this to get to me. He wants to know where I've been and what I've been doing since I left, but it is easier to play to his vices than to actually dodge him. He is still as calculating as ever."

Cyrene still wondered what he actually *had* done all that time away, but it didn't feel like the time to pry. He had given them a lot more than she had expected.

"Which means we need to leave as soon as possible," Cyrene said.

"Yes. There's no way he'll let me out of his sight before the ball. I still think that's our best option."

"He's right," Maelia agreed softly. "I won't be able to get out before then either."

"So, we need a way out," Cyrene reminded them. "And Kael cannot see anyone other than Maelia that he would recognize or he will know what is happening."

"We can't let that happen," Avoca said.

"The Prince goes into the city every day," Maelia filled in. "He won't be a problem here until dinnertime or later."

"Even better," Cyrene said. "If all goes as planned, in a week's time, we will be sailing out of the country with no more complications. Be ready when we do."

21
The BALL

Avoca

AVOCA'S LIPS CURVED UPWARD AS SHE LET CEIS'F KNOW THAT she was in position. He was set to watch Prince Kael for the night so that Cyrene could be seen by the Queen without him noticing. She nodded at Maelia.

The girl smoothed back the sumptuous lily-yellow dress and then folded into the crowd, walking into the ballroom. Once the Queen made her appearance, Maelia would stick to her side as a good little lady-in-waiting.

They all needed to be seen by someone, so it could be confirmed that they were all in attendance. Keeping up appearances for the evening was the only way they could get around the fact that Orden was to enter with the King, and it would be suspicious if they all left before the ball rather than slip away during the festivities.

Avoca just needed to wait for Ahlvie to get here, so he could escort her inside. She wished that she had been able to see Cyrene before leaving, but she had sworn she just needed one more thing from the seamstress before running off.

She tried not to worry about Cyrene. She could take care of herself until Avoca had her in her sights.

"Ready, my lady?" a voice whispered in her ear from behind.

Avoca twisted in her many layers and cursed Cyrene for suggesting the thing. It was a forest-green gown with lace cap sleeves and jewels that shimmered through the rest of the dress. It was the most exquisite thing she had ever put on her body, and she felt completely ridiculous. In Eldora, she wore practical clothing while working and loose dresses that were easily maneuverable otherwise. But she couldn't deny that she liked the appreciative look Ahlvie gave her when she faced him.

"You look stunning."

"Thank you." She let a small smile appear on her face at his attention.

"Shall we?" He offered his arm, and she placed her hand on his expensive black coat.

"Are you certain you won't be noticed?" Avoca asked him once more.

"Kael is the only one who would know me. Unless there are Byern Royal Guard posted inside that room, which we know there aren't, then we should be fine so long as Ceis'f keeps tabs on Kael."

"You're right," she agreed. She was just worried. So much of this was out of her control.

"Plus, I have this handy thing to use as soon as the King and Queen make their entrance." He held up the black mask in his hand.

"I still don't understand how Cyrene got Jesalyn to agree to make the ball a masque," she said as they entered the ballroom.

"She has a way of getting what she wants," Ahlvie said.

"You mean, she's stubborn?"

Ahlvie kept them to the edge of the room. They passed dozens of people dressed in the Queen's extravagant style and the King's style of long black coats and white lace cravats over top starched shirts. The room was decorated in the deep reds and blues of the Aurum.

"Is *stubborn* the best word for her?" Ahlvie asked.

"Headstrong, single-minded, relentless."

"I wasn't going to say it."

Avoca laughed lightly. "She's a challenge."

"A bit scary actually but loyal," Ahlvie said. "She uses the same tenacity to get what she wants in her friendships as well."

Avoca nodded. "In those moments, you'd never guess she was so young."

"She's only a few years younger than me," he said defensively. "She can't be much younger than you. You don't look a day over seventeen."

"Oh," Avoca said, glancing away. She sometimes forgot how young all the humans were. She *was* young for a Leif but hardly young when compared to Cyrene or Ahlvie, who had human lifelines. "Of course." She retrieved her hand from him and stopped. "I think this will do."

She turned away from him before she could see the hurt and confusion that was sure to bloom on his face. She wasn't prepared to tell anyone else about Leifs and her age.

From her position, she could see the entire ballroom laid out before her. If there were any mischief, then she would root it out.

"Should I stake out the room from another angle?" Ahlvie asked, taking a step away from her.

Avoca touched his arm. "No. Stay." Their eyes met, and she tried to remain still, as if she didn't know what her words meant. "The King and Queen will be here any second."

That same flippant attitude that he wore like a shield fell back into place as he stepped into her side. "If you wanted me close, you just had to ask," he said. Then, he winked.

Avoca pursed her lips to keep from smiling and let her eyes wander around the room. She saw Maelia in position with a group of ladies-in-waiting. And she found Ceis'f staring directly at her— specifically where her hand rested on Ahlvie's arm. She flinched away from the penetrating gaze. Only Ceis'f could make her do that. The weight of that gaze bore down on her like a brick. She was the Crown Princess of Eldora, destined to rule. *Then, how come I can't stomach the thought of returning and taking up my destiny?*

She shook the thoughts away and focused on what was ahead.

Avoca saw Cyrene slip into the room through the back door and tried not to smile. She stuck out like a sore thumb, even when she was trying to blend in. There was just something utterly compelling about her. But at least everyone was where they were supposed to be. Orden would enter with the King and Queen and then they could finally leave.

Ahlvie drew her a little closer and her heart accelerated.

"Can I speak with you for a moment?"

She met his gaze. "Now?"

"Just for a moment. We won't be missed."

She opened her mouth to object but then nodded. She was too curious to know what he wanted to say. Just as the King and Queen were announced, he escorted her through the crowd and out the back steps into the gardens.

She suspected she knew what this was all about, but she was going along with it anyway. It was so unlike her. She wasn't afraid of confrontation. With one look, she could stop a man in his tracks and kill him even faster with any number of weapons. Yet here she was.

Perhaps taking her out of Eldora had made her more...human.

Ceis'f would think that was a terrible thing. Emotions clouded judgment. With so many years behind her and many more ahead of her, it wasn't smart to get attached to humanity. Time would pass, seasons would change, and she would still remain. *But, without emotions and feelings, is there much left to live for?*

Maybe she had even chosen to work in the military with a six team because it was one of the few occupations that made her feel alive.

"Avoca?" Ahlvie whispered.

"Yes? I apologize. My thoughts were elsewhere."

"Did I offend you in some way?"

"Offend me? No. No, of course not."

"Of course not?" Ahlvie asked skeptically. He shot her a lazy smile. "Have you met me? I'm entirely offensive."

She let loose a laugh and then quickly smothered it. Few people could make her laugh so easily. "You try."

"Why do you do that?"

"Do what?" she asked.

"Hide your smile." He brushed a loose lock of blonde hair out of her face.

Avoca pulled away from his touch. "I don't."

"You're doing it right now."

"I..."

"You've done it every day since I met you when you busted down the door to my room and knocked out four guards." He stepped forward again. "You're a warrior, fierce and proud. I get it. But when you smile—"

"Stop," she commanded.

Ahlvie didn't even react. He just smiled that easy smile he always seemed to have on his face. "Can I continue now?" he teased.

"No."

"I didn't realize that I needed your permission to tell you how strong you are or how brave"—he leaned forward until he was mere inches away from her—"or how beautiful."

This needed to stop. She couldn't give him hope where there was none. Even if she continued on with this mission, her duty was to Eldora.

In a split second, she had her icy-white knife out of its sheath, hidden away in the confines of her dress. She flipped it in the palm of her hand and then pressed it against Ahlvie's neck.

"You have misread the signs and seek to take that which I cannot provide." Energy poured into her veins at the feel of the knife hilt in her hand, and her body hummed to life.

Ahlvie laughed. The man actually laughed at her. "Oh, Avoca," he whispered affectionately. "I expected nothing less."

What she hadn't expected was for him to knock her elbow back. Her hand flew up to stop him, but he blocked her and then wrenched her hand with the knife backward until her fingers released it. Then, he swung her around, roughly pressed her back against his chest, and brought the knife up to her neck.

"I didn't know that you preferred deadly foreplay."

Avoca's breath came out in spurts, and her mind was full of the adrenaline of the fight. Ahlvie's body was on fire, and she felt the heat rolling off of him. And she just stood there, flush against his chest.

He had disarmed her. She couldn't fathom it. *How did I underestimate him so completely?*

"Tell me I'm not a fool," he whispered. His breath was hot on her neck before his lips found the tender skin. His grip loosened on the knife at her neck, but he just pulled her tighter against him.

"You are a fool, Ahlvie." But she didn't have the conviction she had felt earlier.

She let herself get lost in him, closing her eyes and tilting her head back onto his shoulder. It wouldn't ruin everything to feel something other than duty.

And then she felt Ahlvie being jerked away from her. She turned just in time to see Ceis'f throw a wickedly fast punch directly at Ahlvie's face. Somehow, Ahlvie ducked the punch and barreled forward into Ceis'f's midsection, tackling him to the ground. Ahlvie tried to subdue Ceis'f, but Ceis'f was already lashing out at him.

Ceis'f landed an elbow to the temple, and Ahlvie fell off of him. He rolled on the ground and then landed back on his feet.

"What is wrong with you?" Ahlvie cried.

"Did you think I'd let you near her?" Ceis'f growled.

Avoca groaned and forced herself between them before they could launch at each other again. "That's enough. You both know I am perfectly capable of knocking you out…even in this dress."

"What were you doing with him, Ava?" Ceis'f demanded.

"We were talking."

"That did not look like talking. He was kissing you."

"She's not even interested in you," Ahlvie shot back. "You suffocate her. She can't even look at you."

"Ahlvie!" Avoca snapped.

"You think she's not interested in me?" Ceis'f asked, shaking his head. "You think you can take what is mine?"

"You think she belongs to you?" Ahlvie scoffed. "She's not an object, something that can be in your possession. She's a woman with her own thoughts and needs."

"She doesn't *belong* to me. She is mine."

Ahlvie raised his eyebrows and cracked a mocking smile. "Yours? She doesn't even act like she likes you…let alone loves you."

Ceis'f's eyes shot to Avoca. "He doesn't know?"

"Ceis'f, no," Avoca whispered.

"Know what?" Ahlvie asked.

Ceis'f took a step back, as if he saw where he could win and was taking it. "We are betrothed."

"Betrothed," Ahlvie responded hollowly.

"Avoca is the Princess of her people, and I am the last remaining Prince of mine. We have been meant for each other our whole lives and will be married as soon as she comes of age. No matter what you do, she will never be yours," Ceis'f said, hammering the last nail in the coffin.

"Ahlvie," Avoca said softly.

He raised his hand and refused to meet her eyes. She could see the easygoing guy who had intrigued her and made her laugh so effortlessly draining out of him.

"I understand now. If you'll excuse me," Ahlvie said before turning and walking deeper into the gardens.

Avoca whirled on Ceis'f and slapped him across the face. The sound cracked through the silent night air.

Ceis'f reached out and grasped her wrist in his hand. "What is wrong with you?"

"You have worn out your welcome," Avoca spat at him.

He pulled her toward him and bared his teeth. "We're going home, Avoca."

"Good! Leave, Ceis'f! I did not want you to follow me from Eldora, and I do not need you here now."

"You need me now more than ever. I thought you were a leader, the future Queen. If your mother saw how you were acting now..."

"My mother?" she asked in a deadly quiet voice. "My mother would be ashamed that her future son would think so little of her daughter that he had to babysit her while she was away from home."

"Do you not see—"

"No, you don't," she hissed. She yanked him forward at the last second, twisted so that she brought his hand up to her shoulder, and then reached with her other arm to grab his neck and throw him onto his back at her feet.

"You don't see anything. You don't see why I'm here or what the purpose is in any of this. You would have had me shamed before my own people for my disgrace in allowing six of my team to die in an Indres attack," she told him, leaning over his body. Her eyes were blazing bright, and Ceis'f didn't move at her words. "You see only what you want to see and believe in nothing else. Your parents were killed. Your village was burned. That was twenty years ago. The wounds do not have to heal, but you cannot continue to blame every human for the actions of a few."

Ceis'f rolled to his feet and stood before her, but she continued speaking, almost as if he weren't there anymore, "We have found the first Doma in two thousand years. Do you know what that means for the world? She could fulfill the Circadian Prophecy and restore order to a world devoid of it. We could be welcomed in the Nit Decus castle once more. We could make a difference rather than hide in the trees for the rest of eternity. We were once esteemed counselors and allies. I want that again, Ceis'f, even if you do not. It is an admirable goal to strive for."

"And what of your blood debt?" he asked hoarsely.

"I will happily die for Cyrene to see this come to fruition. If only you were so selfless, Ceis'f."

22

The PRINCESS

Ahlvie

AHLVIE DISAPPEARED INTO THE GARDENS. IT WAS A MAZE HE realized. *Perfect*. He would be happy to be lost tonight.

He already felt it.

He was a fool. Truly this time.

He'd always played the fool. Being quick-witted, a jokester, a drunk, and a scoundrel among other less favorable things had always done him good. He'd never been in a situation where his humor and ridiculous behavior hadn't helped him through it.

He was way into enemy territory. Nearly as far away as possible from the assignment he had been on back in Fen. But it was all to the right end. He knew where he fit into all of this. It all made sense at least. He'd known since he was thirteen where he fit in with it all.

And then Avoca had crashed into his life.

She was a game changer.

"Creator," he whispered into the stillness. "Betrothed and a princess at that."

He hadn't seen that coming. He'd known that there was something between she and Ceis'f. Cyrene had said as much. But he'd mostly assumed that Ceis'f was obsessed with Avoca. He hadn't known the whole story. Cyrene had warned him on their way from Strat. He should have listened. He never followed orders, but he probably should have for this one.

How can I compete with a betrothal to a prince?

"No clue," he murmured to himself as he walked farther and farther into the maze of gardens.

He heard the crack of a twig behind him.

He whirled around. "Who's there?"

There was no answer.

"Avoca?" he said. "Miss me?"

He couldn't help it. The witty tone effortlessly fell off his tongue as he shifted back into his role. At the same time, he slid the blades out of their sheaths at his wrists and toed the ones in his boots.

It smelled like trouble. He could sense someone stalking him. He must have really been lost in thought if he hadn't noticed it earlier. He was usually more perceptive than that.

If it had been Avoca, she would have already called out to him. That meant it was an unfriendly intruder. He was prepared for it. As prepared as he could be for an unseen attacker.

That was when it hit him.

Square in the chest.

All the air rushed out of his lungs as a beast knocked him off his feet. Ahlvie rolled and flipped back onto his feet as it lunged at him again. He was wide-eyed and ready when it came for him again.

He realized it for what it was this time. An Indres.

He would have been glad had he seen the last of those things in the woods the night before he had been captured and dragged to Strat. It seemed his luck had run out.

The small blades in his hands wouldn't do much against the massive creature.

It stood on all fours, glaring at him with bright golden eyes. It came up to Ahlvie's chest, and saliva was dripping from its fangs.

"You're one ugly wolf," he grunted.

As if the Indres could hear him, it tilted its head in offense and then rushed toward Ahlvie. He held his blades at the ready. He wished he'd had a sword on him, but he wouldn't have been able to easily conceal a giant sword that could slay a creature of the dark. He was gifted with knives but not like a sword.

Ahlvie cut at the beast, inch by inch, as it tried to bring him down. The beast was oozing rivers of thick black blood from its many wounds. Its massive fangs jutted out of its mouth, and it seemed to be trying to find a way to get past his blades and to its target.

They circled each other like fighters in a ring.

Ahlvie wondered dimly where the rest of the pack was but thanked the Creator that he didn't have to deal with them. This one seemed to be the Alpha. He didn't need the pack to protect him. Wherever he had come from, his objective seemed to be to kill.

When the beast lunged once more, Ahlvie twisted and slashed a dagger across the beast's throat. It reached out, snarled, and scraped its razor-sharp claws across the front of Ahlvie's jacket. They both fell to the ground.

Ahlvie rolled, gasping for breath.

The front of his jacket was shredded, and he pulled his arms out of the sleeves, discarding the ruined material on the floor.

"I liked that jacket," he spat.

Blood spotted the front of his tunic from the claw marks that were reddening under his gaze.

The beast was slow to get up, but get up, it did. It appeared that the knife hadn't completely pierced his jugular, and he was still moving, despite the blood flowing out of his throat like a torrent.

It was sluggish this time but desperate. Ahlvie barely missed a slash at his sleeve, and at the last second, he kicked up with the dagger in the toe of his boot and drove it into the beast's chest. Ahlvie rushed at him then and brought his final dagger through the Indres's throat, severing his jugular.

It twitched, as if clinging to life, and then fell into darkness.

Ahlvie leaned over the creature, heaving and holding his hand over the open wound on the Indres's chest. He heard howls slice the night air, and he shuddered.

The Indres knew their leader had fallen. They would come for him. Either to take their retribution from his flesh or name him their new Alpha. He could feel them beckoning to him in the chilly night air. His pupils dilated in the dim lighting, and he choked on the summons calling to him from the Indres pack.

"No," he whispered.

I have my own mission. I have Cyrene. Protect Cyrene.

"No, I can't."

The air closed in on him, and then he fell face-first onto the maze floor, next to the fallen Alpha. He busted his lip open, and his forehead split. He gasped for breath as their summons seized him. As he fought to stay away from them, black filled his vision, and he gave in to their request.

23

The

PRINCE

CYRENE ADJUSTED THE RED MASK ON HER FACE TO MAKE SURE it fit snug against her skin. Red feathers were attached to one side, and the rest was studded in jewels. It obscured most of her face, but she had added a bright red lipstick after Avoca had left. She knew that she was supposed to remain invisible, but it wasn't in her nature.

At that moment, King Creighton and Queen Jesalyn made their grand entrance. Cyrene stifled a laugh. Jesalyn had done just what Cyrene had suspected—scrapped the dress she'd had prepared for the occasion and gone with something Cyrene had claimed was all the rage in Albion. The gown was an obnoxious pink color with a million overlapping pieces of ribbon cascading down to the ground over a large tulle skirt. The top dipped in a V lower than Cyrene would ever consider decent and had a wide collar that was hardly flattering.

Cyrene tore her eyes from Jesalyn long enough to search out Kael. To the King's right, he stood in Byern formal clothing. Oh, how she had missed it! Home called to her at the sight of him in Dremylon green and gold.

King Creighton stepped forward to address the crowd, "Lords and ladies, noble houses of Aurum, esteemed guests of House Iolair, I, Creighton Lanett Cavel Iolair, Arrow of the Huntress and Guardian of the Eagle, King of Aurum, and my lovely wife, Jesalyn Adelaida Dremylon Iolair, Queen of Aurum, do welcome you to the first ball of the Eos festival season."

The King drunkenly pitched forward, and Jesalyn quickly stepped in to keep him upright.

"I, Queen Jesalyn Iolair, the Living Huntress and Savior of the Eagle, have prepared this supreme occasion for our honored royal guests. It is my great pleasure to welcome each and every one of you this evening. I am fortunate enough to have my brother, Crown Prince Kael Dremylon of Byern, with us this evening." She gestured toward Kael, who bowed. "In addition to that, this ball marks the end of our time with Prince Dean Ellison of Eleysia."

Cyrene's throat went dry. From behind Jesalyn's left shoulder, a man stepped forward. He was tall with light hair pulled back off his face.

That beautiful face. The hunter from the forest.

No.

She couldn't be this stupid. It just wasn't possible for that Prince Dean Ellison of Eleysia to be *her* Dean. She had thought that he was just some common hunter. With the way his friends had gone on about his father, maybe a merchant's son or even a nobleman's son. *But a foreign prince?*

She'd had her fair share of speaking indignantly to Kael and even Edric, but she never should have acted like that around Dean. She had berated him for his kill, told him to give it over to the hungry, and refused to see him ever again. And he could have been their ticket out of here. A very handsome ticket at that.

"Thank you so much for attending. Now, let's dance."

Queen Jesalyn took the hand of her husband, and they walked out to the center of the dance floor as the rest of their party followed in their wake including Orden. Music started from an orchestra against one wall, and soon, the entire room was flowing with dancers.

Cyrene searched out Avoca and Ahlvie but couldn't seem to find them in the crowd. Maelia had just been asked to dance by Orden, and they were close to the King and Queen.

Cyrene let her eyes fall on Dean. Perhaps that was a better plan after all. If she could get the attention of Prince Dean, then maybe they could have an easier time in escaping all of this. She kept her sights on him as she prowled the room. He danced several dances with different simpering ladies-in-waiting, and she tried to find the best way to intercept him.

She was halfway across the room when Kael Dremylon materialized out of thin air.

"Will you do me the pleasure?"

Cyrene's heart rate skyrocketed, and she reached for her mask to make sure it concealed her face. She covered the movement by pushing a loose lock of hair behind her ear and downcast her eyes. Thankfully, they were still the dull brown Avoca had changed them to.

Creator! Ceis'f was supposed to be here to intercede on her behalf. He was supposed to be watching Kael.

"I...I was just looking for my suitor actually," she stammered.

"He will have to wait then." Kael took her hand regardless and pulled her into the throng of dancers.

Cyrene stumbled over her steps on purpose. The last time she and Kael had danced together, she had decided he was the best partner she'd ever had. She needed to be less than spectacular at the present moment.

"You know, I do think red is your color," he said. "It would be scandalous in my homeland, of course, but red is popular here."

She tried not to let the shock register on her face. He could not possibly know it was her. Yet Edric had said the same thing when she arrived in red for the Presenting and her Affiliate ball.

Cyrene found her voice again and lowered it before speaking, "If it pleases you, my Lord." She cringed at her own simper. But she had to do it.

She had to act like one of those idiotic ladies-in-waiting. If he didn't notice her from her face, then he would certainly recognize her attitude.

His eyes roamed from her face to the clingy red silk dress she had chosen for the occasion.

"It pleases me."

She didn't dare hold back her blush, acting like a good little lady wanting to take home a prized Prince.

The dress itself was a blend between the Byern style Lady Cauthorn had created for her and the bulkier Aurum style. The skirt was full but had layer upon layer of sheer material. The bodice was a long-sleeved silk creation with rubies sewn into the fabric and the same sheer material fanning out along the scoop neckline.

The music started for the next dance, a variation on the Four Queens dance back home. Their bodies moved in sync to the simple steps, and her mind drifted off to the first time she had met Kael and when they had danced the Haenah de'Lorlah in perfect time.

"You dance very well, my lady."

Creator! She had forgotten that she was supposed to dance poorly.

"Th-thank you, my Lord."

He twirled her around in place, and then they interlocked arms to walk in a circle with the other participants. She tripped just twice and stepped on his foot for show. The dance was almost too common to dance at home, but she had seen it many times in the streets during the festival season.

"What troubles you?"

"My Lord?" she asked in confusion.

"All of the other ladies have talked my ear off during every dance, yet here you are, leaving me in silence." He smirked playfully down at her.

"My apologies. Wh-what would you like us to speak about?"

"There you go again," he said cheerfully.

Cyrene scrambled for what a lady-in-waiting would say to grasp the attention of the Prince of Byern. Likely none of the topics she would have spoken to him about. Even when they had first met, they had spoken of her educational pursuits and the advancement of the country more than frivolity.

"Do I distress you?" He turned her to face him and then walked her backward through the next series of steps.

"No, my Lord."

Kael pulled her closer, so they were touching. "Then, I must just make you uncomfortable," he breathed into her ear.

"Of course not, my Lord," she whispered, struggling to keep her voice neutral. But her stomach was in her throat, and she felt like she was suffocating. She needed to get out of this situation.

Where is Ceis'f? Avoca? Ahlvie? Anyone to stop this.

"Please let me know if I am."

"I doubt you could make me uncomfortable," she whispered.

"That is good to hear," he said with a touch of laughter to his voice. "I would hate to sustain another candelabra to the head."

Cyrene gasped and then tried to cover it by coughing. "I don't know what you mean."

But she did. When she had been trying to flee Albion, Kael had intercepted her and in a desperate move, she had hit him on the head with a candelabra to get away.

"Oh, I think you do."

His blue-gray eyes were twinkling in the candlelight. *He had been toying with her! Kael knew.*

She took a step away from him, and he made to follow.

"Mind if I cut in?" Dean asked.

Kael narrowed his eyes. "We have unfinished business."

"Yes," Cyrene said quickly to Dean.

"You mind?" he asked, ignoring Kael.

"No, no. I don't mind."

She nearly flung herself into Dean's arms to get away from Kael. Whatever the mission had been, it was no longer that. They needed to be gone from this place. It wasn't safe.

A new song began almost immediately, but she was practically hyperventilating. While she'd wanted to dance with the mysterious Prince who had dressed like a commoner while out in the city, she couldn't concentrate on that at the moment.

"Are you feeling well?" Dean asked, walking her a few paces away from Kael.

Dean stalled and didn't pull her into the dance.

"Yes. I'm fine." She couldn't bring the simper back. It hadn't worked the first time.

"You seem out of sorts. Do you need me to get you a drink?"

Cyrene took a moment to let her eyes wander the large ballroom. She got a sick feeling in the pit of her stomach when she realized that she didn't see anyone she knew. Avoca, Ahlvie, Ceis'f, Maelia, and Orden were gone. *Did something happen to them, or did I miss a signal to leave?*

The gardens were the alternative exit plan for the group. Maybe that was the best option.

"Actually. I think I need some fresh air."

"Allow me to escort you," he said, offering his arm.

She took it thankfully and left the ballroom with him. As she left, she glanced over her shoulder, but Kael had already melded into the crowd. She didn't believe that he would be gone for long though.

The night air did little to relieve the tension in Cyrene's shoulders. Her friends were missing, and Kael knew that she was here.

Why did he let me go? Did he think that I wouldn't actually leave the premises? Did he detain my friends, knowing that I would come after them?

A million scenarios ran through her head, and she jumped when Dean placed his hand on her shoulder, drawing her out of her thoughts.

"My apologies," he said, withdrawing his hand. "I didn't mean to startle you."

"It's not your fault. I can't seem to find the friends I came with."

"I'm sure they are simply enjoying the festivities."

"Maybe." She doubted it.

"Would it make you feel better if we went to look for them?"

"I think I should probably continue alone. I did not intend to detain you," Cyrene told him. It was as nice a dismissal as she could manage.

Dean stared at her for a minute. "You remind me of someone."

Oh no.

"Who?"

"A woman I met once in the forest."

"I..." she said faintly.

"It is you, isn't it, Haenah?" Dean asked. "I've been looking all over the city, and you were here in the castle all along. Did you come with the Prince? Were you hiding your identity, as I was?"

He sounded so hopeful that she was the woman he had met in the woods. Time seemed to slow as she stared up into the depths of his dark eyes. She actually *wanted* to tell him who she was.

"I don't know who this Haenah is, but..."

Dean confidently took her hand in his. "Do you know how many women I have met who have spoken freely to me? Do you know how many women I have met who not only share my interests but are not afraid to stand up to me when I challenge them?"

"Perhaps more would do so if they did not know you were the Prince," she whispered.

He laughed. "Perhaps they would. Yet, here you are, doing it, knowing that I am the Prince."

Well, he had her there.

"So, tell me how a woman from Byern, traveling through Aurum, makes it to the grand ball without being in the First Class, as you said you were not. Better yet, try to tell me that it's a coincidence that you are here at the same time as Prince Kael."

Cyrene broke away from him. "I…I can't."

"Are you with him?"

"No," she said flatly. Then, she tugged on the string and removed the mask that had been a feeble line of defense against Kael Dremylon. "I am not what you think I am."

His hand traced her face, and she closed her eyes at his touch. It was as if he could see her for who she truly was and not the make-up that Avoca had used on her face.

"I think you are the most spectacular woman I've ever met."

"There's so much you don't know."

"You are the missing girl," he whispered intuitively.

Her mouth opened in shock.

"The one who was kidnapped. They've been scouring the countryside for you."

"How could you know that?"

He smiled. "Because I would stop at nothing less to see you again."

His eyes darted to her lips and then back up. She could see what he was thinking, and she couldn't help but to mirror his actions. She stood frozen. Her mind told her body to move, but her heart disobeyed the command.

The last time she had kissed someone, it had been Edric, and a jolt of energy unlike anything she'd ever felt had tethered her to him. Yet the desire coursing through her at this moment was completely unlike that. *How could I want this from a total stranger?*

His hand found her waist, and she took a step toward him rather than away. She thought he was about to make a move when a gut-wrenching feeling plummeted through her center. She doubled over and gasped for air.

"What's wrong? Are you okay?" Dean asked as she coughed helplessly before him.

Avoca.

Dread filled Cyrene. She would never recklessly grasp for her powers like this. There had to be a reason.

"They're in trouble," she managed to get out.

"Who?" He reached out to steady her.

Cyrene shushed him but used him as leverage as she closed her eyes and reached for her own powers. She needed to let Avoca know that she was coming for her. Give her some hope that Cyrene would answer and help.

As soon as she touched the sparking center at her middle, a deadly heartbeat filled her eardrums. She squeezed her eyes against the onslaught, and her abilities flowed into her like a river emptying into the ocean.

Everything was magnified a thousandfold. She could feel the individual threads in Dean's shirt clutched in her fist, the light breeze touching her skin, and his faint breaths beside her.

Above all, that was the heartbeat. Yet it was *wrong*. Not like the deer at all.

She could sense Dean's heartbeat when she listened for it, but this was otherworldly. It called to her and repulsed her without her having any knowledge of what it was.

Then, she felt it reach out to touch her mind. It was just the faintest brush that, if she had not had her powers to guide her, she would never have felt it. But she had felt that touch before, and she would never again let that happen to her.

Without a second thought, she slammed a mental wall between that and the thing that was trying to reach her. Braj.

The heartbeat remained…and it was getting closer. Too close.

"No," she cried, straightening.

"What's wrong?"

"Give me your weapon."

"My sword?" he asked. His brows furrowed.

"Now!" she cried. Then, she yanked it out of its ornamental sheath before he could object.

She whirled with the sword in hand. It was massive and made for the man behind her, who was much larger and stronger than her. But her powers surged up out of her and flooded the instrument in her hand, lightening and strengthening the steel.

The Braj came out of the shadows at that exact moment.

"Move. Get out of here!" she yelled at Dean.

"I'm not leaving you here!"

She rushed toward the Braj with more determination with the use of her powers than she had felt the last time she killed the Indres. She knew nothing of swordplay, but she let the instrument guide her, let her powers flow freely.

The beast came at her with ease, perilously swinging his poison-laden blade.

Cyrene twisted away from the curved sword. She had known its danger and had been lucky to have survived. She wouldn't give the thing that advantage this time. She felt the irregular heartbeat of the Braj and then used the sword as an instrument to push the magic toward him.

She deflected his blow and drove the sword home. A pulse shuddered through its body, and then it tumbled to the ground. She was forced off her feet as the weight of the Braj took her down with the sword still in her hand.

Her heart fluttered as the power slowly drained out of her, like molasses dripping from a tree. She felt an arm on her shoulder as someone hoisted her onto her feet.

"Are you out of your mind? Next time a Braj attacks, why don't you let me take it out? If his blade had touched you, what would I have done?" Dean asked very seriously.

Cyrene's eyes glazed over and then refocused as she tried to hold on to consciousness. "You…you know about Braj?"

"Don't insult my intelligence," he said, wrestling the sword from the fallen Braj.

"No one knows at home. Everyone thinks…thinks they're…"

"Monsters? Well, they are."

Her legs gave out, and he adjusted so that he was holding her up against him.

"How did you even hold my sword? The bloody thing is too heavy for most of my men, and you handled it like a professional. Did you learn that from your father as well?"

She shook her head, but her body felt sluggish, almost like she was wading through a heavy current. Her powers hummed softly in her, and just as she went to release them at the loss of the threat…another heartbeat filled her ears.

"Dean, there's another," she said softly. Then, she collapsed.

24

The CONSEQUENCES

"Tell them you can't go to Eleysia, Sera," Viktor said.

This time, Cyrene realized immediately where she was. The mind and body connection between her and the last Domina Serafina registered instantly. Perhaps it was because this was the third time that she had been in the woman's thoughts in the past couple of months. She should be worried about her ability to do this, let alone the ease in which it occurred, but Cyrene only felt curiosity.

"You know I can't do that."

There was something in Serafina's voice that hadn't been there the last time Cyrene had been in her head. She seemed stronger, more resilient. Though she still looked upon this man with tender devotion.

"They claim that you have more power than any of the others, and you still let them make your decisions."

For the moment, Serafina looked away from Viktor and down at the slimming red satin dress. Cyrene wished she knew what they were talking about.

"I have no choice. I have not completed my training, so I have very little political clout," she told him.

Viktor took a step back. "You want to go."

"No," she corrected him, "I *must* go. I want to stay here with you."

"Then, stay!"

"Is it always this argument, Viktor? It becomes so draining."

Cyrene noticed their surroundings for the first time. They were in some kind of cottage. It reminded her of the holiday home her parents owned in the country.

"You were the one who separated us, Sera. I've been fighting for us from the beginning."

"By marrying Margana? My best friend?" Serafina snapped angrily. "Your wife is with child, and you stand here, begging for me to do what exactly? I cannot give up my powers any more than you can leave your wife and child."

"I would do it for you." He held his arms out for her.

"Oh, Viktor," she said, falling into his embrace. "Why must this always be so difficult?"

"It has been difficult since the day you stepped into the castle. I feel you drifting away from me more and more, Sera. I can't bear it. You are my one true love. Margana is the person my father chose, not who I chose. My choice will always be you." He grasped her arms and drew her back, so he could look at her. "Find a way for us to be together forever, my love."

"We will be," she whispered.

"No. Use your powers. Then, you will know my love never wavered."

Cyrene woke up to the feel of a soft cushion under her head and silk sheets covering her body. Her mind was hazy. Her head pounded. Her throat felt dry. Her fingers tingled. She blinked away her blurry vision and allowed the room to come into focus.

Where am I, and what has happened?

Her mind was still filled with Serafina and Viktor Dremylon. *Why did they keep coming to me?* She had always adored history, but no history she had ever read said that the supposedly evil Domina Serafina was in love with her archrival and the man who destroyed her, Viktor Dremylon. But the more Cyrene had these visions, the more she questioned if the history she had grown up with was accurate. And how could Serafina use her powers to make their love eternal? Cyrene doubted there was a force on this earth that could do such a thing.

"She's awake," a voice called out with relief.

Cyrene turned her head and saw a young woman looking down upon her. "What's going on?" she croaked.

The woman didn't say anything. She just rushed out of the room. Cyrene looked around at her surroundings and tried to remember what had happened.

Everything came back to her in sharp focus. Avoca had reached with her magic. The pulse of the Braj. Slaying the beast with Dean's sword.

Dean!

She gasped aloud and tried to sit up but crashed back down into the bed as her body tried to recover.

She covered her face with her hands. She had passed out and left him there to fend for himself. He hadn't acted surprised that one was there, but everything she knew about Braj told her that he couldn't hope to defeat one without powers unless he was one of the best swordsmen in the world. That meant...he had likely perished. Her chest tightened at the thought.

Dean couldn't be dead. *Creator!* She couldn't even fathom that. She had only met him twice, but she just couldn't believe it. The first man who had ever shown interest in her without any motivations...and she had likely led him straight to his death.

Cyrene slid slowly from the bed and walked across the small room to bring life back into her limbs.

She had just made it back to the bed when the doorknob twisted. Cyrene turned to face the door, wondering who exactly she was going to see. When the door opened, in strode Queen Jesalyn, and right behind her was Kael.

Jesalyn was smiling like she had just won a prize. Kael looked like the overconfident, mischievous Prince he was. Cyrene stood her ground even though she wanted to drive Jesalyn's smile into the nearest bedpost.

"Haenah, it's so good to see you," Jesalyn cooed. "Or should I call you Cyrene now that we're familiar?"

"Why are you holding me hostage?" Cyrene demanded.

Jesalyn snorted. "We gave you a proper bed and a nice room in the palace, and you say you're a hostage."

"Jess," Kael said softly from her side.

She straightened, and it was easy to see that she really was only sixteen. In Byern, she wouldn't have even reached her Presenting day, and she was here, trying to rule a country. Cyrene would have felt bad for her under different circumstances.

"We're here to bring you back to Byern, where you belong," Jesalyn said.

Kael sighed. He looked frustrated with his sister, but it wasn't like he was letting Cyrene go. "At the present moment, your captors and friends have been detained."

"Detained?" she asked with a cold pit in her stomach.

"Maelia is perfectly safe in the room next door. However, Orden will be charged with kidnapping. Aurum will hand over their Lord to the throne for trial. His accomplices—Ava, Roran, and Ahlvie—will be charged with aiding and abetting a known criminal. I will be escorting you back to Byern at first light. So, get used to your accommodations. You will be home soon."

Cyrene stared at him suspiciously. *Charging all of them for kidnapping?* Kael *knew* that she hadn't been kidnapped. He wouldn't have spoken to her in such a way…toyed with her, if he had thought that someone was going to spirit her away. *Is he doing this because, like Maelia had said, he needs to prove to himself and to Edric that he can do this right?*

"Kael, I wasn't kidnapped."

"You let her address you like that?" Jesalyn asked, raising her nose.

Kael's blue-gray eyes bored into Cyrene, like he was trying to tell her something, but she didn't know what it could possibly be.

Did he worry that since Cyrene really hadn't been kidnapped, there would be an issue with the fact that Byern had sent all these guards onto foreign soil for no reason? Well, that was not her concern.

"You've spent a long time in the company of your kidnapper. Your judgment must be impaired."

"My judgment?" she asked, taking a step toward him. "What happened to Prince Dean? Is he okay?"

When Kael didn't speak up, Jesalyn sighed. "He's fine. He brought you in himself."

Cyrene's hand went to her mouth. *No.* She had trusted him. *And he betrayed me?* Well, at least he was alive, and she hadn't sent him to his death.

Jesalyn huffed. "By the Creator, you are annoying. Why does Edric even want her back?"

Cyrene sagged slightly with relief. She had thought Dean was dead. Knowing he was alive seemed to lighten her, ease some of the tension in her heart, even if he had betrayed her and given her over to Kael.

When she met Kael's eyes a second later, she was shocked by what she saw there. Uncertainty and confusion, and then a second later, there was red-hot jealousy.

She didn't even know how to respond to that when Kael turned on his heel and stormed out of the room. Jesalyn stared after him in confusion. Clearly, this was not part of their plan.

"Well then, tomorrow, I'll have you out of my city," Jesalyn said with a smile before slamming the door shut and locking it.

Cyrene twisted the handle and searched the room to see if there was something she could pick the lock with. But there was nothing. She was trapped in a windowless room, alone, without any hope of finding her friends and escaping to Eleysia after all.

She paced back and forth across the carpet, trying to figure out a puzzle that had no solution.

It was the only reason she heard the click of the doorknob. She took a step back and waited to see what Kael had to say this time. A few endlessly long minutes later, the door cracked open, a torch was thrust into her room, and a familiar face sprang into view.

"My lady," Dean's friend Darmian said, bowing at the waist. He pushed the door the rest of the way open, revealing Faylon and Clym.

Cyrene's eyes searched for the person she was hoping to find, and a second later, Dean appeared, whole and intact with little more than a small bruise on his cheekbone.

"I said I would find you again," Dean said with an enchanting smile.

Cyrene backed away a step. "You betrayed me to Prince Kael."

Dean frowned. "After I dispatched the Braj, I was overrun by Aurum guards. I had to make it seem like I was handing you over. But I was always coming back for you. You can have asylum in my country. In Eleysia. No Byern guards would dare try to take you from there."

Cyrene nearly wept with joy. "You mean it?"

"Of course. You were not kidnapped. That much is clear to me. The rest of the story is your own, but I am free to take you safely away from here, if you will join me."

"Yes," she said with a nod.

Darmian pursed his lips. "Then, let's make haste."

"My friend Maelia is being held next door."

Two of the men dashed to the room next to hers, and soon, Maelia was with them.

"But I have to get the rest of my friends, and I fear they are in the dungeons," Cyrene said.

"Then, we will do what we can to get everyone out of here," Dean said.

"Servants stairs now. As quietly as possible," Darmian said, ushering the girls down the stairs.

Cyrene remembered their mad flight out of Strat only a couple of weeks ago. This time, she swore she wouldn't leave anyone behind. They wound down the stairs until they reached the bottom level and rounded the corner to the dungeons. Darmian, Clym, and Faylon immediately engaged the guards who stood at the entrance, and just then, Cyrene felt a magical pull at her center.

Avoca.

A few seconds later, her friends were barreling out of the dungeons and straight toward her.

"Cyrene!" Avoca cried when she saw her standing at the entrance. "What happened?"

They embraced as she approached.

"We'll talk later," Cyrene answered.

When Cyrene pulled back, she counted all of her companions. She had sworn that she would not leave unless she had everyone.

Orden. Maelia. Ahlvie. Avoca. Ceis'f.

All accounted for.

Dean touched the small of her back. "We should get moving if that's everyone."

She nodded, telling herself that the thrill of his touch was from the adrenaline of the escape. That was all.

Orden knew the hallways better than even Darmian and overtook him for the lead. They took a sharp corner and then another, scaring servants and pushing them out of the way. They didn't have time for pleasantries, not when they had just been imprisoned by the Prince of Byern and the Queen of Aurum.

The hallway revealed a wide opening. They dashed toward it, heedless of where they were going, and ended up at a guarded entranceway that led out of the castle.

Darmian and Orden made quick work of the men who had the misfortune of standing duty, knocking them out and leaving them to be found in a nearby room.

Orden grabbed a lever and hoisted open a door. Footsteps could be heard distantly in the hall behind them.

"Hurry!" Cyrene cried.

"Just go!" Dean yelled.

"Go now!" Orden ordered as well.

The Leifs were the first to dart out through the open door. Whoever was behind them was gaining just as the rest of their party ran toward the city.

Cyrene could see Avoca up ahead, and she felt the gut-wrenching pull of her magic. It was like a magnet drawing her closer, and it only made Cyrene want to pull from her own source now that she could touch it.

Orden was the last to follow. He cut the rope for the door and then ran at full speed toward them. The gate barely missed him as it tumbled down, blocking the entrance. A group of guards yelled from behind the barricade. Arrows were nocked above them, but in the close quarters, only one or two arrows were fired, and they missed their mark.

Their group barreled through the city, toward the docks. Adrenaline fueled Cyrene forward.

The moon glowed bright overhead, illuminating their every move. There was no place to hide in the city. All she could do was hope that they would make it to Dean's ship before the guards caught up to them.

The ship loomed in the distance, proud and true, waving the Eleysian flag.

Her heart hammered in her chest, and everything ached. It felt wondrous and impossible that she had come all this way, and she would finally get to go to Eleysia. Even if nothing had gone as planned, they could still get there after all—and on the Prince's ship, no less.

Dean was keeping pace at her side. She knew that she was the slowest of the bunch.

She could feel her magic thrumming in her fingertips, but she refused to reach for it. Not until she could fully control it. The only time she had ever used it and not passed out was when she found the deer. She hadn't even *done* anything with it. She couldn't afford to pass out at this point.

Cyrene could see that Darmian had already reached the vessel and was commanding the crew to set sail.

"We have to move faster," Dean said.

She didn't dare look behind her in fear of seeing the guards approaching. They were on foot, but drawing nearer.

"I know," she gasped out breathlessly.

"Some more of that magic again would be most helpful," he insisted.

Her feet stumbled over the word, and her mouth dropped open. *He knows. Of course he knows!* He had seen her kill the Braj. Miraculously, he had killed another. But still…hearing that word out of his mouth felt like a dream. She had only just told her Ahlvie. She didn't know how she felt about anyone else knowing, let alone a stranger.

"I don't…"

"Just use it," he said.

Her fingertips tingled. Everything tingled. Her body came to life. She breathed in what she had been holding back for much too long. Her lungs expanded, and her body felt lighter. She didn't know what she was doing or what she was even thinking. All she could feel was the sweet bliss of being filled with the Creator's blessing. It was glorious and eternal.

The fear that had pricked her mind before vanished.

I can control it. I can do it, she chanted to herself.

Without another thought, she recalled the last thing that she had done and pushed the energy blast out behind her. The earth quaked under her feet. The wind roared in her ears. Her whole world shattered.

She flew ten feet in the air and landed heavily on the shaky ground. Dean was a good twenty paces beyond her on the dock. He had somehow cleared the distance and was on safe ground. But where she lay was still trembling with whatever she had done.

Dean screamed her name and gestured behind her. She turned away, and in horror, she saw what was happening.

The beautiful stone houses that had lined the docks only minutes ago were demolished. Rubble.

Her mouth hung open, and she let loose a cry of despair.

The guards lay on the ground. They were alive. She could dimly feel their pulses, proving to her that they were alive, but they were holding on to anything through the trembling of the earth.

Whatever she had thrown at them multiplied and magnified. A ripple passed through the city. She could see the destruction from her magic in its wake. Nothing as bad as the immediate vicinity but not good either.

"Dean, go," Cyrene said. Tears brimmed in her eyes.

For the first time, she felt *wrong* for going on this mission. She had no clue what she was doing. Working with her magic was wrong. It could hurt people. Destroy lives. Wreak havoc. She couldn't do this.

Then, Dean grabbed her by her shoulders and hauled her onto her feet. "Breathe," he whispered so softly that she shouldn't have heard him over the wind in her ears. "Breathe in and out. It will be okay. Just breathe."

She stared into his dark eyes and felt grounded in that gaze. She took a long deep breath and let it out. He nodded, encouraging, and she refused to break her stare.

"That's it," he said. "Just breathe."

Slowly, something shifted within her. Her body loosened. The air died down. The earth stopped shaking. And then her magic vanished. Winked out like a light.

She sagged into Dean's arms, and he held her tight to him.

"There, there," he said soothingly. He breathed into her hair. "If I had known, I never would have suggested that."

"I didn't mean to," she whispered.

"I know. I see that."

"Dean…did I kill all those people?"

He hesitated, like he didn't want to lie to her. "I don't know. I think most people were just knocked down. The important thing is getting you out of here. Can you walk?"

She swallowed back tears and averted her eyes from the rubble behind her. Perhaps everyone had a reason to be afraid of Doma.

"I need you with me right now," Dean said. He lifted her chin until she looked into his eyes. "I said I'd find you. Now, come back to me."

She peeled herself away from him. She couldn't believe what she had just done. How horrible it was to unleash like that. But also how amazing it was to feel all of that power. She was corrupted. She should never touch it again. That much was for certain.

"Come back to me," Dean whispered again.

She swallowed hard and nodded. *Yes, important things first.* She could worry about her magic on the boat. Not how to control it...but how to get rid of it.

Dean helped her move toward the dock, which had taken none of the impact of Cyrene's earthquake. The water was choppy from the wind, but the ship could sail through it.

Just when Cyrene thought she was safe, Cyrene felt a sword at her back. She froze in place. Dean reached for his weapon, but he was too late.

"Don't move."

Cyrene closed her eyes and sighed. *We had been so close. So close.* All she'd had to do was walk onto the ship and leave. But no.

"Turn around, Cyrene."

She took a deep breath and then carefully turned to face Kael Dremylon.

The
FOG

"WHAT ARE YOU DOING, KAEL?" CYRENE ASKED, HER voice hoarse.

"Did you think I'd just let you walk out of the city?" he asked.

"I suppose my answer should be no since you planned to cart me off back to Byern to claim your prize." Her words were as cold as ice.

"And what is my prize?" he asked Cyrene.

Dean shifted an inch, and Kael embedded the tip of his sword into the front of Cyrene's dress. One of the thin straps broke, and a trickle of blood pooled at the spot.

"I wouldn't do that if I were you," Kael said.

Cyrene could feel Dean tense beside her, but he didn't make another move forward.

"In fact, I would move back a few feet."

Dean ground his teeth next to her and then did as Kael had said. Dean had no other choice.

"That's better. I always like a little privacy with you," he said to Cyrene. "So, tell me about this prize."

"Do you think that, if you bring me back, Edric will give you the thing you want instead of keeping it for himself?" Cyrene asked.

"I'll be a hero when I return. I'm quite certain I could have whatever I wanted."

She rolled her eyes. Old habits die hard. "Oh, please. The whole reason you were sent here is because Edric believed I was kidnapped. He wants me back. But I wasn't kidnapped, Kael. You and I both know that. I left."

"And you didn't say good-bye. How inconsiderate."

"I didn't say good-bye to anyone," she reminded him. "Not even Edric."

Her chest contracted but not like it had when she first made the decision to leave. With Edric, everything had been an electric pull, as bright and demanding as her magic hovering at her fingertips. She couldn't let go any more than she could have earlier. The buzz was just as present around Kael. The thought irritated her and infatuated her.

But, with the distance between she and Edric, she didn't feel that pull as strongly. Away from Byern, that pull to the Dremylon brothers felt like a strange, distant dream. As confusing as Serafina's dreams.

Do I have feelings for Edric? Am I attracted to Kael? Or Is it just something that draws me to those damn boys…that draws them to me?

"And, if I return, I'll decide whether or not I'm a prize to be won," she stiffly told him.

"There's something different about you," he said, ignoring her last comment.

"I think I'm the same." But she didn't.

Her magic hummed in her veins, and her worldview had been opened in the last couple of months. Leifs existed. Braj and Indres existed. There was good and bad in everyone. No matter what she believed about Byern, Affiliates weren't everything they were supposed to be. People looked down upon them in the rest of the world and disagreed with what she had been taught. Her education had only taken her so far. It hadn't prepared her for hard travel, swordsmanship, magical training, meditation, hunger in the streets, starvation…women's rights. She had so much to think about. Things she never would have considered before leaving her home.

So, yes, she was different. And she was glad. She never wanted to be that naive girl again.

"No, you don't."

She raised her chin. She had always been defiant at least.

"You're coming with me, Cyrene."

"No, I'm not, Kael."

He reached out so suddenly that she hadn't even seen him coming. He dragged her forward toward him until mere inches separated them. His sword was at her throat, and his bright blue-gray eyes bored down into her own. She felt that jolt pass between them, like a spark igniting a flame. Her head felt foggy…and everything went hazy.

"You're coming with me."

"What?" she whispered. Her eyes grew wide, and she had the strange sense of déjà vu.

"If I have to tie you to my horse and ride with you the entire way back to Byern, you're leaving with me. Now."

"Kael," she breathed. Her voice was a mere whisper, carried away by the breeze.

She felt herself succumbing. Not just succumbing…she wanted to go with him. She shouldn't have left in the first place. Kael knew what was right for her, and Byern could protect her and shelter her from harm. Nowhere else in the world was like Byern. It was her home.

"Come with me," he said.

His lips were so close. Just a breath away. She could lean into that embrace and forget the world. Nothing else existed. Just her and him in that moment. All she wanted was Kael Dremylon.

"Yes," she purred. "Yes, of course."

She was desperate to clear the space between them. To feel his lips pressed against hers. Her mind could process nothing else in the world. She moved toward him and felt his sword bite into her neck.

She cried out, and before he could stop her, she stumbled backward a few steps. Her head cleared suddenly, as if she were coming out of a dense fog. She opened her mouth to say something, but no words came out.

Kael rushed toward her to regain his advantage, but Dean was there. He moved with a Leif-like grace, putting his sword between Cyrene and Kael.

"Give me a reason to kill you, pretty boy," Dean growled. His voice was low and guttural.

He would do it. Cyrene could see it on his face. He would kill Kael in an instant if he made the wrong move.

Kael looked into his face and laughed. "The Prince of Eleysia, Cyrene? Do you bewitch men everywhere you go?"

Her response didn't come. She just stared at Kael in disbelief.

What just happened? She had been yelling at him, and then as soon as he had touched her, she had lost all sense. She had been eager to give in to him and return to Byern. Forget her quest, and be with Kael. *Creator, I tried to kiss him!*

She couldn't connect the dots. *How did that happen?*

"Cyrene, it's time to go," Dean said.

"What the hell did you just do?" Everything was coming into focus. "What did you just do?" she screamed.

Kael smiled slowly. It wasn't the charming smile she was used to from Kael. It was something worse. Something more sinister. Dark and foreboding, like a black shadow sweeping over his elegant features. "You're not the only one with secrets."

Her head whirled. She didn't know what that meant.

Kael turned his attention back to Dean. "Well?"

"Cyrene, go now."

"She's not going anywhere," Kael said.

And then he started pacing his steps. They were fluid and crisp. The steps of a practiced swordsman. Cyrene had never seen him fight before, but she almost didn't need to know how good he was. She remembered the way he danced. Light-footed, sure-footed. Competent and controlled. If he put half as much emphasis on swordplay as he did on everything else in his pampered life, then he was going to be good...great.

But Dean had just killed a Braj. That had to count for something.

She worried what it would mean if Dean and Kael were an even match...and even worse, if they weren't. For as much as she didn't want to return to Byern, she couldn't bring herself to want to see Kael injured either.

"You think you can fight me?" Dean asked.

He sounded so sure of himself. She hoped that pride had been earned.

"No. I don't think I can," Kael said. "I know I can. Fight you and win."

Dean laughed, but he was watching as Kael shifted and brought his sword down toward him. Dean blocked the touch, and steel clanged together. He ground his teeth as they fought against the weight of the blades. Kael barely looked like he was exerting any effort. In fact, he looked like he was having fun.

Cyrene felt a hand on her shoulder and nearly jumped out of her skin.

"It's just me," Avoca whispered. "I left everyone else on the ship. We're ready to sail. You should come with us."

"I can't until we have Dean."

"Should we interfere?"

Cyrene had no idea. She wanted to stop this nonsense. The last thing they needed was bloodshed between the ruling nations. But this fight meant something. Her friends and Dean's companions could overpower Kael, but this moment seemed necessary.

"Leave them," she whispered.

"You believe this fight to be honorable?" Avoca asked.

"I believe it's our way out."

Avoca sighed heavily but didn't say anything else.

Then, the guys moved. Quick footsteps, slicing movements, easy twists and turns. They were both practiced, seasoned fighters. Neither had the advantage, and each was straining to push back and overtake the other.

Kael spun to the right, crossing his sword and striking out at Dean. He missed by a hairbreadth. Dean dropped and rolled away from Kael. They rushed back together, and Dean pushed him backward. Closer and closer to the edge of the dock. The swords clashed off of each other. It looked like Dean was gaining the upper hand. He just needed to finish this.

Damn Kael for doing this! She just wanted to leave. It shouldn't be this hard. She shouldn't have to be this connected to him.

Then, something happened. And her heart stopped.

Kael whirled around so fast that he was a blur. Everything shifted. Even the night air changed directions, as if in connection with him. Dean couldn't move fast enough. He tried to pull up his sword to block the stroke, but Kael was faster, impossibly faster, and his blade slid into Dean's shoulder.

Cyrene jumped forward out of instinct, but there was nothing she could do. She cried out in disbelief.

"No, no, no!" she yelled, dashing to his side.

She didn't even care that Kael was hovering over him. Kael yanked his sword out of Dean's shoulder, and it made a sickening squelching noise. Cyrene shook at the sound. This couldn't be happening.

Kael reared back to finish the deed, but Cyrene jumped in front of him.

"Don't! Don't kill him."

Dean groaned on the ground, and blood was spilling out of his shoulder far alarmingly fast. He needed medical attention.

"Please, please, Kael."

She had no idea how in a split second the advantage had changed. Dean had gone from winning to *this*. She could have stopped this. But, instead, she let the boys have their stupid battle. All for what? Nothing.

"And what will you give me to stop?" he asked.

"Kael," she whispered, pleading. She only had one thing to offer, and she couldn't go back home.

He took a confident step toward her, and she felt the hazy feeling sweep over her once more. He hadn't even touched her, but she was losing focus. It hung just on the edge of her consciousness. It wasn't quite as overpowering as before. More hesitant but still…there.

"What are you doing?" she whispered.

"Showing you just how easy it would be."

Black tendrils caressed her skin, pulling her toward him. The spark that was always there sizzled, and an oily grip drew her toward him. She shivered all over. Panic was laced as much with the need that she felt, but she didn't understand.

"How are you doing this?" she asked. She knew he could feel the fear thrumming through her body.

"I think you know."

Magic.

Creator! Kael Dremylon has magic. Something extremely powerful and completely awful! He shouldn't be able to do this. It didn't make any sense. Viktor Dremylon hadn't had magic. That was why he couldn't be with Serafina. It didn't run in his blood. *How else can Kael possibly have it?*

"Me. Take me," she said. Her heart broke at the words spilling out of her mouth. She'd do anything to save the people she cared about.

Kael held the sword, still slick with Dean's blood, at his side and smiled like he had really just won a prize when the words tumbled from her lips. He circled her wrist with his hand and crushed his lips down on hers.

It was like a jolt of electricity. The touch seemed to amplify his powers, but it also brought hers to life. She had ignored the powers at her fingertips before. She had destroyed buildings and possibly killed men who were doing their jobs. She couldn't risk it again. Even against Kael. Especially against Kael.

But he was pulling it to the surface, and for a second, she let go, and was flooded her with magic.

"There you are," he whispered against her lips.

"You're the rightful heir," she breathed.

"Someday soon, everyone will know." He smirked, triumphant. "Now, go."

He shoved her away from him, and the fog lifted slower than last time. It hovered in her mind with a denseness that wouldn't exactly dissipate.

"What?" she asked in confusion.

"You'll come back to me," he said knowingly. "And, when you do, I'll be waiting."

She shook her head to try to push away her confusion. "You're letting me go?"

"You'll remember this, Cyrene. You'll remember and know…it's all your fault. Everything that happens. You'll remember, and you'll come back to me."

"Never," she breathed.

But he just smiled before turning around and walking off the dock, like they had just had tea instead of fought with swords…and magic.

195

SAFE PASSAGE

CYRENE FELL TO HER KNEES AT DEAN'S SHOULDER AND hastily cradled his head in her hands. She held him against her and fought back the tears and confusion.

This wasn't supposed to happen.

Kael wasn't supposed to win.

And she knew…he had definitely won.

He was letting her go, but there was a price. And she was terrified to find out what that price was. Terrified to wake up one day and discover that he was right, that everything that had happened was her fault. She hated that Kael was inside her head, but he was.

And worse…his magic had gotten inside her head. He was the rightful Dremylon heir. Which meant, as the Braj had told her all those weeks ago, that the Braj and Indres had been sent by *Kael* to kill her. He had been trying to kill her for months. And that contradicted everything else Kael had done since she had met him.

Kael was the one who had warned her not to leave the palace grounds in Byern when the killer was on the loose. He had been furious when he found out that she was gone. He had helped find her when she had gone missing in Albion, even after she had knocked him out with a silver candelabra. He had even made sure that he walked with her to the library, so she would be safe. Then, he'd trekked across Aurum to collect her.

He had been irritating, persistent, and antagonistic from the start but not evil. She had never thought he was out to kill her. And, now, he was just letting her go. *How can I reconcile the man that had tried to save me with the man who had supposedly tried to kill me?*

Her head swam, as if she were trapped under Kael's spell all over again.

"How are you doing?" she asked Dean.

"Hurts like a bitch."

She bit out a laugh and motioned for Avoca to hurry over. "I'm so sorry about this, Dean."

"You didn't ask me to fight him. I thought I had him," he admitted. "I'll get him next time."

"No next time, please. I just want to see you healthy again."

"I can fix this," Avoca assured her. "Ceis'f would be better, but I don't know if he will…"

Dean groaned. "It's nothing. Just…help me up."

"Dean."

"Just help me up. We have to get out of here. Unless you've changed your mind, and you'd like to go back after your Prince."

Cyrene shook her head. "I'm here with the right prince."

He grinned. "That's what I like to hear."

They hoisted him up off the ground, and through a string of curses, he walked onto the ship. Cyrene followed close behind, worried about what would happen to him.

"Ceis'f," she said, dragging him toward her. "Would you heal him? Please."

He stared at her, as if she were insane.

"Please. I know you hate humans. You hate us all. You want to exterminate our race, and the only reason you're here is to protect Avoca. But I say this as her friend. She cares for you but not like this. You are bitter and angry. Maybe you have every right to be—"

"I do," he spat.

She held her hands up. "I believe you. But…please."

He ground his teeth and then shoved past her. "You owe me for this."

She nodded. She knew that. She owed a lot of people for this. She owed everyone.

Ceis'f followed them down stairs and into a room where Dean was carefully deposited on a bed. Once inside, Ceis'f ushered everyone else out, closed the door, and refused to let anyone inside.

Cyrene hurried back out onto the deck just as the Eleysian vessel cast off from the dock. If she squinted hard enough, she could almost see Kael's retreating form on the horizon. She had to be imagining it. But something yanked at her, called to her, pulled her back toward the shore. She couldn't tear her eyes away from the sight.

Ahlvie clamped a hand down on her wrist, dragging her from her thoughts. "It's not your fault," he said.

"What?" she croaked.

"What happened back there is not your fault."

She hung her head.

"I don't know about that," she whispered.

"Well, I do. I don't understand Kael's actions though. He won, yet he yielded. That doesn't sound like him."

"No, it doesn't," she breathed.

"I've fought him before, you know. He's never looked that good," Ahlvie said. "Kael cared more for flirting than swordplay. Unless he's been doing something no one else knew about, he's improved immensely in a very short time."

Cyrene nodded. "Yeah."

"Are you going to tell me what it is?"

Something like magic.

Cyrene kept silent.

Ahlvie sighed heavily. "I can accept that you have magic, but you can't trust me with this thing with Kael."

"I don't know. All right? I don't know anything about Kael. I just had a crazy night. My mind is all fuzzy, and Dean is injured. Kael said that he would let me go, but I'd come back to him, and then everything that happened would be my fault. I don't know what any of that means, Ahlvie. So, maybe I just want to think through it all."

"Okay," he said softly. "It's been a stressful night all around." He looked off pensively toward the ocean.

She thought she saw his eyes flash yellow for a second, but when she looked more closely, it was gone.

"Are you all right?" she asked him.

"I've been better. We all have."

Then, Ahlvie pulled her against him. Tears sprang from her eyes and soaked into his shirt. She hated herself for crying, but all she could do was wait and think and worry. Things she was not any good at.

When Avoca let Cyrene know that it would be awhile before they had news about Dean, Cyrene was taken to the captain's quarters by Darmian where she managed to finally fall into a fitful slumber. He had offered up his accommodations for her on account of her being a special guest of the Prince. She was too tired to even argue how that might come across.

A few hours later, she stumbled out of bed to find a fresh change of clothes lying on a chair. Her heart skipped a beat in panic. She circled the room in desperation.

Where is my dress? Oh no!

The *Book of the Doma* and the Presenting letter were stashed in a hidden pocket she had sewn into the folds of the full skirt. This couldn't be happening. She had spent all that time making sure that, even if they were separated from their belongings, her book would always be with her. And, now, it was gone!

She searched the room high and low. She had left the dress on the floor next to the bed last night before she had fallen asleep in nothing but an oversize shirt someone had offered her. Now, it was missing.

With a frantic pitter-patter of her heart, she stepped into the fresh change of clothes from the chair and darted out of the cabin. She raced toward the stairs that would take her up to the deck, but right before she got there, a body stepped out of the bedroom.

"You're in a hurry."

"Dean!" Cyrene cried. She threw her arms around him without a second thought. She was just so happy to see him alive.

"Ugh!" he groaned as she collided with him.

"Oh Creator, I'm sorry." She hastily stepped back, embarrassed.

She was elated to see him whole and healthy. He had a sling holding one arm up, but as far as she could tell, his shoulder looked repaired.

"How are you?"

"Your friend patched me up as best as he could. It seems Prince Kael tore through some pretty important parts of my shoulder, and even magic couldn't fully heal the wound. Going to have to just let it rest like normal, I suppose."

Cyrene recoiled at the use of the word *magic*. He used it so flippantly, as if he had always known of its existence. As if it didn't matter that it existed at all.

"You speak very freely of magic."

Dean grinned. "Eleysians don't fear it like Aurumians or pretend like it doesn't exist, like the citizens of Byern. We remember the old ways even if the only magic we see comes from the fights against the demon spawn, such as that Braj we saw in the palace. They don't cross to the capital city, but we see them enough in the rest of the country."

"So…Eleysia believes that magic exists."

"Of course it exists. It is everywhere in everything. We just have lost the ability to tap into it."

"I see," she breathed.

No wonder he had been so accepting of her magic from the start. Coming from a world that always believed in it would have been such an advantage. Instead…she'd been born in Byern.

"Speaking of," he said, "the laundress came by your room and returned with this."

He held out the cracked leather book that she had grown so accustomed to, and all the breath left her lungs. She reverently took it between her hands.

"Thank you."

"That book is very old for it to be blank."

Cyrene's head snapped up. "You opened it?" she demanded.

His cheeks colored a rosy red. "I didn't mean any offense. I wasn't trying to pry."

She tucked it away, realizing that she had already made too big of a deal out of it. "Thank you again for everything."

"I think it was all worth it to see you in an Eleysian gown." His eyes ran down the length of her dress.

Cyrene flushed at the words. She hadn't even paid attention to what she put on before rushing out of the room. But now she took note of how well made the dress was. It was of the thinnest, finest Eleysian silk. Featherlight so that it was almost sheer and slimming in all the right places in the softest Eleysian purple.

"Why did you have this on board?" she asked, deflecting the compliment.

"Eleven sisters, remember?"

"Right. I forgot. What exactly was it like, growing up with eleven sisters?" she asked.

He offered her his good arm, and she looped her hand around his elbow.

"Terrifying," he admitted with a laugh. "Eleven *older* sisters, mind you."

Cyrene shook her head in disbelief. She had thought that she had a large family with two sisters and a brother. She couldn't even fathom a family of twelve. Let alone a royal family with that many.

"Why did your parents continue to have so many children?" she asked as they walked up the stairs to the main deck.

"How much do you know about Eleysia?"

"Considering my questions about magic just now?"

"Good point."

She sighed. "And, if my journey thus far is any indication, the things I know about Eleysia are probably not accurate."

Dean laughed and angled them toward the railing. "Well, if what I've heard of Byern is true, you wouldn't even be able to carry on a successful conversation without trying to convert me to your Class system."

"That's ridiculous!"

"Yet to be determined," he said with a smirk. "Anyway, you're probably aware that Eleysia is, in fact, a queendom."

Cyrene nodded. She had heard that in her lessons. She had always thought it sounded like a fairy tale for the Queen to rule. A nightmare in Byern, where Queen Kaliana was a devil. But she had envisioned a benevolent queen as a ruler. Someone like the Leif Queen Shira.

"My mother, Queen Cassia, always wanted a girl, of course. Someone to rule the queendom after she and King Tomas were no longer around. They were lucky to have my sister, Princess Brigette, first. And then, after a while, the running joke became that they couldn't have a son. My mother really wanted a son." Dean shrugged. "So, they kept trying until they had one."

Cyrene felt a laugh bubble out of her, and it felt so good to just relax after the stress of the last couple of weeks. They were on the royal ship bound for Eleysia with the Prince as an escort. She had survived Kael…if barely. She couldn't shake the feeling that there was more to what he had said. But at least she was free of him. For now.

"Seems to have worked out for them," Cyrene told Dean.

"Yes. I'm fortunate to have parents who love me very much."

"Me, too. Though I haven't seen my parents in some time. Not since I made Affiliate." Speaking about her home made her heart contract. She hadn't been able to tell anyone she was an Affiliate since she had left.

"You leave home for Affiliate training, as far as I know, correct?"

"Yes. You move into the castle and work with your Receiver."

"And what was your area of expertise?"

Cyrene snorted. "Expertise is a stretch. I wasn't there that long before I left, and the Queen…well, let's just say we weren't on great terms."

"I met Queen Kaliana. She…left something to be desired," he said.

"That's one way to put that she's a conniving bitch."

Dean's laugh boomed over the bow of the ship. When he looked back at her for a second, his eyes glittered in the early morning light, and she had to take a deep breath. His smile brightened his entire face. Everything changed about him. His features smoothed. His eyes lit up. His body eased. She could just stare up into that face all day.

For a second, when they stared at each other, she forgot that she was a refugee, fleeing Byern to discover her magic, and he was the Prince of a foreign land. They were just two individuals on separate paths that had converged at just the right point. And though she hardly knew him at all, she found herself at ease with him.

His eyes stuttered to her lips and then back. He seemed to realize his error and looked back out at the ocean beyond. She swallowed and was glad that she wasn't the only one effected.

"How much longer?" she whispered, standing shoulder-to-shoulder with him against the rail.

"We should arrive by nightfall. It's only a day trip from Aurum."

She breathed a sigh of relief. "Good."

"You don't like the sea?"

"No. I do. I'm just anxious to be there."

He questioningly raised an eyebrow, and she thought he was going to ask her about why she had left, but the words never came.

"Stay with me," he said instead.

"What do you mean?" she asked cautiously.

"In the palace. We have plenty of room, and I'd love to get to know you."

"And you can't do that if I'm staying elsewhere?" she asked. She knew she was playing hard to get, but in reality, her heart was racing away from her. She hadn't expected a direct invitation to the palace or to have more time with Dean. A thought she was relishing at the moment.

"You know I would come see you every day regardless of where you stayed in my homeland," he said with a bright smile, "but I'd prefer if I could show it to you from my home."

Even though every inch of her was screaming to say yes, she forced herself to consider the offer before jumping into something. "I'll think about it."

27
The
DESTINATION

"SO, WHAT YOU'RE SAYING IS, WE HAVE NOTHING TO GO ON," Ahlvie said.

"Um…not exactly," Cyrene said.

Ahlvie gave her a look that said he knew her too well. He seemed to see right through her. It had always been that way with Ahlvie.

"We know we're looking for two women named Matilde and Vera. They had to have consorted with the likes of Basille Selby, a swindling Eleysian merchant traveler. So, that probably steers us to the underbelly of the capital city, if I had to guess. Otherwise, we don't know what they look like, their age, their trade, or anything about where they could be whatsoever."

"Okay. When you put it that way, there's not much to go on."

"Then, we'll need to split up," Avoca said practically.

"And do what?" Ceis'f asked. "This isn't a six team on a mission, Ava. At the present, this is a melting pot of outcasts. An exhausting, pompous little girl who thinks she's a leader, an Affiliate mute, a drunken fool, a disgraced former Prince, and two Leifs."

"I feel like you fit into at least two of those categories," Avoca said flatly.

"Enough!" Cyrene said. "If we're going to do this, everyone needs to learn to work together. If you two are always at each other's throats, I'm going to go crazy. Are we all here together?"

Cyrene expected Ceis'f to make some smart response to her outburst, but he just sat up straighter. No one else said a word.

"Aye, aye, boss," Orden said, tipping his wide-brimmed hat.

She wasn't sure that he knew how much that meant to her. It didn't matter the troubles they had gone through to get here right now because, in less than a day, she would have her feet on Eleysian soil.

"Okay, good. Well, Prince Dean asked me if I would accompany him to the palace as a royal guest, and I've decided to accept," she said formally.

All the while, her insides were squirming. She couldn't believe she was allowing herself to get lost with another royal. So far, they had only proven to be trouble. But that smile…

Ugh! She couldn't think about that right now.

"So, I'm going to go with him to the palace. I think it will be a good idea to have an insider to search the palace grounds."

Ahlvie snorted, and Maelia hid a smile. Cyrene just glared at both of them. Through the bond, she could sense Avoca had her own concerns about it, but her face was a mask.

"Do you have something to add?"

Avoca frowned. "You can't go to the palace alone."

"I planned to bring Maelia."

Maelia nodded in agreement.

Avoca opened her mouth to protest, but Cyrene cut her off, "It will look more normal if two Affiliates are coming into the palace as a delegation with the Prince than with a whole group. I don't want to draw attention to us."

"But the three of us won't be suspicious," Avoca argued.

"You're suspicious, Avoca." Cyrene hated admitting it, but it was true.

If someone looked too closely at her, they might realize that there was something different about her. She knew most people didn't believe in Leifs, but Dean had said magic was more commonplace. It could be dangerous to bring her into the palace.

"Avoca can go with me," Ahlvie said quickly.

Ceis'f laughed. "Over my dead body."

"That can be arranged."

"Enough!" Cyrene cried. "Enough."

"I'm just saying, if Avoca is suspicious, they'll be doubly suspicious together," Ahlvie argued.

"If she isn't with me, then I'll abandon the mission to be with her," Ceis'f said.

That struck the nail in the coffin.

Cyrene sighed heavily. "Avoca and Ceis'f. Ahlvie and Orden. Maelia, you're with me. End of discussion. We'll split up the city sectors. Anyone familiar with the city layout?" she asked.

Orden sighed. "I've been there. It's all laid out around the harbors. There are five main harbors and seven sectors divided by the river systems on the island—eight, if you include the palace at the center. But it's a big island. This could take a while."

Cyrene nodded. She was prepared for that. They would do what they could. "Draw up what you remember, and we'll separate the sectors for each group."

"Are we just going to not talk about it?" Maelia asked quietly as Orden worked on the map.

Everyone stilled and looked at Maelia. Right away, Cyrene knew what she meant but was afraid to acknowledge it.

"Talk about what?"

Maelia looked up into Cyrene's eyes. "What happened back there? *Everything* that happened since we were imprisoned. I mean…Avoca healed Ahlvie. He had huge gashes across his chest, and a minute later, they were gone. Nothing but a fine line."

"Gashes?" Cyrene asked, her eyes searching out Ahlvie.

He shrugged, and his eyes flashed that yellow color again. "A story for another time. It's not a particularly bawdy one."

"That's the part you're interested in?" Maelia asked, nearly hysterical. "She *healed* him. I study medicine, but this was something else. Just like with Prince Dean. He took a sword to the shoulder, and now, he's *fine*. Then…the buildings and the earthquake." Maelia shuddered. "Why have we not talked about this?"

Cyrene looked around the room and then sighed. "We have. Kind of. Back in Albion, before we left, I told you that I had abilities, and that's why we were going to Eleysia." She shrugged. "At the time, using the word scared me. Magic. I have magic. So does Avoca and Ceis'f. That's how they were able to heal Ahlvie and Dean. That was how I was able to level those buildings. I'm here in Eleysia, trying to find people to help me control it."

"Matilde and Vera," Orden said knowingly.

"Yes."

"If we're really at full disclosure," Avoca said, "Ceis'f and I are actually Leifs."

Maelia's jaw nearly dropped to the floor at that announcement.

"And I'm…I'm Doma," Cyrene said with her chin tilted up. "The first Doma in two thousand years."

"A…Doma?" Maelia asked in surprise. "Like the ancient rulers who subjugated our people?"

"The stories are a lie. Doma had magic, and the Dremylons killed them for it," Cyrene said.

"Wiped out the entire race of Doma," Avoca continued. "Made it so that magic was just a myth in as much of the world as they could touch. We thought all Doma were extinct until Cyrene showed up in our woods."

"And you're actually Leifs?" Ahlvie asked. "Like the creatures who steal children in the night?"

"Myth," Avoca said with a grin. "We used that as our own protection."

Maelia shook her head. "This is a lot to take in."

Cyrene nodded. "I know. I'm sorry to lay this at all of your feet. I've been dealing with it for a while, and I just wasn't ready to share the information. I was too afraid of what I was, and I couldn't accept the fact that this was reality. But…now, I know it to be true, and there's no going back. I am Doma, and I need to learn to control my powers so that what you saw in Aurum doesn't happen again."

Cyrene stood and stretched her legs while Maelia mulled over everything that had just been revealed. She knew Maelia would need time to process the truth. Cyrene certainly had. Orden was the only other person who didn't know, but he acted as if he'd always known. It made her wonder about him more and more.

"I'm just…going to get some air," Cyrene said. She nodded her head at the lot of them and then left to give them all space.

Avoca followed Cyrene above deck. Cyrene could sense her even though she couldn't hear her silent footsteps.

Magic flooded her fingertips as her emotions ran rampant, and she had to forcibly put a hold on it. There was so much there. It terrified her.

What if I destroy everything in my path all over again? What if my emotions keep running away with me, and destruction falls on my friends rather than just my foes? What if I could never control it?

"I am glad you finally got it all out in the open," Avoca said.

"It was time."

"They'll still fight for you. They love you."

Cyrene nodded and clenched her hands. "Your mother was afraid of letting me leave for the very reason that happened back on the docks. I lost control," she whispered. "I...killed people."

"You don't know that," Avoca said.

Cyrene looked down and then up into her impossibly blue eyes. "Yes, I do. At the time, I wanted to believe that the silence after the blast was normal. I told myself, other heartbeats were out there, but once Dean pulled me out of it, the only heartbeat roaring in my ears was my own...and Dean's. I couldn't feel anything or anyone out there."

"You're new to your powers. You could have tapped out at that point."

"I would have blacked out," Cyrene insisted.

Avoca shook her head and looked out at the flat ocean before them. It was in that serene place between lands where nothing existed but the sweet salty air and the endless blue depths below.

"My first kill was a human," Avoca whispered.

"What?" Cyrene asked, stunned.

"It was an accident. I thought I was better than my six team leader, and I wandered off in the wrong direction. Suddenly, I was trapped. I had triggered a bear trapper's metal mechanism. It closed around my ankle, digging through the skin and touching the bone. It was the most excruciating pain I had ever felt in my life, and I had gone through extensive six team training." Avoca didn't meet Cyrene's eyes, and she could tell Avoca was recalling that day. "The man came back for me, thinking I was his next meal ticket. When he saw me, he seemed surprised to see a human in his trap. He quickly went to work, removing the claw attached to my ankle, but I was scared. I was in so much pain. My emotions were high. Everything hurt and was blurry. I didn't know what to do."

Cyrene swallowed. "What happened?"

"My magic went wild. All my training fled my mind, and I was just out of control. Even though he had saved my life and freed me, my magic wasn't honed enough to stop me from making a horrible mistake. That's all it was. One horrible mistake. And then his life winked out of him.

"I spent a good many years paying penance for that deed. I tried to quit the military and my magic, but my mother wouldn't let me. You know what she said to me?"

"What?"

"'This is a lesson, not a punishment. You do this man's death a disservice by not learning how to use your magic properly.'"

Cyrene cringed.

"It hurt at the time, but she was right. I've never lost control like that again, and I use my magic sparingly. Only when I'm at the extremes of my own physical prowess."

They stood in silence for a few moments before Cyrene placed her hand on Avoca's arm. "Thank you," she whispered.

Avoca smiled. "I'm going to make sure everyone is all right below."

Cyrene nodded, and Avoca disappeared below deck. She knew that Avoca was right. She couldn't blame herself for everything that had happened. She would carry it with her. Those nameless lives that she might have harmed in her quest. But she would use that as a reminder of how much worse it could be if she didn't find Matilde and Vera.

"Anything I can help you with?" Dean asked, sidling up next to her.

Cyrene jumped. She hadn't even heard his approach. He might have even more silent feet than Avoca. Or maybe he was just more familiar with the boat.

"Help me with?" she inquired.

"You were planning something in the captain's quarters. Care to share?" Despite the serious question, he had a smile on his face.

"We were just discussing the plans for when we get to Eleysia."

"What would you like to do when you get there?"

Cyrene considered the question. "I've heard about these two women who work with people with magic. Matilde and Vera," she said hopefully.

Dean frowned. "I see. I've never heard of them before, but like I said, while we believe in magic being in everything, there aren't actually people with magic in Eleysia."

Cyrene deflated. "I see."

"But, if I can help, I will."

This didn't change anything. Just because he didn't know people with magic didn't mean Matilde and Vera weren't there. Basille Selby had told her to go there...so these women must exist.

"By the way, have you given more consideration to my offer?"

"Yes."

"Yes, you've considered? Or yes…you'll go?"

"I'll go."

Dean smiled that dazzling smile. All of a sudden, she was swept up into his arms, and he twirled her in a circle. She broke off into laughter and threw her arms around his neck to hold on, heedless of his shoulder. He gently placed her back on her feet. Her cheeks were flushed, and they were awfully close together. She cleared her throat and took a step back for propriety's sake.

"Sorry," he apologized immediately. "I was just so…I'm glad."

"Me, too," she told him. And not just because the palace would give her easy access to more resources, but because it would give her more access to him.

The
RETURN

Daufina

DAUFINA LEANED BACK IN HER QUARTERS IN THE BYERN castle. Home. It was so incredibly nice to be back home. Albion was beautiful and ancient, filled with everything she could ever want. It had been her home once. She had grown up there, and it was a treat to return there on procession from time to time. But she had been in Byern too long now to consider anything else as home.

Now that Edric had given up his hunt for Cyrene, they could begin to move back to order. She would have her Affiliates and High Order to assist. She could plan strategy with the King. She could continue to help plan the Eos holiday. It was all at her leisure.

That was wonderful, considering the tension and anxiety that had plagued the castle.

There had been only one other death since Cyrene had disappeared. Jardana, however unfortunate, was the only one to have perished. No more clues were found. The investigation was coming to a close.

Perhaps, one day…they would all know what had actually happened. Until then, they could get back to business as usual and pray to the Creator that nothing else happened like that again in their kingdom.

A knock at the door drew her from her thoughts.

"Come in," she said softly.

An Affiliate with strawberry-blonde hair hurried into the room, dipping a low curtsy. Daufina had seen her before. She was one of the Queen's favorites. She had always trailed after Jardana and her friends. Adelas.

"Consort," Adelas said.

"Please rise. What is the matter?"

"It's the Queen. She sent me to retrieve you promptly."

"Whatever for?"

This was quite unlike Kaliana. If the Queen sent for her at all, it was through a servant with a letter. Nothing urgent. Nothing that anyone could gossip about.

"She didn't say. She just told me to get you at once." Adelas looked frightened. "If I could be so bold, she was quite out of sorts. I haven't seen her in such a mood since…" She bit her lip.

"Yes?"

"Since her last miscarriage."

That got Daufina right out of her chair. "I'll come at once."

She hauled up her skirts and hurried after the young Affiliate. They took the shortest route. She was uncertain what was wrong with Kaliana and wanted to get to her as soon as possible.

Daufina didn't particularly care for the Queen—her duty was to Edric—but Kaliana wouldn't have requested her if it wasn't important.

They made it to Kaliana's chambers in quick order, and Daufina shooed Adelas away. Whatever Kaliana wanted to discuss with her, it was clear she wanted it to be in private.

"Kaliana?" Daufina said, entering the chamber and closing the door behind her.

No response returned. Daufina walked through the living quarters and toward the bedroom. She heard sobbing coming from the room. Daufina stood there for a moment, debating on whether to go in or not. She knocked gently, but the sobs just came louder.

With a heavy sigh, she stepped into the bedroom and found Kaliana curled into a ball on the floor. She wore nothing but a cream shift. Her hair had fallen out of its careful bun at the nape of her neck. Her cheeks were red and splotchy. Her eyes were puffy and swollen. She looked so young and fragile. Daufina would never have even known it was Kaliana.

"Whatever is the matter?" Daufina asked.

Kaliana looked up at her and then burst into tears all over again.

Daufina hurried over to her side and sank down to her level. "Are you hurt? Has someone hurt you? Kaliana, talk to me."

"I was late," she whimpered.

Daufina drew herself up with wide eyes. "You're pregnant?" she asked hopefully.

"Dear Creator, please let it not be so," she sobbed. Her blue eyes searched Daufina's, and then she leaned her head between her knees, starting to cry all over again.

"What is this, Kaliana? Why are you crying? A baby is a blessing. Edric will want to hear at once."

"No!" she shrieked. "No. He...he can't know."

Daufina had a horrible feeling come over her. "Why? Why can't your husband know of this joyous occasion?"

"Oh, Daufina, how can I ever look at him again?"

Daufina's stomach flipped. She didn't know what Kaliana was talking about. But she didn't like the sound of it.

She grabbed ahold of Kaliana's shoulders and stared her dead in the eyes. "Tell me. Everything."

"I'm late," she repeated.

"You said that."

"I'm a month late," she whispered morosely.

"A month," Daufina said softly.

"I thought it was a mistake. That I was just under stress. I thought this month, when we were back home, things would be different. I would bleed once more," she cried. "But it is not the case."

"You've been pregnant for more than a month," Daufina said. "You're sure?"

"Yes."

"I...I sent Edric to your chambers. He's seen you, hasn't he? Been with you?" Daufina asked.

Kaliana nodded. "He was too late, Daufina. I begged him before that. Begged him. Like a whore," she cried. "And he would not see me. Refused to see me. He loved her so much that he couldn't even look at me. His own wife!"

"So, you did something about it," Daufina said, realizing the horror of what she was witnessing.

"I had to. I thought…"

"You did not think."

"Daufina," Kaliana said. Her eyes begged, pleaded, with her. "Help me."

Daufina shook her head. She couldn't do this. It was treason. What Kaliana had done was treason. Helping her would be worse.

"Who was it? Who did this?" Daufina asked.

Kaliana shook her head. "You can't know."

"I won't help you unless you tell me."

"No!" Kaliana cried. "Is it not shame enough that I am pregnant? With my luck…the baby will miscarry anyway, and this will all be for naught. But I cannot tell you."

Daufina pinched the bridge of her nose and closed her eyes. *How could this possibly be happening?*

"You will tell Edric now. Whether or not the baby survives the pregnancy. If you hide from him, it will look suspicious. You have to glow with the knowledge that you hold the future King of Byern in your womb. Do you understand me?"

Kaliana nodded.

"No one else will know, and if the time comes and the baby chooses to be born after all, then we will say it is premature. I am betraying my King and my country for this. So, you must do *everything* I say from now on. Everything."

"I will," Kaliana said, clutching Daufina's hands.

"He might not even suspect if it is premature since you have never carried a baby to term. But you must act the part and never give away to anyone that the baby could be anyone else's."

"How will I face him?"

Daufina shook her head and stood. She reached down and helped Kaliana to her feet. "Like a queen."

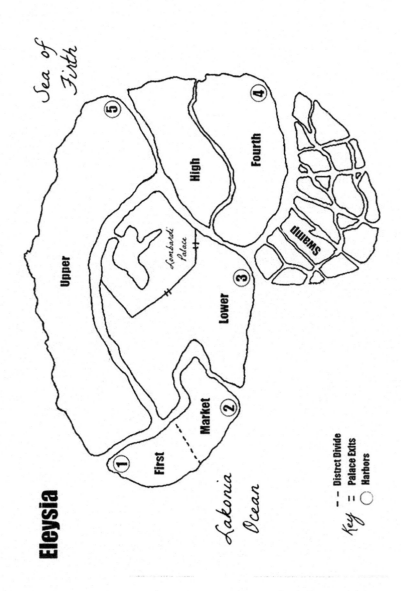

Eleysia

Sea of Firth

Lakonia Ocean

Upper

Lombardi Palace

High

Lower

Fourth

First

Market

Swamp

① ② ③ ④ ⑤

Key
- - District Divide
= Palace Exits
◯ Harbors

THE
BRIDE OF THE SEA

THE ISLAND WAS BIGGER THAN CYRENE HAD ENVISIONED.

Eleysia's capital city was built on an island due west of the Sea of Firth through which they had just sailed. It was isolated from the rest of the world by an outcropping of volcanic islands around it and enormously dangerous rocks on all other banks. Only Eleysian sea vessels could navigate the waters, and their sailors were the most adept in the entire world.

Now that Cyrene was getting a good look at the surroundings, she understood why.

"That's part of the reason we leave at night," Dean said, coming up beside her.

"Why?"

"If we can navigate these waters at night, then less foreign vessels will be able to learn the passageways through the rocks. Plus, the Creator blesses us with safe passages each year. That's why the city is traditionally named the Bride of the Sea."

Cyrene let her gaze drift back to the island. "I like that. The Bride of the Sea."

Their vessel slid through the water and around the gaping rock formations in the dim light of the setting sun. They glided so smooth and precise that Cyrene was certain they would have been able to turn the ship on a pence.

"How do foreign merchants get into port?" Cyrene asked in confusion. "They could end up tossed on the rocks with one wrong turn."

"Ah. Well, foreigners may only enter into First Harbor." He sheepishly looked at her. "Your party will be one of the few delegations not to have to do that. We're entering through the Fifth, the royal docks. But, usually, foreigners always enter and exit through the same pathway."

Cyrene nodded, marveling at the complex structure to their economic system. She would think it would deter merchants from traveling these waters, but she knew Eleysia was the wealthiest country in Emporia. Their dyes were the richest in the world, and it was a huge import into Aurum for their weaving. Not to mention the fact that Eleysia excelled in glassblowing and weaponry. They specialized in pearls of all colors from the darkest black to the softest creamy white. Vineyards were nurtured on and off the islands, and Eleysian wine was a rare delicacy.

Just as the sun winked out from the sky, their ship docked in the harbor. No one in her party had anything, except the clothes on their backs and whatever they'd had with them on the night of the party in Aurum. Everything they had been traveling with had been packed up and placed on a trade ship bound for Eleysia in the days leading up to the ball. Cyrene wasn't sure if the ship would come into port with all of their belongings or not. Ahlvie and Orden had agreed to stake out First Harbor where the merchant was most likely to show.

In the meantime, they had to find lodging on the scarce money they had between them. It would be enough for a few nights in an inn in the less reputable part of the city, but Ahlvie had sworn, he could significantly increase the sum if given a hand at dice.

Cyrene rolled her eyes at the remembered eagerness in his eyes.

"What?" Dean asked.

"Nothing. I was thinking about something else."

"I see. Are you sure your other friends won't come with you to the palace?"

"Oh no. They have business elsewhere. Just Affiliate Maelia is planning to come with me," she said, using her title for emphasis.

"Two Affiliates in the palace," Dean said with a sharp shake of his head. "Never expected that."

"When was the last time Byern sent ambassadors to Eleysia?" she asked curiously.

Dean laughed. "The last time they were sent or the last time they were accepted? Because that King of yours sends them all the time, trying to convince us that it's diplomacy."

Dean's face darkened, and Cyrene winced.

"But I haven't seen one in the palace in…years. Not since I was a kid, I think. I was young enough that the woman gave me a truffle of some sort from your marketplace back home."

"That was nice of her."

"It turns out, I'm allergic to chocolate."

Cyrene's mouth dropped open. "She couldn't have known that!"

Dean gave her a meaningful look. "She was kicked out of the palace soon afterward. So…let's try not to have a repeat."

"I promise, I won't ply you with chocolate," Cyrene said with a laugh.

"But can I ply you with chocolate?"

Her eyes lit up. Eleysian chocolate was a delicacy. "I'm not sure I'd ever say no to chocolate."

"I'll keep that in mind."

Cyrene flushed and turned her attention back to the water.

The ship docked into Fifth Harbor, and their party exited the giant Eleysian sea vessel.

Dean walked down the broad wooden dock with his three men ever present at his side. Cyrene and her friends followed behind them until they stopped in front of a collection of small banana-shaped boats swaying in the water.

"After you," Dean said. "The gondolas will take you anywhere in the city you would like to go. I would love to extend the invitation to stay in the palace to the rest of you, if you all would care to join us."

Orden smiled and shook Dean's hand. "Much appreciated. But we'll be on our way now."

Ahlvie smirked. "Thanks for the ride." They clasped hands, and Cyrene could just barely hear the threat in his voice when he leaned in and whispered, "Take care of them."

Cyrene sighed and rolled her eyes. *Men!*

Orden and Ahlvie disappeared into the first gondola with promises to meet up again soon. She nodded and watched them leave with a forlorn smile. The last time they had split up…her world had turned to chaos.

Avoca clasped Cyrene's arm the way they had during their Bound ceremony. "I don't feel right about leaving you."

"We will be nearby, Avoca. You'll always know if something is wrong."

"But I will not be in the castle to stop it."

"I'll be okay. Let's just follow he plan," Cyrene pleaded.

Avoca nodded once and then hurried into the gondola. Ceis'f followed her without a word. Cyrene watched them go with a sad sigh. Right now, she needed to be in the palace, and she needed everyone else on the outside, looking for Matilde and Vera. It was a big island. *Who knew how long it would actually take?*

"Ready?" Dean asked, offering her his arm.

"Of course," she said.

Darmian offered his arm to Maelia.

"Thank you," Maelia whispered, seemingly surprised by the attention.

"My pleasure," Darmian responded with a smile.

Hmm…curious.

Cyrene stepped into the flat-bottom gondola. It rocked slightly under her weight, but her sea legs were still with her from the journey from Aurum, and she righted easily. She took a seat, and Dean occupied the space next to her. Maelia and Darmian took the seats behind them, followed by Faylon and Clym.

The gondolier pushed off from the dock and began moving them down the main waterway into the city. Lanterns hung from posts that highlighted the channel winding forward before them. Even in the darkness, it was magical.

After passing a few other gondolas on the water, they came to a major intersection, and before Cyrene stretched the expanse of the Eleysian palace grounds. Sand-colored stone walls kept the rest of Eleysia from entrance to the royalty and the enormous palace beyond the walls.

The gondola stopped in front of a metal gate on the river. Upon seeing who was on board, slowly, the gate began to grind upward, revealing its sharp metal spikes. When it was high enough for their boat to safely pass through, the gondolier proceeded through the gate, and they were officially on palace grounds.

"Welcome to my home," Dean whispered into her ear.

They glided to a wooden dock on a vast lake. The castle loomed over them in all its magnificence.

"Is this the only entrance?" Cyrene asked in awe.

"No. There are two main entrances on the grounds, but the waterways are for royalty."

Cyrene shivered. It was so easy to forget that Dean was in fact Prince Dean Ellison of Eleysia.

When she had met him in the forest back in Aurum, he had just seemed like a privileged merchant's son. No more, no less. He was charming and attractive but also thoughtful and honest. She had hidden her true self from him, but it had seemed, even then, like he knew more about her in that moment than most people ever would.

Cyrene half-expected a delegation to be awaiting their arrival, but there was no more than a page boy no older than twelve, holding a lantern for their arrival. The group exited the boat and walked over to the boy.

"Your Highness," the boy said with a low bow. "The lady Queen was expecting your arrival yesterday."

Dean sighed. "Tell my mother, the lady Queen," he said dryly, "that I'll have an audience with her in the morning." His eyes turned to Cyrene. "I have someone for her to meet."

"Yes, Your Highness," the boy said.

He offered Cyrene his arm, and they walked the grounds and into the castle.

Despite the late hour, people milled around in the hallways of the palace. With the number of people Cyrene was seeing on the grounds, the palace had to be close to capacity. Byern's Nit Decus castle was the biggest in all of Emporia, but as far as she knew, it hadn't been near capacity in years. This place was bustling with people.

Dean smiled and nodded at people as he passed and was recognized, but he kept them walking. They went up two flights of stairs and then around a bend before they were finally alone with just their party of six.

"Here you are," Dean said.

"You already had rooms prepared?" Cyrene asked in confusion.

"My mother always has visitor rooms prepped, especially for the holiday season. I think they'll be to your liking. Affiliate Maelia's room is just across the hall."

"Thank you."

"No, thank you for agreeing to come with me."

Dean swept the loose waves of Cyrene's dark brown hair from her face, and she remained perfectly still. His eyes were locked on hers, and for a moment, they dropped to her lips in question.

He bent down and pressed the softest kiss to her cheek. Her body moved toward him of its own accord. He smiled a devious smile, like he knew he had surprised her. But there was something else in his eyes that she couldn't quite read in the dim lighting.

"Good night, Cyrene. Until tomorrow," he said.

His Eleysian accent rolled her name around on his tongue, and she was certain that she would never appreciate it said any other way.

When he and his men disappeared back down the hallway, Maelia dashed to her side. "Did he *kiss* you?"

Cyrene touched her cheek in a daze. "Yes, he did."

"I thought you just met."

"We did."

"Only you could bewitch a king and two princes," Maelia teased.

Cyrene swatted at her. "Oh, shush. I haven't bewitched him," she said, entering her bedchamber. Maelia followed behind her. "I'm sure it was just…a nice gesture."

Maelia's mouth hung open. "So, how do you explain this?"

"I don't know," she breathed.

Before her was a suite…befitting a queen.

30

The
AUDIENCE

"ARE YOU READY?" MAELIA ASKED CYRENE.

Cyrene shook her head.

Despite the fact that she had been exhausted last night, she hadn't been able to succumb to sleep. She had been lost in a nightmare of her magic destroying buildings and mowing down half of the Aurumian army. She couldn't stop thinking about Kael Dremylon using magic, sword fights, injuries, and boat rides in the middle of the night.

And Dean. Whispering in her ear, his fingers in her hair, his lips on her cheek. With everything going on, she should be plotting her next move, but she couldn't stop thinking about him.

There was no jolt of electricity. No tendrils connecting her to him. No current drawing them together, as if they were tethered on a string. No magnets or uncontrollable need that would practically sweep her off her feet.

None of that overpowering obsession.

Just the fluttering of her heart and the flush on her cheeks from the enticing ease of Dean Ellison.

She drew herself out of her thoughts once more and remembered where she was—facing the door to the Eleysian throne.

A man pushed the door open and announced to everyone in attendance, "Affiliate Cyrene Strohm and Affiliate Maelia Dallmer of Byern."

As they walked down the white marble aisle, hushed whispers sprang up all around them. Cyrene was prominently wearing her

Affiliate pin, a gold circle of Byern climbing vines, on the breast of her purple dress. It felt good to have it in place again.

The room was a large rectangular space with ceilings nearly three stories high. Three tiers of balconies were carved into the sandstone walls, and below each one hung a bright royal-blue banner with a winged lion inside the royal crest pictured in white. Rows of seating were set up like a theater and filled with every manner of nobility.

Cyrene assumed they must be the Eleysian Privy Council. The members were elected annually from each of the eight districts and the mainland.

The walkway ended with a royal-blue rug in front of a two-tiered platform and three gilded thrones with cushions in the Eleysian royal blue. Seated on the thrones were Queen Cassia, King Tomas, and Crown Princess Brigette, heir to the throne of Eleysia. There was a row of girls seated to the right, who must be the remainder of Dean's sisters, and a group of men behind them that she guessed were their husbands.

And then there was Dean. She started when she caught his gaze. He had shaven his face to just a shadow across his jaw, and his hair, which had nearly reached his shoulders, had been cut almost as short as the Byern style. Her stomach dropped at how handsome he looked, and she chided herself for thinking of that when there were more important matters at hand.

Once they reached the dais, Cyrene and Maelia each dropped into a proper curtsy. She didn't know about Maelia, but she was definitely hoping that Queen Cassia was less conniving than Queen Kaliana and Queen Jesalyn. Though Cyrene wouldn't mind if Queen Cassia was as benevolent as Queen Shira.

"Rise, Affiliates," Queen Cassia commanded.

Cyrene rose and got a good look at the Queen for the first time. She was a short, plump woman with dark red hair that her eldest daughter mirrored. She wore a simple royal-blue gown made from the sheer material that seemed to be in vogue in the Eleysian palace. A choker of fat white pearls ringed her neck, and she had a sapphire as big as a coin in each ear. It was unsurprising to see that she was heading into her years, considering she had twelve children, including Dean, who was the youngest and fully grown. But for all of that, she was regal and dignified with sharp eyes and unmatched poise.

"Welcome to Lombardy palace and to the country of Eleysia."

They each bobbed another curtsy.

"It is our pleasure, Your Majesty," Cyrene said.

"It has been quite some time since we've had an official delegation from Byern in our homeland. To see two Affiliates in our royal throne room with the blessing of my son warms my heart. Though your presence is most unexpected," she said, letting the words hang in the air between them. "How exactly did we get this great honor?"

"Your Majesty, I have your son, Prince Dean, to thank for all of this. I was in Aurum when we met, but I didn't know who he was."

The Queen's eyebrows rose significantly, and her eyes shifted to her son for a split second before returning to Cyrene.

"We became friends, and then when we were together again at a ball at the Aurum court, he offered to take me and my friend to visit Eleysia. I had always wanted to see the country, and I accepted his kind offer."

Cyrene figured that was mostly the truth. It would have to suffice for now because she wasn't about to get into the specifics.

"I see," Queen Cassia said with a half-smile. "The country is open to visitors of all sorts, of course. Though I would be careful about how you behave in Eleysia."

At the threat in the Queen's voice, Cyrene could feel Maelia tense next to her.

"Previous visitors from Byern have been less than accepting of different...ideologies. It would be best that, while you are here as a guest, you perhaps keep your own beliefs to yourself," she said carefully.

"We understand," Cyrene said.

If she had come here fresh from Byern without spending any time in other countries and kingdoms, without traveling hard across the countryside, and without friends who could guide her through different customs, she would have been uncertain of what that meant. But no longer. She knew many countries believed that Byern's customs should remain their own and not foisted onto anyone else. For a long time, she had thought there was only one right way to rule. Now, she could see that there were as many *right* ways as there were kingdoms...or queendoms.

"Neither myself or my companion have any interest in pushing our beliefs about Byern onto anyone else. In fact, I'm very interested to learn about your own beliefs and customs and to seamlessly assimilate into your court, Your Highness."

Queen Cassia's mouth quirked on one side. "Is that so?"

"Your Majesty," Dean interrupted, "if I might shed some additional light on the situation..."

"By all means."

Dean came to stand beside Cyrene. She warily smiled at him. She had expected it to be tough to deal with the issue of having Affiliates in their palace when they were practically banned from the country, but she hadn't expected Dean to speak up on her account.

"Affiliate Cyrene has my full support. When we met, neither of us knew who the other was. We were not an Affiliate of Byern and a Prince of Eleysia, and yet, we fostered a close relationship. Isn't that exactly what we want from diplomacy with Byern? That is how we enact change. And though I've only known her a short time, she has proven herself greatly," Dean said.

His eyes found hers, and Cyrene took a sharp breath. If she could see the affection blatant on his face, then so could everyone else in the room.

"Pray tell me how," the Queen asked.

"When I was in Aurum, Byern guardsmen came into the countryside, seeking an Affiliate who had been kidnapped. As you can imagine, it was contentious, having Byern soldiers on foreign soil. I thought, surely, war would break out between the countries. But in the end, it turned out, they rescued the girl and detained her within the castle."

"How fortunate."

Cyrene's heart raced as he recounted his version of the story to his parents. She wondered how much he would tell. *Would the whole world soon know about my magic?*

"But the Affiliate hadn't been kidnapped. In fact, she was fleeing the countryside, seeking asylum. When confronted with the ruler who was to bring her back, I fought for her leave, and she selflessly offered herself up to return to her country if I could but live."

The throne room had gone deadly silent. And Cyrene's ears were buzzing. That had happened, but she had never thought of it that way. She just couldn't fathom someone getting hurt for her mission. But the way he told the story made her seem like a hero when she had thought all along that Dean was the hero of the story.

"I see."

"I—" Cyrene began, but the Queen held up her hand.

"If you saved my son's life, then the country owes you a great deal. He is our only son, and I birthed eleven children to get to him. We are in your debt," the Queen said as she inclined her head to Cyrene.

Cyrene's mouth dropped open, and she quickly closed it. Then, she dropped into a deep curtsy. "Your Highness, no debt at all. Prince Dean would not have been in any trouble if he had not helped me."

Dean opened his mouth to protest, but the Queen silenced them both.

"No matter the trouble, you saved my son's life. You are most welcome in Eleysia. I pray that both you and your companion enjoy your stay, and I hope you will bless us with your company at least through the Eos holiday," the Queen said with a smile.

"Thank you, Your Majesty," Cyrene said.

The Queen rose from her throne and signaled an end to the meeting. The Privy Council began to whisper to one another as they circled the room to talk to neighbors. With a pang in her chest, Cyrene realized how much it reminded her of Presentings back at home with all the Affiliates and High Order congregated in one place.

Dean turned to her then, and his smile stretched from ear to ear. "You're staying."

"I'm staying," she confirmed.

Maelia wrung her hands together next to Cyrene. "That was well done."

Cyrene winked at her. "Not so bad as a Presenting, was it?"

"Not half as bad," Maelia confirmed.

"Your Presenting ceremonies are the strangest thing to me," Dean said.

Cyrene shrugged. "When you were raised your entire life for them, they aren't that strange."

"Even when you're not as fortunate to be First Class, like Cyrene, and didn't train your whole life for the opportunity," Maelia said.

Just then, a figure stepped down before them. Dean smiled and pulled his sister in for a hug. The heir to the throne of Eleysia was publicly hugging her brother, as if it were commonplace. Cyrene was definitely going to have to get used to this place. The people in Byern weren't so affectionate.

"We're so glad to have you back, Dean," Princess Brigette said with a sincere smile. "Home wasn't the same without you here."

"Well, I'm back to stay," he confirmed.

"Good."

"You know I could never stay away. Who would I have to nag me all day?"

Brigette raised her eyebrows in a surprisingly accurate imitation of their mother. Dean just laughed.

"Brigette, meet Cyrene and her friend Maelia."

"Pleasure," Brigette said.

"Nice to meet you," Cyrene said, dipping into a small curtsy.

Maelia did the same and nodded in her direction.

"Come," Brigette said, taking Cyrene's arm and pulling her away from Dean. "I think we will be fast friends."

"Oh no," Dean grumbled behind her. He followed, offering Maelia his arm.

"Don't listen to him," Brigette said with a smile. "I haven't met an Affiliate in nearly a decade, and I would love to know everything about your homeland."

"Oh. Well, of course," Cyrene said.

"Perfect. I hope you have found Eleysia to your liking."

"As much as I have seen so far."

"Not much, I'd wager, but we'll fix that. But, first, let me introduce you to my sisters."

Cyrene steeled herself to meet all the girls standing before her. There were so many. She had no idea how she was going to keep them all straight. Even with her quick memory, it didn't seem likely.

"In age order, my sisters, Princesses Susann and Karin."

Both were tall with straight blonde hair to their waists. Susann had a book open in her lap and barely glanced up at Brigette's introduction. Karin had on an extremely low-cut dress and the most makeup. She flounced over to them and curtsied to Cyrene.

"So, you're the reason Dean came home," Karin said bluntly.

"I…" Cyrene began.

"We thought he'd be gone forever."

"Must be important to bring the girl home to meet the family," another girl said, after Karin.

Two other girls followed close behind, and they looked similar with frizzy bright red hair, a splatter of freckles, and round faces.

Brigette pointed at them in order. "The triplets, of course—Princesses Lissa, Lara, and Livia."

Lara pushed past Lissa to get to the front. "Is *that* what this is all about? Dean, have you finally found yourself a girl?"

"And Byern born at that?" Livia cried in protest.

Cyrene's cheeks flushed at the comments, but they wouldn't let her or Dean get a word in edgewise.

"And an Affiliate at that," Lara said in disgust.

"Didn't the last one try to kill him?" another girl with fair hair and big, round green eyes said. Her gown was plainer than the other girls', and she was a bit wider than the rest. She seemed bored by the conversation.

"That's Princess Ruthe," Brigette said. She was making no move to correct the girls or any of their accusations. She seemed perfectly happy to let it continue as she made introductions.

"I distinctly remember the Truffle Incident," Ruthe continued.

Another girl behind Ruthe just shrugged. She was petite with hair the color of burnt copper and a hawk-like nose. "Who cares? She's not here to stay."

"That's Princess Hether."

"If she were here to stay, Mother wouldn't have had an official audience. She's a visitor. No need to get too comfortable," Hether said.

A set of twins nudged Hether.

"You think she's leaving?" one of them asked.

They were the only ones with brown hair in the bunch, but she couldn't tell them apart.

"Of course she's leaving. Don't be absurd, Tifani. It's not as if he's *marrying* her."

Cyrene's mouth dropped open, and she tried to find the words to correct them. They had it all wrong. She wasn't here for Dean.

She hardly knew Dean. It didn't matter in the slightest that he had kissed her last night or the way he'd looked at her or the way he could carry on such an easy conversation with her or that he just seemed to accept her for exactly who she was without pretense, despite his country's prejudice against Affiliates.

"The twins, Therese and Tifani. Though, they're younger than Alise over there."

Alise didn't say a word. She just stared at Cyrene, as if Alise could see straight through her. Through every sugarcoated word Cyrene had said before their mother. Through every reason for why she was here. Through the relationship between she and Dean. And Alise didn't just look curious about what was going on and what was to come; she looked angry.

Cyrene diverted her gaze and turned back to Brigette and Dean.

"Only Alise, the twins—Therese and Tifani—and I still live full-time in the palace. All our other sisters are married with lots of children, so they won't be around as much."

"I see," Cyrene said, trying to keep everything straight in her mind.

Dean sighed heavily. "Well, you've met my sisters. Ready to run yet?"

Cyrene almost laughed. She had faced a Braj twice and Indres. Not to mention Kael's magic. A few girls couldn't be that bad.

"It's nice to meet you," Cyrene said, making sure her voice was strong and level.

They seemed to have one idea about her, but she didn't want to back down from their taunts either.

"You've all had your fun," Dean said with a shake of his head. "Leave her be now."

"No, it's okay," Cyrene said. "They're just protective. I understand that. I'm protective of my brother and sisters. I wouldn't expect anything less."

Several of the girls gave her appreciative looks, and some looked suspicious. But Alise in the back just rolled her eyes. *Well, they are going to be a hard group to crack.*

"They'll warm up to you," Brigette said. "Just give them time." She pulled Cyrene away from the rest of her sisters and began to walk them back through the throne room out of earshot of Dean and Maelia. "It was quite a thing to see my brother stand up for you today."

"Oh, well, I'm sure he was just being kind."

Brigette gave her an appraising look. "He is, by nature, unfailingly kind. But not to the extent where he would speak to the Queen for a stranger."

"I haven't known him long, but I hardly think we are strangers," Cyrene said. She hoped her cheeks weren't as red as they felt.

"You must be very special to him."

Cyrene caught Dean's eye behind her, and he smiled warmly. In that moment, she found that she was perfectly content with being special to Dean Ellison.

SEA BRIDE'S CHAMBER

DESPITE ALL THE FORMAL PLEASANTRIES THAT HAD TO BE made for her visit in the Eleysian palace, Cyrene couldn't neglect the real reason she was here. Basille Selby had told her to come to the Eleysian capital city and find Matilde and Vera. They would be able to help people like her. She hadn't known what that meant all those months ago, but now, she understood.

Doma.

She needed to find Master Domas Matilde and Vera. Somehow, they were still alive even though two thousand years had passed. And it was the sole reason for coming to Eleysia.

With Orden, Ahlvie, Avoca, and Ceis'f searching the rest of the island, Cyrene had concentrated her efforts on the palace even though Dean had claimed that he had never heard of anyone with those names.

Cyrene was right the first time she had walked inside the building. It was crowded. Since the island wasn't all that big, many nobles and members of the Privy Council chose to live on the palace grounds as part of the court. It would be as if every Affiliate and High Order lived in the Byern castle instead of reintegrating into the city after fulfilling their educational components.

That meant she had a lot of ground to cover, all while trying not to look like a suspicious Affiliate snooping around the palace. The only place she had found where no one cared if she looked around was the library, which was enormous and had so many different subjects than what were found in Byern. Her head spun in there.

But still, the first two weeks she had been in the palace, she had no luck. Maelia snuck off the grounds unnoticed to search the Lower Sector, the southern district that attached to the Palace grounds, for any clues. But both of them came up empty-handed, and worse, Cyrene hadn't seen Dean at all. His sisters would come around to get to know her—otherwise known as irritate her to no end, take up too much of her time, and generally try to sabotage her very existence. They told her that Dean had gone back to work after his long absence, but she didn't know what that meant. Princes back home didn't work, not as far as she knew. Prince Kael mostly just fraternized, fornicated, and frustrated her.

She had known that it might take some time to find them, but it was easy to get discouraged when they didn't have any clues and no word from her friends on the outside.

"Any luck?" Maelia asked.

Cyrene jumped on the bed where she had a pile of books sprawled out before her. "How are you so silent? I didn't even hear the door open."

Maelia shrugged. "Years of training with the Guard."

"You're even quieter than Avoca. That's a feat."

Maelia smiled, as if this were a compliment.

"Did you find anything?"

Maelia shook her head. "I think we should go meet with the others and see how their search is going. Try to come up with an easier way to go about this than blind searching."

"You're right. We need to reconvene. I don't want to spend years searching for them. We need to be more pragmatic."

Cyrene followed Maelia out of the castle grounds. In such a short time, Maelia had already figured out the perfect time to get in and out of court without being seen. Cyrene couldn't help but admire that training. While Cyrene had been preparing for her Presenting and learning any number of subjects, Maelia had been learning swordplay, tracking, and other militaristic things from her parents and the guards whom she had grown up with in Levin.

Maelia flagged down a gondola and gave the man directions to where they were to meet the others at an inn in the First Sector. They cut through the water, and Cyrene got her first real look at the city during the day. It was bustling as much as the palace was. Every square inch was built up, and for every waterway that Orden had drawn on the map, there were dozens of other smaller waterways navigating throughout the various sectors. The canals crisscrossed the city in a manner quite like the back roads of any other major city. It was incredible that these boats were the major source of transportation instead of horse or carriage. Though most of the canals had sandstone bridges connecting the various buildings as well as the different sectors.

Their gondola traveled off the main canal and into a narrow waterway in the First Sector. Cyrene could tell immediately that this area of the city was much less reputable than where they had come from. The buildings were more ramshackle, and children ran around barefoot. Taverns littered every corner, offering a drunken reprieve.

"Why am I not surprised that this is where Ahlvie chose to meet?" Cyrene asked when the boat stopped in front of a tavern and inn called The Sea Bride's Chamber.

Maelia laughed and followed her into the inn. Loud music played over the boisterous cheers from the crowd who took up the majority of the space. People were dancing in the center of the room and repeatedly crashing into each other, spilling ale all over the floor. The floors were sticky, and Cyrene was sure she was ruining her silk slippers. She wished she had worn boots, but the weather was so hot in Eleysia that most people didn't even own them.

Cyrene cast her eyes around the room, looking for some kind of gambling table, knowing she would find Ahlvie there. Then, Maelia laughed next to her and pointed up to the stage. There, decked out in full entertainer garb, complete with a flowing mendicant cloak in a mishmash of colors, playing a lute and singing, while the crowd cheered him on was none other than Ahlvie Gunn.

"Way to stay undercover," Cyrene grumbled under her breath.

"He is the most irritating man in Emporia," Maelia confirmed.

"And, somehow, he always figures out what we need to know. So, let's go see if he's figured it out this time."

Cyrene angled toward the stage and started meandering through the crowd toward Ahlvie. She passed a table of men throwing dice and another playing some kind of card game. She was glad Ahlvie was singing on the stage tonight rather than gambling.

He finished his song and swept a deep bow to the room. Everyone cheered and called for another. Cyrene caught his eye then, and his eyebrows rose. His smile grew into that normal devious look she knew all too well. It meant he had a bad idea brewing.

"That's my final song for today, folks. Same place and time tomorrow," Ahlvie called.

"Haille, one more!" someone cried.

"Mardas, sing us your favorite again!"

A cheer went up in the crowd. "Mardas! Mardas! Mardas!"

Cyrene shook her head. Haille Mardas was back. That only meant trouble.

He bowed one more time with a flourish and then hopped down. He found Cyrene in the crowd, and at least a dozen times, he was clapped on the back by happy customers who appreciated his music.

"Ladies, ladies," Ahlvie said, wrapping an arm around Cyrene's and Maelia's shoulders. "Let's get you upstairs where you belong." He winked at a man at the bar and then pushed them toward the stairs.

"You are vile. You know that, right?" Maelia said.

"Horrid, Ahlvie," Cyrene agreed.

"You both love it," he said, squeezing their shoulders and pretending to nuzzle Cyrene's neck for the crowd.

"I am going to kill you," she growled.

Their group made it up two flights of stairs. Ahlvie opened a door into a two-bedroom suite. Cyrene's eyebrows rose.

"You must be throwing dice to afford this room," Cyrene said.

Ahlvie laughed and shut the door behind Maelia. "The owner of the inn lets me stay in exchange for my performances. Seems it brings good business. Better for us to have one place for everyone with ready meals," Ahlvie said. He pulled off the cloak he'd worn for the show and slung it on a hook at the door. "Not better money than dicing, but less chance of getting thrown out."

Cyrene shook her head. "That's because you cheat."

"I take from the rich and stupid and give to the poor and intelligent."

"You give to yourself."

"Exactly."

"Cyrene!" Avoca cried, coming into the main room from the bedroom to the right.

Cyrene felt the connection with Avoca like a gentle thrum. A constant reminder that they were bound together. When they were apart, she could still feel it but dimly. This was the longest she had been away from Avoca since their ceremony.

Cyrene pulled her into a hug. "I've missed you."

Avoca patted her back twice. "Yes. It has been interesting without you around."

Cyrene released her and didn't miss the look that passed between she and Ahlvie. Cyrene wasn't sure if that meant they had finally given in to their feelings or if Ceis'f was being a royal pain.

"Where are Orden and Ceis'f?" Cyrene asked.

"Ceis'f is on watch," Ahlvie said. "And Orden was following a lead in the Market Sector. He should be back shortly."

As if he'd heard his name, Orden trudged in through the door. His oversize hat drooped to one side, and he looked like he had been in some kind of brawl. "No luck," he grumbled.

"What happened to you?" Ahlvie asked with a raised eyebrow. "Met another mistress?"

Orden glared at him and removed his hat. "Don't mess with me, boy. I've had a long day, and I'll be happy to put my fist through that pretty face of yours if you want to keep up the attitude."

Ahlvie raised his hands. "Be careful with the pretty face. It pays the bills."

Orden huffed and then stomped into the other bedroom. Cyrene could hear him washing up, and then a couple of minutes later, he returned. He didn't look all that more cheerful, not that she had ever really seen him cheerful before.

"Cyrene. Maelia," he said, dipping his head toward the girls. "Are we going to bring in Ceis'f?"

Ahlvie shrugged. "I think he's fine," he said casually.

His eyes sought out Avoca again, but she purposely looked away. Whatever was going on didn't seem to be good for anyone here.

"Then, let's get started," Orden said. He leaned back against the wall and crossed his arms. "I assume you girls are here for a reason."

"We came for news, but considering you all look ready to kill one another, I find it hard to believe you have any. Is there *any* good news?" Cyrene took a seat by the unlit hearth. She didn't understand why the room had a fireplace with Eleysia's sweltering heat.

"Ahlvie found out that the boat we were supposed to come in on is supposed to dock at First Harbor tomorrow," Avoca said. Ahlvie tipped his head with a devious smirk. "So, hopefully, it will still have our belongings on it, if they haven't been confiscated or sold."

"I see," Cyrene said. "Well, that is kind of good news."

"Though it seems you have new clothes already," Ahlvie said. He couldn't hold back his smirk.

"Dean has eleven sisters," she explained. "They're doing their best to clothe me in between their everyday sabotage."

Avoca raised her eyebrows. "Anything I need to worry about?"

"Nothing I can't handle."

"They don't know who they're dealing with if they think a little sabotage will stop you," Ahlvie joked with a wink.

"Why, Haille Mardas, that was almost a compliment."

He grinned devilishly. "They haven't seen you take on a Braj."

"Or destroy an entire group of Indres," Avoca said.

"Or break people out of prison," Orden added.

"Or take on the entire Aurumian army and Prince Kael," Maelia said.

Cyrene held her hands up. "Okay, I get it. When you say it that way, it does sound pretty impressive. But you were all there; you know I didn't really do anything. The magic saved my life. I didn't even know how to use it. Everyone else helped with the breakout as much as I did. And…you all are just embellishing."

Maelia touched Cyrene's shoulder. "If that's what you have to tell yourself."

Cyrene smiled at her crew. At least they believed in her, even when she didn't believe in herself. "Well, I've no better luck than you lot. All I've done is spent time in the library and run into a bunch of dead ends. I've had hardly any time without Dean's sisters continually interrupting me. No one has heard of Matilde and Vera. I worry that, if I keep asking around, people will start questioning my motives."

"How about we start with this one?" Ceis'f said. He pushed a man through the open window. He rolled half the length of the room before stopping with a thud.

Cyrene jumped up in shock. "What in the Creator's name?"

"Found him snooping outside the window, listening in on your conversation when I caught him," Ceis'f added.

The atmosphere shifted instantly. Avoca had her knives out from her hidden compartment and was threateningly twirling them. Ahlvie looked laid-back, but she could see his shoulders were tensed, as he was waiting for a fight. Orden reached for a sword at his belt. Even Maelia shifted into a fighting stance. Her hands strayed to her hips, but there was nowhere to conceal a weapon in these flimsy Eleysian dresses. Not that they would have done her much good.

The man grunted when he came to a stop at their feet. His light hair fell forward against his forehead as he hung his head and dropped into a crouch. He wore all black clothing, and a black mask mostly obscured his face.

Cyrene walked forward before anyone could say anything in protest and ripped the mask from his face. "Dean?" she gasped.

"Hello, Cyrene."

When the rest of the room realized who it was, they relaxed their hold on their weapons and shifted back into a neutral stance. But Cyrene didn't move. She just stared at him in surprise. She hadn't seen him in weeks, and now, he was stalking them outside of the palace grounds.

"Why were you outside of that window?" she demanded. "Why are you here?"

He didn't look sheepish even though she thought he should for spying on her. "You and Maelia left without anyone for protection, and I wanted to make sure you were all right, so I followed you."

"I'm getting rusty," Maelia breathed.

"You *followed* us because you wanted us to be safe?" Cyrene asked. "Don't lie to me. You were spying on us. Otherwise, you would have made your presence known."

"I did want you to be safe."

"And…you wanted to spy. Why?"

She had the strange realization that she was interrogating the Prince of the country she was currently in, and one of her friends had just thrown him through a window. If he had other soldiers with him, then they were about to be in a lot of trouble.

Dean stretched up to his full height, towering over Cyrene. "I wanted to know where you were going and why you left the palace grounds."

"I didn't think I was a prisoner."

"You're not, but most people who don't want to be found have something to hide. I don't apologize for following you."

"Just for getting caught?" she quipped.

He smiled, and she tried to ignore the dip in her stomach. "For trying to get closer to you."

Her cheeks heated at that comment, and she tried to regain control of the situation. "There are other ways to get close to me without spying on me!"

"Is he with us or not?" Ceis'f asked.

Everyone turned to Cyrene for the answer. Dean had saved them back in Aurum. There was no reason for her not to trust him after he had risked himself to get them out of the city and then spoken on her behalf to Queen Cassia so that she could stay. But still...she didn't like him snooping around.

Dean raised his eyebrows and awaited her decision. "Cyrene?"

"Is there anyone else with you?"

"No," he answered immediately.

Ceis'f nodded his head in confirmation.

"Fine. Yes, of course he's with us," she said, turning to Dean. "But don't spy on us again."

Cyrene looked to Maelia, who always protested when they added new people to their group. "I know...you don't trust him."

Maelia frowned and then puzzled over Dean. "No. I think I do."

Cyrene balked. "Well then, I guess you are in."

"Can we get back to the matter at hand?" Orden asked.

And just like that, Dean was accepted into their group.

"Mind if I ask what exactly this is all about?" Dean asked. "Is this about the people you're looking for?"

She took a deep breath. "Yes. I know you said you'd never heard of them, but my source told me that they were rumored to be in Eleysia."

"And you've been what? Scouring the island for them?" he asked.

"Something like that."

"I could have helped. I happen to have valuable resources at my disposal."

Ahlvie snorted. "Cyrene is trusting, but even she wouldn't alert the palace to this."

"So, tell me everything about these women. What are their surnames? What do they look like? Where were they last seen?"

Cyrene frowned. "We don't know any of that information."

"So, you've been looking everywhere for these two people off of just names then?" Dean asked skeptically.

Ceis'f threw his hands out and leaned back against the window frame. "I'm glad I'm not the only one who thinks this entire thing is insane."

"Look, Basille Selby told me that I should come here to find them. It must be for a reason. It's not a wild goose chase, and I won't stop looking."

Dean startled forward.

Cyrene gave him an appraising look. "What?"

"Basille Selby? You're sure?"

"Yes. Why?"

"I don't know Matilde and Vera, but I know Basille Selby," he said after a moment, "and I can take you to him."

32

The
UPPER

CYRENE WAS SEQUESTERED WITH DEAN ON A GONDOLA IN THE late afternoon the next day. He had offered to take her to see Basille. He hadn't heard whether or not Basille was back on the island, but most people would return for the holiday season, and it was only ten days away.

Ceis'f was trailing them under Avoca's orders even though Cyrene had assured them it wasn't necessary. She had seen Dean fight and knew he was quite capable.

Avoca had promised to look into ways to track people with her Leif powers, and Ahlvie had readily agreed to help her locate the supplies she would need to do so. Ceis'f had protested, but Ahlvie and Avoca had been out the door and on their way to the Market Sector before he could get a word in.

"How exactly do you know Basille Selby?" Cyrene asked.

"He used to work in the palace," Dean told her.

"Used to?"

Dean frowned and looked away from her. "He used to sit on the Privy Council."

Cyrene started forward, shaking the boat and receiving a glare from the gondolier pushing them through the Upper Sector. "Excuse me? Are you sure we're talking about the same person?"

"It was a long time ago, but I knew him as a child. He always shared wild stories about other lands, and he could keep a crowd captive for hours. I'd say he doted on me. But, after what happened, I'm not so sure."

"The Basille Selby I met in the Laelish Market in Byern did not seem the type to ever be on a Privy Council. He certainly seemed to have stories of adventure, but he was not a nobleman. What happened?"

"He was caught in bed with my sister," Dean said softly.

Cyrene's eyebrows rose, and she gasped. "Which sister?"

"Brigette. But don't mention it to him or her. No one really speaks about it at court anymore after he left the Council."

"The royal heir to Eleysia was caught in bed with a man on the Privy Council."

"A married man on the Privy Council, who was ten years older than her."

Cyrene put her hand to her chest and held on to her seat. "Basille is married?"

"He was, but his wife came down with a fever shortly after that and never recovered. Some blamed him for her death. They claimed that her body couldn't handle the knowledge of his affair. Others claimed that he poisoned her. No one really knows what happened."

Cyrene was reeling. How could all of this be true about a simple peddler? But, of course, he wasn't a simple peddler. Simple peddlers wouldn't have adventure stories or magical books. They wouldn't know the names of Master Domas or realize she had magic. And he *had* known.

"So, how did he become a peddler then?" Cyrene asked, processing all of this information.

Dean shrugged. "I'm not entirely sure. He just disappeared and returned as someone else. I'm sure that story is one he guards closely."

They lapsed into silence as the boat progressed down the narrow waterway. They rounded a bend into a lucrative part of the Upper Sector. Towering buildings were immaculate. It looked about as opposite as was possible from the area of the First Sector where they had been last night.

"Here we are," Dean said, signaling for the boat to come to a stop.

Cyrene admired the house before her. It was a gorgeous building set to mirror the sandstone exterior of the palace. Though it was packed into the street and wedged in between two other houses, it clearly belonged to someone with significant wealth. Much of the other buildings they had passed seemed to have split residences by stories, but this was in a neighborhood where each house was unique. Each had its own dock, and a gorgeous stone bridge arched across the water.

The gondolier docked them at the house, and Dean helped Cyrene off the boat.

"What is this place?" she asked.

"Basille's home."

"He owns a mansion?"

"Unless he sold it, this home in Upper belongs to him. But I doubt he did. It's a family home."

Dean offered Cyrene his arm, and they walked forward. He rapped on the front door. A man opened it a minute later, and Cyrene balked at the person in front of her. This was the man she had seen Basille with in Byern.

"Whaddya want?" he asked.

"Good evening. We're here to see Master Basille Selby. Is he in for the evening?" Dean said formally.

"He's busy. Don' like the looks uh ya."

"Allow me to introduce myself. I am Prince Dean Ellison, and we're here to see Master Basille Selby," Dean said. He took a step toward the man. "Please ring him for us."

The man stuttered before dropping into a quick bow. "Course, Majesty."

Dean and Cyrene went into the enormous house, and Cyrene gasped at its grandeur. Intricate stonework created a mesmerizing pattern on the floor. The walls were a deep burgundy color, and the furniture was antique Eleysian craftsmanship. A large chandelier hung from the ceiling in the entryway.

They walked into a sitting room that was carpeted with deep red Aurumian rugs that must have cost a fortune. Biencan gold platters were arranged on a table beside Kelltic sculptures worked out of the precious metals from the Barren Mountains. Exotic portraits and tapestries covered the walls from Carharan work to novelties all the way from the country of Mastira. It was overdone in its lavishness but also incredible to see all the nations of Emporia together in one place.

"The Prince of the realm," Basille said, entering the sitting room. "To what do I owe the pleasure?"

"Hello, Master Selby," Dean said.

Basille started when he saw Cyrene. "And with an Affiliate."

"Hello, Basille. Good to see you again," Cyrene said.

Basille Selby looked much the same as Cyrene remembered him. He was tall with thick dark hair slicked back. He wore traditional Eleysian garb though, switching out his traveling garments for silks. He must have recently bathed because he perfumed the room with a cloying scent. He was quite handsome, but she couldn't imagine Princess Brigette falling into bed with him. She couldn't picture him married either, not even in his house with all his grandiose ways.

"I'm not sure I can say the same. Cyrene, is it?" he asked, as if he didn't remember.

But she could see his sharp eyes and knew he remembered all.

"You remember my name, Master Selby. You remember everything about our encounter," Cyrene said.

"Is that so?" he asked. He took a seat in an armchair opposite Cyrene. "I meet a good number of people while on my travels. Faces start to blur."

Cyrene slowly retrieved the *Book of the Doma* from her bag and held it up for him to look at once more. It had landed in her lap, because of the man before her. "Do you remember this?"

He smiled crookedly. "So, you made it."

"Of course I did. No thanks to you."

His eyes drifted to Dean and back. "And you manifested?" he asked, cautiously eyeing the book.

"You know I did. Why didn't you just tell me what it meant?"

"Can't talk about those things in Byern unless I want to lose my head."

"Well, can we talk about them now?" she asked.

The man is so frustrating.

"What do you know, Basille?" Dean asked. He had the calm, calculated look of a man who was used to getting what he wanted, coupled with the skill of a man not to be reckoned with.

"You've grown a lot since I last saw you, boy," Basille deflected.

"I'm not a boy anymore."

"That, I can tell. Nineteen at the Eos holiday in ten days' time, if I remember correctly. Did you come to bring my invitation?"

Dean leveled him with a stern gaze. "If you didn't want to risk your neck in Byern, I doubt you would want to risk it here."

"It's been ten years since I was last on the palace grounds," Basille said with a well-oiled smile. "I'm sure my presence would go completely unnoticed."

Cyrene rolled her eyes. If everything Dean had said was true, then he would surely be noticed.

"Where have you been then?" Dean asked.

"Around the world and back again"—Basille flicked the sides of his mustache and then gestured around the room—"as you can see from all my exploits. No world is barred to the man who knows how to access it."

"All but the palace grounds, it seems," Cyrene said casually. "That brings me to the matter at hand. I'm here in Eleysia on *your* word. I am looking for Matilde and Vera, just as you said I should. How do I find them? And don't play any more tricks. I have come a long way to get this information, and I will not haggle with a swindling peddler for it. Just spit it out."

Basille's smile took over his whole face. "My, have you grown since the first time I met you, little Affiliate. Once terrified of your own shadow and throwing your weight around with a title that had barely sat on your shoulders. A title that they give to seventeen-year-old girls with such high opinions of themselves."

Dean took a step forward in anger. "Just answer her."

"Or what?" Basille asked. "Stand down, *soldier*," he said the term derisively. "I will speak to the Affiliate...for a price."

"What price?" she demanded.

"What could you possibly want?" Dean asked.

"I'm a high-standing merchant. Everything can be bought for a price."

Cyrene was certain that Basille did not mean money in this instance.

"Well?" Cyrene said.

"An invitation to your Eos ball is the price."

Cyrene and Dean exchanged a glance. It was an easy enough thing to deliver. The ball was widely open to all nobility. Anyone with a piece of the beautiful Eleysian stationery stamped with the blue royal seal could attend. But why he wanted it could prove more problematic for them.

"You know, if you are discovered on the grounds, you will be in a world of trouble," Dean cautioned.

"That is my battle to fight. You will not be responsible for what happens once the invitation is in my hand," Basille said with a crooked smile.

Dean shrugged his shoulder at Cyrene. "I'll do it. I can get one."

Cyrene looked at him. "Are you sure?"

"Yes," he said, then turned to Basille. "Now, talk to her."

"I reckon I don't know much more about Doma history than you do. Except that I know it all to be true and not some idiotic story that Byern royalty tells the public. Domas lived and ruled with magic in Byern…and they do no longer."

Cyrene nodded. She knew as much. The Dremylons had just been lying to everyone about what had actually happened. The knowledge that Doma had magic would change the entire history of their country.

"How did they lose magic?" Cyrene asked.

"I hear there was a great war, and they lost. But I don't know the specifics. I wasn't there."

"But Matilde and Vera were," Cyrene said quickly. "They were Doma. That's how you knew they could help me."

Basille nodded slowly. "I knew they were Doma in hiding, but…to think they would be alive back during the War of the Light…" He considered this for a moment and then shook his head. "They would be over two thousand years old. That can't be possible."

"Why do you think they were alive back then?" Dean asked Cyrene.

"I don't know. Just a hunch," she lied.

Telling anyone she had been having visions of the ancient Domina Serafina wasn't high on her priority list.

"So, where are they? How do I speak with them?" she asked.

"They're the kind of people who can't really be…found."

Cyrene stood and glared at him in anger. "You sent me here to find them!"

"They're the type who…find you."

"You're unbelievable! How could you make it seem so urgent to get me out of the country and all the way here to Eleysia to speak with them?"

"Because it was," Basille said calmly. "Your magic is a death sentence in Byern. If anyone finds out about it, you will be slaughtered…as they have been doing for millennia."

"What?" Cyrene stilled and felt herself shaking.

"Magic is not welcome in Byern. You are not welcome there. Viktor Dremylon murdered all magical Doma two thousand years ago, and anyone with magic since then has been hunted down and killed. It's cursed."

"But…I lived there my whole life, and nothing strange hap—" She couldn't even finish that sentence. "The deaths. The Braj. All of that was because of my magic. They were trying to get rid of me, as they had done in the past. That makes sense."

"What exactly makes sense?" Dean asked.

"A series of deaths happened in Byern that resulted in a Braj attacking me. I killed it with my powers, but it killed a number of other people who had some kind of relation to me. Do you think they were Doma?"

Basille listened to the news, as if this were an everyday discussion. "Doubtful. It's more likely that *you* awakened magic in ancient bloodlines, and the Braj killed them as it tried to get to the source. I've heard that a particularly powerful magical user can make strange things occur."

Cyrene put her hand on the table to try to process everything that he had said.

"What if someone in Byern knew I had magic?" she asked softly.

"Then, I would advise you to never return to your homeland," Basille reasoned.

She shook her head. That couldn't be it. Kael could have killed her if he had wanted her dead. She had been alone with him any number of times, and on the docks, he'd had her in his complete control, and he hadn't done anything. Not to mention, Edric…if he had magic or had known that she had magic, he hadn't hurt her. In fact, he had fallen for her. She couldn't think that he would do anything to harm her after sending so many guards to collect her. It would have been easier to send someone just to kill her.

"I'll have to think about all this," she said finally. "But are you sure there is nothing else that can be done to get the attention of Matilde and Vera? Are they even still here?"

"I'm sure they're still here. This is their home. They grew up in the Swamp Sector and never could seem to get Eleysia out of their blood."

Dean wrinkled his nose. "The Swamp Sector?"

"What is it?"

"It used to be private homes of the wealthy," Dean said. "The area is technically below sea level, and before I was born, a massive hurricane and an earthquake crashed through the island, hitting the Swamp Sector the hardest. Sinkholes pocketed the district and tore the land apart. The nobility left, and the homes were abandoned to natural vegetation and whoever was desperate enough to live in the flooded conditions."

"It's not all that bad anymore," Basille chimed in.

Dean gave him a questioning look.

"It has a certain charm for the underbelly of the population who don't want to compete with First, Market, Lower and Fourth rivalries."

"And here I was, beginning to think Eleysia was just paradise year-round," Cyrene said.

"It is," Dean assured her.

"In the palace," Basille modified. "Otherwise, you're competing with the various gangs who control the sectors, and you don't want to end up on the wrong side of that war."

"Gangs?" Cyrene said in surprise.

"Do you now see why I followed you?" Dean asked, his voice pleading.

"Ah, young love," Basille said, his eyes moving between them. "Well, it was a pleasure doing business with you. I'll expect the invitation to show up promptly."

"You didn't even give me the information I wanted," Cyrene protested. Her cheeks were heated from his comment, but she tried to control her voice.

"You never specified the exact information you wanted, just that you wanted information. I told you how to find Matilde and Vera. You have to wait for them to find you, and find you, they will. The rest of the information I gave out for *free*," he said, as if he had done her a service. "Now, if you don't mind, I have other business to attend to."

Cyrene swore under her breath. She should have known better than to expect more from Basille. The last time she had visited him, he had given her practically nothing and had his man literally throw her out of his tent. At least this time, she was walking out with dignity.

She stopped at the entrance to the sitting room. "What about the book?" she asked. "Why did you give it to my sister?"

Basille smiled. "If I had known its importance, I would have charged a lot more for it."

Cyrene sighed. "That isn't an answer."

"I don't have magic, Affiliate. Perhaps ask your sister why she chose it. It can't be a coincidence that it passed into your hands."

The
SPORT

CYRENE RETURNED TO HER FRIENDS' INN AND RECOUNTED much of her experience with Basille Selby. It didn't give them much to go on, except that Matilde and Vera apparently lived in the Swamp Sector. They all agreed to focus their efforts in the dilapidated hellhole, and Cyrene reluctantly decided to wait it out. If Matilde and Vera were to find her, perhaps she should just let them.

When Dean returned her and Maelia to the castle, he pulled Cyrene aside and gently kissed her hand. "I'm sorry I could not be of more help."

"No. This was exactly what we needed. Not the best answer, but it's more information than I started with."

"I'm afraid that I have to leave you alone again for a few days. Will you try to stay out of trouble?"

Cyrene narrowed her eyes. "Where are you going?"

"I have some things to accomplish, but I will miss you and worry if you do not promise to stay free of trouble."

"What trouble could I possibly get into?"

He smiled, and his dimples showed, causing her heart to skip. "Wandering alone in the woods, yelling at hunters, fleeing the countryside, breaking out of prison, attacking your Crown Prince, and sneaking out into gang sectors in the middle of the night. Not to mention, taking my sword and killing a Braj! You are walking trouble."

Cyrene laughed. "All right, I'll stay in and be good."

He touched his hand to his heart. "Thank the Creator."

He kissed her hand one more time before disappearing. She sighed, already wishing she hadn't promised. Trouble was way more fun than waiting. She was *awful* at waiting.

Determined to spend her time more productively than she had while stuck in the inn in Aurum, Cyrene retreated to the library. To her delight, as she was browsing the stacks, she found an entire section on magic. Her fingers lovingly brushed the spines. So much knowledge. So much history. Her stomach fluttered, as she knew she could dedicate many years reading everything she could about her ancestors, something she never could have done back home. In Byern, these books would have been destroyed.

She grabbed a stack of books and took them over to a large table she had claimed as her own.

She whittled away the next couple of days, leisurely reading.

One day, in the early afternoon, someone sidled up next to her. "Are you coming to watch?"

Cyrene jumped. Cyrene suppressed a shudder at Alise's appearance. She was the only one of Dean's sisters who hadn't sought her out after their first meeting in the throne room. The others had badgered her with questions about Byern and Dean and Aurum and everything else under the sun. But they'd also offered her new clothing since her gowns had never shown up on the ship from Aurum. Despite their kindness, they weren't exactly friendly. They seemed determined to scare her off, and she was just as determined not to give in. But, above anyone else, Alise put her on edge.

"Coming to watch what?" Cyrene asked.

"Did no one tell you?"

Cyrene chewed on the inside of her cheek and refused to answer. Whatever Alise was referring to, she clearly relished in withholding the information.

"Well, we wouldn't want to be late."

Cyrene finally gave in. "Late for what?"

Alise smiled deviously. "Oh, you'll see."

"I'd really prefer to know ahead of time."

"Cyrene," Alise said softly, "I know we didn't get off on the right foot, but I was just concerned for Dean. Surely, you can understand that."

"Sure," Cyrene said cautiously.

"Let me offer you this. Clearly, you weren't informed."

Well, she was too interested now to refuse. "Okay."

Alise looped her arm with Cyrene's, just as Brigette had done in the throne room, and escorted her out of the library. They walked down a long hallway and then out into a brightly lit courtyard. The courtyard ended in a dirt path leading out of the palace. Cyrene was wary of following Alise onto the grounds, but she could hear voices coming from a smaller sandstone building in the distance. So, she tried to reason that nothing bad could come of this.

"Here we are," Alise said cheerfully.

A guard was standing watch at the entrance of a large stone fence, and Alise pulled her through the opening. When she realized where she was, Cyrene's trepidation peaked.

The fence held a military training arena with seating and a sand pit at the bottom. Two men held swords in their hands. They were bare-chested with nothing but a loincloth for modesty.

Cyrene's cheeks flushed. She hadn't even realized she was prudish until that moment. She had never seen a man with so little clothing on before, and here, an entire crowd was cheering them on.

Cyrene had heard of such buildings for the Second Class in Byern, but she had never been to one, nor was it a sport enjoyed by the First Class. She doubted very much that the military men and women were practically naked when they fought in Byern. She couldn't even fathom it.

"This way," Alise said, directing her toward the royal box.

Cyrene followed her and took a seat wedged between Alise and Brigette, who noted Cyrene's discomfort with a smile.

"What is this exactly?" Cyrene asked.

She watched the two men rush toward each other. Their swords savagely collided. The last time Cyrene had seen this happen, it hadn't been for sport. It had been deadly. Just watching it made bile rise in the back of her throat.

"The soldiers put on a display in the arena," Brigette explained. "It's tradition and the primary way to move up in rank."

"Do people...die?"

"Sometimes," Alise said dismissively.

"But they shouldn't, if they've been training," Brigette said.

"I see." Cyrene tried to ease up.

Things were different here, but that didn't make them wrong. The soldiers who fought for rank and royalty considered it sport. The clothing was practically see-through and put her dresses back in Byern to shame in the modesty department. Their people were more affectionate. She had noticed that as well. Maybe Dean's kiss hadn't meant anything after all.

"Ah...you're just in time," Brigette said with a smile.

One of the swordsmen in the sand pit won by pinning the other to the ground with a sword placed precariously close to his heart. He'd yielded, and the other was named the victor. They ambled out of the arena, and then the next two soldiers were brought out.

These men were different than the last two. Cyrene could see it as soon as they walked out. Their steps were more measured, more precise. Their bodies—*Creator help me*—were more toned and built. She could see the definition in their chest and abdominal muscles. Their legs were like tree trunks, solid and sturdy. Their arms looked like they'd been carved out of stone.

Cyrene's gaze snapped up to one of the soldier's faces, and she jolted backward. "Creator," she breathed in disbelief. "Is that...Dean?"

Alise cocked her head to the side. "Did he not tell you he was competing today?"

"He's a soldier?" Cyrene asked, confused.

"It's tradition for Eleysian princes to join the military. If he wins today, he'll be instated as captain."

Everything seemed to click into place at once. It explained so much about him, like how he had survived a Braj attack and nearly taken down Kael. He had been born with a sword in his hand and grown into a man with it affixed there.

And she was watching him compete...mostly naked.

Her eyes burned, and she wanted to look away, but she also wanted to keep watching. She felt as if she shouldn't see him like this when everyone believed they were romantically involved. Yet Alise had brought her here for a reason.

The pair in the sand faced each other, each holding his sword as if it were an extension of his arm. They were the weapons, deadly and unyielding. The sword in their hand was just the tool at their command.

Without knowing what she was doing, Cyrene leaned forward in her seat, anxiously waiting for the fight. Perhaps there was a thing or two to this sport.

A man flagged for them to begin, and then they were a blur of practiced steps. Their moves were synchronized, as if in a dance that they both knew to perfection. Swords swung and arced. They clashed together, ringing over the crowd who cheered with each thrust, block, strike, and parry. It was mesmerizing.

The other man seemed to get the upper hand and forced Dean backward. Dean dodged the blade and then rolled in the sand pit, grunting when his injured shoulder collided with the ground at an irregular angle.

Dean stood from his roll. He was cradling his hurt shoulder, the one Kael had sliced through, making it clear to his opponent that it was his weakness.

Cyrene almost couldn't watch what happened next.

The man lunged for Dean, thinking he had Dean now. But Dean pivoted at the last minute and swung down with all his might, and the sword went flying from his opponent's hand. He whirled around and drove his sword toward the man's chest, stopping just before impaling him with the deadly weapon.

As they stared at each other, their chests heaved. They were slicked with sweat from the exertion of the activity in the hot, humid Eleysian air. The other man should have surrendered by now, but he just lay there, glaring at Dean.

"Call it," Dean commanded.

"Take the final blow."

Dean pressed the sword against the other man's chest, and Cyrene thought he was going to kill the man, but he stopped.

"Creator, Rob, just call it."

Cyrene was tense as she watched on with the rest of the crowd. "What's happening?"

"If Robard doesn't call the game, then Dean must finish in proper fashion," Alise explained.

"Which means?"

"Kill him."

Cyrene gasped.

"Do it, Princeling," he taunted.

Dean shook his head. Then, he swung his sword, ready to take off Robard's head. Robard didn't even flinch. He just waited for the killing stroke. But, at the last second, Dean threw his sword down into the sand pit.

"I call," Dean said.

The crowd jeered and booed.

Robard smirked at Dean, stood, and held his head high. Cyrene had the distinct impression that Robard had planned for this all along.

"If I have to kill my own brother in arms, then I would rather forfeit," Dean said.

Another man walked out into the sand pit, dressed in a black uniform with a blue Eleysian royal crest on his breast.

"General Jakoby Longe," Alise filled in for Cyrene. "He's our most renowned general."

The General held his hand between the men. "Victory goes to…" He paused dramatically. "Prince Dean Ellison."

Robard's mouth dropped open. "He forfeited."

"Only a true leader would offer his own life in exchange for his soldiers."

"Bias!" Robard cried. "You make him Captain because he is the prince."

"Watch your mouth!" the man said, smacking Robard across the face and sending him flying back in the sand. "He has earned the title of Captain, and you will do well to remember that, as you will be serving under him."

Robard nodded his head and then rushed out of the arena in a tantrum. Cyrene didn't see that arrangement going very well.

The man who had given Dean the title held Dean's hand up in the air, and the crowd roared their approval. Dean's eyes roamed the crowd as he had a confident smirk on his lips. He was completely in his element here. The sweet, charming man from the woods, who had also danced with her in Aurum, was just one part of the soldier standing before her.

Then, his eyes found her. He started forward in surprise and then frowned. He looked almost…ashamed that she was in the audience. She had seen him fight before. *Why would he look at me like that?*

He cast his eyes to the ground, retrieved his sword, and then quickly left the arena.

Cyrene was so confused.

"Come on," Alise said. "Let's go see him in the barracks."

"Are we allowed in?"

"Of course. It's customary for us to congratulate the soldiers after their victories," she said. "Right, Brigette?"

Brigette laughed. "Be easy on her, Alise."

"I'm just showing her the barracks! It's a party. It always is after a fight."

Cyrene hesitated, but Brigette had already turned her attention to someone else in the box, and Alise was pulling her out of the arena.

Alise pushed through the doors to the barracks, and she was right when she'd said that it was a party. Wine was flowing freely, musicians were playing upbeat music to dance to, and there were girls everywhere.

Cyrene's eyes sought out the one familiar face in the crowd but didn't see him. Instead, the person who appeared before her was the man Dean had just fought.

"Robard!" Alise cried. "Do you mind taking Affiliate Cyrene to see Dean? I want to say hello to General Longe."

Before Cyrene could even protest, Alise pushed her to Robard, and Cyrene stumbled into his chest. His well-oiled, very firm *naked* chest. She gasped and then pulled her hand back.

"My apologies," she said quickly. "I didn't mean…"

"No offense taken, Affiliate." He chewed on the word, as if it disgusted him, but he looked at her in the thin red gown that Livia had given her with anything but. "Should I take you to the Princeling then?"

"Um…yes, please."

Robard pushed through the crowd of soldiers and women. He shoved her toward a back room, and there was Dean, standing in nothing but his loincloth, with a half-dozen women clinging to him.

34

The

FIRST

CYRENE GAPED AT THE DISPLAY BEFORE HER.

Then, she closed her eyes for a few seconds and righted her demeanor. This was what Alise had hoped for. She wanted Cyrene to see Dean as immodest, a soldier, and a flirt. She expected Cyrene to give in to her Byern propriety, to be disgusted, tuck tail, and run the other direction.

She felt a hand at her back and realized Alise's other motivation. Robard.

"Hey, Ellison," Robard called. "I brought you something." He raised his eyebrows and didn't remove his dirty hand from her fine clothing.

Dean's eyes snapped up and latched on to her. He opened his mouth to say something, but she had seen enough. She didn't need to see this. It wasn't any of her business. Dean Ellison was not the reason she was in Eleysia. Being a toy in the midst of one of his bitter sisters' plots was not part of her plan.

She shoved Robard away from her and dashed toward the entrance of the barracks. Her magic was firing under her fingertips, like it had done that night in Aurum when Kael coaxed it out of her. Her breathing was ragged, and she couldn't keep her emotions in check.

This was a setup. A ploy. She knew it for what it was. It was something Jardana would have pulled back home in Byern to try to keep Cyrene away from Kael and to diminish her importance at court. But she hadn't had to deal with petty court antics in a while, and her heart hadn't been prepared for it. It was beating fiercely in her chest, and she was terrified of what would happen if she didn't get herself under control.

Am I going to have another accident, like in Aurum? Could I level the barracks this time?

No. Creator! She couldn't let this keep happening.

This was why she needed to find Matilde and Vera. Her magic was out of control. If she wasn't careful, she would do horrible things, and she would have no way to stop it.

"Cyrene!" Dean called behind her.

She turned to look at him as he rushed out after her in nothing but his loincloth. Sweat still coated his skin, and sand coated his skin where he had rolled on the floor of the pit. Up close, he was even bigger and broader than she remembered. And he was blinding to look at.

"I really don't want to talk about it right now," Cyrene said, continuing up the hill to the palace. If she talked to him about what she had seen, her magic might erupt, and she could hurt him or take out the palace or worse.

"Cyrene, please! Let me explain."

"Don't!" she cried. "Don't explain. You have nothing to explain. Just...don't."

Magic burst free from her fingers, and she felt it pool in her body. Life force. Sweet, beautiful power. Raw and uninhibited. It was perfection as it flooded her, and she could do nothing to stop it.

Tears formed in the corners of her blue eyes, and she hated that it looked as if she were crying over Dean. If only a boy was her biggest problem...

"Those girls—"

"Dean, please. Don't."

"I would never do that—"

"Stop!" she cried. She held her hands to her chest.

At any moment, it felt like she would release her powers and destroy the world all over again. She couldn't do that. She needed to hold on. She needed to keep it together. She could control it. It was possible.

But it felt like it was controlling her at the moment.

He held his hands up. "I just defeated my biggest rival, a man I have been fighting with my entire life. He knows nearly every move

I have. It was a fifty-fifty chance, whether or not I would win today. And you bring me to surrender with a glance."

Cyrene's heart raced ahead of her at his words. "We don't even know each other, Dean."

"Then, let me get to know you. I would never be with another woman. That was not what it looked like back there."

"I know it wasn't. Your sister set this all up."

"Which one?" he demanded.

"Alise."

Dean growled low, "She will not bother you again. I will take care of it."

Cyrene shook her head. "I knew what she was doing. She brought me there on purpose, to scare me off."

"And it worked."

"I'm not scared off."

I just need to calm down. Breathe in. Two, three, four. Breathe out. Two, three, four.

"But I'm not here for you either. I don't know what is going on between us. I don't know what your looks mean or the kiss in the hall. I don't know why you're helping me or even why I'm so upset that I didn't get to see you for a couple of days, only to find you doing this without my knowledge."

"I was in training for my Captain's test," he said apologetically. "I didn't think you would want to be there for it. It was the reason I had to return home after spending so much time abroad. And about that kiss…"

He stepped toward her, and she took a step back. Her magic was still hot in her veins, and she couldn't risk hurting him.

"Please," she whispered.

"Our ways are different here than in Byern, I believe."

"Very," she said. Her cheeks heated as she remembered just how naked he was at the moment.

"I thought I was clear when we first met in the woods, but let me be perfectly clear. I want to court you, Cyrene. Just allow me the opportunity to try with you," he pleaded.

Cyrene sighed and looked out toward the lake beyond.

What good would come from allowing myself to be courted by the Prince of Eleysia?

He made her erratic, and her magic burst from her fingertips with the crazy emotions running through her body. She was here on a mission, and that didn't involve another prince. She had enough worries with men back at home.

But, at the same time, the thought of him courting her seemed to settle her heart and her stomach. Her magic lessened and then disappeared…and she hadn't taken out a building.

"Why me?" she managed to get out.

"Because there is no one else like you, Cyrene." He bridged the distance between them, and this time, she let him take her hand. "You are brave and loyal. You fight for what you believe in. You are smart and clever and witty and more beautiful than any woman I have ever seen. And I believe I have just scratched the surface of who you are."

It was so easy with Dean.

No matter her feelings for Edric, the throne had always been between them. The throne and the Queen and the Consort and every other obligation that existed between a king and an Affiliate. Despite his best effort, she had never truly let go with him.

And then there was whatever had happened with Kael. Magic of some sort. Though it made no sense to her. She could never be herself with him. He certainly wanted more from her than she even knew.

But, with Dean, there was none of that. No power struggle. No secrets. No strange pull that she couldn't explain that seemed to link her to him.

Yet Dean was still the Prince of Eleysia, and she was still an Affiliate of Byern. *What could come of this?*

"I don't know what I can offer you," she whispered.

"You don't need to offer anything. My training is on hold until after the Eos holiday. Soldiers celebrate the fights and their advancement through the holiday. I'm yours until then."

"I don't know what to say."

"Just say, you'll come with me to the Eos ball. Every year, we're to come with a date to celebrate the end of another year and the birth of a new one, but I never bring anyone. Be my first," he said.

"I don't know, Dean."

"It is my birthday," he added with a cheeky grin.

How can I say no to that? "Okay, Dean, I'll go with you," she said.

She just prayed to the Creator that she wasn't making a horrible mistake in accepting his invitation.

35

The EXPLOSION

Rhea

"*AHH*!" RHEA SCREAMED FUTILELY. "WORK! BLASTED WORK!"

She stood so quickly that she threw the chair she had been seated in back against the wall. It clattered and dropped to the floor. She didn't even care. Once, she might have. But considering the work her Master Caro Barca should have been doing—that *she* was now tasked with doing—wasn't functional, she just couldn't find it in her to care.

She hadn't seen Eren in over a week. The Eos holiday was today, and she couldn't even leave her stuffy quarters in the Nit Decus castle.

Her master had been relocated to Byern when court returned from procession, and she had been forced to come with him. They had been set up in a nice, rather secluded part of the castle. In fact, she didn't think anyone had been in this part of the castle in *hundreds* of years.

It was a large, open circular room with a glass ceiling that made no sense with the rest of the dark stone construction. The walkways to and from the corridors were so large that she could have fit boats through them, if need be. It was absurd. The rest of the castle had these neat, slim corridors with artwork and gorgeous vines in the molding. But these quarters looked as if someone had wanted them to be fireproof.

It was punishment. She was sure of it. She just didn't know what for.

Captain Merrick had claimed the King had specially given them these quarters, but she doubted it. It was Captain Merrick who was a plague on the King and the country, as far as she was concerned. He had done this out of spite. No more, no less.

And she couldn't do anything to change her lot.

Tonight, Master Barca would be setting off a spectacular display of Bursts fireworks that were unlike anything anyone had seen before. They had spent the last week making sure they would have enough space set up outside of the castle grounds so that they were ready to fire. The only thing left to do was light them tonight after dusk. She should have been thrilled that she could even help him create these contraptions that she had once thought were magic.

But no…Cyrene had magic.

And this was…pure science.

Similar in so many ways. Yet, completely different in others. At this point, she wasn't particularly fond of either—magic or science.

All she had to do was make the mechanism for the fireworks into some kind of contained explosion. She had seen Master Barca do it time and again with Bursts. He just hadn't figured out how to perfectly replicate it. And he had stopped caring about what court demanded of him. He cared much more about his own pursuits.

For what felt like the thousandth time, she wondered what her genius Receiver had been thinking when he created the formula for Bursts.

"I have it!" Master Barca said, stepping eagerly into the vast cavern.

"Have what?" Rhea asked irritably.

"The exact formula!" he said triumphantly.

Rhea warily looked at him. He had said that several hundred times since being in Byern, and every time, it was about something ludicrous that had nothing to do with her work on making explosives.

"What formula?"

"The only one that matters!"

"Master Barca, you're not making sense again."

"What we all search for. What we all want to discover. The ultimate power."

"Whatever are you talking about? Have you figured out how to make your Bursts contain that explosive power? Have you figured out how I can report this to Captain Merrick?"

Master Barca looked at her as if she had sprouted horns. "Why ever would I want to militarize my Bursts?"

"What?" she stammered.

He seemed completely lucid in that moment, and she had been unprepared for it.

"My Bursts are for a merry festival occasion. You'll see them tonight. Putting that power in the hands of the guards would be catastrophic. Did you believe I had not thought of it? Imagine what they could do if they had that knowledge."

Rhea could imagine it. They could conquer the world if they wanted. But she wasn't here for judgments. She was here to advance their society. *What would be the point of all my work if I couldn't even move forward?*

"No, child. This is much more important."

"What is it?"

"The means to attain immortality."

Rhea's eyes widened. "Immortality. Are you sure? I mean…how could you know that?"

"It is not in the knowing. It is in the believing," he said. Then, he muttered to himself, practically speaking in tongues for all Rhea could decipher.

Master Barca disappeared from the door from which he had entered, but Rhea had lost the fire for her quest. She had been trained better than what her current pursuits required. She had been trained to ask why. But the pressure coming from Captain Merrick and the King himself was enough to make her quake in her slippers.

What exactly would be the consequences of creating firepower? And how different would that discovery be from magic itself?

Sure, she wasn't creating it outright from physical prowess of her own body…from something that had been born into her bloodline. But she could mix powders and chemicals together and create an explosion. If she harnessed that, it could be deadly…beyond deadly.

Discovering it for the sake of discovering it was one thing. That was what her master had always done. Pursuit of knowledge was her forte. But should all knowledge be pursued? When that knowledge could have catastrophic consequences, should it be given to people who would manipulate it for their own purposes?

No.

Maybe Master Barca was right.

His Bursts were enough.

No need to finalize the formula for the blast powder.

She would just try it one more time with a clear head and then get ready for the Eos holiday celebrations.

With a resigned sigh, she returned to her work room. Leaning over the various powders she had been working with, she started mixing them together.

Earlier that week, she had pilfered a few Bursts from the festival celebration and deconstructed them to get a better look at what her master had done. But it was difficult to determine when all the powders were already mixed in certain amounts for the Bursts. Not to mention, the blast powder she wanted to create needed to be much more highly concentrated.

She mixed together the ingredients that were used in the Bursts and decided to light it in a closed compartment. The Bursts seemed to pop open in the tightly concealed space. She fitted the powder into a small metal contraption that Master Barca had left on the table. He had a million different such objects floating around that she was sure he wouldn't miss this one.

Carefully placing the object on a table away from her papers, she threaded a wick into the container and rolled it out. The powder itself burned pretty well on its own, so she wanted to make sure she was far enough away in case the fire increased. Luckily, the room was basically fireproof.

Rhea cut the wick and then lit it, standing about ten feet away from the table. The wick burned slowly as it traveled across the distance and then into the metal contraption.

BOOM!

Ring. Ring. Ring.

Rhea's vision was blurry. Her ears were ringing. She placed her hands on them, but that did nothing to stop the ringing. She tried to stand and look around the room, only to realize that she had been thrown all the way across the chamber. Her back had collided with the wall on the opposite side, some thirty feet away from where she had been standing when lighting the fuse.

"What have I done?" she whispered.

But she was shocked to discover she couldn't hear herself speak.

Everything hurt. She had to find a way to assess her injuries, but standing seemed impossible.

Then, there was Master Barca, leaning down toward her and softly cradling her. He was saying something, but she just shook her head. She couldn't hear him. He tried to help her to her feet, but that didn't go so well.

He motioned to her that he was going to go get help, and then he left at a hurried jog, which was really moving for him.

She leaned her head back against the wall and was resigned to her fate when someone else walked into the room.

Kael Dremylon.

An apparition. *What would the Prince be doing here?* He didn't come to this side of the castle. He had been back only for a couple of weeks and had been all but locked in his own quarters.

No. There was no prince here.

Just a dream.

Dream Prince Kael said something to her, but she motioned to her ear. The ringing continued. She hoped this wasn't permanent. *What would I do if I lost my hearing completely?*

Dream Prince Kael nodded and then unexpectedly bent down and hoisted her into his arms. *Am I floating?* This couldn't be reality. She was too weak to protest.

Shouldn't my Dream Prince know that I can't move right now?

Apparently not.

Dream Prince Kael carried her from the room, as if she weighed nothing. Perhaps she did weigh nothing; it was a dream after all.

They walked through the corridors and then reached her small quarters a few minutes later. Dream Prince Kael gently placed her down in the bed, and as exhaustion took her over, she passed out on the covers.

271

Rhea came to again sometime later. She had the distinct feeling of being watched. Her ears were still ringing a little. And her entire body felt like…well, like she had just been blasted thirty feet across a room and into a stone wall.

"Hello?" she croaked into the stillness.

She could hear! Only slightly. Her voice warbled, as if heard through water, but her hearing wasn't completely gone.

"Hello," someone called back.

Rhea turned her head and saw Kael Dremylon sitting in the corner of her room. She had been sure that envisioning him was a dream. His presence made no sense to her.

She opened her mouth to ask him what he was doing in her room, but all that came out was, "Water."

He smiled that charming smile. She was sure that she would have blushed under different circumstances. He *was* the prince.

He handed her a glass of water. "Here you are. I had a physician attend to you and assured Master Barca that I would fetch him when you were awake."

"How long was I out?"

"Only an hour or two."

"And you waited?" she asked in disbelief.

He flashed her another winning smile.

There was something different about him. Rhea couldn't quite put her finger on it. She didn't know him that well, but the prince she had seen before he had left for Aurum was…different. Teasing, flirtatious, jovial, conniving for sure, and manipulative. But this was *other*. He was somehow other. It was like a black shadow had fallen over his body, transforming the man before her. It made her shiver.

"Yes," he said, folding himself back into the chair.

"Thank you, Your Highness," she said, not forgetting her manners.

"How are you feeling?"

"Horrible," she admitted.

"I'm sorry to hear that. I've had a tonic prepared for you so that you can get more rest."

"Thank you," she repeated.

She was waiting for him to say something else. Surely, he wouldn't have stayed here that long for nothing.

"How did you do it?" Prince Kael leaned his elbows against his knees and intriguingly looked at her.

"Do what?"

"The explosion. How did you harness the black powder you've been working with?"

"You've been following my work?"

"Yes," he said.

"I…I don't know," she lied. "It was the first time it had ever succeeded."

"You are friends with Cyrene, are you not?"

Rhea tried not to react to that question, which was so out of nowhere. "I was. We grew up together."

"You do not seem to be in despair over her kidnapping." He gave her a toothy grin that reeked of madness.

"I have been for months, Highness," she whispered.

"Has anyone else told you that you are a bad liar?"

She swallowed. She was nervous now. She fidgeted under his gaze, wondering what he was getting at. "Yes. I've heard that before."

"I would suggest that you do not continue to lie to me. You and I both know that Cyrene was not kidnapped."

Rhea gulped.

"But that will be our little secret."

"Why?" she asked helplessly.

"Because you are going to help me militarize this black powder."

Rhea's eyes widened. "I can't."

"You will create it and teach me how to use it, and in exchange, I will keep the insufferable Captain from bothering you about it."

"I can't," she repeated helplessly.

"And I will not report you for withholding information from the King during a murder investigation." He drummed his fingers together and stared at her with his piercing gaze. "I'm not sure your friend Eren would appreciate that either."

Rhea sank further into the bed. *Checkmate.* "All right," she breathed. "But the King and Eren must *never* know."

He grinned with victory. "I'm very good at keeping secrets."

The
CELEBRATIONS

Daufina

"IS THAT THE LAST ONE, CONSORT?" THE DEMURE AFFILIATE Bitta asked.

Daufina pushed the last piece of paper away from her and nodded. "Yes, I believe so." She stood regally and surveyed all of her hard work.

The Eos holiday was exceptionally important in Byern festivities. It was the day the Creator had first walked the earth and blessed Emporia and also the day of Byern's independence from the dreaded Doma. Each year, they would have a celebration for the entire country. People would travel far and wide to see the famed Bursts go off overhead and to eat, drink, and be merry.

It was also significant for all the Second and Third Class children who had turned seventeen that year, officially coming of age in Byern. For those individuals, a Presenting ceremony would be held at court to determine their Class as well as to be assigned to their Receivers. This day would determine their entire future. Since so many children came forth, it would be slightly different than for those children of the First Class, who could afford an entire ceremony for one person, but it was still held to much importance.

Part of her key duties as the Consort was to work with the King on placement for all of these children. It was a long process, and many advisors would be brought in to lessen the load. They still had a country to run after all.

"Shall I deliver these to His Majesty for the arrangements this afternoon?" Affiliate Bitta asked.

"Yes. All, save for the First Class ones," she instructed. She glanced over at High Order Ceron, who had been patiently awaiting orders. She passed a small stack of papers to him. "Take these to High Order Garrison. He'll know what to do with them."

"Yes, Consort."

He procured the paperwork and left at once.

There were so few this year. Even less than last year. But Presenting letters would need to be written for those who would change into First Class. It was tradition.

Affiliate Bitta retrieved the rest of the letters and carefully filed them to be delivered to the King for the ceremony.

Daufina left her work behind and strolled leisurely to her chambers to get ready for her part in the ceremony today. After a good, long soak, she changed into a tiered purple dress woven with diamonds. Her hair was arranged into silky waves that flowed down her back, and her face was artfully painted. The Presenting was a big show, and she needed to look the part.

A contingent of guards escorted her to the chamber where Kaliana and Edric were already waiting. Kaliana was practically glowing in her blue dress. She had even let her hair hang loose over one shoulder instead of wearing it in the sharp bun she usually preferred. Edric looked as regal as ever, and it was truly shocking to see him standing by Kaliana's side with one hand on her shoulder. Kaliana adoringly gazed up at him.

"Are we waiting on Prince Kael?" Daufina asked.

Kaliana flinched slightly, and Daufina narrowed her eyes. Kaliana had been doing very strange things indeed since the Prince had returned home from Aurum. Daufina wouldn't even consider what the reasons were for Kaliana's odd behavior.

"He should already be here," Edric said. "But he is frequently late, and if he does not arrive soon, we will start without him."

Daufina nodded and sat down just as the door opened again. In walked Prince Kael. He wore an all black doublet, and his dark hair had been swept back from his face. It appeared he hadn't been sleeping much as dark circles were painted under his vivid blue-gray eyes. Daufina gauged Kaliana's reaction to his arrival and didn't like what she saw.

"Were you waiting for me?" Kael asked with a sneer at his brother.

Their interactions had been even worse since Cyrene had left. Daufina had never believed one girl could cause so much unrest.

"We hadn't planned to," Edric said. He was smiling though. Kaliana's pregnancy had left him more jovial than he had been. He reached out his arm to Kael, who clasped it with his own, almost to the elbow. "Brother."

Kael nodded and then released him. "Well, let's get this show on. So much to do, so much wine to drink, so many beds to warm."

Edric sighed and then held his arm out for Kaliana. She took it without looking at Kael again, and they strode to the entrance.

Guards opened the doors, and in went the King and Queen of Byern. Daufina followed next with her head raised, and Kael brought up the rear. He slipped into a seat in the first row while the three of them sat down on immaculate gold thrones on top of the dais in the throne room.

One by one, children came forward and received their Class information and Receiver positions. Each one swore allegiance to the King, the throne, and the country. Then, they were sent on their way. A select few—only five this year—moved up to First Class. Joy broke on their faces at the declaration, and their expressions would be forever ingrained on Daufina's mind. And of those chosen few for the First Class, only *one* had been given over to be made a High Order, the highest rank he could have attained. Daufina thought the small Third Class boy, Aubron, from the mountain town of Fen, had been about to faint at the news.

But, in due course, everyone was selected into their proper stations, and until next year, all would be well for the Second and Third Class families. Thankfully, she thought the First Class Presenting was planned for much later next year, which would give them a reprieve from the work.

Once all but the Affiliates and High Orders were left in the room, Edric stood to address them with a smile, "My fellow countrymen and women, thank you so much for celebrating this blessed Eos holiday with me. The Creator herself once walked on our earth on this day. Byern is forever grateful for her blessing, and

277

I encourage you to celebrate this gift." Edric raised his hands as his enraptured crowd cheered. "I do have one announcement before we leave this hall and enter the streets for merriment and a special presentation of Bursts, prepared by Master Barca, all the way from Albion."

A hush fell on the crowd as they awaited his announcement. Daufina even waited with bated breath to hear him.

"It is with great joy that I announce that Queen Kaliana is with child!"

There were some gasps and faint whispers, but Daufina suspected that most people had already guessed why the Queen had been acting differently lately. Why the King and Queen had been acting differently together.

"Soon, we will have a Dremylon boy fit to rule as my heir. I could not have asked for a better blessing from the Creator on this great day. Go forth and be merry, for your country is the greatest on earth."

The Affiliates and High Order cheered his bold statement as Kaliana stood next to Edric, beaming up at her husband.

For some reason, Daufina let her gaze shift away from the smiling couple and over to the shadow in the corner of the room. Kael looked like a thundercloud, dark and ominous. Her stomach twisted. He could not even conceal his distaste for his brother at the announcement of his own baby nephew. *What must he be thinking...plotting?*

Kaliana would never...Kael would never...

No, Daufina wouldn't even think it. Her hand went to her stomach as she forced down the thought.

This was a day of celebration, and she had every intention of enjoying herself. Politics could be left for another day.

37

The
EOS HOLIDAY

EVERY MORNING ON THE EOS HOLIDAY, CYRENE'S PARENTS would wake her up bright and early just as the sun was rising on the horizon. She would dress in her best golden gown and run downstairs to wait for the presents from her family. She and her siblings—Reeve, Aralyn, and Elea—would feast on her mother's sweet cakes and marvel at the ribbons and gowns and chocolates that her parents gave them as blessings from the Creator on her day.

After the morning meal, they would bundle up in their warmest clothing and find a place on the streets to await the court with Rhea and the rest of the Gramm family. The court would parade through the city with the King, Queen, and Consort at the end of a column of Affiliates and High Order.

The mountains would loom overhead with their snow-topped peaks. And, if they were lucky, snow would hit the streets for the first day of the season. They would be exempt from lessons for the day. While a large group of Second and Third Class children of age were brought to Nit Decus castle for their Presenting ceremony, the city dwellers would play in the snow, and an annual snowball fight would break out in the streets.

Once Cyrene had reached a certain age, she was forbidden from the fights, but by then, she could join the festival in the city where everyone wore white ribbons in their hair and danced in the various banquet halls.

At night, her family would sit around the hearth and remember all the things they were thankful for on this day for the Creator. They would go to bed, full of love and chocolate and blessings.

Rhea would sneak into their house through the second-story window and snuggle with Cyrene and her sister, Elea, giggling at cold toes and their adventures from the evening.

This Eos holiday, there would be no snow.

No mountains.

No family.

No Rhea.

Cyrene never thought she would miss the cold. Colder temperatures wouldn't hit Eleysia for at least a couple of weeks, and even then, it would be nothing like home.

The door to her room opened, and Cyrene jumped. "Oh, it's just you," she said, when she saw Maelia's face in the doorway.

Maelia toed the door closed behind her. "Happy holiday to you, too," she said.

Cyrene sat up in bed and pulled the covers back. "Come sit with me."

Maelia smiled brightly and dashed into Cyrene's bed. For a minute, she could almost imagine Maelia as a kid with her Captains of the Guard parents easing up on her on this one day.

"This is my first year away," Cyrene whispered.

"Mine, too."

"I thought I would be in the parade in Byern. People would look up to me as I walked through the city. I'd been dreaming about it since I was a girl."

"I'm glad I'm not in a parade," Maelia admitted. "I just wish I were standing on top of the perimeter wall in Levin with my parents. It was the one day of the year when I was permitted to see the world from so high up."

"I bet that was freezing," Cyrene said.

Levin was even farther north than Byern, and they always had bitterly cold winters.

"You don't notice the cold after a while."

A knock sounded from the door. Both girls started and then giggled at the interruption.

Cyrene called, "Come in!"

The door opened, and there stood Dean, looking ever the part of the Eleysian Prince. He smiled when he found them in bed together. "Am I interrupting?"

Cyrene laughed. "No, we were just reminiscing about Byern."

"And the snow," Maelia said.

Dean shuddered. "The snow? Why would you miss the snow?"

"It's home," they said in unison.

"I see. Well, I came to bring you an Eos present, Cyrene. Maelia, I know that Darmian was asking around about you," Dean said.

Cyrene's eyes widened. "You and Darmian?"

"Don't get any of your ideas. I'm sure it's just...business," Maelia said, already getting out of bed.

"'Business,'" Cyrene said, making finger quotes.

Maelia rolled her eyes and shut the door behind her.

"Present?" Cyrene asked.

She got out of bed and stepped into her dressing robe. She didn't feel comfortable dressed just in her night shift around Dean even though she sometimes thought the Eleysian clothing bared more than her Byern shift.

Dean walked around the enormous four-poster bed and casually took a seat on the down comforter. If someone had found out about that happening in Byern, the entire court would be talking about it. But he seemed so comfortable and confident in the space that she took the seat next to him.

He offered her a small box. She arched an eyebrow and then tore into it. She removed a bag from within and was delighted to find decadent Eleysian chocolate.

She popped one into her mouth and moaned. "Creator, this is delicious."

"I did say I would ply you with them."

Cyrene laughed. "Feel free."

"But I have one more thing," he said. He removed a tiny box from his pockets and opened it for her.

She stared at the contents within and went still. It was the most beautiful string of milky-white pearls she had ever seen. When she couldn't find the words to respond, Dean removed them from the box and held them out for her to see.

"Dean," she whispered, "they're beautiful."

"A family heirloom."

"I can't," she breathed. "It's your birthday and you're giving *me* gifts."

"Ah, but you're going to the ball with me. That's gift enough. And trust me, the pearls will look much better on you when you wear them tonight than sitting in a box," he told her. "Allow me."

She shifted her back to his chest until they were nearly touching. She could feel the heat radiating off of him. It took everything in her not to lean back toward him and let his warmth seep into her. She pulled her long dark tresses to one side. He placed the pearls around her neck, and then he clasped the necklace into place. His fingers trailed along her neckline, and she shivered.

"There," he whispered, his breath hot on her shoulder. "Perfect."

"Thank you." She touched a hand to the pearls and faced him. "They're amazing."

Dean laced their fingers together. That one small gesture disarmed her. It was so simple yet meant so much. His thumb stroked her hand while the other hand came up to cup her cheek. Her breathing hitched as her eyes landed on his lips.

Dean smiled sweetly, and she could feel the tension blooming between them. She could distinctly remember the feel of his lips on her cheek all those weeks ago, and he hadn't made a move since then. This was the closest they had been since he had asked to court her.

He must think her Byern modesty precluded kissing. Just when she thought that she was going to have to show him that it didn't, he pulled back and stood.

"I have duties the rest of the afternoon, but I wanted to see you before I left." He brought her hand up to his lips and kissed her, his eyes boring into her all the while. "Until tonight."

Then, he turned and left her room.

Cyrene flopped back onto the bed and let loose an exasperated sigh. *What have I gotten myself into?*

Cyrene stared at her reflection in the mirror. She was to meet Dean at the entrance to the ball any minute now. She touched the pearls at her neck once more. They meant something. She knew they did. Maybe everything. And none of the trepidation that she had first felt with him lingered within her.

She hadn't found Matilde and Vera, but her magic hadn't acted up either. Dean's presence seemed to have a calming effect on her. Something that she noted happily.

But it did sour her mood that she had fled home and everything she loved for a mission that she couldn't possibly accomplish. Even if she had found Dean in the process.

Cyrene felt a slight tug in her stomach as a someone approached her room from down the hallway, and a smile tugged at her features.

"You're here!" Cyrene said when the door opened. Cyrene didn't have to turn around to know it was Avoca who stood behind her.

"Happy Eos, Cyrene," Avoca said with a small smile. "We're all in position for the party."

"Good. Let's hope we fare better at this ball."

Avoca nodded. "I think we will."

Cyrene stepped down from the pedestal in front of the mirror and motioned for Avoca to follow her out of the room. They walked through the corridors on the way to the Eos ball. "Are you going to tell me what's happening with Ahlvie and Ceis'f?"

Avoca's smile froze. "Nothing is happening with either of them."

"And Dean didn't give me a family heirloom to wear to the party," Cyrene said sarcastically.

"He's openly courting you, Cyrene. You know he wants to be with you."

"And Ahlvie and Ceis'f feel the same with you. Have you decided what you will do?" Cyrene reached for her hand.

"No. I can't be with Ceis'f, and I will outlive Ahlvie," she whispered. Avoca squeezed her hand, as if that was the end of the discussion, and then melted away.

Cyrene could feel a slight tug on their bond and wished her good luck.

Cyrene couldn't worry more about Avoca's issues, for she was approaching the rather large royal Ellison family. She took a deep breath and then proceeded down the hallway to meet Dean.

Everyone was milling around and chatting before they were to be announced to the holiday ball. Nearly all the daughters were married, and they had brought their husbands and children to the ceremony. Brigette didn't have a date, but Cyrene noted with displeasure that Alise was on Robard's arm. Therese and Tifani both had dates whom Cyrene didn't recognize.

Dean intercepted Cyrene before she had made it all the way to the ground. "You're stunning," he murmured. He drew her into him for a heated embrace. He fingered the pearls around her neck. "They go perfectly with the gown."

She smiled and stared up into his handsome face, basking in his affection. She had chosen an ice-blue gown, so light that it was almost the color of snow. She had almost chosen Byern gold but decided at the last minute that it might not seem proper. She still proudly displayed her Affiliate pin. She couldn't hide who she was, but she didn't have to flaunt it. And Dean didn't care either way.

"We'll be first," Dean said, shuffling them to the front of the line.

Cyrene saw there were a few well-placed stares at the necklace around her throat, but Dean didn't stop to let anyone ask any questions.

"First?" she squeaked.

"We go in reverse birth order."

"I see."

Dean loosely wrapped an arm around her waist, drawing her toward him. "I'll be right here the whole time."

They approached the double doors to a large ballroom, and an announcer hit a solid cane to the ground twice to gain the crowd's attention.

"Prince Dean Ellison of Eleysia, accompanied tonight by Affiliate Cyrene Strohm of Byern," the man cried for everyone to hear.

Cyrene's mouth went dry, and she froze. She couldn't go out there. Everyone in attendance would judge her for being an Affiliate. They would all hate her for it. She had never backed down from anything, but with the new knowledge that the world despised the one thing she had always wanted in life—to become an Affiliate—she was wary of what that meant for her future.

"I can't," she whispered to Dean in panic.

He smiled down at her, as if nothing was amiss. "You can."

"No."

"I want to show you to the world, Cyrene," he breathed. "Show the world you are mine."

"Dean…"

"And nothing will change that."

She opened her mouth to protest but found that she couldn't. *How can I fear this moment when I didn't even stop to consider what to do in the face of a Braj in Aurum?*

Cyrene looped her hand into the crook of his elbow and then nodded. They walked into the ballroom, and applause broke out. As she walked with Dean down the stairs, Cyrene couldn't tell if people were happy to see her or not, but she tried not to care. Dean had just called her *his*. That was all that was important.

The room was decorated completely in white. All the tables had expensive white silk cloths that draped to the floor. The glasses were white frosted. White flowers of every variety were artfully arranged into centerpieces, so the entire room was perfumed with the fragrant scent. Servants were dressed in sheer white frocks and carrying trays of clouded drinks. The whole room looked blanketed in snow, and the familiarity of it lulled her.

They walked to the center of the room where space had been left open for the royal family. Introductions followed for all of his sisters. Therese and Tifani along with their dates were next. Then, Alise and Robard made it into the room. Robard shot Dean a dirty look, and Alise looked pleased with herself. She smiled brightly at Cyrene and waved like they were old friends. She was a dangerous one for sure.

The rest of his sisters filtered into the room.

Just when it was time for Brigette, the announcer cleared his throat, and a page ran toward him. He looked down at the piece of paper he had been given and nodded.

"Her Royal Majesty, Queen Cassia Ellison, the Matron Bride of the Sea, and the King Regent Tomas Ellison," the man declared.

Cyrene looked up at Dean in surprise. "Where is Brigette?"

The whispers throughout the room proved that everyone else had noticed her absence as well. Brigette had been there when Cyrene and Dean were outside of the ballroom, and now, she was missing.

"I don't know," Dean said. He looked worried.

"Should we go check on her?"

He shook his head. "It would be best not to draw any more attention," he whispered as his parents made it to the circle.

The Queen raised her hands, gesturing to the musicians to begin playing. But then, just as the first chord struck in the room, the announcer dropped his cane again.

Everyone swiveled back to the entrance to see what the commotion was. *Someone was to be announced after the Queen and King?* That simply wasn't proper.

The announcer cleared his throat, and when he read the new piece of paper, his eyes enlarged to twice their size. It was noticeable, even from where Cyrene was standing.

"Her Royal Highness, Crown Princess Brigette Ellison, the Maiden Bride of the Sea, and"—the announcer looked up at the crowd in shock and bewilderment—"Master Basille Selby."

38

The
HUMANITARIAN

"OH CREATOR," CYRENE WHISPERED, "WHAT HAVE WE DONE?"

"You mean, what has Brigette done?"

Cyrene looked up at Dean, but he just shook his head.

"There is nothing we can do to fix this. Brigette dug her own grave. She's going to have to lie in it."

"What will your parents do?"

"Nothing in public. They'll wait until everyone is distracted."

Queen Cassia looked ready to rush over to her eldest daughter and filet her alive.

To Brigette's credit, she didn't even flinch under her mother's gaze as she strode into the ballroom in a royal-blue gown with Basille Selby on her arm. The whispers erupted all around them, and Cyrene could already tell that the old gossip was circulating the room.

Brigette stepped up to her mother with a wide smile on her face. "You remember Master Selby, don't you, Mother?"

Queen Cassia smiled at him, but her eyes were murderous. "It has been nearly a decade since I've heard that name."

Basille bowed to the Queen. "And not a day goes past that you haven't missed hearing it, I'm sure."

"I'm sure," the Queen responded icily. "Maestro, a dance to celebrate my eldest daughter's eternal wisdom and grace in all matters."

Cyrene jolted. She barely knew Brigette, but she almost wanted to go save her from the wrath in the Queen's look and the disgust in her cool voice.

But Dean put a hand on Cyrene's back and pulled her into his arms just as the music began. "Not a battle for you to fight, my little warrior."

"Me?" she gasped. "I'm not a warrior." Her feet slid across the floor with Dean leading the way.

"You run into battles headfirst without a thought for your own safety," he whispered against her hair. "That sounds like a warrior to me."

Cyrene remembered the last time someone had called her a warrior. She'd had her warrior ceremony in Byern. After finding out that Affiliates and High Order had started as the warriors from Viktor Dremylon's army when he killed off the Doma, she'd had to prove her warrior status, and she had just barely survived.

"Perhaps I just desire to help the people I care about," she reasoned. "Maybe that doesn't make me a warrior. Maybe it makes me a humanitarian."

Dean quirked an eyebrow up. "A humanitarian? For someone with your particular…skill set, I find that a bit ironic."

"Why is that?" she demanded. "Are you saying that I can't care about humanity?"

"Not that you can't care, but I would think you'd be a Domatarian," he said, making up a word on the spot. "And, as far as I've read in the history books, that makes you a warrior."

He twirled her in place and then drew her back to him, but by then, she was fuming. She couldn't even help it. She just couldn't believe that he would say those things. As if she couldn't care about humanity when she had spent her entire life thinking that she was human. The very distinction between Doma and human had created a war and extinguished an entire race and all magic.

The dance ended, and Cyrene abruptly dropped her hands. Her magic fired under her fingertips as her emotions battled inside her. It wasn't as erratic as the last time it had happened after Dean's fight to become Captain, but she was upset.

"Excuse me."

And, without ceremony, she turned and walked off the dance floor.

She needed a drink. Something to cool herself down. Creator, she just missed the mountains and the cold and the snow. She grabbed a flute of some icy liquid and tipped it back. Her head spun, and she shuddered. Whatever that was…was not punch. And it was much stronger than the wine they drank at court. Also, it was a very bad idea. She needed control tonight. If she were on edge and lost control of her magic, many people could suffer.

"What's going on?" Avoca whispered, grasping her forearm in the crowd. She was in a shimmering green Eleysian dress that fit her like a glove.

"Nothing."

"This isn't nothing, Cyrene."

"I have it under control," she spat at Avoca.

For the first time since they had been connected, she wished that Avoca couldn't feel her powers or know what was running through her. "Just let me be for one night. I'm fine. *Nothing* is going to happen."

Avoca steeled her with a sharp glare. "I have a debt owed to you, Cyrene."

"One I did not ask for."

Avoca looked hurt, and Cyrene instantly regretted her rash actions.

"I understand." Avoca let go of Cyrene, and before she could say anything more, Avoca rushed into the crowd.

Cyrene groaned. "Avoca," she cried, following after her.

"Leave it, Cyrene," Avoca said, brushing her off and disappearing effortlessly into the crowd.

"I'm sorry," she whispered in despair.

Cyrene shook her head and then exited out onto a balcony overlooking the courtyard below. It was blissfully cooler here. She didn't feel like she was burning up from the inside out. Even if there weren't snow or mountains, it was quite beautiful. It just wasn't home.

Ache hit her in the pit of her stomach. She needed to stop this. Picking fights with Dean and Avoca wasn't going to get her back to Byern—if she could *ever* go back to Byern. Basille had said that it was impossible for her to return, and that coupled with how strongly she missed her favorite holiday celebration only made everything worse. This magic was a curse, not a blessing. One she couldn't ever hope to control.

Dean walked out onto the balcony. "Cyrene?" he whispered.

She wiped a tear from the corner of her eye but didn't face him.

"Why did you leave? Did I upset you?"

"No," she said. But it was a lie. She was upset with him, with everything really.

"Tell me what's wrong, so I can fix it. I thought we were just having fun."

"We were," she agreed.

"But…"

"But there is so much about me that you don't know."

"Then, tell me," he insisted.

"I'm not a *warrior*," she spat the word. "I never want to be, yet I'm so conflicted. Affiliates started out as warriors for the Dremylons during the war. They killed Doma. They killed my ancestors. Yet I'm one of them."

"I didn't know," he admitted. "We don't study Byern history as thoroughly as our own, except for learning that Affiliates and High Order were created. I didn't know that would trigger you."

"Creator! It's not even that," she said, turning to face him. "It's everything. What am I even doing here, Dean? I'm getting nowhere. Maybe I should just go home."

Dean reached out and cupped her cheek in his hand. He tilted her chin up until she looked at him, and the affection in his eyes nearly stole her breath away. "You could leave, but I don't know how I would bear it."

Under his careful hands, her magic diminished until it was nothing but a soft simmer under her skin. *Or is that the heat from his hands?*

"Dean—"

"You're not a warrior. You're not a humanitarian. You're not even an Affiliate," he said. "You aren't a label, Cyrene. You are everything you want to be and more. I see it in your conviction in everything you do. And though I know you could be anything you wanted, all I can possibly want is for you to be mine."

No response was necessary.

Dean covered her mouth, and it was like the heavens opened up over them. His lips were soft but commanding, prying life out of her willful mouth. His hands were rough and callous from endless hours with a sword in his grasp, but he treated her so lightly, as if she might break.

But she did just the opposite. She latched on to his shirt and drew him against her. A tide broke between them, and she couldn't seem to get enough of him. She had been waiting weeks for this moment. She hadn't even known it at the time, but every touch and nudge and gentle caress had been stoking a fire in her veins. And the feel of him awakened her body and calmed her magic to a gentle thrum while also calling it forth between them.

Dean gasped against her mouth, and his gentle hands betrayed him, latching on to her waist with force. Whatever was passing between them felt like she was opening herself up and feeling the force of her magic for the first time. But it wasn't scary, and she felt perfectly in control.

When he pulled back, he leaned his forehead against hers and sighed. "What was that?"

"I think you just kissed me."

He chuckled and wrapped his arms tighter around her. "That was more than a kiss."

"Mmm," she groaned.

He kissed her one more time. "Yes. Much more than a kiss."

Cyrene rested her cheek on his chest and sighed. All thoughts that had been troubling her today fled her mind. This moment was perfect, and Dean was right. It was so much more than a kiss.

"Prince Dean," a voice called behind them.

Cyrene immediately broke away from him, but he kept her hand, as if knowing her propriety would drag her from him.

"Yes?"

Darmian walked out onto the balcony. Cyrene could see Maelia standing just behind his shoulder. By the flush on Maelia's cheeks when Cyrene glanced her way, she had to assume Darmian had gotten out of guard duties to be with her.

"Sorry to disturb you," Darmian said. "But Queen Cassia and Princess Brigette are beyond reason. They're yelling at each other down a hallway, and guests can hear them."

Dean blanched and cursed. "Thank you for letting me know. Let's go, Darmian." Dean kissed Cyrene's hand. "I will return to you."

"You always find me again somehow," she said with a smile.

He kissed her hand once more and then followed Darmian off of the balcony.

Cyrene glanced at Maelia. "So, Darmian?"

Maelia colored. "It is not how it appears."

"Oh, please let it be."

"You're in a good mood." Maelia raised her eyebrows in question.

"Yes, I am. And, oh!" Cyrene started forward and clutched her chest.

"What? What is it?"

"Avoca," Cyrene gasped. "I don't know what's going on, but she's upset. Oh Creator, I'm sure this is my doing. I need to find her."

"I last saw her with Ceis'f. They were walking out of the ballroom."

"Which direction?"

"I'm not sure. Back toward your rooms, I would guess."

Cyrene doubled over. She let loose a word befitting a sailor. "She's never pulled this much power before. I need to go to her. Now."

Cyrene ignored Maelia's pleas to wait and dashed off the balcony. Avoca was not an overly emotional person. She kept herself completely in check. Something must have seriously upset her for her to be drawing so much power.

Ignoring the confused glances from partygoers, Cyrene left the safety of the ballroom and darted down the hallway. A figure appeared in her way, and she nearly groaned aloud.

"In such a hurry?" Robard asked.

He was huge and sturdy up close, and despite the fact that Cyrene had magic, she shrank from his form.

"I'm looking for a friend. You didn't happen to see a couple go by here? A young woman in a green dress with a man, and both have fair hair?" Cyrene didn't even know why she bothered. She could feel Avoca was in this direction somewhere. The strength of her magic pulled Cyrene toward her.

"Sure," Robard said easily. "The girl seemed like she was ready to fight the man, or she was just intoxicated and hoping for something else."

Cyrene sneered at him. Avoca was not *looking* for something. *Men!* "Thank you for your assistance."

"Here." Robard offered her his hand. "I can show you the way."

Cyrene balked at his suggestion, but then she realized, it wasn't a suggestion. He took up a large portion of the hallway, and he wasn't going to let her pass.

"I'm grateful," she ground out.

Robard was leading Cyrene in the general direction where she could sense Avoca. Cyrene wanted to just run far, far away from this man. She had seen the angry gaze he shot to Dean when he had won, and she knew this was not a man to be trusted. But her manners had taken over, and for some reason, she just couldn't say no.

Then, Avoca's magic disappeared. It happened so suddenly. The connection fizzled out.

Cyrene's mouth dropped open. That couldn't mean something had happened to her. She would know. She had to know if that'd happened. It felt more like when she walked out of a dark room and into the light. Her system was shocked, and she couldn't see properly.

She had been so in tune with what was happening internally that she hadn't even been paying attention to where Robard was taking her.

"Hey, where are we?" she asked, trying to break away from him.

"I think they went in there," Robard said. He pointed at an open door.

"No, I don't think—*oopb!*"

Robard had shoved her through the door. She turned to run out of it, but he slammed it in her face. She tried the handle, but it was locked.

"What are you doing?" she screamed.

A face appeared at a slit opening in the face of the door.

Alise stared back at her with a conceited grin. "Hello, Cyrene."

"Alise…let me go."

"Have a nice night," Alise said cheerfully.

Cyrene let loose a bloodcurdling scream, but wherever they had led her was far enough removed from the party that no one could hear her scream.

39

The TRIANGLE

Avoca

AVOCA DIDN'T REGRET HER DECISION.

She ground her teeth together and wove through the pressing crowd of strangers in the Eleysian ballroom. The smell of so many bodies together in one enclosed space was almost suffocating. She was sure, to normal humans, it didn't smell bad at all. They wouldn't be able to sense what she did, but it was perfectly clear to her. And it was giving her a splitting headache. Not to mention, the two glasses of icy liquid she'd had earlier and Cyrene's behavior.

Ugh, Cyrene!

Avoca owed her a blood debt. Cyrene had saved her life during battle, and for that, Avoca would always be eternally grateful...and eternally trying to make up for the shame of it. But Cyrene did not make it easy on her to do any of those things. Cyrene's unconventional ways had gotten them this far, but it always felt like she was diving into the unknown. And then she had just blown her off when Avoca was only doing her duty.

She marched out of a pocket of overly perfumed women in deep purple dyed Eleysian dresses and continued toward the open air.

She needed air. She needed earth. She needed to feel her magic and connection to the ground.

This island with so many inhabitants was almost worse than Aurum had been. Every inch of land outside the palace was either water or a building. It drove her earth powers mad.

An unmeasurable feeling of homesickness took her over. She missed the trees and canopies of Eldora along with her mother.

Avoca swallowed back her emotions and forced the mask of indifference back on her face. Her greatest weapon was keeping herself in check and dousing her emotions. She was a trained Leif fighter, a powerful magical user, and the heir to the throne of Eldora. She damn well had to act like it.

"Ava," Ceis'f said.

He appeared like a wraith out of nowhere. If she hadn't had the two glasses of whatever that liquor was, she would have seen him coming. She should have felt him coming.

"What is it, Roran?" she said, using the fake name Ceis'f had taken since being on the road.

"You didn't even see me coming," he accused.

"I don't want or need your company tonight. Leave me be."

"I don't trust you on your own in your...condition."

"My condition?" she spat at him. "I've had two drinks. Do you know how many you used to imbibe when you first came to Eldora?"

Ceis'f froze and glared at her. She was being purposely hurtful, but she didn't care. The way Ceis'f had been acting since they reached Eleysia had pushed her over the edge. She could hardly even look at him, and he was her only string tethering her to home.

"I had reason," he snapped.

"Of course you did."

She turned her back to him and pushed down another corridor. This time, she could tell he was following her.

She stopped in the middle of the hallway and whirled on him. "Stop following me!"

"I will not let you go wandering off onto the palace grounds on a holy night with a temper while you're full of drink," Ceis'f said calmly.

There was fire under his words, and she could practically see the flames licking at his fingertips. She had upset him enough to draw out his magic.

"On a holy night in Eldora, I would have my hands in the earth, and my body would be full of energy. I wouldn't need a drink because there would be enough power within me to satiate my thirst. But we're not in Eldora, and right now, I'm not a princess for you to look after. So, leave me alone tonight," she commanded. She tilted her chin up, like the princess she was.

"Like it or not, Ava, you're stuck with me."

"Ugh!"

That was the last thing she'd wanted to hear.

Avoca took off down the hallway. She could hear voices coming from an adjacent lot and saw the Queen and her daughter, Brigette, facing off with each other.

"But I *love* him, Mother!" the Princess yelled. "You cannot do this!"

"I am still Queen, Brigette. And so long as you are heir to the throne and live in my palace, you will do as I say until I draw my last breath, so help me Creator!" the Queen said.

Avoca shook her head and kept running. That felt all too familiar. And though she had never loved another man while in Eldora, she could feel the weight of the one who had been forced upon her, chasing after her down the hallway.

Avoca nearly ran headfirst into a large man blocking the hallway.

"*Ooph*," she said, stopping short. He looked like a guard, but he was in party attire. "Excuse me."

Ceis'f caught up to her then, and the man looked them both over and then stepped aside.

Avoca took another turn, opening herself up to her magic and finding the source of the earth. It led her out a back exit of the palace. She was facing a large lake and could see the beautiful palace grounds stretch before her. She took a healing breath and held on to it. Her magic listened to her call, and she dropped to the ground to soak up the energy from the earth, as if satiating the hunger of a starving man.

"Creator," she breathed. "Thank you."

"Ava," Ceis'f called. "You're practically blinding with power. Cut it loose."

She shook her head and drank more in. "It's amazing, Ceis'f."

"You need to stop," he demanded. "There's water everywhere. You don't need so much earth."

She rounded on him. "That's easy for you to say. Your main element is everywhere," she said, gesturing toward the sky.

"And it all smells wrong, Ava! I'm used to the forest air…the mountain air," he said softer. "This is city air. It hardly calls to me the same. Now, get up, and let it go. If you want to feel in your element, then we should get off this island with hundreds of filthy humans and go home!"

"Leave her alone," a voice sounded behind them.

Avoca lifted her head at the sound and smiled. *Ahlvie.* "You're here."

"Stay out of this," Ceis'f growled. His voice was low and dangerous.

He had unconsciously shifted into a fighting stance. Avoca could see his flames licking at the palms of his hands.

Orden grabbed onto Ahlvie and tried to haul him back. "Come on, Ahlvie. This isn't your fight."

"Yeah, listen to the old man," Ceis'f taunted.

Orden glared at him. "I've stuck up for you through all of this. Tried to stay out of your business. Tried to keep all of you together. But you're all determined to kill each other, aren't you?"

"If that's what it takes," Ceis'f growled low. The flames traveled up his arms, igniting with his rage.

"Then so be it," Orden said, releasing Ahlvie and crossing his arms.

Ahlvie cocked a smile and took light, easy steps, as if he didn't' see Ceis'f's flames. "Nice trick," he teased.

"There's more where this came from."

"Ceis'f, stop it," Avoca said. She glared at him. "You're acting like a child."

"This is a long time coming, Ava," Ceis'f spat. "We're going to have to settle this here and now."

"There is *nothing* to settle!" Avoca cried.

"She's right. When are you going to get it through your head?" Ahlvie said. He actually smiled.

That was the thing about Ahlvie. Everything was a joke and carefree. But she knew, underneath that facade, he was very serious about his friends and extremely loyal, not to mention a skilled fighter.

"She doesn't want to go home. She doesn't want you to try to control her. She just doesn't want you."

Ceis'f glared, and without a second thought, he shot a fireball toward Ahlvie. Ahlvie's eyes grew, but he threw himself out of the way. He rolled into a ball and then landed back on his feet.

"Can't take the truth?" Ahlvie taunted.

"That's not the truth."

Ceis'f pushed a burst of air right at Ahlvie. He couldn't dodge that blast quickly enough and ended up getting knocked backward ten feet, landing on his ass.

"If it's not the truth," Ahlvie said, staggering back to his feet, "then why are you fighting me?"

"Because you're a lying, manipulative, wretched human, just like the rest of them!" Ceis'f yelled, losing it.

He pushed another blast of air toward Ahlvie, but Avoca had had enough.

She drank in the magic that the fresh earth had given her and rocked the ground at Ceis'f's feet. He tried to stand against the onslaught, but even he couldn't avoid the effects of her magic. She was stronger than him. Only barely.

"No more, Ceis'f," she commanded. "It's over."

She reached for more and more. She took water from the lake, swirled it around his body, and then threw him backward. He landed several feet away from her. She could see the anger clearly written on his face, but he would never come after her.

"Ava…"

"Ahlvie is *not* like the people who killed your family!" she yelled. "Not Ahlvie. Not Cyrene. Not Orden. Not Maelia. They are good and kind and flawed. Flawed like everyone is! If you cannot see that and accept that, then you are worse than the people who took your village from you. The loss of Aonia was horrible. So many Leifs were lost at one time due to savagery and the unknown, but holding on to the hatred and letting it be the fuel for your every action has poisoned you! And I could *never* be with someone who hates so fiercely." Avoca turned from Ceis'f and looked at Ahlvie. He was staring at her, wide-eyed but unafraid. "I want someone who loves."

Their eyes met, and her heart leaped at the possibilities in that one gaze. She had no idea what she was doing. Getting involved with a human was…a terrible idea. She would live for hundreds, likely even thousands, of years, and he would have such a short life in comparison. The notion of loving someone she would lose was terrifying and horrifying, but she couldn't let that fear rule her life the way hatred ruled Ceis'f's.

Avoca could feel the wrath coming off of Ceis'f, but she just didn't care. She was tired of the control and the tiptoeing around Ceis'f. She wanted this. *What else matters?*

She cleared the distance between she and Ahlvie, put her hand on the back of his neck, and pulled his lips down on top of hers. Her magic fled her body so suddenly at his touch that it left her body numb. In that moment, all she could feel was Ahlvie's lips on her mouth, the hungry way he seemed to devour her, and the need rolling off of him. It had been growing for months. She had been an idiot for ignoring it.

She would rather live, truly live, with him for even a short life than live without him for eternity.

And then she heard a scream, as if it were ricocheting throughout her skull, and the bond that tethered her to Cyrene exploded. Avoca broke from Ahlvie's lips and nearly fell over as she gasped for breath.

"What? What's wrong?" Ahlvie asked, reaching for her.

"Cyrene," she whispered.

40

The RELEASE

CYRENE GRABBED AT THE DOOR HANDLE AND PULLED WITH all her might. She rattled it, using her weight to try to wrench it open, but it was no good. She couldn't open the door. Alise and Robard had locked her inside a dark room in the middle of who-knows-where in the palace.

"Help!" she screamed at the top of her lungs.

She screamed and screamed for someone to find her until her entire body ached, and her voice was hoarse. If she kept this up, she would lose her voice, and then no one would ever find her.

This couldn't be happening. She had been so tuned in to what was happening to Avoca that she wasn't even paying attention to Robard.

Creator! I am such an idiot.

She hadn't felt comfortable with Robard, yet she had allowed him to lead her. Of course, Alise was in league with him all along. She had thought that Alise was angry and bitter, but she had thought that it was over. Cyrene should have known that Alise was plotting while she was silent. She didn't even know why Alise hated her so much!

Is it simply because I am an Affiliate? Or is it something more…something to do with Dean? It couldn't just be that she was overprotective. There was protective, and then there was locking your brother's girlfriend in a dark room, away from the rest of the palace.

Cyrene's frustration built. She could not stop here and let herself waste away in this stupid room until someone stumbled upon her. Alise didn't know whom she was messing with, and Cyrene had every intention of proving it to her.

Her magic tingled under her skin. Fear pricked at her. Without Dean, there was no way she was going to be able to control this. Her whole body quaked as she opened herself up to the infinite power. It was too much. She knew already that she couldn't do anything in small doses. The energy swelled in her. With this much, she could destroy this whole room. With much more…the whole palace could come crumbling down on top of her head. She wasn't focused on an enemy, as she had been in the past.

She steeled herself and bit back a sob. She was going to hurt someone. But she didn't know if she would ever find a teacher to tell her how to control her magic. She would just have to figure it out on her own. If she didn't use her magic now, she would never get out of here.

Cyrene took a few steadying breaths, trying to remember Avoca's meditation practices in the woods. But she couldn't sense anything around her. Just stone and more stone. Nothing to grasp on to. Nothing to tether her to the world, except the pulse of her magic within her and the bond she shared with Avoca.

Reaching for the bond, she stretched her hands out toward the door. Through the pain of the energy filling her up to the brim, she released her hold on everything but the bond.

The wall in front of her exploded with such force that Cyrene was knocked off her feet and whooshed back against the far wall. Her head cracked against the sandstone wall, and she slumped on the ground. Dust was everywhere, and she ached all over.

She held strong and fast to the bond with Avoca as dizziness crashed over her, and she felt herself slipping toward unconsciousness.

Her fingers went to her head. A huge knot was already forming where she had crashed against the wall. No wonder she was almost losing consciousness.

Avoca.

She called to Avoca through their bond but had no response. She had no idea if it was even possible for Avoca to hear her. Still, Cyrene tugged on the bond and hoped Avoca would hear her.

Cyrene pushed up onto her feet and stared down at her ice-blue dress in dismay. It was covered in dust and torn at the bottom. Nothing she could do about it now.

Cyrene lurched out of the room and stared at her handiwork. A giant crater was carved through the wall of the room and barreled through other rooms as far as Cyrene could see. She shuddered at the full weight of her power and continued down the hall. She put her hand on the wall for support, trying not to lose consciousness.

Cyrene turned the corner and saw two women striding toward her. "Help me!" she called to them in a hoarse whisper.

They looked at each other and then curiously back at Cyrene. One of them nodded to the other.

"Yes, I see her," the other woman said.

"Please help," Cyrene said again.

"Serafina, what are you doing, roaming the castle grounds?" the woman asked. She was about medium height with brown skin and long spiral, curly black hair.

Cyrene startled. "What?"

She turned to the woman standing next to her, who looked very similar to the other woman. A little bit taller perhaps but with the same dark skin and black hair in slightly looser waves with so much body and volume that it almost looked out of control.

"What have we told you a hundred times over? You can't just wander around the grounds at night. You're more closely connected to the elements on holidays, and it's even worse for someone like you."

Cyrene stumbled forward. "What...what did you call me?"

"Serafina, you need to be careful," the first woman said with a shake of her head. "You can't use yourself up. We heard the commotion. We know you're struggling again."

"I'm not Serafina," Cyrene said, latching on to the wall.

The women looked at each other with raised eyebrows.

"You mean...this isn't a dream?" the second woman asked. "I could have sworn we were sleeping again."

"Sera only shows up in dreams. That was a long time ago."

"Did you...know Serafina?" Cyrene asked carefully. A splitting headache was ripping through her, but she felt more alert with the strangeness that was happening before her. "Domina Serafina?"

"Well, she was just a Doma when we knew her," the first woman continued. "She didn't become Domina and rule the council until a few years later," she rambled.

The second woman jabbed her in the side.

"Oh!" the first woman squeaked.

"What is going on?" Cyrene asked.

Both women closely studied her.

"You're not a vision?"

Cyrene shook her head.

"Then, who are you?"

"My name is Cyrene Strohm. I'm an Affiliate from Byern. I came to Eleysia with Prince Dean."

Both women recoiled.

"That can't be."

"An Affiliate?"

"No, there hasn't been one in years."

"Certainly not one like her."

"Um," Cyrene said, "excuse me?"

"Don't mind my sister. She's always been a little hotheaded," the first woman said.

"And you're as cold as ice," she spat back.

"Don't even start with me, or I'll make you wish your flames could withstand an ice storm."

"Excuse me!" Cyrene said louder, halting their fast speech. "You wouldn't happen to know anyone by the names of Matilde and Vera, would you?" Her heart leaped with hope that, perhaps through all of this horrible mess, something good would come of it.

"Where did you learn those names, child?"

"Basille Selby sent me here to find two women named Matilde and Vera. You're them, aren't you?"

"Basille Selby," they said in unison.

"Yes. He gave me a book," Cyrene said. She felt her body weakening and slumped forward. "I'm sorry. I...everything hurts."

The second woman walked forward. She reached her hand out and touched Cyrene's face. She took a deep breath, her eyes widening. "How much did you use?" She turned back to the other woman. "You're going to need to do this."

Her sister stepped forward until she was eye level with Cyrene. She cupped Cyrene's face in her hands and closed her eyes. After a pregnant pause, Cyrene felt ice ripping through her body. Her teeth chattered, and she arced away from the woman's touch, but she held on tightly.

Then, suddenly, it was over, and Cyrene was left with a lingering chill in her bones. But everything else was gone. She was completely healed. Her headache was gone. Every ache and pain in her body was removed. Her body naturally healed quickly, but this was more.

This was magic.

"I am Vera," the woman whispered. "And this is my sister, Matilde. Though we do not go by those names at court in this generation. You can call me Mari, and Mati goes by Kathrine."

Cyrene nearly sobbed. "I have been looking for you everywhere."

"I assure you, Cyrene, we have been looking for you for much longer."

The
MASTER DOMAS

MATILDE AND VERA. KATHRINE AND MARI.

Whatever they chose to be called, it didn't matter to Cyrene. All that mattered was that they were real.

They were real. They were here. And, as much as she hated to admit it, Basille Selby was right. They had found her.

Running footsteps pattered on the ground behind them. Cyrene stood hastily and turned to face whoever was coming their way. She almost put herself in front of Matilde and Vera to shield them from the intruders, but then she realized how ridiculous that would be. Two Master Domas who had managed to evade notice for two millennia had to be infinitely more powerful than she was, and surely, they needed no protecting.

Avoca rounded the corner. "Cyrene! You're alive! Oh Creator! I'm sorry. I shouldn't have left you." She looked between Cyrene and the two women at her sides and frowned. "What's going on? What's wrong?"

Matilde purposely tottered forward. "Well, if you aren't the spitting image of your mother."

Vera shook her head. "Grandmother, I'd wager, Kathrine."

Avoca frowned. "What?"

"We have been gone from Eleysia for too long, it seems," Vera continued.

"Absolutely too long," Matilde said.

Avoca's eyes were as big as saucers. "Cyrene, who are these people?"

Ahlvie and Orden appeared around the corner. They both doubled over with their hands resting on their knees.

"Creator, Avoca!" Ahlvie cried. "Warn me before you go running off like that."

Orden seemed to assess what was going on and straightened up. His chest was still heaving from exertion. "What's going on?"

Matilde raised an eyebrow at Cyrene. "Friends of yours?"

"Yes," Cyrene confirmed. "This is Avoca, Ahlvie, and Orden."

"And who are you?" Ahlvie asked.

"Manners on that one," Vera chided.

Ahlvie flashed her a smile.

"He means," Orden said, "who the hell are you and what are you doing to Cyrene?"

"This," Cyrene said with a dramatic pause, "is Matilde and Vera."

All three of her friend's mouths dropped open at the same time. Cyrene wasn't sure if they had even believed that Matilde and Vera could be found. They had been away from home for so long, searching and searching with such little information.

Cyrene would be the first to admit that she had been losing hope, but everything had changed. All it had taken was for her to lose control of her powers and cause a massive explosion—the very thing she had been avoiding since she got here.

"Thank you for the introductions," Vera said politely. "However, in the palace, I go by Mari, and my sister goes by Kathrine."

Avoca reverently ambled forward. "It is an honor to meet you both." She pressed the tips of her fingers to her lips in a sign of deference.

"Oh, I have missed Leif manners," Vera said with a smile.

"You know about…Leifs?" Avoca asked.

Matilde snort-laughed. "Know about them? You have much to learn."

"Perhaps they should not learn it while out here, in the middle of a tunnel," Vera suggested.

"Yes, of course, Mari. I was just getting to that."

"Shall we depart then?"

"Yes, I think so."

Matilde and Vera walked forward at a rapid pace. Cyrene jogged to keep up with them. She had no idea where they were walking to, but she knew that she desperately needed their teachings. Her friends followed in her wake.

"I suppose we'll have to get her out of the country," Vera said.

"I think Ika Roa would be perfect this time of year," Matilde said.

"Yes. I do hate that we have to leave so soon after the Eos. I would have preferred to show more respect to the gods with the elements so near."

"I believe the gods just gave us a blessing."

Vera glanced over at Cyrene. "Yes. Ika Roa then."

"That way, we can start from scratch. She has the power and something else I'm not sure about," Matilde continued, as if Cyrene wasn't standing right next to them. "Something powerful though."

Vera nodded. "I feel it, too. We'll have to discover what that means at a later date."

"Yes. We should bring the Leif girl. She's young, but they always look that way."

"What exactly are you talking about?" Cyrene asked in confusion. "Ika Roa?"

"We need to leave the country immediately," Vera said as they rounded another corner.

"What?" Cyrene gasped. Why?"

The women looked at each other and then proceeded up a flight of stairs without answering. They took their time climbing to the top. Matilde griped under her breath about flying, and Cyrene just stared at her in confusion.

"Don't mind Kathrine. She misses the sky."

Cyrene nodded, having no idea what that meant.

Vera took a deep breath when they reached the top of the stairs. "Ika Roa seems like the perfect place to begin your training. And you must be trained, or you'll be a danger to everyone and everything."

"At the rate you're going, you'll burn yourself out," Matilde warily told her.

Cyrene shuddered at that thought. She couldn't lose her magic, and she didn't want to harm anyone. *But leave the country?*

She was about to say something, but Matilde turned her attention to Avoca.

"Shira is still Queen in Eldora, isn't she? I heard she took the throne after Eve'a fell in battle."

Avoca's eyes widened again. Matilde and Vera were talking about something that had happened two thousand years ago.

"Yes," Avoca peeped.

"Perhaps we should go there," Matilde said dreamily. "We haven't been in Eldora in so long, Mari. Just think about the woods…"

"But if she's anything like Sera, then it will be water first. The rivers aren't enough. We'll need all of the Lakonia."

Cyrene's head was spinning. "You have to take me out of Eleysia to train me?"

"Yes, and we should move with haste," Matilde said irritably. "Are the boys coming with us?"

Vera cast her gaze over Ahlvie and then Orden. "They might as well. They already know too much."

"Wait!" Cyrene cried, silencing their endless tirade. "I can't leave Eleysia. Why can't we train here?"

"Just like Sera," Matilde mumbled under her breath.

"Let me guess…something to do with this Prince Dean you mentioned?" Vera said.

Cyrene's cheeks heated, but she couldn't deny it. She didn't want to leave Dean. She wanted to see what could be with him. At the moment, he felt essential to her magic. Maybe it was selfish to want this…him. But she had walked away from Edric without even a backward glance. Her heart couldn't do the same to Dean.

"Yes."

"Oh, how history always finds a way of repeating itself," Matilde said. She shook her head and looked at Vera, as if to say, *You reason with her.*

"Especially when they erase it and have no hope of learning from their mistakes," Vera said in response. She shrugged her shoulders at Matilde. "I philosophize; you implement, Kathrine. So…implement."

Matilde grumbled under her breath and tossed her wild hair to one side. "Must we stay in Eleysia? Is this Dean so important?"

Cyrene nodded. He had become so important to her in such a short period of time, but he *was* very important to her. She had to see this through.

"Can you still train me here?" Cyrene asked.

Matilde huffed in protest and looked to Vera. They seemed to be speaking their own language for a moment.

"We have to," Vera said to Matilde.

"Always making things difficult." Matilde wrenched a door open. "In, all of you, before I change my mind."

"Should I go find Maelia?" Ahlvie asked Cyrene.

"There are *more* of you?" Matilde asked. "How many people actually know about your powers?"

Cyrene bit her lip. "Um…more than one."

"Gods!" Matilde cried, walking away. "We're nearing a two-millennia ban on magic and the Circadian Prophecy's potential conclusion. And the first magical wielder we've seen with any strength in hundreds of years is running around with a Leif, proclaiming herself to anyone who knows what to look for. If we felt that disaster, Mari, then you know we weren't the only ones!"

"Do you mind sealing the room before you start going off on philosophical diatribes?" Vera asked, pursing her lips.

"That's normally your area of expertise," Matilde said.

Matilde dramatically waved her hand in the air. Avoca's eyes widened again. Even Cyrene, who had practically no knowledge of magical properties, could sense that what she had done was powerful magic. And she had wielded it effortlessly.

Vera smiled at her sister and then sank into a chair. Cyrene looked around and saw that they were in a quaint sitting room. There weren't any rugs down. Only a few wooden chairs rested against the wall before a low table. A few cushions were tossed in front of the table. And there were old, really old, paintings on the walls.

"Please have a seat," Vera said.

Avoca immediately dropped onto a cushion, as if it were the most natural thing in the world. Ahlvie took the one next to her, but he looked significantly less comfortable sitting on the floor. Orden leaned back against the wall, crossed his arms, and stared around at the lot of them. Cyrene dropped into one of the chairs, but Matilde remained standing, pacing back and forth across the room. She didn't seem to be able to stand still.

"So, by my estimation, you have a long way to go," Matilde said, walking to one end of the room and then back. "What exactly were you doing in that hallway anyway? The amount of energy you used could have had disastrous consequences."

"I…was locked inside," Cyrene said.

Vera tilted her head. "Why?"

"Honestly, I'm not sure. Dean's sister, Alise, and one of his soldiers, Robard, locked me in there. I don't know what their motive was or what they were doing. At first, I thought it was because Alise hated me and didn't want Dean to be with me, but I think that's such an extreme. The reasoning doesn't make sense."

"We can get to the bottom of the issue later," Matilde said. "All I'm gathering is that you used a very powerful energy blast to *unlock a door*?"

"Um...yes," she whispered.

"That's child's play. I can give you five hundred different ways to use the energy you possess to open a door without destroying half of the palace."

"Well, I don't know any of those," Cyrene said. "I had to get out of there, and that was all I knew how to do. At least, I didn't black out."

"You've been having blackouts?" Vera asked softly, her voice serious and concerned.

"Yes, nearly every time I use my magic in any significant capacity. You can be upset with me for how I got through that door, but I'm not trained. The only training I've had is with Avoca in the woods, and she has Leif magic, which is different than Domas." Cyrene sprang to her feet. "Neither of you knows the difficulties I've already gone through to find you so that *you* can train me. I did the best I could, and that got me here. I think the very fact that I'm still alive—despite half of the Byern and Aurumian armies, three Braj, and a pack of Indres tried to capture or kill me—is pretty impressive."

Vera and Matilde looked at each other, and then huge smiles spread across their faces.

"Good, they said.

"Good?" Cyrene asked.

"We wanted to make sure you were ready," Vera said.

"How did you get that I was ready to train out of *that*?"

"You faced adversity and came ahead, all on your own. Most Doma who go untrained don't last past seventeen. None of your strength," Matilde informed her.

"So?"

"So, you're ready," Vera said. "We'll train you."

"When do we start?" Cyrene asked, clapping her hands together.

"Now," Matilde told her.

"Now?" Cyrene blurted out.

Vera stood. "Yes, I think now sounds perfect."

42

The

TRAINING

CYRENE FOLLOWED IN VERA'S WAKE AS THEY EXITED THE castle a short while later and hurried out to the docks. This wasn't exactly how she had pictured celebrating the Eos holiday, but she couldn't have been more excited.

Matilde had left at once to begin preparations for whatever was to come. Meanwhile, Cyrene had sent her friends off to tie up loose ends. Orden had rushed to find Maelia and let her know what had happened. Avoca had gone to collect the *Book of the Doma* and Cyrene's Presenting letter from her rooms. While it had been up to Ahlvie to find Dean and let him know what had happened. Cyrene had really preferred to do that one herself, but once everything was underway, Vera had bustled her along to collect the things she needed. It seemed that Vera was as anxious to get started as Cyrene was.

With book and letter in a leather pouch, Cyrene and Vera met Matilde siting in a gondola on the water. There was no gondolier in sight.

"All right. In you go," Vera said, prodding her forward.

Cyrene carefully eased herself into the boat and dropped her bag onto the floorboard. Vera followed in behind her, taking the seat next to Matilde.

Matilde smirked at her. "Are you ready for your first lesson?"

"Absolutely."

"Row our boat to the Third Harbor. We have a lot of work to do, and we'd like to get started as soon as possible."

Cyrene skeptically eyed them both and then glanced at the oar. "You're serious?"

"Very," Matilde said.

Vera nodded her head.

"I've never rowed a boat in my life. Well," she said, "just once in my life, and that was because I feared it was life or death."

"Then, fear this is life or death," Matilde told her.

Cyrene saw that they weren't going to budge on this, and she shakily stood. She walked to the stern of the boat and reached for the paddle. She wanted to tell them how ridiculous this exercise was going to be. She had no idea what she was doing, it was the middle of the night, they were going to lose the entire night for training. A gondola wasn't like the little dinghy she had used to navigate the underground waterways in the Byern castle. But she steeled herself and decided she would give it a try before giving up.

Taking the paddle in her hand, she pushed off from the dock and rowed out onto the open lake. She rowed it about halfway across the lake before her arms were aching, and her breathing was heavy. With every stroke that she pushed, she appreciated what the gondoliers did. They must have the most powerful arm muscles in the world to get across the water so effortlessly all the time. And back muscles. They were going to hurt in the morning. She just knew it.

"Is there a point to this?" she asked as she finally approached the gate to exit the lake.

"We were just seeing how long it would take for you to realize that you should use your magic for this," Matilde said dryly.

Cyrene froze. "But I thought you were going to train me to do that."

They glanced at each other, as if they were reading each other's minds, and then up at Cyrene.

"We are," Vera said simply.

"I'm dangerous though. I could destroy the island if I tried to move the boat."

"We would never let that happen," Matilde told her. "But you must start somewhere, and this is where we'll begin. Now, grasp for your powers."

"Gently," Vera amended. "Like a lover's caress."

Cyrene reached for her powers, and they came all too readily to her fingertips. It was euphoric.

"Now, each power has its own thread."

"A pulse?" Cyrene asked. "That's what Avoca called them."

"Similar, yes, but within you, not within the substance. If you want to manipulate water, you have to first find the energy within yourself to do that work," Vera instructed calmly. "The number of elements you can manipulate determines how many different energies you can feel within. You clearly have all five, and Spirit is the strongest. But to work with Spirit safely, you need to master the other four elements. Let's start with water, shall we?" Vera took a breath. "I'll show you what I mean."

Vera put her hand out in front of herself, and a warm band of gold light wrapped around her arm to her wrist. She slowly and deliberately let Cyrene see the thread of power between her and the water as their boat drifted forward of its own accord.

She dropped her hand and smiled. "Now, you try."

Cyrene closed her eyes and fumbled for the thread within her that called to the water. She had felt the energies within her for months. Now, she just needed to figure out how to harvest them.

Vera was right. Spirit was the most powerful. It almost seemed to push all the others out of the way when Cyrene stretched down inside herself. She didn't even know what it could do, but it was so blinding and begged for attention that she almost wanted to open herself up to it. But she pushed the urge aside and took ahold of the line that brought water to her fingertips. She used the movement to push the boat forward, just as she had seen Vera do.

But instead of flowing smoothly, the boat jerked out of control, as if propelled by a tidal wave. A gust of water came over and crashed down onto Cyrene, knocking her from her feet and shoving her onto the floorboard of the boat. The boat stopped moving just before hitting the gate that let them exit the royal grounds.

Cyrene was coughing up lake water as she pushed herself into a sitting position. When her eyes met Matilde and Vera, they were both still seated calmly and serenely. Not a drop of water was on either of them while Cyrene was sure she looked like a fish out of water.

"Very good," Vera said.

"Adequate," Matilde said. "But not the worst we've ever seen."

"I'm drenched," Cyrene groaned.

"That means you were able to access water...even if it seems as if that is not your issue," Vera said.

"Too much power, if anything," Matilde agreed.

"We'll need to start smaller."

"Much smaller."

"Are either of you going to clue me in on what's going on?" Cyrene asked. She was thankful for the warm weather for once because she would have been frozen solid if in Byern.

Matilde shook her head, as if Cyrene's question was of little import. "Vera will guide us out of here, so we can get to our desired destination before sunrise. Feel your powers, Cyrene, and follow her lead, but don't try to do anything. Just learn the way she does it."

The gate rose before them. Cyrene wasn't sure if that was the result of the guards who were usually stationed overhead or magic, but she didn't pay any further attention. She just focused on what Vera was doing. She couldn't *actually* see the magic Vera was using. And she didn't entirely know how she was doing it. But there was a sense or a feeling to it. When she concentrated, she could tell what was happening and how much power was being used. If that was common, then she understood why they had freaked out about the amount of magic she had used to get out of the cell Alise and Robard had thrown her in. Moving the boat forward was a millionth of the amount of power she had harnessed to do that.

The journey to Third Harbor was much smoother with Vera leading the way. Soon, they were docked, and despite the fact that Cyrene was still sopping wet, she followed Matilde and Vera off the boat and to a much larger vessel.

Matilde spoke to a man for a few minutes, and Cyrene surveyed him. He was a burly man with a large jagged scar across the right side of his face. He had long hair tied back into a knot at the base of his head with a captain's hat on his head.

Cyrene's jaw dropped. "Captain De la Mora?" she asked.

The man raised an eyebrow at her as his eyes crawled over her wet body where the sheer material clung to her. "Do I know you, girl?"

Cyrene crossed her arms over her breasts. "We met in Albion earlier this year."

"I don't remember you," he said dismissively.

Oh, but Cyrene remembered him. She would remember him anywhere. He was the jerk who had refused her, Ahlvie, and Maelia a trip to Eleysia. Captain Lador had agreed to take them out of the harbor, providing their only way out, but he had died. The Braj who had come after Cyrene had killed him. And the new captain, Captain De la Mora, was prejudice against Affiliate and High Order.

"You should," she said stiffly. "You were leaving the country and refused to let me aboard your ship."

The Captain narrowed his eyes at her and then frantically looked between Cyrene and the twins. "An Affiliate. Did you know what she was?" he asked Matilde and Vera.

"Yes, we're quite aware. Now that all of the pleasantries are out of the way, we need to leave straight away."

"I don't transport Affiliates," Captain De la Mora argued.

Matilde shot him a furious look. "You will do just the sort today and every day we need you henceforth."

She walked onto the boat without a backward glance, and Vera followed her. Cyrene gave him a smile and walked forward, but he roughly grabbed her arm.

"Let me pass!"

"I trust these women with all that I am. That's the only reason I'm letting you on this ship. But if you try any funny business…"

"You'll what?" she asked him.

"I'd be happy to throw you overboard and leave you behind," he spat. Then, he pushed past Cyrene and stormed onto the boat.

Cyrene grumbled under her breath but followed him on board. She hadn't even done anything, and people everywhere accused her of being corrupt. Her people had such a bad name, and it frightened her. Now that her eyes were open…she wanted to do something about it.

First things first…her magic.

Captain De la Mora made it perfectly clear to the crew that she was to be avoided at all times, and by the time they finally stopped, Cyrene felt sufficiently isolated. Even Matilde and Vera had stayed together below deck, murmuring to themselves. Cyrene had so many questions for them, least of all how they had survived for two thousand years, but they didn't seem the type to allow questions until they were ready to give answers.

"Be back before sundown, Geof," Matilde said sharply. She was holding a metal bucket and waved it at him.

"I will. Of course, my lovely Kathrine," he said as cheerfully as he could muster. "And Mari."

"You're a good man," Vera said. She patted his arm twice and then walked toward the rope ladder that one of the men had thrown down for them.

Cyrene smiled halfheartedly at the Captain, who just glared back at her. Then, she climbed down the ladder and onto a small boat. They arrived at shore on what looked like an isolated volcanic island. It was utter paradise with tropical palm trees, crystal-clear blue water, and pearly-white sand. The mountain loomed high above them, and Cyrene hoped there wasn't going to be volcanic activity anytime soon. There hadn't been an eruption in her lifetime, and she hoped to keep it that way.

Once the boat was nearly out of eyesight, Matilde and Vera cleared a spot in the sand and took a seat. Cyrene gingerly followed their lead.

"Before we begin," Cyrene said quickly, "can I ask you one question?"

"You just did," Matilde responded quickly.

"I think one will be enough. There's so much to teach you," Vera said.

"And I have so much to tell you. Like about this," she said, reaching into her bag and producing the *Book of the Doma* that had brought her here in the first place.

Matilde and Vera gasped at the same time. Their eyes in the early morning light were bright and violet as they widened with surprise.

"Where did you get that?" Vera murmured reverently.

"My sister bought it off an Eleysian peddler named Basille Selby, and it was given to me as a gift for my seventeenth birthday," Cyrene told them.

"May I?" Vera asked.

She reached for the book, and Cyrene regretfully offered it.

"Basille must not have known," Matilde said, "or else he would have brought it to us."

"No. How could he have known?" Vera asked.

She flipped through the pages, and Cyrene was sure that she had never looked happier than with a book open in her lap.

"Have you tried to read it?" Matilde asked. Her eyes darted up to Cyrene in panic.

"I did try to read it at first, but I lost minutes and then hours of time. It started to scare me, especially since I was the only one I knew who could even see the words."

They both nodded in understanding.

"Yes. It is Doma made. The secret of its construction was lost before we were even accepted."

"I haven't told you everything," Cyrene admitted. "The first time I used my magic was to save my own life, and I blacked out. I had a vision or a dream or something of Serafina going through her own Presenting."

Matilde and Vera shared one of their meaningful looks.

"When you had this vision, were you looking at Serafina, or could you interact with her?" Matilde asked

"No. I *was* her," Cyrene told them. "At least, I was trapped in her body, going through all of the motions of what she was doing. I mean…I met Viktor Dremylon. They were in love and wanted to marry before she left to be a Doma."

Vera startled. "You found that out in your vision?" She thoughtfully chewed on her lip. "Most people don't know that anymore. They are just bitter enemies instead of bitter lovers."

"Yes. How tragic," Matilde said sarcastically. "Tell us more about this vision. You went through her Presenting?"

"Yes. I was there with her through the tunnel. I opened the book. I saw the words written on the wall. When I got back to my body, I could read the pages. They suddenly made sense."

Both women stared at her wordlessly. She had clearly shocked them.

"What does that mean?"

"That means, Cyrene," Vera said shakily, "that you are the first person in two thousand years to be given access to Doma secrets and the ability to truly unlock your Doma power."

"When I was in Eldora, Queen Shira told me it was the lost *Book of the Doma*. I've read some of it, but I couldn't do anything the book said. I had a block against my powers that I had to work against before I could even access them."

"Yes, that's right," Matilde said. "This is the lost *Book of the Doma*, and eventually, you will learn how to access its secrets, but this doesn't change anything at the moment. You are much too inexperienced to be able to work from the book. The only thing more powerful for Doma, besides this book, was the Domina diamond, and that, I fear, has been lost forever."

"Then, we should get started," Vera said. "This is just another sign."

"A sign of what?" Cyrene asked.

Matilde pursed her lips and glared at Vera.

"Look, everyone keeps mentioning the Circadian Prophecy and how I'm a part of it, but I don't know what that means. Does it have to do with this?" Cyrene asked, shoving her Presenting letter in front of the women.

They read the crumpled paper.

WHAT YOU SEEK LIES WHERE YOU CANNOT SEEK IT.

WHAT YOU FIND CANNOT BE FOUND.

THE THING YOU DESIRE ABOVE ALL ELSE RISKS ALL ELSE.

THE THING YOU FIGHT FOR CANNOT BE WON.

WHEN ALL SEEMS LOST, WHAT WAS LOST CAN BE FOUND.

WHEN ALL BEND, YOU CANNOT BE AS YOU WERE.

"Where did you get this?" Vera asked. She ran a finger down the paper.

"It is my Presenting letter from court when I was made an Affiliate. I thought the first two lines meant that I had magic because I couldn't seek it, and it couldn't be found, but I don't really understand any of it."

"This is a small section of the Circadian Prophecy, yes," Matilde verified. "Many who have studied this part have no better understanding of it. Educated men and women have worked on interpretations of the Prophecy for generations. We can only follow the portents the way that we view them."

"And how do you view them?" she asked desperately.

Vera sighed. "That we were spared in the War of the Light for a reason, and we will do what we can to help bring balance back to this world."

"And, to do that, you need more training," Matilde cut in. "So, let's get started."

43

The WATER

CYRENE SPENT THE REST OF THE DAY LEARNING TO REMOVE exactly one drop of water from the bucket and transferring it to another bucket. If she had thought she was wet from trying to row the boat, she was wrong. She had no control over what she was doing. She was more likely to drown herself with the water then she was to pick up a single, solitary droplet.

By lunchtime, she'd had no success. She could dump the entire bucket onto her lap over and over and over again, but moving a single drop was not possible. She was starving and could eat an entire feast table, but Matilde and Vera had only packed a light meal. Not to mention, she was exhausted as she hadn't had any sleep the night before.

After eating, Cyrene concentrated again and felt a familiar burst of energy rush through her. She knew she should push it back and only use a small amount, but rationing the power was more difficult than drawing so much to her body that she couldn't breathe.

"This is hopeless," she grumbled under her breath.

It didn't help that Matilde and Vera were endlessly patient. Two thousand years seemed to have given them more patience than the average person.

"Hopeless is only for those who give up," Vera said.

"You will keep trying until you have it," Matilde said. "There is no other option."

Cyrene ground her teeth and focused on the task at hand. *One droplet. Just one tiny droplet.* She could tear down a building but not move one droplet of water. Just as she was cursing herself, a tiny drop of water rose out of the bucket. Cyrene shrieked and jumped into the air. The water fumbled and then fell down onto the beach, disappearing into the sand, but she couldn't even care. She had done it.

Vera smiled. "See?"

"Again," Matilde said. She was smiling, too.

By the end of the day, Cyrene could successfully move one droplet of water from one bucket to the next. She couldn't do it very confidently and definitely not when there were distractions. She also couldn't move much more than that without soaking herself all over again. But it was a start.

When Captain De la Mora's vessel appeared on the horizon, Cyrene could barely stand on her own two feet she was so tired.

Matilde quickly grabbed the buckets and sloshed the water out onto the ground. "Pretty good," she said.

"Pretty good?" Cyrene asked. "This morning, I couldn't even feel the water element inside me, let alone move one droplet on its own!"

"But try to move a whole ocean," Matilde said.

"Or find water in the desert," Vera countered.

"Or stop a hurricane."

"Or do anything with a distraction at hand," Vera said with a smile.

"Okay," Cyrene said sullenly, "I get it. Baby steps. But it's an improvement."

"It is," they agreed.

The ride back to the capital left Cyrene feeling ragged and beyond hungry. Her stomach growled, and she had to force down the desire to beg the Captain for any food. He didn't like her as it was.

The Captain insisted on sending a gondolier with their party, which Cyrene was thankful for even though she was sure he hadn't done it for her. But she didn't exactly want to be the one to try to make the boat move on its own all over again. She wasn't entirely sure that Matilde and Vera wouldn't make her do it either.

When they arrived back within the palace gates, Cyrene could see a figure pacing the deck, as if waiting for them. Once they got closer, Cyrene could tell that it was Avoca. She frowned and hoped that her friend was all right. The last time something had happened to her, Cyrene had known by her burst of magic.

Oh. Cyrene had been using magic all day. Avoca must have been worried even though she had known what Cyrene was doing.

Cyrene quickly got out of the boat once it had docked and rushed to Avoca.

"You're all right?" Avoca asked. "You were using small portions but constantly. I could feel how drained you were."

"Starving actually," Cyrene said with a smile. "And tired."

Matilde and Vera appeared behind them.

"Hello, Avoca," Matilde said.

Avoca gave the formal sign of deference for her people.

Vera produced a smile. "If I heard correctly, you said that you felt Cyrene's powers while she was using them?"

Avoca and Cyrene glanced at each other, and then Cyrene shrugged. They had to know one way or another.

"We're Bound," Cyrene told them.

"Well, *that* explains it," Matilde said, looking to Vera.

"Yes, it certainly does." Vera reached for Cyrene's wrist at the same time as Matilde reached for Avoca's. They each ran a finger over the spot where the gold tattoo lay, and it sparkled iridescently in the sun.

"The first in two thousand years," Vera whispered.

"And it still takes the shape of a dragon," Matilde said.

"As it should."

"Who performed the ceremony?"

"My mother," Avoca said.

Both women's lips curved up into wicked smiles as they released their wrists.

"I see. In Eldora?" Matilde asked.

"Yes," Cyrene confirmed. "Avoca saved my life and offered me a blood debt, but her mother suggested we be Bound until her blood debt has been paid."

"I see," Vera said.

They glanced at each other again with huge smiles on their faces.

Then, Vera nodded. "Avoca, you will appear for training with Cyrene at dawn every day henceforth."

"Yes, ma'am," Avoca said confidently.

"Now, off with you, Cyrene. Eat a hearty dinner. We have much work to accomplish tomorrow," Vera said.

"And get a lot of sleep," Matilde warned.

Cyrene nodded. She already realized how exhausting it was, working with her powers. She would need a lot of food and rest to get through all of this.

Cyrene and Avoca walked away from the docks. Cyrene was excited for food, sleep, and a change out of her wet clothes. Her hair had mostly dried, but she was sure she looked less than presentable for society.

"I didn't want to say anything in front of them," Avoca said when they had reached the kitchen.

"Say what?" She loaded her plate up, not caring who saw how much she was about to consume.

"I know you didn't mention Ceis'f to them last night, but he's missing," Avoca told her.

"What?" Cyrene gasped, nearly dropping the plate she was juggling. "What do you mean, missing?"

"Last night, we got into a fight about Ahlvie. I finally made my choice, and now, Ceis'f is gone."

"Ceis'f wouldn't just abandon you," Cyrene said logically. "He loves you. Whether or not you chose him, it's his duty to stay with you. Do you think he's just hiding out?"

"No, I don't. I told him to leave, to go home."

"You've been saying that since we left Eldora."

"This time was different. I was…cruel. Beyond cruel. I used my magic to push him away from me in a vortex of water."

Avoca looked so afraid that Cyrene was afraid for her. Avoca was normally so stoic. The thought of what could frighten her didn't sit well with Cyrene.

"I don't think he's gone. He couldn't just be gone. He's probably just fuming, and he needs to walk it off. Do you truly think he would leave?"

"I don't know," Avoca said. "I'm going to go out and search for him. Rest up for tomorrow, and I'll meet you at the docks."

Cyrene nodded and watched her friend leave. She dug into her food, all the while thinking about everything that had changed in the last day. It felt surreal that she was finally being trained. She had so many questions left unanswered, but the fact that she had made even a tiny bit of progress made her so happy that it almost didn't matter. She would learn everything she needed to know in time. She finally felt justified in leaving her country behind for this. She had been right all along.

By the time she finished eating, she had no energy left. She knew that all she needed now was to find the nearest bed and never leave again.

Staggering down the hallway, she didn't even look up when she heard her name.

"Hmm?" she asked.

"Cyrene, there you are!"

Someone grabbed her shoulders, and she tipped her head to look up into the most beautiful brown eyes. At the look on Dean's face, she smiled and felt a renewed burst of energy flow through her.

"Hey," she whispered.

"Where have you been?" he asked desperately. "I have been waiting for you all day. Ahlvie told me that you had left with Matilde and Vera, but he didn't exactly give specifics. I was worried about you."

"I'm so sorry. I thought that Ahlvie would alleviate your worries. They agreed to train me," she said, dipping her voice lower.

"Cyrene, that's amazing!"

"This is what I've wanted to do since I left Byern, and now, everything is falling into place."

"I'm so happy for you."

Dean threaded his fingers through hers, and a shiver ran up her back. He glanced around the empty hallway and then tugged her away from the main corridors. She turned a corner, and Dean pressed her back into a darkened alcove. His mouth was only inches from hers.

Her exhaustion was wearing off from the excitement of being with him.

"I was really worried about you," he breathed.

"You don't have to worry about me," she said, trapped in his gaze. She teetered on her tiptoes and nearly brushed their lips together. Her heart was racing ahead of her. This felt almost better than reaching for her magic. Definitely better than moving one drop of water at a time all day.

"You're wrong." Then, he softly dropped his mouth down on hers. His lips were tender and slow as they caressed hers. "I will always worry for your safety."

Cyrene's cheeks heated, and she sighed, leaning back against the hard stone of the alcove. "I didn't mean to worry you."

His hands pushed up through her hair and tilted her head back up to look at him. She closed her eyes and sighed. She was so tired, and just the feel of his fingers was lulling her to sleep.

"That feels good."

His mouth found hers, and despite her exhaustion, she pushed back against his lips with more force. She refused to let the fact that she was tired get in the way of her time with Dean.

"Whoa," Dean said, pulling back from her. He rested his forehead against hers, and she could tell he was breathing heavily. "As much as I want this, and I do, I want to make sure you're okay. This didn't scare you away?"

She shook her head. "*This*, most certainly, does not scare me." Then, she kissed him again for good measure.

He laughed. "Good. Because I know Eleysia is different than Byern, and I've been wanting to kiss you since I met you in the woods in Aurum."

"You have not!" she insisted.

"Are you kidding? A gorgeous, feisty woman who wasn't afraid to put me in my place the first time she met me? Someone who pushed back and didn't care about my title?"

"I didn't know about your title."

"And it didn't change a thing."

Cyrene shrugged. "A title is just a title. The person underneath the title is the only thing that matters."

His smile was electric. It was as if no one had ever bothered to see past the prince to the man underneath.

Her legs quivered as exhaustion hit her anew.

His smile turned to concern. "Are you all right?"

"Just tired. I've been training all day and can barely stand."

Dean smirked down at her, and then, before she knew it, he scooped her up in his arms. He held her as if she weighed nothing, carrying her down the empty corridor without a backward glance.

"Dean, what are you doing?" she whisper-shouted at him.

"You've had a very draining day. You should be resting, but I'm not willing to give you up just yet."

"Well, wherever we're going, I can walk there!"

He laughed. "I think I like this."

Dean toed open a door at the end of the hall. Cyrene was about to demand he release her, but the comment was lost on her lips. The room she entered was inherently masculine. All dark colors and hardwood furniture. It was impressively clean with books neatly arranged on a bookshelf that took up an entire wall and a desk full of more books.

But Dean kept moving and opened up another door. This brought her into a darkly furnished sitting area, which connected to a bathing chamber as well as a bedchamber.

Dean gently laid her down on the sofa, and even though she wanted to protest, the comfort of the sofa and the softness of the pillow under her head immediately soothed her.

"These are your rooms?" Cyrene asked shyly.

He nodded and took a seat next to her, resting his arms against the back of the sofa. "Yes."

"They're nice."

Dean shrugged dismissively, as if he wished he could minimize the opulence of his rooms. But he seemed comfortable here, more laid-back. It was like seeing him back in the woods, away from his courtly duties.

Just a man. With a woman. In his rooms.

Cyrene bit her lip and averted her gaze. She needed to slow her thoughts down. Dean had brought her here because she was exhausted, and he wanted more time with her. Nothing else.

"So, tell me everything. What happened? How did they find you?" Dean asked.

Cyrene looked back over at him and smiled. "They were at the party. With a little thanks to your sister, they found me. Just like Basille Selby had said."

"My sister?" Dean asked, confused.

"Alise."

"Creator," he said, running a hand back through his short hair. "What did she do now?"

"She and Robard…locked in a room, and I…kind of blasted the room apart, trying to get out," she confessed. "I was the explosion."

Dean cursed violently and stood. He started pacing angrily. "What was she thinking? And then that explosion. How did you survive something like that? It rattled the palace."

"I don't know what Alise was thinking. I would really like to know what her real problem is with me because it's going past bitterness over you."

"I have no idea what's bothering her. This is beyond ridiculous. She is endangering your life." He ground his teeth. "I thought I made myself clear with Alise before, but I will talk to her again. She needs to stop this business right now."

"I agree, but will you come sit down? You're making me nervous," she said. She could feel her eyelids growing heavy. All she wanted to do was sleep, but Dean was making her want to stay awake.

"Yes. My apologies."

Dean moved forward, and she thought he was going to take his previous seat, but instead, he gently lifted her head from the cushion and sat where her head had last been. He placed the pillow back in his lap. She rested back against him, and he ran his fingers through her long hair. She sighed and snuggled against him. *This is bliss.*

"You're so exhausted."

"I know," she murmured. "Matilde and Vera have been training me to control my powers. It's exhausting."

"Well, get some rest," he encouraged. "I'll be right here."

"What happened to Basille and Brigette?" she murmured in the silence.

Dean sighed. "Basille left Eleysia again. My mother has forbidden them to wed, and Brigette hasn't left her rooms."

"That's so sad for them."

"My mother can be unbearably stubborn when she wants to be. Thankfully, she likes you."

"She does?" Cyrene asked, surprised.

"You're still here, aren't you?"

"Mmm," Cyrene said. She wasn't sure that was the same thing.

Cyrene felt herself drifting off. Him playing with her hair was like a lullaby. She couldn't keep her eyes open. Nothing else existed in the world, except being with Dean right here, right now. He bent down and kissed her forehead, and then she succumbed to her exhaustion.

THE BOUND EFFECT

CYRENE STRETCHED HER ARMS OUT AND YAWNED exaggeratedly. Light filtered in through the window, and she peeked one eye open in protest. She was so tired. Every part of her body hurt. Sleep was her new best friend.

She yawned again, kicking her foot diagonally across her bed when she encountered a body. She squeaked and sharply sat up. She wasn't in her bed, and she had woken up next to someone else.

Creator! How tired was I?

She glanced down at her figure and saw that she was still in the Eos dress she had worn to the party, but it was rumpled and a disaster after the hours of it being soaking wet and then her sleeping on it. She glanced over at the body with rumpled light brown hair—almost blond in the early morning light—a five o'clock shadow against a strong jawline, and the bare back of a very handsome and sleeping Dean Ellison.

Her heart skipped a beat at the sight, and she scooted a little further away from him. *How did I end up in his bed?* The last thing she remembered was Dean running his fingers through her hair on the couch. Not good. She had been so out of it that he had transferred her into his bedroom without her even waking up.

Then, her head snapped to the side as realization hit her. "What time is it?"

Dean's head popped up, and he looked over at her with a crooked grin on his face. "Good morning," he breathed.

Her heart melted a little bit more at those words. *Creator, he is attractive and distracting, and I'm late!*

"I'm late! I was supposed to be at the docks at dawn!"

Cyrene jumped out of bed and rushed for the door. Dean followed after her. He grabbed her hand before she reached the door.

"Let me go! I have somewhere to be. I'm late!"

"Do you really want to be seen running out of my bedchambers in the morning in the clothes you wore to the party?" he asked.

His hands slid down her arms, and she shivered.

No. No, I do not want that. She shook her head.

"Come on. Go this way."

Dean shrugged on a shirt, and she couldn't help but stare at the rippled muscles before they disappeared from view. She was not sad to see him put a shirt on. Definitely not. She was late…not thinking about how defined his chest was. Okay, she definitely was thinking about that.

Dean took her through a back passageway that led her through a much quieter section of the palace and dropped her off right at the corridor where her rooms were.

"Thank you," she said.

She threw her arms around his neck without thinking about it, and he dipped his head down to kiss her. Her breath caught in the early morning. She was seriously reconsidering this leaving thing. She had woken up in his bed after all…and he was making it very hard to walk away.

"I have to go," she said regretfully. "I'm late."

"I start security procedures soon. I won't be around as much," he told her.

"I know you'll find me," she said with a smile before dashing to her room.

She changed as quickly as she could before practically flying down to the docks. Matilde, Vera, and Avoca were standing around a gondola, looking less than pleased, to say the least.

Cyrene was out of breath when she reached them. "My deepest apologies. I don't know how I didn't wake up. I'm never late," she insisted.

"You weren't in your room," Avoca accused.

"Um…"

"And your face is bright red."

"I just ran here!" Cyrene cried.

"What were you doing out all night? You were supposed to be sleeping!"

"I was. I just woke up."

"No one knew where you were," Avoca chided. "So, where were you?"

Cyrene looked to Matilde and Vera for backup, but they seemed perfectly fine with Avoca's methods. "Dean's, but—"

"Cyrene!"

"It wasn't anything bad. I just slept!"

"If anyone had seen you though—"

"Well, no one saw me. Can we go now?" Cyrene asked.

"Yes," Vera said. "I think that is a good idea."

"Agreed," Matilde said. "As long as you are here at the right time tomorrow morning, I don't care who you're sleeping with."

Cyrene put her hands over her eyes and grumbled under her breath. Today was off to a bad start after waking up in Dean's bedchamber.

The worst part was that, in her haste, she hadn't had time to eat, and by the time they made it to the island to train, she was starving and knew today's work would only increase her hunger. She placed her hand on her stomach as she took a seat next to Avoca in the sand. Today was going to be a long day. But when Matilde and Vera began to speak, she put all thoughts of her grumbling stomach out of her mind. This was why she was here in Eleysia after all.

"We'll begin where we left off," Matilde said. "But, this time, instead of Cyrene picking up the water and moving it by herself, we want you two to link and move it together."

"Ideally," Vera said, "all of your magic should be able to flow seamlessly, individually and together, so that when you're linked, using your powers in tandem will be like breathing. I want you to each grasp your powers and then reach out for the other. Since one of you is Leif and the other is Doma, the magic will feel a little different, but that is perfectly normal. When you touch, you should actually be able to see what the other person is doing. Give it a try."

Cyrene took a breath and pulled her magic to herself. It came to her so easily this time. She and Avoca reached for each other at the same time. It felt comforting like touching her hand.

She prodded Avoca's magic, as if it were a separate entity from herself, but then, with a sigh, it seemed to wrap around her. They had done this before in their Bound ceremony, but Cyrene hadn't known what it was at the time. And it felt amazing. So much more strength and power, and from Avoca's end...control. Years of practiced control. It gave Cyrene a sense of calm and understanding. They were better as a team than she could ever be alone.

"I didn't know this was possible," Avoca breathed in surprise.

"Good," Vera said. "Now, begin."

With Avoca's guidance, they moved on from droplets to moving buckets of water to feeling the wave of the ocean on the beach. It was so much easier with her, but when they weren't linked, Cyrene still had trouble with the control. She knew that she shouldn't use Avoca's control as a crutch, but it was undeniably easier with her assistance.

Matilde stood up and paced at the tenth time when Cyrene couldn't move water from one bucket to the next without being linked to Avoca. "There's something else!" she cried.

"Kathrine, sit," Vera said.

"Something is wrong. You can feel it, too. I know you can."

"I'm doing the best I can," Cyrene said.

"But something is holding you back. I can't place my finger on it."

Vera sighed. "Cyrene, when you were Bound to Avoca, how was the ceremony performed?"

Cyrene explained what had happened with everything, except the specifics between their visions.

"And Shira used powers to bind you at the end?" Vera confirmed.

"Yes," Avoca and Cyrene said in unison.

"This might seem strange, but...you haven't been Bound to anyone before this, have you?"

Cyrene opened her mouth to immediately contradict that statement, but then images of her Rose Garden test back in Byern came to her mind. "I...I'm not sure."

Matilde's head snapped to her. "What do you mean?"

She chewed on her lip and looked away. She knew it was ridiculous to hide Byern secrets from them, but the thought of telling them about what had occurred was horrifying. It made her

334

stomach knot up and her body tense. She wasn't supposed to tell anyone about this. She had given the Byern royalty her word that she would never speak about this.

"Are you all right?" Vera asked.

Avoca reached out and touched her head. "You're all clammy."

Cyrene took a deep breath and then forced the words out, "When you become an Affiliate, you go through a loyalty ceremony called the Rose Garden ceremony. It is similar to what happened with Avoca, but magic couldn't have happened in Byern. It doesn't exist in Byern."

Matilde and Vera looked at each other in horror. There was a moment of stunned silence before everyone began speaking at once.

"How could you never mention this?" Avoca asked.

"What happened in the ceremony?" Vera asked.

"Those Dremylons! I can't believe they would do this," Matilde spat.

"Slow down!" Cyrene cried. "I didn't realize how important this was. I had to declare my loyalty to Byern by drinking out of a vial. I had...visions, and at the end, they told me not to speak of it to anyone."

"At the end, was any kind of magic used? Did you feel anything out of the ordinary? Anything at all?" Matilde pressed.

Cyrene thought back and realized it with a shock. "A jolt. I felt this electric pulse go through me. I didn't know what it was at the time—"

"Gods," Matilde murmured.

"What does that mean?" Avoca asked shakily.

"It means," Vera said, "that Byern has been binding people to them...to the country and the land and the entire Dremylon line."

"I thought only people with magic could be Bound," Avoca said quickly.

"So did I," Matilde said. "But it explains so much. These are just done to Affiliates and High Order?"

"Yes," Cyrene confirmed.

"Somehow, the Dremylons have figured out how to get around the laws of magical nature, and in binding people to the country and the line, they are forcing these people to work in Byern's interests. It starts with the conditioning and is solidified with the Bound ceremony."

Cyrene swallowed. "No. That can't be it. I'm here. I went against the wishes of the Dremylons and Byern. I used my powers and escaped. I'm here!" She didn't want to believe that to be the truth. It would mean so much more of her life was a lie.

"Have you felt drawn to go back home? A need to return? An unnatural need for either of the Dremylon boys?" Vera asked clinically.

Cyrene looked down and swallowed. "Um…yes. But it's been diminishing since I started using my powers."

Matilde and Vera looked at each other and seemed to come to a resigned conclusion.

"Sit," Matilde ordered. "We'll tell you a story."

"Once upon a time," Vera said with a sad smile, "we were much like you. Young and ambitious. We traveled all the way from Eleysia to Byern to join the Doma. Matilde's powers manifested when she was extremely young, and mine showed up just before I turned seventeen."

"We passed the ritual like your Presenting and were temporarily placed with a Doma because we had shown…exceptional skills," Matilde continued. "We were shipped out of Byern and went deep into the frozen tundra in the Haevan Mountains. We had never been in cold before. It was devastating."

Vera cleared her throat. "Details, sister. We were to be trained with a select group of Doma and Leifs. It was tough work. Harder than we'd ever thought possible, and at the end of it…we were Bound."

Avoca leaned forward with her mouth agape. "You're not saying…"

Vera smiled. "I think Avoca knows of what we speak. We were part of an ancient group called The Society. Some called us Dragon Bound."

Cyrene's mouth dropped. "Dragons?"

"Yes," Matilde confirmed. "Dragons have exceptionally long life spans. Longer even than most Leifs. And, after the fall of the Doma, our dragons were not welcome anymore in Emporia. They fled our world, but as long as they live…so do we, which is how we have survived these last two thousand years."

"Why didn't you leave with them?" Avoca asked.

"The curse," Vera said.

"Curse?" Cyrene asked.

Vera nodded. "Magic has been contained within Emporia for all these years. In an attempt to rid the world of our kind, we were trapped at the end of the War of the Light, so Viktor Dremylon and his army could hunt us down and kill us. Rid the world of magic. There were so few Doma left, and where the most magical blood still existed—Byern—any potential Doma were killed before they could reach safety."

Cyrene shook her head in horror. "How am I alive?"

"We have to assume, the strength of your powers," Matilde said. "And your determination to get away. I cannot think your desire for adventure is a coincidence."

"So, as you see"—Vera revealed her wrist, and Matilde stretched hers out as well. As with Cyrene and Avoca, they had shimmery gold tattoos that appeared bright as they ran their fingers over them—"our bond has diminished with distance and time from our Bound mate, but it is still there. It is entirely possible that the connection you feel to Byern and anything in Byern is drawing from your strength as it tries to pull you back."

"That's…horrible. And I did it unwillingly."

"No," Matilde corrected. "No one can be Bound unwillingly. You might have done it without knowledge of the consequences, but it had to be done willingly."

How naive she had been to think that all she could ever want in life was to be an Affiliate, to be tied to her homeland. She certainly hadn't been able to grasp the full realm of what that ceremony meant at the time, and now, somehow, she was Bound for life.

"Can I…remove it?" Cyrene asked hopefully.

Matilde and Vera sighed and exchanged worried glances.

"I'm afraid that is outside our area of expertise," Vera said. "If there's a way to break a binding, we haven't found one."

Matilde gave her a long level look. "And, believe us…we've tried."

The
SPRING

WINTER CAME AND WENT WITHOUT A SINGLE SNOWFLAKE.

And, as the time passed, Cyrene's powers grew, her control improved, and she was lost more and more to this boy.

"Just one more," Dean said, wrapping his arms around her waist and trying to hold her to him.

"I have to go. You always make me late," Cyrene chided.

He dropped his lips down on hers again, and she sighed into him. *Creator, I could do this all day!* He swung her around in his room and backed her legs up against the footboard of his bed.

"Skip training for one day," he encouraged.

"And would you skip a day of your military training?"

"For you, I would do anything."

He planted a kiss on her lips and then across her cheek before moving down the curve of her neck. She felt breathless.

She had to fight not to give in and skip training for the day. Matilde, Vera, and Avoca would kill her. But it was getting harder and harder to pull away from Dean. Harder and harder to remind herself to stop and not to give herself away. Many people back home had thought that Cyrene was Edric's mistress, and despite the fact that it wasn't true, Cyrene did not want the same rumors to fly about her and Dean. He wasn't married, but it simply wasn't proper to move forward. But curse her body for wanting to.

"I have to go," she reminded him.

"You said that once."

"You will be the death of me, Dean Ellison."

She tugged away from him, but he grabbed her hand and gently kissed it.

"You are the life of me, Cyrene Strohm."

"How do you expect me to leave when you say things like that?"

His brown eyes lit up, and that gorgeous smile that had won her over lit her up from the inside out. "I don't."

"I have work to do."

"How is that going?" he asked sincerely.

She knew he was just trying to keep her with him longer. He would do it every day they were together, and that was most days after he had talked to Alise and convinced her to leave them alone. She had been under the impression that Cyrene was just going to disappear, but the longer Cyrene had stayed, the clearer it had become that she wasn't going anywhere.

"Good," Cyrene said. "Making progress."

"Moved on from water?"

Cyrene frowned and shook her head.

Despite her limitation of being Bound to Byern, Cyrene had been working twice as hard to master her powers. Matilde and Vera had warned her that it normally took years to be able to manipulate all of the elements, but Cyrene didn't want to hear it. She felt ahead of the game since she was Bound to Avoca. They had spent all winter on the water element, and they had to be getting close to mastering it. Cyrene was anxious to move forward with her training.

"No, but I will, if you let me go," she rebuked.

He groaned in protest, but then he leaned down and kissed her one more time, wrapping his arms around her. "Come back to me today. I'm going to miss you."

"You'll be too busy beating Robard to miss me," she said with a wink before scurrying out of his arms and rushing to the door.

Training went much the same as it had been going.

She'd wake up exhausted and go to bed exhausted. Her powers were growing, but she never felt like she used as much energy as she had against the Braj or Indres. No more blackouts. No more Serafina visions. Just the endless, tiresome work of making water do her bidding.

She and Avoca linked, and together, they reached toward the ocean and pulled up a huge amount of water. Cyrene took lead and began spiraling the water in the air, creating a spherical cyclone. Avoca twisted, and Cyrene could feel what she was going to do before she even did it. Avoca jerked her hand, and the cyclone rose into the air, picking up sand, rocks, and even more water. It rotated and enlarged as it spiraled upward.

All the while, Matilde was shooting dangerous flames in their direction. The first time she had tried that, both Avoca and Cyrene had needed new clothes because their gowns had been singed beyond repair by the end of practice. Now, working as a team, they could dodge the flames while still raising the water formation overhead.

"Now, freeze it," Vera said.

She jabbed at Avoca with her magic, and Cyrene could feel the ice hit her in the sternum.

"Ugh!" Avoca cried, nearly losing focus.

Cyrene reacted on instinct to protect her and take more of the energy for herself. She felt the burst of release as her powers rushed from the depths within her. She took a deep breath and forced herself to keep going. She was never as good at freezing the water as Avoca, but it was a test. Vera had taken Avoca out of the equation for a reason.

Cyrene shot her hands forward, and in her moment of clarity, the sphere shook and cracked. Then, before her eyes, there was a perfectly round ice crystal. The bits of sand and rocks and seaweed were trapped within it, but it was so flawless that Cyrene nearly cried.

She brought it down toward them, and as it drew near, the water was so cold that it made their breaths come out in puffs in front of them. Cyrene giggled and then did something on instinct. She ruptured the ice crystal into tiny snowflakes and let them softly rain down on them, as if they were in the Taken Mountains.

She held her tongue out in front of herself and danced in the snow. Avoca laughed along with her, and soon, all four of them were twirling around in the snow on the middle of a deserted tropical island.

"First and last snow of the season," Cyrene murmured.

"In spring," Avoca said.

Matilde nodded with a smile at Cyrene and Avoca.

Vera looked pleased as well. "I think that concludes the water element."

"What?" Cyrene asked in surprise.

"You have more to learn, but you could not have done what you just did without significant control and understanding of the element," Matilde said.

Vera nodded. "The Bride of the Sea ceremony is coming up this week to praise the start of spring. We'll break until then and start up on the next element henceforth."

"What will we be working on?" Cyrene asked.

"Earth," Matilde said automatically. "Avoca has a perfect grasp on it, and you should know how to manipulate her element, as she does yours."

Avoca looked ecstatic. "I can't wait."

The girls returned to the capital with a feeling of giddiness between them. Avoca almost immediately disappeared to go find Ahlvie. He still wasn't staying in the palace because he appeared to like his new job as an entertainer, but he had relocated closer to the grounds to be near Avoca and Cyrene.

To both Cyrene's and Avoca's dismay, Ceis'f had not returned. Avoca had sent a messenger to Eldora to ask her mother about him, and her response had been disheartening. No sign of Ceis'f back home either. If they hadn't had training...and if not for Ahlvie, Cyrene was sure Avoca would have gone out to look for Ceis'f. But he had done what she had asked of him, so she tried to block him out.

Since today was the first day in months they had ended early, Cyrene decided to go down to the training barracks and check in on Dean. But, when she got down there, it was mostly empty, and no one had seen Dean at all that day. She found that strange but decided not to panic about it. She hurried back up to the palace and looked everywhere for him. She finally was about to give up when Robard abruptly stopped in front of her.

Cyrene stood her ground with fire in her eyes. "What do you want?"

"The Queen has requested your presence," he said smoothly. "If you'll follow me."

"What? So, you and Alise can trap me again? I think not. You can tell me where to find her and be on your way."

"I'm under orders."

"And I don't care."

"From Prince Dean," he bit out.

Cyrene's brow furrowed. "If you make one wrong move..."

"No worries, Affiliate," he said dryly. "I think where you're going will be bad enough."

Cyrene opened her mouth to ask what he was talking about, but he grabbed her elbow and unceremoniously yanked her down the hallway. She was lost in her thoughts about what the Queen could possibly want from her, let alone why Robard was collecting her on Dean's orders.

When she stumbled forward into the throne room with Robard on her heels, the tension was unbearably high. Queen Cassia, Princesses Brigette and Alise, and Prince Dean were standing together, arguing. Each was yelling over the other, trying to be heard.

Queen Cassia snapped at them to be quiet, and everyone turned to stare at Cyrene at once. She had the distinct sense of déjà vu from the time when everyone in the castle had thought she had been murdered. Edric and Kael had rushed to her side because they had been so worried. But, for some reason, she didn't think that was the case here.

The Queen was holding a piece of paper in her hand, and despite her regal appearance, she seemed ready to hurt the first person she got her hands on. Brigette looked like she hadn't slept in weeks. All of her energy had left her. Alise seemed smug, whereas Dean looked irritated.

When his eyes met Cyrene's across the room, instead of the happy man she had been falling head over heels for, she saw he was guarded.

"You requested to see me, Your Majesty," Cyrene said, falling back into her proper ways with ease. She dipped a low curtsy to the Queen before rising with her chin held high.

"Yes. It seems that your presence in my city has become an international matter," the Queen said.

"Pardon?"

"You are to immediately leave Eleysia and return to your homeland," she commanded.

Cyrene's eyes widened. "You're making me leave? But why? I've been here for months. I thought I had proven myself."

"It's not a matter of proving yourself," Queen Cassia said. She held up the paper in her hand, and from where Cyrene was standing, she could see that it was a letter. "It's a matter of this."

"Mother," Dean said urgently, "can't you reconsider?"

She raised her eyebrows at him. "You spoke for this girl once. I don't think you can do any more for her."

"What is that?" Cyrene asked.

"It is a personal letter from the King of Byern, demanding your immediate return upon receipt of this letter," Queen Cassia said.

Cyrene's mouth fell open. "He did what?" she snapped.

"He's sending an army to retrieve you, in fact," Alise said with a self-satisfied smile.

"An army?" Cyrene squeaked. "He would never—"

"Do it again," Dean finished for her.

She opened her mouth to protest, but what could she say? Edric *had* sent an army into Aurum to retrieve her. No matter how validated she felt about leaving and finding the key to unlocking her magic in Eleysia, she couldn't deny what he had done or why he had done it.

She had spent the last couple of months trying to forget the Dremylon men and all the trouble they caused...and what they did to her heart. But she refused to return at Edric's summons. She was not a toy. She might be bound to Byern, but she'd *rightfully* made her own choice to leave.

"I'm not leaving Eleysia to go back to Byern," Cyrene told them.

"You absolutely will!" Alise said.

The Queen shot her younger daughter a fierce look and then turned back to Cyrene. "We're not starting a war over one person. You haven't acted like other Affiliates here in Eleysia—I will say that much—but that does not mean we want Byern's might knocking on our doorstep."

"Let her stay, Mother," Brigette said.

"No."

"Do you want to break your son's heart?" she whispered. But everyone could hear her.

Dean winced at the blow, as if someone had struck him. Cyrene wanted to reach out to him, but she knew that it wasn't appropriate.

"I love my son, but I will not risk my country for him," the Queen said. "And that's final. I will write to King Edric and inform him that you will be returning to Byern promptly. Since we are not sailing out of the harbors in the next week, due to the Bride of the

Sea ceremony, you will have a few days to settle your affairs here.
But I can offer you nothing further." Queen Cassia nodded her
head and then left the room.

As soon as the door closed behind her, Cyrene thought the
room might return to an uproar. But Brigette didn't say a word.
She just left. Alise shared a look with Robard that turned Cyrene's
body to ice.

In fact, after her afternoon on the beach, she could feel her
body temperature dropping as her magic filled her. It had been
weeks since her magic had gotten out of control. She realized she
was shaking.

"Did you do this?" Cyrene asked Alise.

Alise just smiled. "Do what?"

"Did you?" she demanded. "You've hated me since the
moment I walked in here. You've tried to get rid of me, and now,
you've succeeded."

"I've no idea what you're talking about," Alise said as she
breezed past Cyrene to Robard.

Cyrene clenched her hands into fists. "You're messing with
people's lives, and I've never even done anything to you!" She
reached out and roughly grabbed Alise. Robard unsheathed his
sword, but she didn't even look at him. As if a sword would scare
her after what she had seen. She knew Alise had something to do
with this, and she wanted her to confess. "Just tell the truth."

"You're hurting a princess of the realm," Alise said with her
nose in the air. "If you want to leave here on good terms, I'd
suggest you unhand me."

"Cyrene," Dean whispered, "just let her go."

Cyrene threw Alise backward and had to catch herself from
using her magic to do it. "I know you did this."

"So what if I did?" Alise asked. "However it happened, you'll
be out of here in a few days."

Every fiber in Cyrene's body made her want to lunge forward
and throttle Alise, but she resisted the urge. It wouldn't help
anything at this point. She hated letting Alise get away with this,
but she needed to figure out how to stop it...not kill the person
who had started it.

"Fine," Cyrene said with a shake of her head.

Robard sheathed his sword and then followed Alise out of the
room.

That left Cyrene completely alone with Dean. She nearly crumpled as the realization of her circumstances fully hit her. If she didn't find a way out of this, then she would be leaving Dean and be on her way to Byern.

"Is it true?" Dean asked when she finally faced him again.

"Is what true?"

"Were you involved with the King?"

"Where did you hear that? Was that in the letter?" Cyrene asked anxiously.

She shouldn't have felt nervous about this line of conversation, but the unease on Dean's face didn't calm her nerves.

"What does it matter? Is it true?" Dean sighed and ran a hand back through his hair. "Of course it's true. Why else would he send an army to collect you...twice?"

"It doesn't change anything. I'm not with him now, and not that I should have to explain my previous...relationships to you, but we were never really together either."

"Cyrene, this changes everything."

"Why? Why does it have to change anything?"

"Because you're leaving!" he cried, finally loosening the anger he had been holding tight like a whip. "Because he's coming to claim you."

"Well, I'm not going back! I left the country for a reason, and anyway...I'm with you," she said softly. Her blue eyes were pleading with him. She reached out and placed her hand on his arm. "I'm with you."

"Why didn't you tell me?"

"About Edric?" she asked.

He cringed at Edric's name. "Yes."

"I didn't think it'd matter to tell you the truth."

"It matters."

"Why?" she demanded. "Why does my past change anything about you and me?"

"Do you love him?" Dean asked. He looked like her answer could plunge a knife through his chest.

"It's complicated, Dean," she said.

"So, you do."

Cyrene sighed. *How can I explain Edric to Dean?* She had never wanted to have this conversation. What she'd had with Edric was completely separate from what she currently had with Dean.

Thinking about them as a comparison felt wrong. And, at this point, she wasn't even sure how much of her time with Edric had even been real.

"No," she said finally. "No, I don't."

He pulled her against him and buried his face in her hair, breathing her in. "I can't lose you," he said softly.

"You won't. I promise."

She hoped that was a promise she could keep.

46
The ARMY

Daufina

DAUFINA WALKED BRISKLY FROM HER CHAMBERS AND DOWN the back hallways that led between her and Edric's rooms. Ever since he had gotten that blasted letter from the Eleysian Princess, claiming that Cyrene was in their country, he had lost himself in the hunt again. Daufina couldn't believe it when she'd read a copy of the letter Edric had sent her.

An army!

He was amassing an army to send to Eleysia to retrieve one girl. Daufina wanted to bury her face in shame for what was happening to her country. *How could he be so stupid?*

In the time that Cyrene had disappeared off the face of the map, she had seen Edric become renewed. He had been somber about her disappearance, but the news that Kaliana was pregnant had brightened his mood. It was treason to even think about what Kaliana had done to get the baby, but Daufina couldn't deny that she had been happy with the results thus far.

Edric had been acting like a doting husband. Perhaps not loving, like he had been with Cyrene, but still, he had been taking his marriage seriously once more. It had made all the difference, and they had even announced Kaliana's pregnancy to the entire country at the Eos holiday.

All of that for nothing.

"You're truly sending an army?" Daufina called, barging into his war room.

Edric stood before a large table scattered with maps, measurements, paperwork, supply readouts, drawings of new techniques and maneuvers. Merrick stood just to his side. His right-hand man. He was whispering something into the King's ear. *Poison.*

"Hello, Daufina," Edric said coolly.

"Edric, be reasonable. Send an envoy to collect her. Think of diplomacy, for Creator's sake. We can reopen trade negotiations with Eleysia. If Cyrene has been there, then we could use her knowledge of the country to acquire an ambassadorship. This could open up Byern to a world of new possibilities."

"Diplomacy," Merrick spat. "It is past time."

Daufina drew herself tall. He could not speak to her like that. She was Consort after all. "Captain, perhaps you should remove yourself while I discuss this with His Majesty."

"No, stay," Edric said. "I'll need your views on how best to infiltrate their defenses. We don't have a detailed map of the islands surrounding the country, and with so few ports, we'll have to be cautious. Their navy is supreme if we have to engage on water to get there."

"Edric! Are you listening to yourself?"

"Enough!" he yelled. His blue-gray eyes were molten. "They took her, Daufina. They are holding her. I have given them a sufficient amount of time to return her, but if they do not, I need a contingency plan. And I *will* follow through on my statement. It was not a threat to Eleysia; it was a promise."

"You would go to war for her." It was a statement.

Daufina always knew that he would. For *her.* She'd known it the day he sent troops into Aurum. He would do anything for *her.*

Edric's eyes softened for a moment. "I would go to the ends of the earth for her."

"Can you not wait a few days for a reply?"

"It costs money and time to mobilize an army. That, I cannot wait for if they refuse," he told her stiffly.

"I know the cost of war. It's that very thing I believe you are overlooking."

"Do not belittle me, Daufina," he growled. He flicked his hand at Merrick, who bowed and retreated from the room. Clearly, whatever he wanted to say, he preferred to be in private.

"I am not belittling you, Edric. I am thinking past Cyrene. I'm thinking of the country, of the land and the people. War is blood and sweat and tears. It is tragedy and heartbreak," Daufina said, hoping that he would understand where she was coming from. "It is lives lost…and over what?"

He shook his head and looked away from her. He seemed lost in thought, and she almost spoke but waited for him to address her again.

"Do you know that it has not rained a single day since she has been gone?"

"What?" Daufina asked.

"I spoke with one of the High Order about weather patterns. We've been having issues with crops. He said that it had not rained a single day since Cyrene had been kidnapped and dragged out of our country," Edric told her.

"I don't…you think that is somehow related?" she asked warily. "When I hear that…all I think is that you want to send good soldiers…good men to war during a dry season when the crops aren't growing. You are sending them to fight for you while the countryside is already bleeding."

"There is something about her, Daufina," he said. He held his head between his hands.

He looked pain-stricken. *I want to go to him, but what could I do to cure what is ailing him? Nothing.*

"She is calling to me, pulling me toward her. It's like I can still feel her. Here." He grasped at his chest. "It's faint, but I cannot escape her."

"Edric," she whispered.

"I sound mad. I know. Believe me, I know."

"It is obsession. You feel tied to her in some way because of something you had for such a short period of time. Then, she was taken away from you. It is no more than that."

Edric sank down into a chair behind the table. He looked worn, as if Cyrene's absence had hollowed him out. Daufina had thought that Kaliana's pregnancy would revive him. She had believed it was in the process. But it was just a patch for the wound. She saw that now. He would not rest easy until he had Cyrene back. That desperation made him very, very dangerous.

"All those months ago, you told me to make my country whole again," Edric told her. "I cannot see a way to do that without bringing Cyrene back. And I will…by whatever means necessary."

THE
FINAL DAYS

"I HAVE EXACTLY THREE DAYS TO FIGURE OUT HOW TO FIX THIS disaster."

Cyrene stared around the crowded inn suite. A sense of urgency lit up the room. She couldn't believe this was happening, and after her conversation with Dean, she was more determined than ever to fix this.

She knew that she couldn't get a letter to Edric in time before Queen Cassia shipped her out of the harbor. *And what would I even say in the letter anyway?*

Sorry, I wasn't kidnapped. I had to go chase down a pair of two-thousand-year-old Doma who your ancestors had forgotten to murder.

She didn't think that would go over well.

"How did Edric even find out you were here?" Ahlvie asked. He was kicked back in a chair with his feet up.

Eleysia had been good to him, she could see. It was strange to think about how much she had missed him now that he was in front of her. He and Maelia had been her constant companions for so long.

"Yeah. It's been months," Maelia said.

"Someone must have leaked the information," Orden said.

Then, his eyes traveled around the room, as if he was trying to figure out which of them had done it. *But how can I blame anyone in this room?*

"What about Ceis'f?" Ahlvie asked.

"No," Avoca said automatically.

"It's plausible," Orden said. "He has motive."

"Ceis'f would never betray me."

"Well, I'd bet he'd think he was only betraying Cyrene," Ahlvie said.

"Same thing!"

"He doesn't think like that though, Avoca. You know he doesn't. You are Leif. We are Other."

She sighed and rubbed her face. "It's a possibility."

"I don't want to think that Ceis'f would do that, but it's not ruled out. There is another option though. Dean's sister Alise has been plotting to get rid of me," Cyrene said. "So, it could have been her. And, as much as I would love to get back at her for her ridiculous, petty sabotage, I need to figure out how to stay first."

"I hate to say this, Cyrene, but maybe we should just go," Avoca said. She had her arms crossed over her chest, and even in the dark purple Eleysian gown she was wearing, she looked like a warrior.

"We came here to find Matilde and Vera, and look," Ahlvie said, gesturing to the two women who had thus far remained silent by the door, "there they are."

"I know, but—"

"As much as I like Eleysia, I wouldn't mind a change in scenery," Orden said.

"Yes, but—"

"There's nothing tying us to Eleysia now that we have what we were looking for," Avoca continued. "It would be reasonable to just take the news that we have been asked to leave as a sign and disappear before anyone knows otherwise."

"I understand what you're saying, but what will happen to Eleysia if they don't hand me over?" Cyrene asked.

Orden stroked his beard and tipped back his big, floppy hat. "Diplomacy. They would say that you disappeared, and Edric would send a small group to investigate, but it would be the truth, so it would blow over."

"No way," Ahlvie said. "Edric isn't thinking clearly right now. It would be war before he'd act diplomatically to someone taking Cyrene. Are you all forgetting Aurum?"

"And what about Cyrene?" Maelia said from the corner.

She looked even paler and smaller than normal. Cyrene had thought the weather would raise her spirits and give some color to her, but it seemed to have had the opposite effect.

"Yes, what about me? Um…what about me?"

"Dean," she filled in.

"Oh."

"And Darmian," Maelia added. She coughed twice and then looked away. "My apologies. I've been a bit under the weather."

"I know this doesn't pertain to the entire group, but Maelia is right. I'm not willing to leave Dean."

"You would go back to Byern instead of fleeing for this Prince?" Orden asked.

"I understand how you feel about him, Cyrene, but it's not reasonable," Avoca said practically.

"Then, there has to be another way. I don't want to leave Dean. Maelia doesn't want to leave Darmian. None of us want to split up, except Ceis'f, who abandoned us and maybe sold us out!" she grumbled. "Yet I've been summoned home. What do we do?"

"Perhaps I could offer a third scenario?" Matilde said with a wry smile.

"Kathrine," Vera said softly, "you're not honestly suggesting what I think you're suggesting, are you?"

"What's life without a little risk?"

"A big risk."

"It would work."

"You don't know that."

"Could you perhaps fill us in on what you're considering?" Cyrene asked. She was desperate enough to try anything.

Matilde explained what she had in mind, and by the time she finished talking, everyone was staring at her, slack-jawed.

"You want us to do what?" Cyrene asked.

"I know it sounds risky," Matilde began.

"It sounds like suicide," Avoca said.

"It just might work." Ahlvie nodded his head. He had always liked his plans to have a little bit of insanity to them.

"It is never going to work," Maelia said. She pursed her lips and looked like she might pass out.

"Do you need someone to look at you?" Cyrene asked.

Maelia shook her head. "No. I've done what I can. It will pass."

Cyrene frowned but nodded. She wouldn't push Maelia. "I've no idea what is going to happen in the next three days, but if you think this will work...if you think I'm ready for this, then I'm in."

The rest of the room agreed with her.

Matilde stood up a little straighter. "Just like old times, right, Mari?"

"I hope it doesn't end up like old times."

"We're older and wiser. Plus, I'll let you do all the real planning."

Vera rolled her eyes. "Of course you will."

Two days later, Cyrene was standing on the docks at First Harbor with her heart in her throat. She could barely see the outline of Ahlvie and Orden in the torchlight. She couldn't believe they were actually going to go through with this. She couldn't believe *she* was actually going to go through with this. It felt...crazy. And maybe it was, but it was the only way, and she would do it. She had made a promise to Dean.

"You have everything?" Cyrene asked.

Ahlvie patted his shirt pocket. "All here. Are you going to tell me what the letter says?"

Cyrene shook her head. "It's private, but if talking to Edric doesn't work"—and she didn't think it would—"then give him the letter. That should settle things."

"I can't believe, after all of this, I'm on my way back to Byern."

"I know. Maelia is in position to make sure no one knows, not even Darmian, that you are leaving tonight."

"Good. You know I'll do what I can to get this all straightened out." His eyes drifted upward, searching out Avoca.

Cyrene knew Ahlvie hated leaving Avoca behind, but she needed Avoca to get through this.

"And you'll return to me safe and sound and in one piece," Cyrene instructed him. She reached out and touched his arm. "And to her."

"Is she coming?"

Cyrene was glad for the low light. She could normally sense Avoca when she was near, but she didn't feel a thing. Cyrene had expected her to be here, but her mood had been so sour after they had finalized their plans that Cyrene also wasn't that surprised to find that she was gone. She had already lost Ceis'f. Even if they had fought all the time, she hadn't actually wanted him to leave. And she definitely didn't want Ahlvie to leave.

"I don't know," Cyrene finally answered.

"She'll be here," Ahlvie said confidently. "She has to be."

"I'm sorry that we have to split up."

Ahlvie shook his head. "It's a necessity, but she knows how I feel. Nothing is going to change that in the time it takes for me to get to Byern and back."

"You love her, don't you?" Cyrene asked.

"I know I'm a jokester and a drunk and a gambler and anything else people want to call me," Ahlvie said. His eyes were still fixed on the end of the dock. "But none of that matters when I'm with her. But I haven't told her, and I need to tell her."

"I'm sure she knows."

"Time to go," Orden called from the deck of the ship. "We need to get out of here. Storm's a-brewin'."

Ahlvie gave Cyrene a wry smile.

"Be safe out there," she told him.

He pulled her to him and squeezed her hard. "You be safe, too. You won't have me to watch your back."

Cyrene laughed. "I'm pretty sure I watch your back."

Ahlvie's eyes wandered down to the end of the dock again, and then he shook his head in despair. "Will you tell her I love her?"

"Tell her when you come back," Cyrene insisted. "You'll have all the time in the world then."

He nodded, and with one last forlorn look, he hurried after Orden and got onto the boat. The Eleysian vessel disappeared out onto the water. It was already choppy. Unseasonably troublesome.

She would have smiled if she wasn't so sad to see her friends go.

A figure appeared next to her, and Cyrene would have startled if she hadn't sensed her coming.

"Why didn't you say good-bye?" Cyrene asked.

Avoca shook her head. "I can't say good-bye to him."

"He was devastated that you weren't here."

"He'll come back. He has to come back."

With a flick of Cyrene's magic, she linked herself with Avoca. The feel of their magic together was about as intimate as Avoca got. She wasn't one to break down and cry or ask for a hug. But this, Cyrene could offer her. It wasn't enough, but it was something.

"Everything falls into place today," Maelia said in Cyrene's room the next morning. Her hands were shaking as she pulled on the pale yellow Eleysian gown for the Bride of the Sea ceremony.

Cyrene's own gown had been delivered this morning. When she had opened the box, she had gasped. It wasn't the gown that she had ordered. It was something so much more beautiful. The cerulean and gold dress was so light and buttery soft that it slipped through her fingers. The dress was strapless with a sheer slip that went over the bottom layer of the dress before falling long and flowy to the ground. She wore the string of Eleysian pearls Dean had given her at Eos around her neck.

"I know." She looked at herself in the mirror and adjusted the pin in her hair. "Are you sure that Darmian is none the wiser with our plans? I don't want him to run to Dean."

She nodded. Her eyes were distant. "I'm certain."

"Good. Are you going to be okay?"

Cyrene glanced back over at her friend, who looked as if her illness was getting worse. The pale yellow did nothing to improve her coloring.

"Stop asking me that," Maelia snapped.

Her irritation level was through the roof, and Cyrene couldn't figure out why.

"What's going on with you?"

"I'm just…frustrated." Maelia dropped her eyes to the ground. "I feel like I'm betraying my country if I follow you and betraying you if I follow orders."

"We can't go back there, Maelia. You know that, right?"

"Why not?" Maelia asked. "Not that I don't want to stay to be here with you and with…Darmian." Her voice dipped as she used his name. "But country comes first, Cyrene. It always comes first."

Cyrene frowned. "I know what you're saying, Maelia. If I thought there was another way or that Byern would be accepting of the person I am, then I would go back." She reached out and grabbed Maelia's hands. "I miss Byern. I miss the castle and the mountains and the river and the smell of home. I miss the Laelish Market at high season and riding my horse through the streets instead of taking stupid boats *everywhere*."

Maelia laughed, and a tear leaked out. "I miss those things, too."

"I miss Rhea and my family and court…"

"And Edric?"

Cyrene nodded. "And Edric. But you know what I don't miss?"

"What?"

"The naiveté I had about the rest of the world and the pedestal I put Byern on before leaving. Our home is not perfect. It's broken, and it's done horrible things to the rest of the world…to people like me. If I go back to Byern, I want it to be for the right reasons and not because some *boy* demands I return, like a child who got his toy stolen."

The
CALM

CYRENE AND MAELIA ARRIVED OUTSIDE OF THE THRONE ROOM, their arms locked for support. Cyrene wasn't even sure Maelia should be out of the rooms. She was burning up. But, every time Cyrene had told her to just lie down, Maelia would snap and tell her she was fine. She knew that Maelia was really there to be supportive of Cyrene, and on a big day like today, she wouldn't miss it.

Then, Cyrene saw Darmian's eyes light up at Maelia's appearance. She almost laughed. He was the real reason that Maelia had refused to stay in bed.

Darmian immediately approached them. He looked fine in his royal-blue military uniform. "Affiliate Cyrene," he said in deference. "Maelia."

"Darmian," they said in unison.

"Maelia, you look…" He trailed off as he just stared at her, starry-eyed.

"Thank you," she said with a bright red blush on her cheeks.

"May I?"

Cyrene let Maelia go when Darmian offered her his arm. They walked away, revealing Dean standing by the door.

Even from here, she could tell he looked nervous. He was pacing back and forth before the door. His head was tilted slightly downward, and he seemed to be muttering to himself. He shook his head once and then started over. She almost laughed, but then nerves set in with her. If things didn't go as planned, tonight would be their last together.

Trying to remain positive, she pushed her shoulders back and walked over to Dean. He was so engrossed in his own thoughts that he hadn't even seen her coming. She tapped him on the shoulder, and he jumped.

"Cyrene," he said when he turned to face her.

"Hi, Dean."

"You look stunning," he said, drawing her against him.

She closed her eyes and breathed him in. She wanted to remember every detail. The way his hard chest felt beneath her cheek. His musky sea-salt scent. The way his fingers dug into her back, as if he refused to ever let her go. The quick beat of his heart at her nearness.

"Thank you," she said softly. "I don't want this to ever end."

Dean sighed into her hair. "It won't." And he sounded determined.

When he looked back down at her, she could still see anxiety coursing through him. But something else was there, too—defiance or hope or love. That four-letter word, she hadn't dared let herself think about. The last time she had been set to give her heart away, she had been prepared for it to be broken. But with Dean…there were no boundaries. He knew her, all of her, and she couldn't lose him. She wasn't ready for that kind of heartbreak.

She stretched up onto the tips of her toes, snaked her hand around his neck, and fiercely kissed him without thought for who was around to see them together. Passion hit them with a ferocity that both of them would tiptoe around when they were alone. Not that she wasn't willing to move forward, but she had always been too afraid to give her heart away completely. Those thoughts were rapidly dissipating in her mind.

"Ahem!"

Cyrene slowly released Dean but couldn't drag her love-struck gaze from his face. She even reached back up and planted one more kiss on his lips before moving away again.

The Queen stared between them with a thoughtful look on her face. "It is time to begin the ceremony."

Dean took Cyrene's hand in his.

Queen Cassia frowned. "This is a religious moment of prayer to the Creator for her blessing on the seas. It is the royal family's duty to uphold the honor. Cyrene is not a part of the royal family.

As I told Alise, Robard could not come with us, and thus Cyrene is not to accompany you either."

"Cyrene is coming with me," Dean said defiantly. "You are forcing her to leave in the morning. All I have is today."

"That is precisely why she should not be on the royal boats." Queen Cassia wasn't a hardened ruler. She seemed sympathetic to her son's problem. But the threat of war still loomed, and she wouldn't allow anything to hurt her people.

"I refuse to go without her, Your Majesty," he said, his voice formal.

The Queen held her head higher, as if the title alone threatened to weigh her shoulders down.

"But I implore you, as your son, to allow me this one morsel of happiness before you rip it from me."

Queen Cassia closed her eyes, and for a second, she looked like she was going to fight Dean. But then she nodded. "Okay, but make sure she knows how the ceremony works." The Queen turned on her heel and disappeared into the throne room.

"Well, that went better than anticipated," Dean said.

Cyrene let loose a breath. "I didn't mean to put you in this position, Dean."

"It's not your fault, but I'm not going to let anyone dictate my time with you from here on out," he told her. He ran a hand back through his hair and then diverted his eyes.

"You seem a little nervous," she said softly.

He laughed, his voice rising an octave. "Do I?"

She nodded. "A little. But it's okay. I get it. I'm a little nervous too and sad about everything that's happening."

He took her hand and placed a kiss on her knuckles. "I am nervous, but I don't want you to be sad. I would do anything I could to change that."

Just then, the Queen and King and all of Dean's sisters and their husbands walked into the throne room. Dean offered Cyrene his arm, and they ducked into the back of the line behind Brigette.

"Okay, so fill me in on this ceremony," Cyrene whispered.

"The Bride of the Sea is the biggest holiday in Eleysia. Eos is big, of course, but since Eleysia has always relied so heavily on sea travel, we celebrate the coming of spring in a very traditional way."

They walked out of the palace and down onto the grounds. A group of boats just a little bigger than the normal gondolas were set up on the docks.

"Traditionally, the royal family takes the official family boats out and rides through the city. The Queen speaks to the crowd, and a priestess says a prayer over the Bride's Ring."

"The bride has a ring?" Cyrene asked in confusion.

Dean nodded. He offered her his hand as they got into the boats. They were seated with Brigette behind them and Alise and the twins in front of them.

Alise turned around and sniffed at Cyrene. "Who let her on board?" she asked.

"Mother," Dean said. He gave her a look that begged her to argue with him.

"She wouldn't let Robard ride with me."

"That's because Robard is a soldier. He always has been and always will be."

"Who knew you were obsessed with nobility?" Alise sneered. "That's not how I remember it."

Dean glared at his sister, and Cyrene's cheeks heated. She didn't want to know what that meant.

"Mind your own business, Alise," he said.

The boats started moving, and once they were out of the gates and on the main canal, Dean took a deep breath and continued his story, "Where did I leave off? Oh, right, the Bride's Ring. It's a special gold band inscribed with the date of the ceremony. It symbolizes our marriage to the sea. So, after the prayer, in front of everyone in the queendom, we pass the Bride's Ring down the royal family line. It begins when the priestess gives the ring to the Queen, who passes it to the King. It goes down the line of their children before finally reaching Brigette, the Crown Princess, Maiden Bride of the Sea."

"So...you pass a ring to your sister, and that's it?" Cyrene asked.

They were already moving past crowds of people on their way to this ceremony, and she wanted to make sure she understood what would be happening.

"No. Brigette says a prayer and then tosses the Ring into the holy pool. This is an offering to the Creator for safe sea travel for the next year and serves as a remembrance of her blessing upon us.

This completes the official ceremony. The Eleysian people also toss Bride's Rings into the water all over the city in remembrance today. After they have celebrated separately, a festival is held on the water, and the palace throws a huge ball."

"That seems simple enough. I'll just follow along as we go," she told him.

He kissed the top of her head and held her hand as they made their procession through the city. The closer they got to their final point, the more nervous Dean got. The crowds were thicker, and people were craning their necks and pushing people out of the way to see into the royal boats pass.

She even thought she'd heard her name being called a few times, but that couldn't be. *How would anyone know my name?*

Their boats finally stopped in front of a temple on the water. It was made of the same sandstone as everything else in Eleysia, but it was simple and elegant. The crowds were swarming, and gondolas clogged the passageway as nobility sought to witness the ceremony.

The priestess walked out of the temple. Her pale hair fell to her waist, and she was dressed in an all-white robe. She had a serenity about her that Cyrene had never seen on another. Byern wasn't exactly pious even though everyone celebrated the Creator and honored her on holidays. Temple wasn't required, so few would go, and there weren't religious ceremonies like this. It was beautiful and humbling for Cyrene to be a part of this.

A guard escorted the Queen out of the boat, and she stood next to the priestess.

Queen Cassia tilted her chin up. "Ladies and gentleman of Eleysia, thank you so much for gathering today for the honoring of our Creator and her blessing we receive each year." Her voice boomed over the crowd.

Cyrene glanced over at Dean and squeezed his hand. He met her eyes and shot her a half-smile. She listened as the Queen went on to talk more about the Creator and another year of safe sea travel. It was much the same as what Dean had just told her.

The priestess stepped forward. She looked so fragile, but when she began to pray, Cyrene knew she had an incredible inner strength. Cyrene bowed her head with the crowd and sent up her own prayer to the Creator, asking for help to make the right choices and for guidance in the coming trials.

Then, the priestess produced the tiny gold Ring. Cyrene could barely see it from her prime seat. She couldn't imagine anyone else could. The Queen passed it to the King, and then it went down the line.

Tifani finally handed it to Dean, and for the first time, Cyrene could see that it was actually a very pretty ring. The gold shimmered and glittered in the morning light. The engraving was in a beautiful script that shifted in coloring, and Cyrene nearly jumped out of her skin. She hadn't seen that flowing writing since she had given the *Book of the Doma* to Matilde and Vera a couple of months ago.

But there was Doma magic in that ring. Cyrene would bet her life on it. She looked around the venue and wondered how much of this had been constructed by Doma and how much of the ceremony had come from Doma.

She was lost in thought about what all this could mean when Dean cleared his throat.

She snapped her head back to him, expecting to see him pass the ring on to Brigette, but instead, he was holding a different ring. An exquisite ring with a large oval diamond held into place by gold filigree that almost looked as if it were waves. The band was intricately designed with smaller diamonds and tiny onyx pearls that Eleysia was famous for.

Her hand flew to her mouth, and she looked up into Dean's dark eyes.

He smiled crookedly and then sank to one knee in front of her. "Cyrene, you are my light and my life. I don't know how I lived before you or how I could ever hope to live after you. I never want to find out. Would you do me the honor of being my wife?"

Cyrene's mouth fell open, and tears pooled in her eyes. "Yes! Yes! Oh Creator! Of course, I'll marry you."

Dean slipped the ring onto her finger, and tears fell onto her cheeks. She reached forward and kissed him on the mouth. Everything made sense now. Why he had been so nervous. Why he had insisted on her coming on the boat. Why he had promised that they would be together.

He had been planning his own way for them to be together while she had been planning her own means for it. Her emotions were running so hot that the boats rocked in the water.

Dean laughed and held on to the side of the boat. "The waves even seem to agree with us."

She laughed, too, and looked down at the ring in shock. She had never thought about this moment or whom it would be with. She had always just assumed it wasn't going to happen for a long time.

Dean handed the Bride's Ring to his sister, who stoically stared at him. "Sorry to surprise her in the middle of the ceremony."

Brigette took it from his hand. "I hope you're happy." Then, without a word of prayer or blessing, she tossed the ring over her shoulder into the water.

She crossed her arms and looked away from the crowd. "Can we leave now?"

49

The
BEFORE

WHEN THEY WERE BACK ON SOLID GROUND OUTSIDE OF THE palace, Cyrene and Dean were bombarded with congratulations. Most of his siblings weren't around much and didn't know that tensions had been running high among the court or the fact that Cyrene was supposed to be getting on a boat to head back to Byern tomorrow.

But the ones who did know what was going on held back from the group. Brigette seemed indifferent, but Cyrene suspected she was nursing a broken heart. The very thing Cyrene and Dean were trying to avoid. Alise looked furious. Cyrene still didn't know what her problem was, but she looked ready to spit fire at Cyrene. And she was very glad that Doma blood didn't run in the Eleysian royal family.

The Queen, however, ushered everyone away from Dean and Cyrene and stared them down. "That was a very clever thing you did today."

"I'll take that as congratulations," Dean said.

"I am happy for you both, but marriages of royalty are a matter to be determined by me and your father. If you think that by proposing in front of half of the queendom will change my mind about sending her off to Byern tomorrow, you're wrong. Expect a long-distance engagement. I refuse to let this stand until I've had word from King Edric that he will allow this. His Affiliates are his to give away as much as my son is my responsibility."

Cyrene's heart sank at the words. That couldn't be true. Consort Daufina had said that her father had married someone against the wishes of the court. But Cyrene highly doubted that, if she went back to Byern to ask for permission, it would go over very well…or at all.

Dean seemed to come to the same conclusion. "You can't ship her back to Byern!"

"I at least need approval from King Edric for this marriage. He wants her back, and we don't need a war over one girl," the Queen said. "We have a celebration to get ready for tonight. I expect you to be on your best behavior after that debacle." Queen Cassia left them standing at the docks.

Cyrene was sure they were supposed to follow her inside, but the last thing she wanted to do at this point was face his family after that conversation. She had the sneaking suspicion that Edric would never agree to let her marry Dean…or anyone really.

She looked down at the ring on her finger and felt her magic jump at the sight of it. She was engaged. And she had no idea if she would ever get married.

"Cyrene"—Dean grabbed her hand and kissed the finger that the ring was on—"you said yes."

She laughed hoarsely and tried to hold the tears back. "I did. I mean…you proposed! You want me to be your wife. Are you sure that's what you want?" she asked, her fears getting the better of her. "You're not just doing this so that I won't have to leave?"

"Of course I don't want you to leave, but that's not the reason. It was going to happen anyway."

"It was?" she asked softly.

"Yes. I love you, Cyrene. I love everything about you."

Cyrene smiled wide and threw her arms around his neck. "I love you, too."

He squeezed her tight. "It is so good to hear that. I feel like I've been holding that in for months. But I'm glad you know now. I'm not going to let one letter get in the way of us. You're not going back to Byern unless it's what you want to do. It's not, is it?"

She shook her head. "No. I want to stay here with you."

He sighed. "Good." He kissed her hard on the mouth. "Come with me. I kind of had something planned in case you said yes."

"Did you think I wouldn't?" she asked, following him back out onto the boat.

"I wasn't sure if it would be too soon with you. I knew I wanted it, but I didn't want to rush you. We have our whole lives."

"I'll admit, it wasn't high on my priority list. I have a few other things I want to figure out before getting married. A lot of things actually, but that doesn't mean it feels wrong with you."

He leaned back in the gondola and kissed her as they sped through the canals to their destination. His lips were tender, as if her words had sparked a fire within him. His fingers threaded into her intricate updo, and he grumbled as he kept hitting pins.

Cyrene laughed and pulled his hand away from her hair. "Leave it be. I have to be presentable for the party later."

He groaned and leaned his head back.

She ran her thumb along his hand. "So, where are you taking me?"

Dean smiled but didn't fill her in.

A few minutes later, they were docked in Fifth Harbor, and Dean was pulling her toward a large ship. She followed after him and got on board.

"Another boat?" she asked in confusion.

"A celebration," he said. "I wanted to do something special for you."

"We're celebrating on a boat?" she asked again.

"Well, at sea. I hired a small crew to take us out on the water. It is the Bride of the Sea ceremony today. And since you will be my bride at sea and are wearing a bride's ring, I thought it was appropriate."

"About as appropriate as it gets," she agreed.

The crew cast off, and Cyrene watched the capital city grow smaller in the distance. She could still see it as a speck on the horizon, but they were closer to some of the other volcanic islands in the area. It was a beautiful sight to behold. It was the first time she had ever seen the island like this. The last time, they had come into the city at night. Now, she was seeing it as it would appear to a stranger.

The crew stuck to themselves so well that Cyrene basically never even saw them.

They had lunch above deck, out of a basket that Dean had filled with Eleysian delicacies. He spread a blanket and placed a few cushions out for them, and they toasted their engagement with a bottle of bubbly champagne that went straight to her head.

When lunch was over, they didn't have that much time left before they needed to go back for the party, but neither of them seemed ready to leave.

Dean's fingers trailed up her arm and to her shoulder. Goose bumps broke out across her flesh, and she leaned into his touch. He kissed her shoulder and then her collarbone. She sighed.

"Creator," he groaned. "That sigh is going to kill me."

He stood, hoisted her into his arms, and carried her below deck. She didn't even protest when they entered the bedchamber. For the first time since she had found her magic, she felt out of control, and she loved it.

Dean set her down on the bed and lay next to her. She had slept in his bed more than once in the months since she had come to Eleysia, but never had it felt more intimate than the moment when she was looking up at her future husband.

His fingers threaded back up into her hair, and he slowly removed the pins, one by one. Her dark tendrils fell out of its style until it cascaded down her back. Then, he pushed his hands through the mass of hair once more.

"I like it better down," he told her, brushing it to the side and gently kissing her on her bare shoulder.

"Then, I'll wear it down," she told him.

Their eyes met in the dim lighting, and it was as if everything in the world made sense. She might have been sent to Eleysia to find Matilde and Vera, but finding Dean along the way wasn't a coincidence. And she loved him.

They moved together at the same time. All those months they had been holding back cracked open between them. Their lips touched and tongues explored.

He leaned her back on the bed and covered her body with his. The pressure of him against her just made her crave more. His hand slid under the fabric of her dress and caressed her calf, knee, and thigh. Her own hands were clutching his chest and back, trying to get him closer.

Fire built within her body as magic seemed to come alive with their connection. Every place his hands touched her was a shock to her system, both intense and jolting. She had never felt so alive.

When she pushed him back to tug his shirt over his head, her heart was hammering in her chest. She was entirely exposed and vulnerable to him. But Dean gazed at her with the most caring and wonderful look in his eyes. Those eyes swore to her with everything he was that he loved her…and they were going to be together.

"Are you sure?" he asked.

She nodded. Her body was shaking. Her powers were alive and pooling inside her, like she was about to release more energy than she ever had in her whole life. It was a buildup that could tear down kingdoms or re-create the world.

"Yes," she confidently told him.

And then, as their bodies came together, she released that energy. Every last ounce of it, she let flow from her, and with all her might, she pushed it out into the world. It was like heaven and bliss and sweet pleasure. It was the best feeling in existence.

There was a split second of perfection. A perfect calm. A perfect stillness. A perfect being.

And then the waves started.

50

The
STORM

CYRENE AND DEAN MADE IT ABOVE DECK JUST AS THE FIRST wave crashed on board. She almost lost her footing as water sloshed over her dress and under her silk slippers. Dean caught her at the last minute. He shoved her toward the railing.

"Hold on!" he cried over the sound of the storm.

Wind whipped her hair around her face and whistled in her ears. Her heart was still hammering after what had happened. Then, she looked all around her in horror.

The water that had been a little rough when they first went out on the water was now devastating. Thick black clouds hung overhead. Sheets of rain could be seen in the near distance, and it was traveling fast. The waves themselves were already ten feet high and growing. She dipped with the rocking of the boat, thankful for her sea legs.

"When did this start?" Dean called to one of the crew working on the deck.

He had huge frightened eyes. "Just now, Your Majesty. It came on so suddenly. We had mostly clear skies, and then, out of nowhere, the world erupted."

Dean shook his head. "That's impossible."

"I saw it, too, Your Majesty," another sailor confirmed.

Cyrene felt sick about what the sailors had said. The storm had just come upon them. With no expectation for a storm of this magnitude. Her hands were shaking with the realization.

"Dean…" she said shakily. She could barely be heard over the wind.

"Not now. Let me find out what's happening. Go below deck, and get out of the rain," he said.

"Dean!" she cried.

He turned to her with concern in his eyes. He took her hands. "Please, go below deck. We have a very small crew, and this looks like a full-blown hurricane. I have to help get us to safety. I don't think there's time to get us back to the capital."

"I can help," she said warily.

"No. Even if you were a sailor, you don't know these waters." Dean shook his head. "The Creator must be punishing us."

"What? Why?" she demanded.

"Brigette threw the ring in the holy water without a prayer. She did this." Cyrene was about to open her mouth to protest, but Dean shook his head. "She's cursed us. Now, please, get somewhere safe."

Dean ran off to help the sailors on board, but she could see that it was no use. The waves were too high. The hurricane was coming in too fast. The rain was too heavy.

And she had done this.

When she had pushed her magic out into the world, she had called forth this storm. She, Matilde, Vera, and Avoca had been working on pushing a storm out into the ocean to prevent Ahlvie and Orden from being pursued and to hopefully prevent the Byern army from coming into open water after her. Matilde and Vera had told her that it would never be of full magnitude because they couldn't go out on open water, and they didn't want to push Cyrene too much. She was the first magical user in two thousand years with abilities to control the weather...and she had just brought a hurricane down on top of herself.

Dean could try all he wanted to get them to safety, but she had to do what she could to try to stop this. No matter what happened, she couldn't unleash this on the world.

Bracing herself against the wind and rain, Cyrene reached into herself for her magic. She nearly gasped when so little of it came to her. She had used so much to draw in this hurricane, and she hadn't even meant for it to happen. She had been so caught up in Dean that her magic had just worked its own way, feeding off of her adrenaline and energy to create something beautiful...and terrible.

Cyrene held on for dear life as the boat dipped and curved with the force of the waves. She dug deeper and deeper into her core, demanding more energy. She needed to control it, contain it. There were consequences for tampering with the weather, especially to this degree. She didn't want to find out what would happen if she couldn't stop this. But she hadn't used this much magic without being linked to Avoca since she had fought off the Indres. And that felt like a lifetime ago.

More magic filled her veins, but it wasn't enough. She could almost cry. It definitely wasn't enough. She was depleted and drawing this much out of her reserves was painful. She could feel it singeing through her fingertips and down to her toes. If she drew more, she could black out...or worse, burn out.

But she couldn't stop.

She swirled the water back in the way it had come. When she had released before, she hadn't even thought about it. It had left her body, fully formed. Now, she needed to counteract everything she had done, and the scary part was that she didn't even know how to do it. They had only worked on starting the disaster...not fixing it.

Fear pricked at her. She didn't want to let this thing run its course.

"What are you doing?" Cyrene heard Dean yell, even over the sound of the wind.

That broke her concentration, and she felt some of her magic dwindle. She contemplated ignoring Dean's call, but then she heard an unexpected voice.

"Did you think you would just get away with it?"

Cyrene frowned. "Robard."

How had he gotten on board? She hadn't seen the crew, but she was sure that Dean would not have included him as part of this. Her stomach dropped. She had a horrible feeling about this. Holding on to her magic as best as she could, she gave up her position on the deck and dashed toward the sound of Dean's voice.

She found Dean and Robard squared off on the slippery deck. They both had their swords in their hands, and their feet were planted in defensive positions. She was facing Dean, but when he saw her, he actually looked fearful. That must have gotten Robard's attention because he turned around and lunged for her.

Cyrene screamed and dived out of the way. On instinct, she called up a wave to push him away from her as she ducked and rolled. Her shoulder was already throbbing from the impact. When she looked back up, Robard was a few feet away from her, drenched from head to toe. He looked at her as if he couldn't believe what had just happened.

"Witch!" Robard called. He regained his footing and looked ready to attack her. "Is this why you've been harboring her? She's a black magic user?"

Cyrene nearly laughed at him, but she wanted to get as far away as possible from him. He had murder in his eyes. She scrambled to her feet and dashed to Dean. He held his sword high to protect her even though it was clear that she could hold her own. At least until she depleted her energy source.

"You have no idea what you're talking about," Dean said.

"She just used an evil spell on me."

"I did nothing of the sort," Cyrene said defiantly. "All I did was keep *you* from attacking me!"

"What is this all about, Robard? Why are we fighting? You used to be like my brother!"

"*Like* your brother," Robard cried. "Close but never close enough. You were promoted as an officer first, and you became Captain first. You've gotten everything because you are the Prince."

"I've worked hard for what I've achieved. Maybe if you stopped complaining and put that energy into something worthwhile, *you* could have made Captain instead of trying to cheat me into it," Dean cried.

"I put everything into my training. I came from *nothing* and worked harder than anyone. I lived in the training facility, but it was never enough. There was no way I could ever be the prince. Then, she walks into your life," Robard cried, pointing his sword at Cyrene, "and suddenly, everything is just perfect. Now, you're going to wed, and once again, I have nothing."

"What does Cyrene have to do with anything?"

"Because the Queen, your mother, refused to give me Alise's hand!" Robard roared. "I did everything I could to show her just the kind of person Cyrene was. Then, even when she is forced to go back to where she belongs, you find a way to get around it."

Cyrene gasped. "Wait, this was your doing? Did *you* send the letter to Byern?"

"I had Alise officially send it," Robard taunted. "But everything was my plan, and it would have worked, too, if Dean hadn't proposed!"

"You dirty bastard! Can't have everything you want, so you try to take away my happiness! You will pay for your sins."

Then, Dean hurled himself at Robard.

It was as if Cyrene were watching the two fight in the sand pit to see who would become Captain all over again. Except, this time, there was no general to determine the winner, and she doubted either of them would stop before the killing blow.

Robard countered Dean's attack, and then they paced together in a choreographed dance. They knew each other's strengths and weaknesses. The last time she had seen their sword fight, Dean had won, but Robard had forced him to concede to his weakness. He couldn't kill his friend. Cyrene saw that Dean was not going to have that problem today, but Robard seemed confident. Recklessly confident. If he overestimated Dean's ability to forgive him, then he would be in a world of hurt.

Cyrene hurried out of their way so she could fix this. Because she had to fix this. She concentrated on what was going on around her and felt her powers push out into the atmosphere. She didn't know what she was doing, but she had to try.

Holding on to her powers with a tight leash, she propelled them outward until she could feel almost a residue of what she had done before. Her powers were everywhere. In every drop of water and every air current and every cloud. The ocean teemed with her magic. It was too much and not enough. She could have sat in this trance forever, like a purgatory for her powers.

Then, she felt it…like a thread that connected everything together. Her energy was depleting. She wasn't strong enough for this. Maybe with Avoca to bolster her, she could have done it. But, now, her breathing was labored. Her body ached. A fever burned through her system. She closed her eyes and gritted her teeth against the distant sound of swords clashing together.

Still, she latched on to the thread and began to unravel it. She took one piece and pulled it apart and then the next. The boat rocked, and she fell forward onto her knees. The wood beneath her fingers singed, and she gasped as she realized *she* had burned the wood.

Everything was relying on this one moment, and she had to keep going. She picked at the thread until she was trembling and writhing in agony, lying on her back. If she didn't stop and let it go, she wasn't just going to burn out her powers; she was going to die.

But there was so little left. She could do it. She could right this wrong.

She opened her eyes to try to gain just one more ounce of strength from the world around her. She tried to pull from the great giant ocean, but she had to have the energy for it. She pushed herself to her knees and prayed for this to all end.

Then, she heard a squelching sound and watched as Dean's sword slid through Robard's body. He dropped to the deck, and blood pooled all around him. Dean sank to his knees. She couldn't tell if it was the rain on his cheeks or hot tears streaming down his face, but what she did know was that Robard was dead.

For an instant, she reached out toward the blood and the heat and life force calling to her on the deck. She could feel Robard and his body and the power within him. She could take it. So easily. She could use it to fix this catastrophe. She could right the world with that much power.

She breathed in, feeling the tingling subside in her body. She almost did it. She almost let go. But she knew there were consequences. Robard, no matter how awful, didn't deserve that. He had called her a dark witch, and if she used his essence to stop this hurricane, even for a good cause, he would be right.

Forcing aside the lust of that feeling, she concentrated on what she could control, and with her last burst of energy, she pushed her magic out into the world. Her body fell back onto the deck just as their ship wrecked onto land. She went flying, but before she landed, her body gave out, and she fell into darkness.

51

The

BLOOD

CYRENE WOKE UP IN A DARK ROOM.

There was a torch burning in a corridor, illuminating a staircase. She felt refreshed but nervous. She almost yelled out for someone, but then she saw who walked inside.

"Viktor," she breathed. "You're late."

Then, Cyrene realized where she was. The last thing she remembered was the boat crashing, but here she was, in the past, with Viktor and Serafina. Once again, she was trapped in Serafina's body.

"Sera," he said. He hurried forward and pulled her into his arms. "My apologies. I had to…"

"What is it?" she asked.

"Margana," he whispered.

Serafina cringed away from him. Cyrene couldn't believe he was bringing up his wife in front of her or that Serafina was meeting him again after he'd gotten married.

"She went into labor."

"She did?" Serafina asked.

Cyrene could tell her heart was breaking.

"Yes, but I came anyway. I had to come for you."

"A boy or a girl?" she asked.

"Sera."

"Just tell me."

"A girl," Viktor said.

Serafina closed her eyes and breathed through her mouth. "Did you get everything?" she asked shakily.

"Yes."

"And are you sure about this?" she asked.

He gripped her hands and kissed them hard on each knuckle. "I want us to be together. You said this would keep us together forever. That's what I want, Sera. I'll do anything to have that."

"Anything but give up your family."

"Anything but give up your magic," he mirrored.

She pulled her hands away from him and looked down at what she had been working on. Cyrene saw the ingredients but had no idea what it could be. She worked for a few minutes in silence.

Finally, she placed a small vial in front of Viktor and one in front of herself.

"I don't know if this is going to work." Her hands were shaking, and it was one of the few times Cyrene had seen Serafina really nervous. "It's only supposed to work between magical users, but...are you sure you want to go through with this?"

"Will we be together forever?"

Serafina nodded, a lump forming in her throat.

"Then, I'll do it."

Viktor disappeared upstairs, and when he came back down, he was holding a perfectly swaddled little baby girl.

Serafina's eyes burned as she looked at her. "You don't have to. It could be anyone..."

"You said it's stronger when it's flesh and blood and someone close to you. I could think of no one closer," Viktor said.

Cyrene had a horrible feeling come over her. She didn't know what was about to happen, but it couldn't be good.

"Okay. We'll...we'll begin." Serafina picked up a book and handed it to Viktor. "You know what to do? It's different than Doma magic since it's not inherent within you. We don't know the consequences."

After skimming the page, he swallowed hard. "Blood magic," he whispered. "I can finally have my own magic, and it will bring us together."

"It's not permanent. It requires sacrifice. A sacrifice that you have to be prepared to harness. Each person has an essence or a fire...and when you take a life, you can wrest that magic from the source," she said warily. "It's taboo to even speak of it in the castle."

"I'll do it."

And then he withdrew a long knife from his belt.

Cyrene wanted to turn aside and not witness what was about to happen, but Serafina seemed determined to watch. She was trembling, and tears rolled down her cheeks, but she didn't turn away. They were in this together.

As Viktor slid the blade across his baby's neck, Serafina released a small sob. She covered her mouth with her hand. Blood pooled in Viktor's hands and onto his feet as the life left his firstborn child. Tears were pouring down his face, but he didn't stop.

He just chanted the words, "Life freely given. Power freely taken. Drawn from you. Give thus to me. Cast off the light and plunge into darkness. I surrender."

She felt the air shift in the room as Viktor took the blood sacrifice and harnessed control of the power from his child's life essence.

Cyrene was sickened and disgusted. *How could Viktor Dremylon kill his firstborn?* All of this was to harness magic for some kind of ritual. It felt surreal. She couldn't believe that Serafina had let him do this…encouraged him to do it.

Viktor placed the baby on the floor between them, and he and Serafina clasped arms.

Serafina read from the book to begin the ritual, *"The Bound ceremony is a sacred act set up to strengthen and combine the magical properties from the originators. Three qualities above all link us together—loyalty, trust, and acceptance."*

Cyrene gasped as realization hit her. He had harnessed magic so that he and Serafina could be bound together for all of eternity.

"The circumstances of our binding will test for loyalty, trust, and acceptance between the hosts. Do you wish to be tested for the Bound ceremony?"

Viktor answered, "Yes."

Serafina met his eyes and nodded. "Me, too."

"Know that the trials might be difficult, and once you start, there is no going back."

There was already no going back. Cyrene could see it in their eyes.

"Do you accept the circumstances?" Serafina asked.

Their eyes met again, and they smiled.

"Yes," they whispered together.

They each grabbed a vial of liquid and tipped it back.

Viktor and Serafina had been Bound two thousand years ago.

Cyrene sat straight up and gasped for air. *It couldn't have been real. It couldn't have been. That had never happened. It was just a dream. It was just a dream. It was just a dream.*

"Cyrene!" Dean cried next to her. "You're alive."

She crashed back down into what she realized was sand. The skies were dark, but the rain had stopped, at least for the moment. She worried they were in the eye of the storm and that if they left this spot, everything would start up all over again.

"Creator," she breathed. "What happened?"

"We're shipwrecked. The storm crashed us into some rocks, and then we landed on this island." He threw his arms up in defeat. "You've been out for hours. I thought you were...dead."

"How did we get on the island? Where is the rest of the crew?" Cyrene asked.

Dean's face looked bleak. "We were sinking. I grabbed you and found something to paddle with. I swam us onto shore. I haven't seen anyone else. They might still be out there."

"And Robard?" Cyrene asked.

She couldn't believe what had really happened. Dean couldn't have thrust his sword through Robard's chest. His blood couldn't have called to her to use it to stop the hurricane. Like Viktor had used it to harness blood magic from his firstborn child. None of that was real.

"He's..." Dean's voice cracked, and he looked away. He buried his head in his hands. "Gone. I've known him my whole life, and now, he's gone. Dead."

She reached out and touched his leg. "He was trying to kill you."

"We've fought thousands of times. I could have stopped him. I could have made him surrender."

"He would never have surrendered."

Dean looked away. "I don't...I don't want to talk about it. We need to find shelter for the night, and in the morning, we'll find a way to get off this island."

They scouted out a place in the nearby trees. Cyrene was weak and could barely move. Dean had to carry her halfway, and he didn't look too good himself. She knew that they needed to eat something to replenish their energy. But they couldn't find much more than a coconut in the dark. It would have to do until morning.

Cyrene rested back against Dean's chest and closed her eyes. She was beyond exhausted. The couple of hours that she had slept while blacked out wasn't enough with the amount of energy she had used. She didn't even want to think about trying her magic right now. Her whole body was sensitive. She doubted it would be a good idea.

Closing her eyes, she tried to use Dean's warmth to chase away the demons. Sleep quickly took her, but soon enough, she awoke, screaming at the top of her lungs. Blood was everywhere. On her eyelids and on her hands and in her hair. She clawed at her face, trying to get rid of it.

Dean grabbed at her hands. "Cyrene, calm down. You're safe." He pulled her to him. "You're safe."

She lay against him until she stopped shaking. By that time, the sun was already on the horizon.

"Come on," Dean said. "Let's go see if we can find a way off this island."

He helped Cyrene to her feet, and they slowly trudged back through the woods and out onto the beach. She was starving, and her stomach grumbled loudly. Her head also hurt, which likely meant that she was dehydrated. If she had a container, she could purify the salt water to drink. Matilde and Vera had taught her how to do it. But she wasn't equipped while stranded like this.

They walked around the island until her thirst got the better of her, and she pitched forward into the sand.

"Hey," he said, reaching for her, "why don't you go back to the site of the wreck? I'll keep looking. Do you know how to build a fire? We could try a smoke signal."

"Yes," she said weakly. Thank the Creator she had learned how to make a fire in the Hidden Forest at the beginning of this journey because fire was not something she could control magically…if she could even use her magic right now. "I can do that."

By the time Dean returned, she had a huge bonfire in the middle of the beach, outside of where they had shipwrecked.

Under normal circumstances, she might have been frightened about the enormity of the fire in front of her but not today. She had started and hopefully ended a hurricane all in one day. She was pretty sure that she could douse a fire if she wanted to.

Dean had some local vegetation for them to eat, and then they waited. It felt like hours passed while they just sat there on the beach and roasted by the fire. She didn't know what they would do if no one found them. Nothing else was in sight of the island they were on, and the island itself was tiny and deserted. She didn't know how much food was on it, and Dean had only found a small spring for water. Not much to go on.

Cyrene retreated to the comfort of the tree line when she felt like she was losing more water than she was bringing in. So much for a romantic post-engagement excursion. Nothing like being marooned on a desert island.

She splashed some water on her face from the spring and then drank two handfuls. She immediately felt refreshed, but her body still hurt all over. Whatever she had done last night hadn't been her best idea. She was starting to think that control was less about knowing how to use her magic and more about being able to separate her emotions from the use of her powers.

At this rate, she wouldn't have reason to use them again.

"Cyrene!" Dean called. "Cyrene! Come down here!"

She dashed back down through the trees and out onto the beach. She sank to her knees in the sand when she saw what was out on the water. A boat. A real boat. She almost cried with relief.

She ran over to Dean where he was jumping up and down and waving his hands.

"Over here!" he yelled. "We're right here!"

The ship came to a halt a short distance from the island and then dropped a tender with a small crew inside. They rowed toward shore. Dean ran out into the water until he was knee deep, and Cyrene followed.

As the boat approached, Cyrene sighed with relief. Two of Dean's men, Faylon and Clym, were in the boat. She was surprised that Darmian wasn't with them. They were a matched set and always had been since she had met them in the Aurumian forest.

"We're so glad to see you," Dean said to his friends.

They clasped his forearms and pulled him on board.

"You have no idea how happy we are to see you, Your Highness," Faylon said.

"We've been searching ever since the storm passed through," Clym told him.

Dean reached for Cyrene and hoisted her out of the water. Faylon and Clym exchanged a look before turning around and making their way to the ship.

"What happened out here?" Faylon asked.

"We got caught in the storm and were shipwrecked. Lost the whole crew…and Robard," Dean said softly. "We barely survived."

"Thank the Creator you did," Clym said.

"Yes. Thank the Creator," Cyrene whispered.

They reached the boat, and Faylon and Clym climbed the ladder to get back on board. Dean offered Cyrene to go up next, and then he followed up behind her. As soon as they were on board, Dean seemed to relax.

"Let's go home," Dean said with an easy smile.

"I apologize, Your Majesty," Faylon said. "But you're not going to like this."

"Like what?"

Clym reached out and grabbed Cyrene.

"Hey! Unhand me!" she yelled.

Dean jumped forward, but Faylon was there, and together, he and Clym wrenched Cyrene's arms behind her back.

"What the hell do you think you're doing?" Dean demanded. "That is my betrothed. You're harming a future Princess of Eleysia."

Faylon cleared his throat. "We have orders to arrest Affiliate Cyrene on sight."

"You what?" Cyrene cried.

"Explain yourself. Under whose orders?" Dean demanded.

"By orders of Her Majesty, Queen Brigette," Faylon announced.

Dean stumbled backward a step at the name.

"Queen…Brigette," Dean said, his body caving in at the title.

"For conspiracy to murder Queen Cassia and King Tomas."

52

The CONSPIRACY

"I DIDN'T CONSPIRE TO KILL ANYONE!" CYRENE CRIED FOR what felt like the hundredth time.

Dean had said the same thing over and over to his men, but ultimately, their orders had come from the Queen. So, there was nothing to be done about it until they got back to the capital.

Faylon and Clym had taken her below deck and chained her to a thick wooden bed. There was no way that she could get away. Not that she was going to try since she hadn't done anything wrong. She had no idea why she was even being accused, and Faylon and Clym wouldn't speak about it in front of her. They'd just shoved her into the room, chained her to the bed, and locked the door.

The worst part about the whole thing was that she couldn't be up there with Dean while he dealt with the deaths of his parents. No, not the deaths. The murder of his parents.

She couldn't imagine what that must feel like. And to have to go through it alone on top of the death of one of his oldest friends. Even if he had eleven sisters to mourn with…none of them were here now. But she was, and she wished with everything that she could be up on deck with him right now.

Cyrene wasn't sure how much time had passed while she was stuck below deck when she felt the boat slow and then finally stop.

Faylon came to collect her. "Don't try anything," he warned her.

She held her arms out where they were chained in front of her. "These don't exactly give me the opportunity," she sneered.

"Just don't do it."

"I didn't do anything. I was with Dean this entire time. I have a solid alibi for this. I've been here for months. Why would I conspire to kill the Queen and King?" she asked him.

"I'm just following orders, and you should, too."

He chained her hands behind her back and then ordered her to go above deck. She was placed into a small boat. She straightened her shoulders and lifted her chin. She had done nothing wrong.

Her resolve broke a bit when Dean got into a different boat. He sadly glanced at her but then was rushed away. Cyrene's gondola followed behind Dean's.

The canals were empty, and Cyrene could see the result of the hurricane. Debris was everywhere in the water. Some of the houses were crumbling. Others had completely collapsed. People were somber as they transferred precious belongings to other locations. Still, others helped the people who had lost everything.

A few people noticed Dean as he passed by, and a cheer rose up in the crowd. "Prince Dean!"

He managed a small wave, but Cyrene could see how defeated he looked, even just in the set of his shoulders. To her surprise, she heard her name again. Just like she had yesterday on their way to the Bride of the Sea ceremony. It was hard to believe that had only been yesterday.

Then, she heard it again.

She glanced over to the crowd, and another cheer went up. "Princess Cyrene! Our new Princess!"

Tears welled in her eyes at their cheer. They were…applauding her. Excited to bring her into the royal family. She tried to smile at the crowd, but soon, the boats were whisked away, and the cheers disappeared. None of them had any idea that she had been arrested. She hated to think what they would say if they saw her passing by after they'd found out.

She wouldn't think about that right now. She would talk to Brigette and figure all of this out. Brigette couldn't seriously believe that Cyrene had done anything to hurt her parents. She hadn't always gotten along with Queen Cassia, but Cyrene didn't want her dead.

Dean would convince them. He knew her. He knew she would never do this. It would all work out. Just a misunderstanding. They had no proof.

The boats meandered onto palace grounds and docked on the lake. A retinue of soldiers was waiting for them on the dock. Once she was off the boat, Faylon and Clym took either of her arms and hauled her toward the palace.

Dean grabbed Faylon. "Unhand her. She can walk on her own. I won't have my fiancée being treated like a criminal with no proof."

"Thank you," she whispered.

"Let's just go," he said, moving forward.

She swallowed hard and hurried to catch up with him. It was awkward, walking with her hands bound behind her back. She almost reached out for her magic, but instead, she just sent up a call to Avoca. Cyrene couldn't sense Avoca nearby, but that didn't mean she wasn't. After the amount of magic Cyrene had used, she didn't know what was normal.

Instead of walking inside, the soldiers hurried them into a packed courtyard. Nobles filled the space, jockeying for the best view of whatever was happening. When they saw that it was the Prince, an alley opened up for Dean to walk through.

None of the cheers from the outer wall were heard in here. Most people glared at her, and a few people even threw things at her. She kept pace with Dean and felt utterly humiliated by the walk of shame for something she hadn't even done.

When they finally reached the front of the courtyard, the crowd had gone deathly quiet. Cyrene's eyes found Brigette seated on a dais, overlooking the crowd. She seemed to have aged fifteen years overnight. Dark bags were under her eyes, and she appeared worn and hardened.

"Prince Dean," she said when she finally saw them.

He bowed deeply, and Cyrene dipped into the best curtsy she could manage with her hands tied behind her back.

"Queen Brigette," he said. Cyrene could tell the words hurt him. "Is it true?"

"Queen Cassia and King Tomas were murdered last night in their sleep by an assassin who was apprehended after the incident."

Brigette gestured off to her right, and Cyrene looked around Dean to see whom she was pointing at. When she saw who was on her knees in chains before the throne, Cyrene gasped aloud.

"Maelia!" she cried.

Cyrene jerked forward, as if to run to her friend, but Faylon grabbed her shoulders and held her in place. Her knees gave out beneath her at the sight of her friend shackled to the ground. Bile rose up in her throat, and her breathing was ragged. Her entire body trembled with the view before her.

It made no sense.

"Cyrene! Cyrene, please!" Maelia cried. Tears streamed down her cheeks, and she coughed in between sobs. "I didn't. I didn't. Please help me."

Cyrene just stared at her friend as she tried to stay upright. "She couldn't have done it. She didn't," she whispered.

Dean questioningly looked from Maelia to Cyrene.

Her eyes found his. "She couldn't have."

"If that is how you plead," Brigette said coldly, "then bring forth the witness."

The reason that Darmian hadn't gone out to look for Dean materialized before her. He walked out before his Queen and bowed formally in his royal-blue military uniform. He also seemed to have aged overnight.

"I apprehended the murderer, Your Majesty," Darmian said. His voice lacked all emotion. He was strong and stoic and refused to even look at Maelia.

Cyrene could see how much that broke Maelia. Her head dropped, and all Cyrene could hear was the sound of Maelia crying.

"Please recount what you saw," Brigette said.

"I was intimately involved with the suspect and had planned to surprise her in her rooms that night." He delivered that news without a trace of embarrassment or remorse. "When she wasn't in her quarters after the ball, I went in search of her. I found her leaving the royal wing of the palace. She was crying and shaking and rubbing her hands together, as if she were trying to get the blood off of them."

Cyrene cringed.

"And then the alarm went up. The Queen and King had been found dead in their bedchambers. There was an assassin loose. Even though I did not want to do it, I searched Maelia because of her suspicious behavior. What I found was this." Darmian retrieved two sharp blades and laid them before the Queen as evidence. "She sliced their throats open. She is guilty."

"I didn't," Maelia repeated over and over again. "Your Highness, please. I never wanted to hurt anyone. I never wanted to. I was forced to. I resisted for as long as I could. I tried to stay away, but it called for me. It made me."

Cyrene's mouth fell open. Maelia was admitting to it. She had actually committed this heinous crime. *How is that possible? Poor, sweet Maelia.* She was good with a sword, but two Captains of the Guard had raised her. She wasn't an assassin. She couldn't be. *Could she?*

Then, Cyrene really thought about it…all those times she had known just when to go in and out of the palace, unnoticed, how everyone seemed to pass right over her in a crowd, the utter stillness of her feet…

"Creator," Cyrene whispered. "You did…"

Dean sharply looked at her, but her eyes were focused on Maelia. She couldn't get in enough air.

Maelia was her friend. She had been her friend from the first day when she was made an Affiliate. Not once had she suspected that her friend could do something like this.

Is this why she had been so sick? She was trying to resist assassinating the crown?

Cyrene felt like an idiot, and she was also utterly terrified. *What was to become of Maelia for her actions?* Despite everything, Maelia was one of her closest friends.

Brigette looked indifferent. "You admit to your crimes and say someone forced you to do it. Who forced you?"

Maelia was trembling from head to toe. "I wish I could tell you. I wish they would let me."

Brigette shook her head. "She's mad. The punishment for the murder of the Queen and King of Eleysia is death. Does anyone here speak otherwise for this girl?"

Maelia looked up into the crowd for someone, anyone, to say something. Cyrene wanted to. She desperately wanted to defend her friend. She stepped forward to do just that, but Dean put his hand on her arm and shook his head. She pushed past him anyway.

"I will! I speak for her," Cyrene called.

A ripple ran through the watching crowd.

Brigette fixed Cyrene with an icy glare. "You have no voice here, Affiliate. You have been summoned for conspiracy to murder. We already believe that you conspired with your Affiliate friend here to end the lives of our Queen and King. You used

Prince Dean to enter the country, seduced him to lull us into a false sense of security, and then sent your assassin to do your dirty work," she said with venom in her voice. "Your trial awaits you after we deal with this murderer. So, unless you want to follow her onto the block immediately, then I suggest you step back."

Brigette flicked her hand toward Maelia, and a handful of guards began unchaining her.

Cyrene stepped back in horror. They believed that she had seduced Dean to get close to the royal family. They believed she was responsible for this. But since they hadn't caught her red-handed, she wasn't on trial yet, like Maelia was.

Cyrene could barely watch as Maelia was dragged onstage to a block. She was forced to her knees in front of everyone. Her sobs could be heard over the jeering crowd as she slowly lowered her head down onto the wooden block.

Cyrene turned her head away from the display. She couldn't watch.

But Faylon jerked her head over. "Watch what you've done."

She tried to pull away, but she couldn't. She was pinned in place, and nothing and no one was going to stand up for Maelia.

Queen Brigette raised her hand. "For the murder of the Queen and King of Eleysia, I hereby sentence you to death."

Cyrene felt like she was hyperventilating. Her body was going insane, yet...she didn't feel her magic. Not once. Not an ounce of power came to her body. She trembled with that realization as her mind tried to avoid what was happening in front of her.

A man in a black hood held an ax high overhead, and then when Brigette dropped her hand, he brought it down onto Maelia's neck. Cyrene screamed as her best friend's head dropped into a basket, and her body crumpled.

She jerked away from Faylon and tried to rush forward to Maelia.

She was dead.

Her head was disconnected from her body.

Gone.

Cyrene struggled and pushed against the people holding her as tears flooded her eyes. She reached for her magic again and again, trying to make the pain stop. She needed to make the ache in her chest disappear. She needed to fill that hole within her.

Maelia had murdered the Queen and King.

Maelia was her friend.

Maelia was a murderer.

Maelia had had a gentle laugh.

Maelia was an assassin.

Maelia had helped her when no one else came to her defense.

Maelia had slit the rulers' throats.

Maelia had hugged her after they were reunited.

Maelia had bloody knives.

Maelia was dead.

Cyrene collapsed. *Maelia couldn't be. She just couldn't be.*

She sobbed. Her heart was broken.

"How could you do this?" she shrieked.

"She killed my parents," Brigette said emotionlessly. "She got less than she deserved."

"Dean," Cyrene said, searching for him. He took a step back from her. "Dean, please."

He looked at her with that same empty look that Brigette had on her face. "You're to be tried for conspiracy to murder. You were part of the plot to murder my parents. How was I ever stupid enough to think that I loved you?"

Cyrene's mouth fell open. "You can't believe this! Dean, I do love you!"

"I can't hear any more of this. Take her to the dungeons where she will await trial," Dean said to his men.

Cyrene screamed. She reached for her magic and came up empty.

"Knock her out if necessary. None of you know what she's capable of," Dean said, devoid of emotion.

The last thing she saw was Dean's empty dark eyes. Then, the pommel of a sword hit her temple, and she lost consciousness.

To Be Continued...

ACKNOWLEDGMENTS

THANK YOU TO EVERYONE WHO BELIEVED IN THIS STORY. It was a long time coming, and I'm immensely proud of where it has ended up. And there is no way that it could be where it is today without people who helped me along the way.

Big thanks to Rebecca Kimmerling, who was the champion for this book from the start. I appreciate all the late nights and random editing questions. Thank you to Anjee Sapp for beta reading the book and loving it to pieces, theorizing and brainstorming with me, and all around keeping me sane. Thanks to Robin Segnitz and Katie Miller for your help with the book and overall inspiration. Meera Bhardwaj and Kiran Bhardwaj for the invaluable help on Matilde and Vera. Their brilliance would never have manifested without all those months I basically lived with you.

Thank you to my publicist, Danielle Sanchez, who devoured this book in one sitting and spearheaded the campaign on it! Thank you to my agent, Kimberly Brower, who fought tooth and nail to get this series what it deserved and never gave up. And mostly for realizing it wasn't a princess book. It was the anti-princess book. Thank you, Jovana Shirley, for the intense editing on a tight schedule and beautiful formatting. Thank you to Lauren Perry for the amazing photograph used on the cover of this book! As always, thank you to the wonderful Sarah Hansen for the most beautiful cover I've ever seen! For taking my vision and making it a reality.

I appreciate my family, especially my two sisters who were deeply invested in this from the start and helped me with all the more sinister planning. And, of course, my loving husband, Joel. Without him, I never would finish any book, let alone one of this magnitude. Thank you for watching the puppies, brainstorming, watching *Supernatural*, taking me for ice cream when I'm down, holding me when I cry, and celebrating the triumphs.

Being married to an author isn't easy, and I appreciate everything you do for me.

And, of course, to the fans! Thank you for loving this series, recommending it to your friends, writing reviews, and gushing to me online and in person. I can never thank you enough!

ABOUT THE AUTHOR

K.A. LINDE GREW UP AS A MILITARY BRAT AND CREATED fantastical stories based off of her love for Disney movies, fairy tales, and *Star Wars*. She now lives in Lubbock, Texas, with her husband and two super adorable puppies. In her spare time, she is an avid traveler and loves cruising, reading young adult novels, and dancing.

Additionally, K.A. has written more than a dozen adult novels and is a *USA Today* bestselling author. She does not encourage anyone younger than eighteen to pick those up!

K.A. Linde loves to hear from her readers!

You can contact her at kalinde45@gmail.com or visit her online at one of the following sites:

www.kalinde.com

www.facebook.com/authorkalinde

http://twitter.com/AuthorKALinde

CPSIA information can be obtained
at www.ICGtesting.com
Printed in the USA
BVOW08s1425150117

473536BV00002B/111/P